Praise for *A Daughter's Choice*

"'A Plain woman who doesn't know her place'—that's how Henrietta Miller describes herself. Her devotion to animals means she doesn't quite fit with expectations, especially in the eyes of her bishop father. When Nicholas Byler, a veterinary assistant with opinions as strong as Hen's, arrives in town, their spirited clashes kindle a connection neither expects. With warmth and insight, Kelly Irvin delivers a quietly powerful tale of love, identity, and finding where one's heart truly belongs."

–Suzanne Woods Fisher, bestselling author of *A Healing Touch*

"Henrietta Miller had my heart the minute she refused to let a man boss her around. Now that is a woman I can identify with! In *A Daughter's Choice,* Kelly Irvin tugs the reader into a conservative Amish community, and then drops an opinionated heroine with a steel backbone right in the middle of it all. You will fall in love with all of these characters, especially Hen! Irvin is a master storyteller, and this is a story you won't want to miss."

–Patricia Johns, *Publishers Weekly* bestselling author

A Daughter's Choice

KELLY IRVIN

YOU are the reason we do what we do here at Barbour Publishing. We promise that we will always use our God-given talents to produce content with you in mind—and that we will remain biblically faithful, no matter what.

Thank you for being the heart of our business.

Print ISBN 979-8-89151-221-4
Adobe Digital Edition (.epub) 979-8-89151-222-1

All scripture quotations are taken from the King James Version of the Bible.

Cover Design: Kirk DouPonce, DogEared Design

Published by Barbour Publishing, Inc., 1810 Barbour Drive, Uhrichsville, Ohio 44683, www.barbourbooks.com

Our mission is to inspire the world with the life-changing message of the Bible.

Printed in the United States of America.

To my little animal lovers Brooklyn, Carson,
Henry, and Stanton, love always.
GRANDMA

GLOSSARY OF PENNSYLVANIA *DEUTSCH*[*]

aamen: amen
ach: oh
aenti: aunt
bopli, boplin: baby, babies
bruder, brieder: brother, brothers
bu, buwe: boy, boys
daadi: grandpa
daed: father
dat: dad
dawdi haus: attached home for parents when they retire
denki: thank you
dochder, dechder: daughter, daughters
dumkoph: blockhead
eck: corner table where newly married couple sits during wedding reception
Englischer: English or non-Amish person
eppy: cookie
fraa: wife
gaul: horse
gelassenheit: a German word, yielding fully to God's will and forsaking all selfishness
gern gschehme: you're welcome
Gmay: church district
Gott: God
groossmammi: grandmother
guder daag: good day
guder mariye: good morning
guder nammidaad: good afternoon
guder nacht: good night
gut: good
hallo: hello
hochmut: pride
hund: dog
Ich bin gut: I'm good

jah: yes
kaffi: coffee
kapp: prayer cap or head covering worn by Amish women
kind, kinner: child, children
kinnskind, kinnskinner: grandchild, grandchildren
kossins: cousins
lieb: love
maedel, maed: girl, girls
mamm: mom
mammi: grandma
mann: husband
mei naame iss: my name is
meidung: also called shunning or the ban. Community members avoid contact with an individual found to have committed a serious infraction of their district's rules.
mudder: mother
narrisch: foolish, crazy
nee: no
neis: niece
onkel: uncle
Ordnung: written and unwritten rules in an Amish district
rumspringa: period of "running around" for Amish youth before they decide whether they want to be baptized into the Amish faith and seek a mate
schee dich zu dreffe: it's nice to meet you
schtumm: stupid
schweschder, schweschdre: sister, sisters
sei so gut: please (be so kind)
suh: son
wie bischt?: how are you?
wunderbarr: wonderful

*The German dialect commonly referred to as Pennsylvania Dutch is not a written language and varies depending on the location and origin of the Amish settlement. These spellings are approximations. Most Amish children learn English after they start school. They also learn high German, which is used in their Sunday services.

CHAPTER 1

Raising goats and raising children didn't seem all that different. Not that Henrietta Miller had any children of her own. Yet.

"Stop that, Petunia." Henrietta nudged the baby goat—aptly called a kid—away from her voluminous skirt. Too little too late. Hay, dirt, and goat hair decorated her apron, even though the sun had just kissed the April morning sky. Hen's younger sister Ruby would *tsk* over the frying bacon at breakfast. Her dad would scowl over his first cup of coffee. No matter. "Behave yourself. No amount of cute will get you fed first, my sweet."

The kid was used to getting her way. After all, Hen had been bottle-feeding her since it became apparent that her mother didn't have enough milk for Petunia and her twin, Penny. Her big chocolate eyes full of hope, she led the small herd in an enthusiastic chorus of squeaky bleats. All the kids jumped, skipped, hopped, and tumbled to their own music. Their antics were a comedy routine that never failed to make Hen laugh.

Even the manure smelled like perfume on this fine day in southwest Pennsylvania. The dairy goat herd was healthy and happy. Hen's family had plenty of milk to sell and for making cheese, yogurt, caramel candies, and Hen's favorite—goat milk fudge. And soap, of course. The tourists loved the goat milk soap. "I know, I know. I'm hurrying, you sweet beasties, I'm hurrying. I'll be back in a jiffy, I promise."

She closed the pen, latched it, dodged Tigger, a tiger-striped kitten that insisted on being underfoot anytime a sip of milk was remotely possible, and zipped across the grass to the large shed where she kept the does. Immediately Sam, the rooster, took the kitten's place. His *cock-a-doodle-doo* could wake the dead in the next state. "Come on, Sam, I know this is your territory. I promise not to steal it."

His response? To crow again. "Seriously? Move it, chatterbox. Go find Sassy." Sassy was the matron and top egg layer in the chicken coop. She'd put Sam in his place. "I've got work to do."

Sam deigned to trot from her path, only to take up his march behind her. He was the king of the yard—in his mind.

Feeling like the animal pied piper, Hen picked up her pace. She was behind this morning. She still needed to milk the mama goats, clip their hooves, and shave their udders. Then they could be returned to their kids after a night apart. That allowed Hen to gather a nice haul of milk and the kids to drink their fill during the day.

"Hen, Hen, come quick!"

Hen glanced up from unhooking the shed door's latch. Her sister Philomena—who knew why their parents had given such a tiny girl such an enormous name?—dashed across the yard toward her. Yellow-Belly-Buster, the dog they shared, ran circles around her. "I have to milk the mamas. You'll have to wait. While you're waiting, run get your coat. It's April, not July."

The five-year-old was always in too big a hurry for coats. At least she had shoes on. Spring in Pennsylvania meant they could still see their breath and find ice on the water tanks at dawn. Mena always wanted Hen to do everything in a hurry. Catch night crawlers. Feed frogs at the pond. Get her a cookie. Climb a tree. *Now* was never soon enough.

"It's not that cold. Jack's worse." Philomena scooped up Tigger and plopped him on her skinny shoulders. "He's still not eating. *Dat* called the vet."

Philomena was a mini Hen. She insisted on caring for the animals—much to their brothers' chagrin. They claimed the little girl was mostly in the way. Hen had more patience. "We probably need to adjust his diet. He's getting old—even for a Morgan. I've been reading up on it."

"What if he's got bad colic?" Philomena's lower lip trembled. Her blue eyes were teary behind the thick lenses of her brown-rimmed glasses. "Or what if it's Cushing's disease?"

"Don't borrow trouble, *lieb*. Jack's digestion doesn't work as *gut* as it used to. We just need to give him some extra lovin'." Hen strode across the yard double-time. She squeezed the tiny tornado of a child in a big hug.

Their elderly horse was well into his early thirties—a nice long life for a Morgan—a breed prized for their longevity. Which was good, because he was a member of the family. The older Miller children had learned to drive a buggy with Jack in the lead. The twins still needed their turn, as well as Mena, who would be the last. "We'll get him fixed up."

Jack's troubled neigh greeted Hen as soon she entered the barn. Their mare Lucy whinnied in response. She was expecting and getting close to foaling, so Dad had started bringing her into the barn at night to protect her from the cold and allow him to keep an eye on her better. Jack's predicament probably stressed her too.

Philomena, Buster, and Tigger, who'd decided he preferred walking, trailed behind Hen. Sam chose to stay outside. He didn't care for the barn. Which was good. The horses didn't need his incessant crowing and preening.

Jack didn't look happy at Hen's approach. This was a huge red flag. Hen adored Jack, and he adored her. "Come on, buddy, it's me. Your best bud."

He shook his head and stomped his feet.

"I get it. You don't feel gut. You're grumpy. You'll be fine, I promise."

"I hope you're right."

Dad didn't sound particularly happy either. He stood in Jack's stall, his hand smoothing the Morgan's withers as he murmured in the horse's ear. Jack had his head lowered. He didn't raise it as Hen and her entourage moved closer. His normally shiny bay coat had turned dull. His supper of fresh hay from the previous evening lay uneaten, and his water bucket was still full.

"Mena says he's worse." Hen opened the stall door. Ignoring the disappointed woofs and meows, she allowed only Mena to follow before she closed it again. "He hasn't pooped in two days."

"I'm aware." Concern deepened the lines around Dad's brown eyes behind smudged wire-rimmed glasses that had slid down his nose. "I hear rumblings in his intestines. I reckon he has gas pains he can't pass."

"I can walk him." Mena thrust herself between Hen and their father. "Jack likes me. He'll walk for me."

"You're supposed to be helping your *schweschder* make breakfast." His expression flared with a combination of frustration and resignation. He sighed. "Go, now. After breakfast, you'll help her with the dishes, mop the floor, and sew your new dresses. The one you have on is too short."

"Dat—"

"Don't backtalk me, *kind*."

"But—"

"Mena, do as Dat says." Hen placed her hands on the girl's skinny shoulders and propelled her toward the stall door. "Save me a piece of toast and some apple preserves, *sei so gut*."

Her face filled with disappointment, Mena trudged through the open door and out of the barn.

"I've told you before you don't want to be a bad influence on her, Henrietta." Dad was the only one who called Hen by her full name. He smoothed both hands across the stallion's back. The horse dipped his head and nickered. "It's bad enough that you ignore your household chores. Don't encourage Philomena to do the same."

Here we go. In other words, he didn't want Mena to grow up unsuitable to be a Plain wife. The right man would come along for Hen. She was sure of it. God had a plan. At least that's what Dad had said in the endless number of messages he delivered in church since drawing the lot to become bishop of their Smicksburg north church district. God had a plan for everyone.

Which meant God's plan had included Mom's death from an allergic reaction to an antibiotic given to her for a urinary tract infection compounded by the flu. Philomena had only been two years old. Too young to even remember her mother.

No one died from a UTI. What kind of plan was that?

The question pestered Hen nightly when she curled up in bed with Buster at her feet and Tigger nestled on her pillow, but she'd never had the guts to pose it to her father.

"Are you listening to me, *Dochder*?"

"*Jah*, Dat."

"Ruby and her special friend will no doubt marry soon. That will leave you in charge of the house until..."

His uncertainty written all over his prematurely lined face, Dad faced Hen. His thoughts were so obvious they stung like a horde of wasps. He didn't believe Hen would ever marry. Her sister, younger by two years, would marry first. It happened. The oldest didn't always find a mate first.

"I'll marry one day."

"Can you see yourself?" Dad waved his hands at her. "Dirt on your face and your apron. Goat manure on the hem of your dress." He sniffed. "It's barely dawn, and you already stink. Do you even know how to darn a sock?"

"Of course I do. *Mamm* taught me." Hen froze. She took a big chance bringing up her mother. Even after three years, Dad tended to roll up tighter than a roly-poly bug when she or her siblings mentioned Mom. As if they could pretend she hadn't gone from their lives far too soon. Mom had taught Hen to do everything a woman needed to know. And then some. The *then some* didn't cancel out her womanliness. "The goat herd brings in gut money that helps us feed and clothe our family."

Dad's Adam's apple bobbed. A second or two passed as if he considered his response. Would his lips move with the word *mamm*? "The fact that your mamm isn't with us anymore isn't an excuse for letting yourself go. Neither is your goat herd an excuse for turning yourself into a tomboy. Or flaunting your opinion in front of your elders."

At least he uttered the word *mamm*. But that wasn't the real bone Dad wanted to pick with Hen today. He was upset because of her impromptu speech urging the expansion to a secondary business with Angora goats. She'd interrupted Dad while he sat at a picnic table with the other men after church Sunday discussing new ways to earn income as farms became less profitable. Instead of serving the sandwiches and walking away, she'd waxed enthusiastically about opening new doors to new products, like wool and yarn. Her cheeks warmed. His scowl was engraved on her brain. Not just discomfort but embarrassment. "I'm sorry, Dat."

"But not sorry enough to curb your tongue or mend your ways. You're twenty-two. When was the last time you went to a singing?"

Hen searched her memory. It hadn't been that long. Had it? What was the point? Goofy sixteen-year-old boys acting silly, trying to impress girls who were hopping around like popcorn seeds in oil in a hot cast-iron pan worrying about which boys would give them buggy rides home. Hen could drive her own buggy, thank you very much. "It's been a month or two."

"Lying is a sin."

"I mean a year or two."

"Or three."

"Let me take Jack for a walk. He needs to pass some of that gas. It may be all he needs to feel better."

"Your schweschder is going to help out at the school now that the teacher's assistant has married." Dad handed her the halter. "You'll need to take over in the house starting on Monday."

A daughter didn't contradict her father. Hen swallowed angry words. "But the goats need me."

"Your *brieder* will take care of them. They're livestock. They won't know the difference."

That wasn't true. Dad knew better. He was punishing her. Hen bit her tongue until she tasted salty blood. Her brothers didn't care about the goats the way she did. They were far more interested in working with Dad training horses. "For how long?"

"Until school is out. Understood?"

The end of April. Not so long. "Jah, understood."

Hen quickly put the halter on Jack. His ears didn't perk up. In fact he peered at her with accusatory eyes. She patted his muzzle. He whinnied. "Come on, *bu*, let's go."

She led him from the stall and headed for the barn doors. He usually had her scampering to keep up. Jack preferred the great outdoors. Today she had to encourage him to keep moving.

Buster's barking didn't help. The dog raced toward them, his concerned woofs gaining volume. "Buster, stop it. What's wrong with you?"

"Where are you going with that horse?"

Hen raised her hand to her forehead to shield her eyes from the sun creeping above the horizon. A young man tall enough to loom over her five-foot-eight body stood in her path. That explained the barking. "Buster, hush." The dog halted next to Jack. His bark died until it became a low growl in his throat. "That's enough, *hund*."

Hen squinted at the newcomer. Chestnut hair sticking out from under his straw hat, pale complexion, gray eyes. Body hidden in a black wool coat. Definitely not someone she'd met before. "Who are you?"

"I'm the vet's new assistant." He stepped into the shadow cast by the barn. "Nicholas Byler. If that's the horse Bishop Miller called Dr. McDonald about, you best get him back in his stall."

"What do you mean? Doc's new assistant?" Hen swallowed a deluge of angry words. She'd applied for that job. She had all the knowledge needed. She'd lived on a farm with goats, cows, pigs, chickens, dogs, cats, and horses her entire life. And no one loved animals more than she did. "I didn't think he'd filled that position yet."

"He hired me last week." Nicholas' forehead wrinkled. His eyebrows rose. "I started on Monday, but you don't need to worry. I know what I'm doing. You need to take that horse back to his stall. I'll examine him and then consult with Dr. McDonald. We'll determine the best course of treatment."

Doubtful. No way this stranger knew as much as Hen did. But he had one thing going for him. He was a man. That had to be it. Heat roasted Hen's cheeks. She dismissed a surly comment on Doc McDonald's poor judgment. "This is Jack, and he needs some exercise." The man's know-it-all tone coupled with his assumption she'd do whatever he said was like walking barefoot through a burr patch. "He'll pass some gas and be right as rain."

"You're wrong." Nicholas Byler didn't move out of Hen's way. This stranger was bossy, and he lacked manners. "The last thing he needs is vigorous exercise."

"No one said anything about vigorous exercise. A nice walk in the corral."

"He needs to go back in the barn so I can examine him properly."

A ginormous burr patch.

CHAPTER 2

This woman apparently didn't know lima beans about caring for a geriatric horse. Nicholas Byler heaved a breath. No excuse existed for not taking proper care of animals. Neither did that give a person an excuse for being rude. She was bossy, and she lacked manners. His clenched jaw hurt. The gangly woman whose rumpled prayer cap didn't cover her brown hair was clad in a stained lilac dress and gray coat buttoned wrong. She probably didn't know any better. Not that ignorance was an excuse.

"I need to examine him before we decide if a walk is the best medicine." Nicholas forced a smile. "You don't want to make the poor thing's pain worse, do you?"

"Sei so gut, don't talk to me like I'm ignorant." The woman's dark brown eyes flashed. In a minute she'd stomp her foot. "The first time I rode Jack, I was in diapers. I've been taking care of him since I was old enough to walk."

"Then you should know to call the vet at the first sign of colic and wait for him before you decide to treat the horse yourself." Nicholas advanced toward her. He reached for the lead line. She backed up. A bit like a finicky mare that needed to be reassured. But not at all like any Plain woman Nicholas had ever met. "I'll take him back inside if you want to go get your *daed*. I assume Bishop Miller is your dat."

"He is." She still hadn't released the lead line. "You just said yourself you're not a vet. Where's Dr. McDonald?"

Nicholas had laughed the first time Dr. McDonald introduced himself. Which hadn't gone over well. Surely Nicholas wasn't the only one who found the name McDonald—as in Old McDonald had a farm—a funny, if suitable name, for a veterinarian. "He's delivering a breach calf at the Shiracks' farm."

"Fine. I'll take Jack back to his stall." She patted the horse's muzzle and then turned him back toward the barn. "I'm sure Dr. McDonald will come as soon as he can."

Nicholas opened his mouth to contradict her, then closed it. A bespectacled man sporting a dark brown beard streaked with silver strode through the barn's open doors. "You must be Nicholas."

"I am. You're Bishop Miller?"

"Adam." The bishop jerked his head toward the barn. "Henrietta, we'll let Nicholas examine the *gaul* before you walk him."

The stubborn woman had a name. Henrietta murmured in the horse's ear. Jack nuzzled her cheek. A person couldn't fault her loving touch. The horse obviously adored her. That would go a long way toward his recovery.

Nicholas followed them to the barn. A quick, deep inhale of the familiar scents of hay, horses, and manure steadied his mind. A white-and-black cat halted in his path, drilled Nicholas with a fierce scowl, hissed, and shot into the last stall. A beautiful sorrel raised her head and whinnied as if to welcome him.

"Don't mind Willow. She has a new litter of kittens she's protecting," Henrietta called out. "And Lucy is expecting. She's bigger than a house and not happy about it. The other three horses are ones Dat is training for *Englischers*."

"I see. Your daed has his hands full, then."

She shrugged and nodded, apparently done sharing.

Nicholas didn't need to talk to do his job. He examined Jack, took his temperature, listened to his digestive system, and asked a series of questions—most of which Adam answered after shooting a frown at his daughter, quieting her.

"How much time does he spend out to pasture?"

"If we're not using him for the buggy, quite a bit, I suppose."

"Horses are grazers. He's probably eating fresh grass more than he should. Morgans are notorious for being overweight. And as he's gotten older, his ability to digest the fresh greens is reduced."

"Jack's not fat—"

"Henrietta."

The woman quieted in the face of her father's stern gaze.

Nicholas examined Jack's teeth. Not good. "Given his age and the state of his teeth, it's not surprising he's developed colic. His teeth are so worn down, he can't chew the stocks of hay anymore."

"We've never had a horse live this long." Adam adjusted his wire-rimmed glasses up his nose. His hands were chapped and red. "I've had a few with dental problems, but not so that they couldn't eat. It's not like we can give him dentures."

"True. Start soaking and chopping up his hay. Add beet pulp to his diet. I reckon he weighs about a thousand pounds, so give him fifteen pounds or so a day while reducing his forage by 25 percent. Give him smaller meals a few times a day."

"What about the pain?" Unlike most Plain children, Henrietta hadn't learned to keep quiet in her elders' presence. Or maybe it was only because she cared so much about Jack that she couldn't force herself to remain silent. Someone whose love for animals rivaled Nicholas'. "He's not going to eat as long as he's in pain."

"Dr. McDonald will have to give you the pain medication." If only Nicholas could go to veterinary medicine college, then he could prescribe drugs. But that was off the table—for now. His father had sent him to Smicksburg to care for his grandfather. Family came first. Nicholas would make do with what he learned from books and working with English vets. "As soon as he gets done at the Shiracks'."

No point in telling them his employer had given Nicholas a cell phone to use for as long as he worked for him. Dr. McDonald said communication was critical when animals' lives hung in the balance. Not only because livestock played an important role in an agricultural economy, but also because animals often were considered members of the family.

Becoming a veterinarian would mean Nicholas would have to leave his faith, his family, and his community. Having a cell phone was a step in that direction. His bishop back home would say one small step on the road to hell. What else could he say? On the other hand, maybe only a weak faith would be swayed by a piece of electronic equipment.

Or was that Satan talking?

"I'll go into town to the tractor supply store for the beet pulp."

Henrietta's morose expression had disappeared, replaced by pure concern for the animal. Maybe her reservations about Nicholas' expertise had been allayed. "I can stop by Dr. McDonald's and double-check with him if you want, Dat. I'll have to pick up the medication anyway."

Or maybe not.

"I'll pass my notes on to Dr. McDonald as soon as he returns to the clinic." Nicholas replaced his stethoscope in his backpack. "If you can point me to the faucet, I'd like to wash my hands before I head out."

"Dochder, go tell your schweschder we have a visitor for breakfast. And get cleaned up before you touch the food."

Did Henrietta even try to hide the horror that rippled across her face? "Nicholas probably has other stops to make, what with Dr. McDonald being occupied."

Nicholas had no desire to go where he so obviously wasn't wanted. "I should get back to the clinic. We have regular appointments waiting."

With another frown aimed at his daughter, Adam shook his head. "I reckon you left home without breakfast this morning. You have time to eat."

Nicholas' sister had made breakfast, but Dr. McDonald's call had meant Nicholas didn't have time to eat. His stomach rumbled.

A smile replaced Adam's scowl. "Decision made."

When the bishop smiled, he looked like a completely different person. Younger. Less burdened.

"After breakfast I'll go to town." Henrietta had a one-track mind. "The boys are already milking the goats."

"No you won't." His smile was gone as quickly as it came, and Adam's tone suggested his words held a message for his daughter that was for her alone. "I'll make the trip to town. You have floors to mop."

"But Dat—"

"Dochder."

Henrietta kissed Jack's forehead. Head held high, her posture stiff, she slipped past Jack. She took her time latching the stall. "I'll be back later, Jack, to take you for a walk."

How could a person argue with sheer stubbornness when it involved caring for an ailing animal? Since he was old enough to walk, Nicholas had been just as devoted to animals. He named chickens, hogs, and cows—to his father's chagrin. It was hard to slaughter livestock and eat them after

Nicholas gave them names and let them follow him around all day long.

Adam's rueful smile said he had plenty of experience dealing with a similar situation. "The sink's over here."

Nicholas followed him to the front of the barn. The bishop said nothing while Nicholas washed up. He gave a smile back—albeit a pained one—as he offered Nicholas a holey towel. "Henrietta loves her animals."

"I can't fault her for that." Nicholas dried his hands and draped the towel over the sink. "Her concern for the horse's health is admirable. I wish all people were as dedicated to their animals' well-being."

Adam's gaze was fixed somewhere over Nicholas' shoulders. His troubled expression matched clouded eyes. Even a man like Nicholas could read that look.

His new bishop was worried, and the why had something to do with Henrietta.

CHAPTER 3

One special friend did not an expert on men make. Fighting the urge to tell Ruby as much, Hen dumped still-sizzling sausage links onto a platter next to a mound of bacon strips. Her sister thought four years of courting the same man meant she could spout endless advice to her older sister.

"First of all, he's a know-it-all, bossy man who took the job I applied for. Second of all, Nicholas Byler could be married for all we know." Hen inhaled two of her favorite aromas—bacon and coffee. Her mouth watered, and her stomach rumbled. She leaned in front of her sister to set the platter on the table next to a mammoth bowl of scrambled eggs. Ruby was two years younger and five inches shorter. And by all accounts, a lot prettier than Hen. "And third of all, I'm not so hard up for a beau that I'll jump at the chance to try to catch any Toby, David, or Henry who comes my way."

"If you don't hurry up, all the Tobys, Davids, and Henrys will be married."

Time to reroute the conversation. "Why didn't you tell me you're going to help out at the school starting on Monday?"

"I didn't know the school board asked Dat until last night. You were asleep." Ruby poured orange juice in short glasses for the little ones. "It's only for two weeks. School is out at the end of the month."

Everyone knew the school year ended April 30. "Dat says I have to take care of the house while you're at the school."

"He just wants you to practice your wifely skills. I reckon Nicholas Byler would like that too."

"Enough with Nicholas Byler already."

"Who's Nicholas Byler?" Micah ambled into the kitchen. Where their younger brother tread, his smaller shadows Luke, Devon, and Dillon wouldn't be far behind. "And if Ruby can get a beau, anybody can. Even you, Hen."

"Nice. Thanks for your words of support, *Bruder*. Wash up." Hen swatted his hand before he could swipe a sausage. Her brother was nothing if not predictable. At nineteen he was a regular at singings. If he had a special friend, he kept that tidbit to himself. But that didn't mean he didn't think he was an expert on relationships. At his age and being a man, he thought he was an expert on everything. "Nicholas is Dr. McDonald's new assistant."

"You shouldn't hold it against him that he took the job you wanted. He didn't know you wanted it. Plus, you weren't even in the running. Doc McDonald mentioned to Dat that you'd applied, and Dat told him not to consider you. That you're needed at home." Ruby added more toast to an already impressive stack. It took a full loaf to feed the entire family. "At least he didn't embarrass you by telling Doc McDonald you applied after he told you not to."

"He didn't! How could he? He knew how much I wanted that job." Hen wrung the threadbare dish towel between her hand so hard it ripped. She'd filled out the application because she'd been sure her father would change his mind if Doc McDonald actually offered her the job. The extra money would've come in handy in feeding and clothing a family of eight. "I can't believe he did that to me."

"To you? I can't believe you went against his wishes. He said he didn't want you working with an Englisch man every day." Ruby's indignant tone made her sound just like their father. No doubt, she'd be a good parent someday. "Plus, I need you to help me with taking care of this family. I can't believe you don't see that. Did you even think about all the work to be done around here when you put pen to paper at the clinic?"

Hen turned her back to her sister. She went to the cupboard and pulled out the sugar so she could fill the sugar dish. In that respect, Ruby was right. She shouldn't have to bear the brunt of the hole left by their mother's death. Hen had let her do it because she was good at it and Hen wasn't. But Hen could help in other ways too—like bringing in additional income.

"Come on, Hen, let it go." Ruby side-arm hugged Hen. "It was a long shot anyway. Doc McDonald always hires men. I'm surprised an Amish man got the job, for that matter. I wonder where Nicholas Byler is from. He likely had to do a phone interview, which probably didn't make his family happy, either."

Hen returned the hug. Ruby's observations were also true. No point in taking Dad's treachery out on her. "Who knows? I didn't have time to grill him. Nor the interest."

She was too busy trying to restrain her instant dislike. Ruby was right. Nicholas had no way of knowing the job would've been perfect for Hen. Still, he didn't have to be so bossy. He did seem like he knew what he was doing. Jack was in good hands. She'd have to be satisfied with that. The thought rankled. Why did women always have to settle?

"That's gut, because I'm not all that interesting."

Nicholas' voice reverberated in the suddenly quiet room. Hen dropped a stack of napkins. Embarrassment burned through her. She knelt to pick them up. Unfortunately Nicholas was still standing in the doorway when she rose. She forced her best smile. "Have a seat. The food's getting cold."

Nicholas slid into a chair in the middle of the long hickory table that seated twelve. "I'm from Bird-in-Hand. Me and my sister Lenora came to stay with our grandpa Moses Byler last week. And jah, I'm twenty-three and single. Anything else you'd like to know?"

His brief bio delivered in a playful tone only served to cause a dozen more questions to sprout up like an unruly patch of thistles in Henrietta's brain. Why come from halfway across the state to live with his grandfather at this stage in his life? Was it because of the job, or did he get the position after he moved to Smicksburg? How did he become so learned about animals? Why wasn't he married at twenty-three?

He probably hated that last question as much as Hen did. A person didn't have control of when love decided to knock on the door, or whether the other person would open that door. Plus, it was no one's business.

"Welcome to the community." Ruby filled a mug with coffee and handed it to Nicholas. He probably wondered how the two could be related. Ruby had their mom's blond hair, blue eyes, and tiny build. Hen was built like their father—tall, rangy, with brown hair and caramel eyes. They were also as different in temperament as winter and summer. "Your *groossdaadi* used to come to church regularly, but I haven't seen him in a while. During the summer, he and your *groossmammi* always brought watermelon straight from the garden for the meal afterward. Before she passed."

How long ago had that been? Hen racked her brain. She remembered the Bylers but not well enough to know about the watermelon. She was too wrapped up in her goats and her business. "Did you come out here because of your groossdaadi?"

Pain flitted across Nicholas' face. He took a sip of his coffee, the cup and his hands shielding his lower face for a few seconds. "Jah. He's not doing well."

Having witnessed Dad's struggle to overcome his pain at losing Mom, Henrietta had a clear picture of how Nicholas' grandfather was doing. "Melancholy because of your *mammi*'s passing?"

"I suppose, but he also has dementia." Nicholas cleared his throat. "Most days he doesn't remember Mammi is dead. He keeps waiting for her to come back from town and make him supper."

Sad and hard for grandkids to deal with on their own. "Your schweschder must have her hands full. I've heard folks with dementia tend to wander."

Nicholas took a long drink of water. His gray eyes were dark, almost stormy. His fair skin had pinked up. Whatever he was thinking, it wasn't good. Maybe she shouldn't be pummeling him with so many questions. Mom used to tell her she was far too curious for her own good. But how did a person learn anything, if she didn't ask? Nicholas studied his water as if searching for answers. "He does take off now and then, but so far, he's managed to make his way home. Our Englisch neighbors know. They've brought him home a couple of times. They're real kind."

"Let's give our visitor a break from the questions, sei so gut." Dad pulled out the chair at the head of the table. It scraped the pine floor. "Sit. Time's wasting."

The naysayer had entered the kitchen so quietly, Hen hadn't noticed. She whirled and took the seat farthest from him.

Luke, who was fourteen, grabbed the chair next to Nicholas. Devon and Dillon, eight-year-old twins, engaged in a brief tug-of-war over the chair on the other side. Devon won, so Dillon, his expression sulky, took the next chair down. Dad's silent prayer lasted seconds, but the quiet stretched out afterward, broken only by silverware clinking on plates and the passing of bowls and platters. The Millers took their food consumption seriously.

Nicholas must've thought they were pigs. Or not talking because of his presence—which was far from the truth. They always ate like they'd been deprived of food for months. Mom would've been horrified and put a stop to it. Dad didn't seem to notice.

"These eggs are gut." Nicholas held up his fork, a chunk of said eggs clinging to it. "Lenora's are either runny or dry."

So Hen wasn't the only one who sometimes failed in the kitchen. Although her eggs were fine. Mostly.

"I collected the eggs." Mena beamed. "I'm Philomena. They call me Mena. I help Ruby cook. But I like helping Hen better."

Ruby sighed. Hen elbowed her. Their little sister was simply being honest. Mena proceeded to introduce everyone—even Hen and their father. "Everybody calls Hen the goat whisperer."

It was Dad's turn to sigh. The boys giggled. Hen jumped into the silence that followed Mena's pronouncement. "I know Nicholas. He examined Jack."

"Is he going to be okay?" Mena's face crumpled. From sunshine to rain in zero seconds. "He's not going to die, is he? My mamm died—"

"He'll be fine, Philomena. Nicholas is seeing to that." Dad hid his expression by patting his lips with his napkin. "Less talking and more eating. You have chores to do."

Mena might not remember her mother, but she was aware of what she was missing. What other little girls and boys had. Her lower lip quivering, she ducked her head and picked up a slice of toasted sourdough bread overloaded with peach jam.

"Your dat is right. Jack will be fine." Nicholas' words brought up the little girl's head. "I promise. With a diet more suited to his age, he'll feel better in no time."

His snarkiness disappeared when he spoke with animals and little girls.

"You're smart. Isn't he smart, Hen?"

"It's his job to know." The words sounded churlish even to Hen. "Besides, I found the same information on the internet."

Oops. Loose lips and all that. Hen tried for a smile. Dad didn't return it. He scowled, but he said nothing. Not in front of company.

"Hen's smart too," Mena said. The little girl could be so oblivious. "But she doesn't have a special friend."

"Philomena—"

"She couldn't have a special friend." Devon chortled. "Her clothes are always dirty."

"And she smells like goat." Dillon mimicked his twin's tone and his giggle. "Who wants a special friend who smells like poop?"

"That's enough—"

A strident *beep-beep-beep* saved the boys from their father's sharp words. The annoying sound seemed to come from Nicholas' pants. His face turned redder than an overripe strawberry. He shoved back his chair and stood. "I'm so sorry." He pulled a cell phone from his pocket. "It's Dr. McDonald. He insisted I carry a phone in case—"

"Take the call outside." Dad clipped each word like he was chipping ice from a block.

Nicholas darted from the room.

"A vet always has a lot of emergencies." Why did Hen feel the need to defend this know-it-all stranger who took her job? It wasn't about Nicholas. She always took the opposite side from her dad. "It makes sense to give him a phone."

"He should know better than to bring it into the house." Dad pushed back his chair. "Everyone has chores to do this morning. You best get busy."

"If you hadn't pulled my application, I could've been the one assisting Doc McDonald."

Dad stood. His glasses on the end of his nose, he glared at her. "I told you not to do it. You disobeyed me. You forced me to have an embarrassing conversation with Doc. Now he thinks I can't handle my own dochder."

"I just thought—"

"You don't think. You're selfish. You want what you want with no thought for anyone else. That's the problem." Dad threw his napkin on the table. "Help your schweschder. She shouldn't have to shoulder all the responsibilities with your mamm. . ." His voice went hoarse and petered out. "Set an example for the other *kinner*. Especially Philomena."

In so many ways, Dad was right. But Hen could do so much more. She could help earn money to pay for the family's needs. "I'm not a kind anymore—"

"Then don't act like one. You're still my dochder. Until you marry, you live in my house. You do as I say."

Or what? He'd take a switch to her behind the way he did when she was in the third grade and took the buggy to town to buy ice cream? This was going nowhere. She was making it worse for herself and for Dad. He had enough on his plate, being both father and mother to her brothers and sisters. "I'm sorry, Dat."

His expression softened. "I know you are. That's what makes being your daed so hard. But you must learn. Surely you see that."

Hen did see it. He was not only her father but her bishop. A widower with seven children and all the responsibilities of a church leader. All she did was make it harder for him. "Are you sure I can't go into town for you?" Hen busied herself stacking plates. The boys were already on their way out. "Ruby says she needs a few supplies from Needles and Notions."

"They can wait." Ruby leaned past Hen to gather up the water glasses. "I'd rather have help with the floors and the dusting. I—we—need to bake bread. We're almost out."

"You heard your sister." Dad clomped from the room before Hen could argue. Hen blew out air. She grabbed serving bowls and handed them to Ruby at the sink.

Her expression sly, Ruby took them. "You didn't tell me the vet's assistant was so handsome."

"Ruby!" Looks weren't important, especially when the man wearing them was like a pair of pliers pinching the tender skin under Hen's forearm. She set a stack of plates in the hot water bucket in the sink. "You have a special friend. What would Peter think?"

"Peter knows I'm only thinking of you. This fellow is hardworking, smart, pleasing to the eye, and most importantly, available."

"You figured all that out in the time it took to eat eggs, bacon, and toast?"

"He was doing great until he brought a phone into the house."

For once Ruby was right, and Dad as well. The *Ordnung* forbade phones in the house for a reason. People should pay attention to those in front of them, not someone calling in the middle of family time. No one needed to be that connected to the world. But Ruby hadn't heard Nicholas try to boss Hen.

"Can I have an *eppy*?" Mena had climbed on a chair and pulled a cookie jar filled with chocolate chip cookies across the counter. "And one for Buster. And one for Tigger. Willow might want one too."

"Philomena Katherine Miller, you just had breakfast. Get down from there."

Ruby whirled and shot across the kitchen. Mena's whine following Ruby, Hen used the diversion to slip from the kitchen. She'd return later to dry and put away the dishes. Right now, she needed to learn more about Nicholas Byler. He had the job she wanted. She was always interested in learning more any way she could. No doubt he would move back to Bird-in-Hand one day. That job might still be hers. She'd wear Dad down sooner or later.

One other intriguing thought buzzed around Hen's brain as she trotted out the door. Nicholas Byler ignored rules. He might somehow understand Hen's predilection for doing the same—for the right reasons, of course.

One of Dad's frequent observations always delivered in a weary voice rang in Hen's ears. *"The road to hell is paved with gut intentions, Dochder, don't be in such a hurry to get there, sei so gut."*

CHAPTER 4

Holding the phone tightly against his ear, Nicholas paced in the Millers' front yard, careful to zig around a striped cat and zag past an orangey-yellow dog, both of whom seemed determined to join him for the call. Having a phone for emergency communications was only half the battle. He should've asked his van driver to wait. Instead, he'd gone to drop off two other riders. Dr. McDonald wasn't happy about that.

"Lou's only five minutes out." Nicholas managed to squeeze in this information when his boss paused long enough to breathe. The man always uttered fifty words when ten would do. And all the while urging Nicholas to hurry. "He'll get me back to town in fifteen minutes."

"Sooner would be better rather than later. Lou is the slowest driver in the state." In other words, he observed the posted speed limits. Dr. McDonald was more worried about his animal patients than Lou's human passengers. "Prod him a little if you have to. I'll pay him extra. Have him take you to the clinic. Pick up the meds. Meet me at the Brodericks' farm. Got that?"

"Got it." The Brodericks' prize bull had an ear infection, of all things. "I'll see you as soon as I can get—"

The phone emitted a shrill beep in Nicholas' ear. He jerked it away from his face. The number from his grandpa's shack phone appeared on the screen. Lenora would never call unless it was an emergency. "I have to go."

"What, is Lou there?"

"No, but—"

"Is Adam's mare in trouble?"

"No, but—"

"Get here as quick as you can." Dr. McDonald hung up.

The phone connected to the new call. Lenora started talking before Nicholas could speak. "It's *Daadi.* He didn't want to take his pills this morning. He said they make his brain foggy. When I tried to insist, he locked himself in his work room. He won't come out."

Gott, *have mercy, sei so gut.* Nicholas did an about-face, intent on a return to pacing. He ran smack into Henrietta. She stumbled backward. He caught himself by flailing his free arm. "*Ach.* Sorry. I didn't see you there."

"See me where?" His sister's voice squeaked with irritation. She had the patience required of a teacher with a one-room schoolhouse full of students—which she'd once been—but she sounded on the edge of losing it. "What are you talking about?"

"Nothing." Nicholas held up his hand to ward off Henrietta's attempt to speak. He could only handle one conversation at a time. "Just wait it out, Schweschder. He has to come out eventually."

"He doesn't have a coat. It's cold in there." A half hiccup, half sob punctuated his sister's words. Lenora never cried. She could stare down a half-dozen back-talking ten-year-old boys intent on throwing spitballs in the classroom without batting an eye. "He's supposed to drink a lot of water. He hasn't drunk any. He needs to take his pills."

"I get it. I get it. There's not another key to the workshop?"

"If there is, I don't know where it is. I've searched his bedroom, the desk, and the living room, even the bookshelves. Can you come? He'll listen to you. He likes you. He hates me."

"He doesn't hate you, and he doesn't even remember me." The two of them hadn't spent enough time with Grandpa growing up for him to remember them now. He was more likely to call Lenora by Grandma's name Mary. And Nicholas favored his dad enough to be Amos to Grandpa. As much as Nicholas wanted to help his sister, he couldn't. Not and keep his job. "Dr. McDonald needs me—"

"Daadi needs you."

"What can I do to help?" Henrietta flapped her arms in front of Nicholas as if he couldn't see her standing there in his personal space. The unadorned concern in her face—despite still smelling like manure—improved her appearance a hundredfold. Behind the bluster hid a pretty girl. An hour ago she'd been aggravated with him for taking a job she coveted. Now she wanted to help. "Can I do something for Dr. McDonald? I know a lot about birthing foals."

As if she could help a veterinarian with a degree and ten years' experience on the job. She did have faith in herself. Nicholas shook his head. "Thanks, but he needs me to open up the clinic and get him some supplies, including drugs."

"So what's the problem with your daadi?" Hen accepted his rejection and moved on. Another point for her. "Maybe I can help there."

And she was determined to be helpful.

"Who are you talking to?" Lenora sounded peeved again. "I know we need you to keep the job, but Dr. McDonald will understand."

Not likely. The veterinarian had tunnel vision when it came to his patients—which was a good thing for them—not some much for people. "Just give me a minute."

Nicholas rubbed the spot on his temple where a headache bloomed. He put his hand over the phone and explained the situation to Henrietta.

Her lips pursed, she squinted her eyes and chewed on her lower lip for a few seconds. "I *can* help, then. Your daadi used to have a crew that constructed buildings, mostly barns, sheds, and businesses, right? He drew up the plans, didn't he?"

"He did, but now—"

"But now he can't. But he doesn't remember that." Henrietta tapped her cheek with her index finger, inadvertently making a smudge of dirt bigger. "I'll go to the farm and tell him I need him to draw up plans for a new goat shed."

The sound of an engine joined the cacophony of birds, dogs, and cats, along with the distant bleating of goats. The van. Time was up. Nicholas' stomach burned. "I won't lie to Daadi."

"I don't lie to anybody. I do need another goat shed. I want to start a herd of Angora goats."

How would her father feel about that? Lou's dusty van rounded the curve. No time to contemplate Henrietta's statement now. The driver would be in front of the house within ninety seconds. Nicholas took his hand from the phone. "Schweschder, Henrietta Miller is on her way over. She'll explain the plan when she gets there."

"If Daadi won't listen to me, he surely won't listen to a stranger."

"Henrietta has a plan. Just follow her lead."

Nicholas disconnected. Henrietta whirled and dashed in the direction of the barn. "*Denki*," he called after her.

She didn't turn around, but her voice carried on the brisk spring breeze. "Tell Dr. McDonald we'd still like for him to come by to check on Jack in a few days. Just to make sure he's on the mend."

She too had tunnel vision.

Which, when it came to animals, was still a good thing—no matter how annoying her inability to trust his treatment was.

Nicholas climbed into the van. Lou had already received a call from the vet. Relieved, Nicholas leaned back. He rolled down the window. The spring breeze was preferrable to the van's stuffy air.

"Hey, where's Hen?" Hands on her hips, Ruby stood on the porch. "Did you see where she went?"

Nicholas stuck his head through the window. "We have a situation with my daadi at the farm. She offered to go help out my sister with him."

"She's supposed to be drying the dishes and mopping the floors."

"Sorry!"

Nicholas withdrew into the van. Dry dishes. Mop floors. Or go lure an elderly man from his locked fortress. Which was a more suitable task for a young Amish woman? The bishop would have one answer to that question, his daughter another.

One thing was for certain. Henrietta Miller was unlike any Plain woman Nicholas had ever met.

CHAPTER 5

The Bylers' wooden, two-story A-frame could use some paint. Time for a frolic. When was the last time Henrietta had been at the Byler farm? Probably for church. The front porch steps needed work too. The third one squeaked and gave under her weight. "I'm not that heavy."

She reached for the screen door.

"I'm out here!"

The shout came from behind her. Hen whirled and retraced her path down the steps and past her buggy.

A woman with chestnut hair a shade lighter than Nicholas' and the same gray eyes strode across uneven ground covered with more clover and weeds than grass. A sleek black Labrador followed close on her heels. "You must be Henrietta."

"Call me Hen." Hen rushed to meet her. "You must be Nicholas' schweschder."

"I am."

"And who is this beauty?" Hen held out her hand to the dog. Her tail wagging in ecstasy, the lab sniffed and licked her fingers. "Such a sweet kiss. Denki."

"This is Daisy. She's Nicholas' dog. She also belongs to our little sister, but he refused to leave her in Bird-in-Hand, and she refused to be left." Lenora's tone lightened. "She was busy sulking because Nicholas didn't take her with him this morning. Now that we have company, she's all smiles and kisses."

Nicholas was a dog lover. A point in the positive column, but it would take several more to move the know-it-all over to it. "Gut for her. Is Moses still in his shop?"

"Jah, only now he won't even answer me when I call to him." One hand on her crooked prayer covering, Lenora rushed ahead of Hen. Daisy woofed and raced past them both. "I'm afraid he's passed out."

"Does he do that?"

"Not really, but there's always a first time. He was talking. I told him you were coming and what you needed. He said okay, and that was that."

"Then all is well."

"How do you know?"

"If I were him, I'd be working on the plans."

Lenora's frown faded. "I suppose you're right. I *hope* you're right."

Someone, likely Moses, had applied more recent elbow grease to the workshop. The white paint was fresh and clean. Planters filled with asparagus ferns adorned either side of the path leading up to the door. Even the glass in the windows sparkled. "He spends a lot of time out here."

"Sure. But he never locks the door. I'm able to bring him a sandwich for lunch. A thermos of *kaffi*." Lenora tugged on the door. It didn't open. "I start a fire in the woodburning stove sometimes, because he doesn't think of it. He doesn't even seem to notice the cold."

"He's living in another world."

"Do you have dementia in your family?"

Hen shook her head. "*Nee*, but my favorite librarian retired after she was diagnosed with Alzheimer's disease a few years ago. She was so smart. She'd read every book in the library and then some. I could ask her any question, and she'd either know the answer or know how to get it."

Which kept Hen from having to use the internet to find information. Her father didn't approve of her using computers. The Ordnung allowed it for businesses, but he refused to concede that Hen ran their goat business. If anyone did research, it should be him or Micah. Neither was so inclined.

Lenora touched Hen's arm. "I'm sorry. Family or friend, it still hurts."

Nicholas' sister was nice. Nicer than he was. "I saw her once on the street in Punxsutawney. She didn't know me. Her husband apologized. Really he shouldn't've. It wasn't his fault. Or hers."

Which led to the question, whose fault was it? Dad would say disease in a world full of sin could be traced back to Adam and Eve. Why should a librarian suffer because a woman was tricked by a serpent into eating a forbidden fruit? Hen shrugged off the thought like a heavy winter coat that was too warm in the spring weather.

"Nicholas said you had a plan for getting Daadi to come out. Care to share it?"

"Here we go." Hen rapped on the workshop door. "Moses? Moses! It's me, Hen Miller. I came to see if you've made any progress on those plans for my goat shed."

Silence. "Moses?"

The door opened. Moses peered out. The man Hen remembered from church had shrunk into a wizened figure with bent shoulders and rheumy, faded blue eyes behind thick-lensed glasses. "Henrietta, the bishop's daughter. Does he know you're here?"

Moses might have had dementia, but he hadn't forgotten what a stickler Dad was. "I left him a note."

True. He wouldn't be happy, but then he never was when it came to Hen's thoughts on expanding and improving their goat business. "I want to be able to show him how we can raise a second small herd without taking up too much land. The shed doesn't have to be huge. We'll still have pasture enough for both herds as well, along with the horses."

At least that was the idea. The fact was she intended to build the shed herself with help from her brothers. It didn't have to be fancy. She'd watched a bunch of videos on the internet, and DIY was the way to go. That didn't mean the shed wouldn't benefit from actual plans drawn by an experienced contractor.

"Come on in, then." Moses moved aside long enough for Hen to slide by. But then he stepped back into Lenora's path. He raised a gnarled finger and shook it at his granddaughter. "But not you. I don't know you."

"Daadi, it's me. Lenora. Your *kinnskind*."

His forehead wrinkled. He frowned. "Nee. Lenora's in Bird-in-Hand. Go on. Git."

Hen backpedaled a few steps until she stood beside Moses. She shivered and wrapped her arms around her middle. "Even with the sun out, it's still cool today. I sure could use a cup of hot tea. What do you say we head over to the house and get warm? We can talk there."

Moses ran his hands up and down his arms. "It is a bit nippy. Mary, go make us some tea. I'll get my supplies. We'll be right behind you."

Somehow it seemed better that Lenora's grandfather thought she was his wife than a stranger he didn't recognize at all.

Her gray eyes damp with tears, Lenora nodded. "On my way. Chamomile or peppermint?"

"You know better, *fraa*. Black tea for me. With honey. When have I ever drank anything else?"

"Right."

In less than five minutes they were seated at the kitchen table, Daisy sprawled on the rug by the back door, with Moses' oversized paper, pencil, and ruler spread out in front of him. He had already drawn a preliminary sketch. "Do you want to go with prefab, or do you want to do Sheetrock? Either way, we can paint it. Do you want regular doors or a roll-up door like a garage door? How big is your herd? Do you have a size in mind?"

That his mind cranked itself up for this moment seemed unfair. Hen glanced at Lenora. Standing at the stove with a teapot in one hand, she dabbed a tissue to her cheeks with the other. Another tenderhearted person. Hen turned back to Moses. "I would say we'll want at least six to start. That's probably all we can afford, but we need an enclosure big enough to hold twelve. That's my long-term goal. They'll have *boplin* every year. According to what I've read, we should figure sixteen square feet for each goat. They don't like to share, and they don't like the cold. Our winters will be brutal for them. It needs to be sturdy and have room for individual feeding stations and heat lamps."

"You've done your homework." Moses' pencil made scratching sounds as he bent over a notebook. His forehead wrinkled, he did math faster than Hen ever did in school. "That's a good-sized building. Plus you'll need pasture for them. Did you consider that?"

Just a shed. All Hen needed—all she could afford—was a shed designed to keep the goats warm and dry in cold and wet weather. And enough acreage for them to graze. "We'll need at least two acres for six goats, but that's not a problem. Dat is only planting alfalfa and corn on a hundred acres this year."

That left eighteen acres for produce and pasture. The alfalfa would be sold as hay to bigger farms, along with the corn.

"I don't know anything about raising goats." Moses sat back. He stroked his curly silver beard. It reached to his waist when he sat. "But I reckon it comes with a lot of overhead. A building like this won't be cheap. I'll have to talk to my crew about a starting date after I work up an estimate for you."

"Daadi, you don't have a crew anymore." Lenora set a steaming mug of tea in front of Moses, along with a jar of honey and a spoon. "You're retired, remember?"

A befuddled expression passed over his wrinkled face. "What are you talking about, Dochder? I have plenty of good years left in me. And what are you doing here? Where's your mamm?"

"My mammi died, remember? My mamm is Hannah." Her voice soft, laden with sadness, Lenora added honey to her grandfather's tea, stirred it, and laid the spoon aside. "I'm Lenora, your *kinnskind*. Drink your tea. We need to warm you up."

The man sitting across from Hen no longer burst with energy. He deflated under her gaze. "So bossy," he grumbled. "Everyone wants to tell me what to do."

Nevertheless he lifted the mug to his lips and sipped.

"We just want you to be healthy, that's all." Lenora went to the counter and returned with another mug and a platter of muffins. She set one in front of Hen. "Look, Daadi, your favorite. Banana nut muffins. They're still warm."

"Humphf." When he didn't reach for the muffin, Lenora took one and placed it on a napkin next to his mug. "You didn't eat your breakfast. We need to get some food in you."

"Bossy. I'm a grown man. I'll eat when I get hungry."

This had to be so hard. Hen shot Lenora an encouraging look. "Who worked on the crew with you, Moses?"

Moses chose to take a healthy bite of muffin instead of responding.

"Nicholas mentioned Wilbur Nettles took over your business," Lenora offered. "Maybe you can still work up the plans and then ask him to use them to build Hen's shed."

It wouldn't be necessary, but bolstering Moses' sense of usefulness came first at this moment. If the name Wilbur Nettles meant anything to Moses, he didn't show it. He picked up the spoon, stirred his tea, and stared into his mug with a faraway expression on his whiskered face.

"It's okay. One step at a time." Hen glanced at the clock on the wall next to a calendar. "Ach, I better get home. I have chores to do."

"I'll walk you to your buggy." Lenora grabbed a shawl from a rack next to the back door. "I'll be right back, Daadi."

No answer.

"It must be so hard, yet you're so patient." Hen followed her to the back door. "My groossdaadi lives down the road. I can't imagine what it would be like if he didn't remember me. Or thought I was someone else."

"I try to be patient. It's not his fault." Lenora nudged Daisy, who yawned, stood, and sashayed over to Moses' feet where she plopped down again. This allowed Lenora to open the door for Hen. "Mostly it makes me so sad. He keeps asking where Mammi is. Nicholas and I have to take turns telling him she died. It's like he has to go through the grief of losing her all over again. It breaks my heart."

"Maybe it would be better to tell him she's gone away to visit family. That she's coming back. Why cause him that grief when he isn't going to remember anyway?"

"Maybe. But lying to him doesn't seem right." Lenora chewed her bottom lip. It was already chapped and red. "We have to take him to Pittsburgh next month to see his doctor. Maybe we can ask her what's the best way to handle it."

"Definitely. And you could use the computers at the library in Punxsutawney to research it." That's what Hen did. How could educating herself about an important topic be wrong? There was so much information available at their fingertips. Which was why the elders didn't approve. It was too much like being connected to the electrical grid. They might get swallowed up in the world. That would never happen to Hen. Dad should trust her on that. "It helps to educate yourself."

"Does the *Gmay* approve of that?"

"It depends on the purpose. It's allowed for business, but I think health is another good reason."

"Same with our Gmay in Bird-in-Hand." Her shoulders sagging, Lenora rubbed her temples. "I'll call my mamm and see what she thinks."

"Gut idea." Getting her new acquaintance in trouble would not get them off to a good start. Hen untied the reins from the hitching post. Zane neighed his approval. Standing around waiting for her wasn't the gelding's favorite use of his time. "It must be hard moving to a new place and leaving behind the rest of your friends and family."

"I loved teaching, but family is more important." Lenora's eyes reddened again. "Mostly I miss my *schweschdre* and my mamm. Isn't that silly? I'm nineteen."

"It's not silly. I know what it is to miss a mother." At least Lenora could still visit her mother. "I'd be happy to spell you anytime if you want to go into town to shop, or just get away. Moses seems to know me."

"That's so sweet of you." Lenora smiled for the first time. She could be her brother's twin. "And much appreciated. Maybe we can talk about it after church Sunday."

"Sounds like a plan."

Hen climbed into the buggy. With a wave, she took off.

She'd made an unexpected friend. If her plan to start a new goat herd helped Moses feel useful, that was a good thing too. A day that started off gloomy was now full of possibility.

At least until Dad chewed her out for leaving Ruby with only Mena to help her. And threw a damper on her plans for building a goat shed.

Maybe she'd wait to mention that part.

CHAPTER 6

Hen's father and bishop pulled a suitcase from the back of a van when Hen turned off the dirt road that led to their house. He'd want a word about where she'd been sooner rather than later. A Plain woman talked to the driver through his window, her hands gesticulating. A visitor. They weren't expecting anyone. Mena, Ruby, Tigger, Willow, Buster, Sam, the boys—the whole gang had gathered around. Mena turned three cartwheels in a row. Buster woofed and rolled in the grass. Somebody good, it seemed.

Then the woman turned around. Aunt Ginny, known to the rest of the world as Ginny Burkholder or Joel Burkholder's wife, had come for a visit.

If Dad hadn't been standing there, Hen would've jumped from the buggy and turned her own cartwheels. Dad's sister was the best. Even he would smile for as long as she stayed around.

"Hen, there you are." Aunt Ginny hollered and flapped her arms like a bird taking flight. "Get down here and give me a hug, sweet pea."

Most Plain people were short on physical affection. Not that Mom and Dad didn't love their children. They simply didn't go around handing out hugs in abundance. But Aunt Ginny loved a good hug-a-thon.

No two siblings could be more different. Aunt Ginny smiled morning, noon, and night. She was short and round to her brother's tall and lanky. Her cheeks were pink and dimpled. Her brown eyes sparkled as if she knew a joke and was about to tell it. Her brown hair started turning gray in her mid-twenties. She was a year older than Dad but acted much younger.

Hen hopped from the buggy and skipped toward her. Not even Dad's disapproving gaze could tamp down her joy. A woman her age shouldn't skip, but a visit from her favorite aunt deserved a celebration. "I didn't know you were coming. What a glorious surprise!"

"Your dat figured you all could use a pick-me-up." Aunt Ginny's arms squeezed Hen hard enough to take her breath away. She smelled of Dove soap, baby wipes, and peanut butter cookies. "Besides, it's been far too long since we had a good visit."

Hen backed away in time to see a look pass between her dad and Aunt Ginny. What was the word for it? Hen racked her brain. She'd never been good in school, mostly because she was itching to get outside to play softball and volleyball. Collusion. That was it. This was no casual visit. No matter. She'd drag it out of Aunt Ginny later. "Jah, indeedy, it has."

Avoiding her dad's gaze, Hen picked up the suitcase and marched it up the porch steps. "What's in your suitcase? It weighs a hundred pounds."

"You always did love to exaggerate." Aunt Ginny pranced up the steps. She really did. For a rotund person, she was light on her feet. "Books, clothes, shoes, more books, stationery, stamps, stuff."

Aunt Ginny loved to read. Mostly mysteries. But some biographies too. And she was the only person in the world—according to Dad—who read cookbooks just for fun. She also belonged to half a dozen round-robin pen pal clubs. She wrote a ton of letters. Hen used to love to "decorate" the letters with smiling faces and kitty cats for her aunt when she was younger. "You must be planning a long visit. What does *Onkel* Joel think about that?"

"You know your onkel Joel. He's busy working. As long as he has his kaffi, his chess, and his crossword puzzles in the evenings, he's content. Besides, your *kossins* are there."

If Aunt Ginny was the social butterfly in her Plain community, Uncle Joel was the man who rarely spoke. He farmed, and he worked on his crossword puzzles. Just don't ask him to make conversation with all the words he learned from those puzzles. Only two of their six children were still at home. Charlotte would do the cooking, and Xavier would help with the farmwork.

"Their loss is our gain." Ruby held open the screen door for them. "I can't wait to try your new recipes."

Leave it to Ruby to talk about recipes. Hen squeezed past her and caught up with their aunt. "What's going on with your horses? Is Xavier riding Captain yet? How are Lilac and Juniper?"

Lilac and Juniper being the family's two milking cows.

"Captain is a perfect gentleman now. Mena could ride him." Aunt Ginny blew Mena a kiss. The little girl followed behind with Tigger in her arms and Buster on her heels. "Those two cows are giving us plenty of milk, butter, cream, and ice cream."

Once the suitcase was open on the bed's Flying Geese quilt, Ruby left to set a place at the table for Aunt Ginny. Mena followed whining for cookies—one for her, one for Aunt Ginny, and two for Tigger and Buster. Hen settled on the bed and propped her sneakers on the cedar chest nestled at the foot. "Okay, they're gone. So tell me what you're really doing here."

"What do you mean?" Aunt Ginny had perfected the look of innocence Hen often used herself. She hung her shawl on a hook and went to her suitcase. "I've been planning to visit for a while."

"Not until this summer, last I heard. Is everything all right in Lancaster?"

"Everything's fine."

"Then what are you doing here?"

A teal dress in her arms, Aunt Ginny plopped down next to Hen. She patted her knee. "You are such a nosy kind."

"I'm not a kind."

"Nee, you're not." Aunt Ginny could exaggerate a sigh with the best of them. "I'm here because your dat is worried about you."

"What? Why? That's ridiculous—"

"Save the theatrics, *neis*. He wrote me a long letter about your shenanigans."

Hen was pretty good at exaggerating a sigh herself. "There were no shenanigans. I just wanted to get a job as a vet's assistant."

"And you went so far as to fill out the application after your dat told you not to."

"I thought he would change his mind if I actually got the job." Mom used to say Hen was just like her dad—in other words, just as stubborn. "Especially when he saw how much it paid."

"So then to add insult to injury, you jumped into a conversation among the men after church one fine Sunday and embarrassed your dat by insisting he should consider starting a herd of Angora goats."

Hen also had a brain and knew how to use it. Shouldn't Dad be proud of that? "Why does that embarrass him?"

"I reckon you know the answer to that question." Aunt Ginny snorted. "Don't play the *dumkoph* with me. He's the bishop. You're the bishop's daughter. You're old enough to know what that means."

"He's afraid no one will ever marry me, and we'll both be the objects of pity." Hen threw up her hands in frustration. "People will whisper behind our backs when he's ninety, and I push his wheelchair to the front of the room on Sunday morning, me an old spinster."

"He wants you to be happy."

"If he wanted me to be happy, he'd let me work for the vet and raise my goats in peace, instead of making me take care of the house while Ruby is off helping at the school."

"Someday you'll have your own house to keep. This is practice." Aunt Ginny gave Hen a one-armed hug. "It's not so bad. I'll help you with the house."

"That's the plan, then. He brought you here to whip me into shape so he can marry me off."

"He brought me here because you seemed to be meandering off the path. Every Plain girl dreams of marrying. You can't tell me you're the one exception in the whole of this country."

Hen threw herself back on the bed. She spread her arms wide and stared at the ceiling. "I do want to get married and have boplin. I look forward to that day. I just want to do a few other things first. Didn't you want to accomplish other things before you perfected your diaper changing and baby rocking skills?"

Aunt Ginny lay back and wiggled on to her side, so she faced Hen. She propped her head on her hand. "Nee, not that I can remember. I saw Joel, and I was smitten. Smitten, I tell you. I love being a mamm. You will too. You'll take all the love you pour out on animals and channel it into your kinner. That's a promise."

"I don't know." Hen groaned. She rubbed her face with both hands. Dare she speak the words aloud? "What if I'm a bad mamm? What if something happens to one of them? What if it's my fault?"

"Whatever are you talking about? Are you saying you're afraid your *bopli* will die?"

"Everyone dies." Hen rolled on to her side with her back to her aunt.

"Stephen died. He was only three weeks old. Then Mamm died for no gut reason."

Sure, her animals died, but she knew from the beginning that they had much shorter lives. She could prepare herself. No one prepared for a parent to go to the hospital for a simple infection and come home in a casket.

Aunt Ginny had stayed with the family when baby Stephen died, asleep in his crib one minute, no longer breathing the next. A perfectly healthy baby. Then she'd come back for almost four months when Mamm died. She'd sung Mena to sleep, held the little boys when they cried, cooked meals, and cleaned the house. She knew how hard Hen and the others had taken it. "It's been three years. There's no specific time a person grieves a loss, but sooner or later you have to accept it and learn to go on. Gott's—"

"If you say Gott's will be done or Gott has a plan, I will most certainly barf all over your dress."

"You don't believe Gott has a plan?"

"Jah, I do." Hen stared at the framed cross-stitch of a little girl on her knees in a nightgown praying by her bed that hung on the wall over the room's only chair. "I don't like His plans. They stink."

She whispered the last words and waited. Lightning would split the sky, burn a hole in the roof, and strike her dead.

Nothing happened. Even Aunt Ginny said nothing. Instead she wrapped her arm around Hen and pulled her close. Memories of her mother's soft touch and smell of Ivory soap flooded her. Aunt Ginny tried hard, but she wasn't Mom. Mom would understand. She would have answers to the hard questions.

"My sweet *maedel*. I don't think we're expected to understand Gott's plan. I do know that if everything was easy, our faith would be flabby. Hanging on to faith in hard times hones that faith."

"It sounds like an excuse someone thought up."

"That someone was the apostle Paul."

"I thought it sounded familiar." Shame made it hard to swallow. No one else in the world would hear Hen's doubts and not judge her, only Aunt Ginny. *Denki, Gott, for* Aenti *Ginny.* At least she knew when to thank God for blessings. That was worth something, wasn't it? "But he was a man too, wasn't he?"

"And I'm only a woman. I'm no gospel scholar. I only know it gives me comfort to think Gott is in charge. We don't have to understand. We simply have to believe."

"So Gott judges us on whether we believe in the hard times?"

"Have you talked to your dat about this?"

An image of her dad's face reddening and smoke billowing from his ears assailed Hen. "Are you crazy?"

"He's also your bishop." Aunt Ginny's voice was low and sweet. "He can help you with your questions."

"Exactly my point."

"What about the deacon who taught your baptism classes?"

Robert had a supply of unending patience, but Hen's doubts had come after her baptism. What kind of timing was that? "That was before Mamm died."

"Ah. When you still thought believing was easy."

Hen had gladly entered the Plain faith. It had never occurred to her to do otherwise. Life was good. God was good. "Jah. Nee. Not that it was easy. I didn't even pray about it. I figured Gott had us covered. I figured Gott would reward faith. That He wouldn't let bad things happen to the people I love. After all, I believe. Mamm believed. Dat believed enough for all nine of us. That's why he drew the lot, isn't it? He's the biggest believer of all, and yet Gott took his fraa."

"That's what you think happened?" Aunt Ginny lifted Hen's chin, forcing her to look at her aunt. "Gott didn't take your mamm. Disease that runs rampant in a fallen, sinful world took her."

"You sound like Dat."

"I don't nap during the sermons on Sunday morning. I listen. I'm not always sure of much, but of this I *am* sure." She smiled, the picture of a staunch believer. "Gott didn't take that bopli. Satan wants us to doubt. He wants to worm his way into our minds and, worse, our hearts. You can be sure of one thing, if nothing else—Gott didn't take that sweet bopli. He allowed it, but He didn't do it."

Satan. According to her aunt, Hen had opened the door and Beelzebub strutted—or maybe he tiptoed—through it.

The windup clock on the nightstand ticked loudly in the silence. Hen examined the dirt under her ragged nails. She curled her fingers into her palms to hide the offending sight. Her fingernails weren't the only parts of her that were dirty.

"I'm sorry. I shouldn't have unloaded on you." She wiggled from Aunt Ginny's grasp and stood. "You must be hungry after your long trip. And thirsty. Ruby made some fresh peppermint tea yesterday. Add sugar and it tastes like peppermint candy. Slakes your thirst and freshens your breath."

"You can't fool me, neis. But don't worry, your secret is safe with me. You'll find your way. I promise." Aunt Ginny went to the hooks and hung up her dress as she talked. "I'll pray. There's a man waiting for you somewhere along the road. Gott will lead him to you when the time is right."

"There you two are." Dad stuck his head through the doorway. "What's going on in here? Ruby's got lunch on the table."

For once no disapproval marred his words or his expression.

"We were catching up." Aunt Ginny squeezed past him. "I'm starved. Let's eat."

Dad lingered in the doorway. "What excuses did you give your aenti for running off instead of staying here and helping your schweschder maintain our household?"

So much for the lack of disapproval. So much for being all smiles during Aunt Ginny's visit.

"None. Not one."

Thank goodness Aunt Ginny could be trusted to keep a confidence. Dad could never know about Hen's doubts. They'd likely kill him.

CHAPTER 7

The crack of ball against aluminum bat reverberated in Nicholas' ears, along with the friendly trash talk of the players and the folks who sat in their fold-up lawn chairs along the sidelines of the makeshift softball diamond that filled the Yoders' backyard. Or what passed as trash talk from a group of Plain people fresh from a three-hour Sunday service.

The scent of fresh cut grass mingled with the aroma of grilled hot dogs cooked by Simon Yoder, the Gmay deacon. Jackets, sweaters, and shawls had been cast aside as the sun warmed the late April afternoon air. A game of softball had always struck Nicholas as the perfect antidote to a numb behind after sitting on a hard bench for the service. His dad called it the pent-up wiggles release.

The loudest cheers and jeers seemed to come from the girls' team currently on the field. Led by none other than Henrietta Miller. Not surprising. The woman did have a mouth on her.

"You should play." Lenora coupled her sentiment with an overzealous elbow in his midsection. "You were the best player at our school back in the day."

"That was a long time ago." Nicholas rubbed his rib cage. His sister didn't know her own strength. She stood next to him, a plastic cup of iced tea in one hand and a monster cookie in the other. She seemed to be following him around. Like him, she needed to make friends in their new community. "Why don't you play?"

"Because I was awful. Go on. It'll be a gut way to meet other people your age."

"Women, you mean."

"I see Hen out there. You need to thank her for helping out with Daadi last week. She was super gut with him."

Lenora was right, of course. When Nicholas returned from work on Thursday night, Grandpa had been engrossed in creating plans for Hen's goat shed. He'd even eaten his supper and taken his pills without complaint, all the while telling Nicholas about the girl who'd come for a visit. He didn't remember her name, but he remembered the project.

"When she comes off the field."

"Don't be a dope."

"Hey, Nicholas, do you play?" Bat in hand, Micah Miller approached. He had his father's dark eyes and hair, height, and lanky build. Only the silver-streaked beard was missing. He swished the bat back and forth. "We could use someone who can hit. We're short players today."

"See there." Lenora nudged Nicholas again. "Nicholas is a gut player. A gut hitter, and he pitches."

"I'm pitching this game, but there's always room for a backup pitcher." Micah flipped the bat around so the handle faced Nicholas. He held it out. "It's all yours."

"Denki."

Nicholas shot Lenora a scowl. She didn't seem to notice. Her gaze was still on Micah. Her mouth hung open. Her cheeks were pink. Her hands fluttered as if they had a mind of their own.

Seriously? Nicholas shifted his gaze to Micah. The man was staring at Lenora. That appreciative stare, Nicholas recognized. No man liked seeing a guy ogle his sister. Wide smile, eyes sparking. Yes, sparking, not sparkling. "Hey—"

"You're Lenora, right?" Micah's smile stretched, revealing deep dimples and even teeth. "The girls could use some help too. We're slaughtering them."

"Ummm...I'm not much of a player, but I'll give it a shot." She smiled at Micah. "It'll be fun."

"You hate sports—"

"Hush," Lenora growled as she slipped past Nicholas and made a beeline for the other side of the field where church benches did double duty.

Would wonders never cease? Nicholas followed Micah to the cluster of players gathered near the backstop someone had constructed of wooden planks and chicken wire. After a quick round of introductions, he found himself standing at home plate, facing a stocky pitcher with an exaggerated windup. The first pitch went wide. The second one was a straight shot down the middle. Nicholas swung and missed.

It'd been a long time since he swung a bat. His timing was off.

"Hey, batter, with a swing like that, you're going down. You couldn't hit the side of a barn!"

He'd recognize that voice anywhere. Nicholas took a few practice swings, making sure to end with the bat pointed in the vicinity of second base, where Henrietta Miller stood, legs bent, hunched over, pounding her mitt with her fist. Two could play this game. "I can see why they call you Hen. You squawk like one."

Long drawn out oooohhhs accompanied by laughter filled the air.

"You swing like a doddering old man." Henrietta smacked her mitt harder. "You swing like a three-year-old."

"We'll see about that."

Nicholas dug into the chalk-outlined batter's box. He lifted the bat over his right shoulder and wiggled it. The pitcher went into that windup that made her resemble a girl with a rattlesnake in her underwear.

Easy does it, wait for it, wait for it.

Nicholas connected. Boom. Surprise held him captive for a second.

"Go, go, run, go!" The shouts of his teammates sent him hurtling down the first-base line. "Keep going, keep going!"

He rounded first and headed for second base. Midway, an outfielder slung the ball to Hen. She nabbed it and held her glove out. No way around her. No way through her.

Nicholas reversed course. The first baseman, a chunky girl with a mass of freckles decorating her red cheeks, blocked his return. Hen's toss beat him to the base.

His first at bat in four years, and he was caught in a pickle. In a hot box. In danger of being run down in no-man's-land. In a goose chase with two girls, no less.

"Get him, get him, Hen, get him!"

"Run, Nick, run!"

The crowd's raucous shouts mingled with laughter.

He skidded to a stop, pivoted, and headed back to second.

"No you don't." Hen came straight at him. "You're mine."

Not really. Another reverse. The first baseman had the ball again.

At this rate he'd wear a new path in Deacon Yoder's backyard. Time to reverse again.

Hen leaped in the air to grab the first baseman's throw. This time she didn't wait. She came at Nicholas full tilt.

No time to turn around. He backpedaled.

Big mistake. He tripped over his own feet and fell on his back.

A second later Hen's body slammed into his. Her sweaty, red face, eyes wide and startled, stared down at him, only inches away.

The crowd's laughter died. So did the shouting.

"Oops, sorry." She scrambled to her feet. Her tag was none too gentle. "By the way, you're out."

Stunned, Nicholas remained sprawled on his back as he watched her stroll away, the ball held high. If the mishap had embarrassed her, she didn't let it show. "That's three outs. We're up, *maed*."

A smattering of applause grew into a chorus.

If Hen could brush it off, so could he. Nicholas hopped to his feet, dusted off his pants, and trotted to the sideline. Micah met him at the backstop. "Are you all right?"

"Fine. I need a glove."

"Use my brother's. He got sidetracked taking his girl for a buggy ride." A guy Nicholas didn't recognize tossed him a mitt that had gone more than a few innings. "You can take his spot at third."

More than good. He wanted a chance to redeem himself after the fiasco with Henrietta.

"Sounds gut."

"I'm sure you're all over it." The man grinned. "Kind of like Hen was all over you out there."

"Not funny, Ralph." Micah wasn't smiling. "That's my schweschder you're talking about."

"Just joking."

"Not funny."

Definitely not funny. Micah clapped Nicholas on the back. "Let's go score some points. The girls need to be taken down a peg or two."

Especially one in particular.

CHAPTER 8

Mortification heaped upon mortification. Careful to avoid glancing at the spot where her dad sat with Aunt Ginny, Mena playing with her doll at their feet, Hen strode to the sideline. Too bad she was up next in the batting order. What she really ought to do was dig a hole and hide there for the next forty years. Maybe by then Nicholas would go back to Lancaster.

The horror on his face flashed in her mind's eye. His knee in her belly. His warm breath on her cheek. His scent of soap and sweat in her nose.

"You can't even play softball without getting carried away." Her whisper filled with aggravation, Ruby thrust a red plastic cup of water at Hen. "You couldn't just tag him? You had to tackle him?"

No point in wasting her breath explaining the fall was an accident. If Ruby wanted to believe the worst of Hen, so be it. "I got him out, didn't I?"

"You embarrassed him. You spoiled any chance of him wanting to ask you to go for a buggy ride with him."

"Like he would've anyway. He's too busy tooting his own horn about being the vet's assistant. He's such a know-it-all."

"Takes one to know one."

Hen worked to rein in her irritation. Ruby thought she should fill the gap left by their mother's death. It wasn't possible. Or necessary. "I'll apologize after the game, okay?"

"Okay. If you can. I'm not sure Dat will let you get anywhere near Nicholas now."

"Maybe you can head Dat off at the pass."

"Or you could toss out an 'I'm sorry' as you pass Nicholas on the field."

When push came to shove, Ruby would have her back.

"If you two are through gabbing, you're up, Hen." Pitcher Adele Plank, also Hen's best friend since first grade, held out Hen's favorite bat. "We're behind by five runs. Let's try to keep our eyes on the ball. So to speak."

Hen took the bat and marched up to the plate. Micah was pitching as usual. They'd played softball together since they were old enough to bean each other with wild pitches. She knew his stuff. "Try to get it over the plate, little bruder."

"Why are you standing so far from the plate, big schweschder?" He pretended to draw a bead on her with the ball. "Are you afraid I'll bean you? Don't worry, I can thread a needle with my pitches."

He knew which buttons to push. Hen inched closer to the old patio chair pillow serving as home plate. She took an easy practice swing, waggled the bat, wiggled her hips, and stared at her brother. "Do what you've gotta do."

The pitch sailed straight down the middle. Hen smacked it into left center field and took off like a gold-medal Olympic sprinter. The ball landed between the outfielders and rolled. They raced after it while Hen ran past first and headed for second. By the time the center fielder picked up the ball, she was on her way to third.

The center fielder had a good arm. The ball snapped into Nicholas' mitt a second after Hen landed one foot on the base. Nicholas waved the ball at her. "Maybe you'd like to make a run for home plate."

"I think I'll wait."

Nicholas tossed the ball to Micah.

Her gaze riveted on her brother, Hen edged away from the base. Micah was good at picking off runners.

Nicholas took his place a single step from the bag. They were as alone as they would ever be. Hen exchanged glares with Micah. He slung the ball to Nicholas. She made it back to base with plenty of time to spare. "Stop showing off and pitch, Micah."

"Don't tell me what to do, Schweschder."

Micah threw a pitch. The catcher did his job, leaving no chance for Hen to steal home. Stealing home would be a coup. Plus it would get her away from Nicholas. She edged away from the base. "I hope I didn't hurt you when I fell on you."

"You didn't." Nicholas pounded his fist into his mitt. "You're not that heavy."

"That's gut. I think." What did that mean? Not that heavy. "I am sorry, though, if I embarrassed you."

"I'm not embarrassed. Are you embarrassed?"

"I'm not embarrassed."

"Gut."

"Gut."

Trash talk from both sides filled the space between them. Hen edged away from the base, one step, two, three. That was plenty.

"So how's Jack doing?"

A safe topic—even if it did reek of arrogance. Everyone knew he was the vet's assistant. He didn't have to rub it in. "He's much better. He's eating and pooping again."

"That's gut news. He's a gut gaul."

"He is. He's the best."

Micah shot the ball to Nicholas, who whirled and tagged Hen with it. "You're out, by the way."

"What? No I'm not." Hen looked down. She'd been so busy talking with Nicholas she hadn't realized how far from the base she'd wandered. He'd broken her focus. She'd let him. "Hey, that's not fair."

"All's fair in love and softball."

"Whatever."

Hen trudged from the field to the sound of catcalls, laughter, and applause. The families watching didn't know what she and Nicholas were talking about, but they knew the phrase *tit for tat*.

Nicholas had only been in town a short while, but he already knew what made her tick. Get her talking about animals and she could think of nothing else.

He was smart, and he loved animals almost as much as she did. So she'd give him a point for that. Maybe two.

Plus he wasn't half bad at softball. Another point. Maybe two.

The points were starting to add up.

"What was that all about?" Adele had her hands on her hips and a frown on her face. "That's not how we score points."

"I know. Sorry."

"Tell me you didn't get so flustered by Mr. Bird-in-Hand you forgot where you were." Adele rolled her eyes. "He's not that handsome."

"No chance. He took the job I wanted."

"Ah, he's the one." Adele took a hard practice swing. "In that case, we really do need to beat him."

That attitude right there was the reason they'd been best friends since first grade. "If you could hit it right over his head, just out of reach, that would be exactly what the veterinarian ordered."

Adele hooted. "I'll do my best."

"Hen, over here." Aunt Ginny's wild gesticulations from behind the church benches forced Hen to leave Adele to her practice swings. Aunt Ginny's smile seemed forced. Hen squeezed past her teammates and went to her. "Gut game, isn't it?"

"I tried to get your attention before you went up to bat."

"What's up?"

"Your dat wants you."

The spectators roared. A loud round of applause followed. Adele had smacked the ball into far-left field—right over Nicholas' head. Hen clapped so hard her hands hurt. "Now? The game's not over."

Aunt Ginny leaned closer. She touched Hen's arm. "It is for you."

Ach. She glanced toward the spot where her father had been sitting. He was gone. "Where is he?"

"He's rounding up the kinner." Aunt Ginny sped ahead. She moved fast for a portly woman. "I'm in charge of rounding you up."

"I'm a little old for rounding up."

"He opined that you are too old for softball games."

Never. "Because I fell on Nicholas Byler?"

"From where we sat it seemed like you tackled him."

"I would never do that intentionally. All I had to do was tag him. It's softball, not football." Hen sucked in a breath. No sense in taking her frustration out on Aunt Ginny. "I just wanted to get him out."

"With no thought for what the people watching would think?"

In the moment, honestly, no, she hadn't thought of what others would think. That wasn't how a person played the game. She had to be all in to win. Wasn't that how it was done? "What was I supposed to do?"

"I'm sure your dat will cover that in depth."

Aunt Ginny was right. Reins in his hand, Dad stood next to the buggy, waiting for her. His expression darkened as she approached. "You should see yourself." Sighing, he shook his head. "You're such a mess."

"What do you mean?"

"Look at yourself."

Hen glanced down. Grass stains, dirt, and chalk dust covered her apron and Sunday dress. She probably had some of each on her face as well. No doubt her prayer covering was crooked. All signs she'd played with gusto. "I got a little dirty. Sometimes that happens where you're having fun."

"Was it fun charging a man like a bull? Knocking him to the ground?"

"It's part of the game." Hen tried to squeeze past him. Dad moved into her path. She stopped, straightened her shoulders, and stared at him head-on. "No harm done."

"You tackled a man in broad daylight in front of the entire Gmay. Can you not see why this was unseemly for a young woman?"

"I didn't tackle—"

"Don't argue with me." He didn't raise his voice. It wasn't necessary. His disappointment delivered in a low, hoarse voice did its work. Which one was more disappointed in her? Her father or her bishop? "I saw it with my own eyes. As did everyone else."

"No one was hurt. It was a hotbox. A pickle. It's part of the game."

"You're not a softball player. You're a Plain woman."

As if she needed reminding. The fact followed her everywhere, hanging on her skirt, and tightening her prayer cap strings. "What would you have me do—let him pass?"

"Jah. Is that so hard to understand?" The angst that seeped into his voice heaped guilt on Hen. She wanted to be good. Surely he could see that. "Step aside. Simple. Dignified."

"That's not how you win the game." Had Dad forgotten what it was like to play softball or volleyball or even cornhole? Had he forgotten the thrill of a win? Had he forgotten the days when he played hooky from work on warm summer afternoons to teach Micah, Ruby, and Hen how to bat and catch? How he'd cheered when she connected with his underhand pitch or caught her first pop-up? "The men were ahead."

"We don't play to win. We play for fun. For the joy of it." The muscle in his jaw pulsing, Dad tugged at his beard. "We play to keep our bodies in shape as Gott would have us do."

"I understand that. I really do." He deserved her respect. He wanted what was best for her. And he loved her. This was his way of showing it. Maybe it was the only way he knew how. Which didn't make it any easier. "I just don't think Gott minds a little healthy competition. Aren't we made in His image?"

With a sigh, Dad lifted his black church hat from his head and resettled it. He shook his head. "Get in the buggy, Dochder."

His tone labeled Hen a lost cause. Gritting her teeth, she did as he directed. The boys were scooched together in the last row. Mena sat on Luke's lap. They'd left the row closest to the front for Hen and Micah. Ruby's beau would take her for an afternoon drive. The rest of Hen's siblings stared up at Hen with anguished faces. Nobody liked it when family argued. "It's okay. We're just having a discussion. It'll be fine."

Mena scooted from Luke's lap. She wrapped her arms around Hen's neck and laid her head on her shoulder. She smelled sweet like peach jam and watermelon. "I don't like 'cussions. They hurt my ears."

"Me neither, kitten." Hen held her close. "But sometimes people have things to say that have to be said."

She settled onto her bench and pulled Mena into her lap. Everyone was here except Micah. "So Micah didn't have to leave the game?"

"Micah is a man now." Dad stared straight ahead. He snapped the reins and the buggy jolted forward. "He'll make his own way home."

Dad had missed her point—intentionally, no doubt. Micah could do what he wanted, when he wanted. Men received buggies on their sixteenth birthdays so they could start courting. Dad and Mom had given Hen a cedar chest to fill with linens and dishware for when she married.

None of this was news. She'd chosen this life when she was baptized. Why did the yoke strangle her now?

Because no man had parked his buggy outside her house? Because she was secretly afraid no man ever would? It wouldn't be the end of the world. She'd have her goat business. She'd play mama to her siblings. She'd be an aunt to nieces and nephews. Life didn't hinge on marriage.

Unless a person was a Plain woman.

CHAPTER 9

The best part of planting a spring garden during a work frolic—aside from getting Hen out of cleaning house for a whole day—was the smell. The sweet aroma of freshly turned earth warmed by the sun on this last week of April filled the air. Inhaling so deeply she could smell the dirt in her bare toes, Hen turned off the rototiller and surveyed her work. Dozens of evenly spaced rows delighted the eyes and spoke to her of the promise of fresh vegetables to come for the Bylers. So far her fear that she'd have to face Nicholas hadn't materialized. He was busy painting the exterior of the house with a dozen other men. That should keep him busy most of the day.

Now if she didn't run into him at mealtime, all would be good.

A giggle interrupted her reverie. Hen tore her gaze from the soon-to-be-garden. Lenora, followed by Daisy, whose tail wagged so fast it was a blur, pushed a wheelbarrow full of onions, tomatoes, peppers, and pea plants through the grass toward Hen. Seed packets of beans, corn, squash, cucumbers, cabbage, carrots, lettuce, okra, radishes, sweet potatoes, and eggplants had been tucked into the corners. "What are you laughing at?"

"You." Lenora muscled the wheelbarrow closer to the garden's edge. She reached for the onion seedlings. "You're sniffing the air like a hund. What were you thinking about?"

"Thinking how nice it is to know winter is over, and summer is around the corner." No way she'd tell Nicholas' sister about her other thoughts. With any luck, Lenora wouldn't bring up that awful collision on the makeshift softball diamond. Hen dug her bare toes into the dirt and breathed in the calm. "How are you doing, Daisy? You look happy as a puppy with a bone."

Hen held out her hand. Daisy sniffed and smiled. Her tail whapped even faster. "How do you like your new home?"

Daisy woofed, plopped in the grass, and rolled over on her back. "Ah, that good?" She gave the dog's belly a quick rub. Her tongue hanging out in ecstasy, the dog stretched and let her legs stick straight out. So unladylike. Nicholas had a dog who could be Henrietta's lifelong friend. "So does Nicholas have any other pets?"

"We've adopted two cats since we arrived. By the time summer rolls around, I'm sure there will be two more. The man can't resist those sad faces." Lenora chuckled and shook her head. "Peppercorn and Snowball. They're already sleeping in his bedroom at night. People seem to think it's fine to just drop off unwanted pets in the country, like farmers need more animals to feed."

Nicholas had a soft heart for rescuing animals. Maybe it would balance the scales against his know-it-all, bossy attitude. Maybe. "They're blessed you took them in, for sure and for certain."

"We're also blessed to have everyone come out to help us." Lenora's free hand went to her heart. "I don't know how we would've gotten the house painted, the porch fixed, and all the other repairs made. Plus planting the garden by myself."

"That's what frolics are for." Hen scooped up her share of the onion seedlings. "Besides, I'd rather be outside than doing spring cleaning at home."

For once Dad hadn't insisted Hen stay home. As the bishop, he had a responsibility to lead by example. Frolics involved everyone.

"I admit I'm happy Ginny and the other women are taking charge of making new curtains." A dusting of freckles adorned Lenora's nose. Her cheeks had turned pink from the sun. "My sewing skills are fine, but it's not my favorite thing to do."

A possible friend and ally? "What are your favorite tasks, then?"

"I like to bake. If you ever need a bunch of desserts or breads for a bake sale fundraiser or a wedding, recruit me." Lenora knelt. She dug a hole with a trowel then plopped in the onion seedling and covered the roots with dirt. "Voila. One down, three dozen to go."

Her chuckle tickled Hen's funny bone, despite her disappointment.

Baking? She laughed. The only cooking she liked to do involved goat milk and selling everything she made. "I'll have the tomatoes planted lickety-split."

Which would give her time to pick Lenora's brain. "So how is your daadi doing?"

"Better. Much better, denki to you. He's been on fire with the plans for your goat shed. He was excited to find out you were coming over today. He can't wait to show you. It sounds like your goats will have top-notch lodging."

"I'm glad he's excited. So am I."

"He needed to feel useful."

Now to find the right time to approach Dad with the plans. Of course his first question would be how much would the building cost—on top of the cost of the Angora goats.

"Do you think Moses can give me a ballpark figure for how much the shed would cost?" Top-notch lodgings might be more than her nest egg would allow. "My dat is very conservative when it comes to spending money."

"That makes sense. I don't know if Daadi still has that math in his brain. It's weird. His favorite hymns are there and stories about growing up in Lancaster County and his parents. More recent stuff is gone."

"Makes you wonder..." Hen bit back the remainder of that sentence. It was bad enough she'd expressed her doubts about God's plans to Aunt Ginny. Not to a woman she barely knew. She'd scare her off forever. "What about Nicholas? How's he settling in?"

"You mean has he recovered from getting bested by a girl on the softball field?"

"Is that how he saw it?" Hen wiped her face with her sleeve. It came back damp. The air was warming. "I don't. It was an accident."

"You got him out." Lenora held up the trowel like a trophy. "He didn't like getting caught in a pickle his first time at bat in front of a crowd of strangers."

"I didn't mean to embarrass him." Or Dad. It was just a game. When did playing a game become so filled with opportunities to break rules of propriety? Being a grown-up was no fun. "Besides, he got me out. We're even."

"Don't worry, he'll get over it."

Men with their tender egos. "I suppose so."

"Don't worry about it, really. He said you apologized."

"He talked to you about it?"

"Sure. Nobody else he can talk to. Same with me." One hand on her back like an old lady, Lenora straightened and stretched. "It's just the two of us rambling around in this big house with Daadi."

"You're always welcome to talk to me."

"In that case. . ." Lenora's pink cheeks darkened to apple red. "How come Micah didn't come today?"

Micah. *Aha.*

Hiding her grin, Hen ducked down to plant another onion seedling. Aunt Ginny and Dad were intent on marrying off Hen. Turnabout was fair play. Time to do her own matchmaking for her brother. "He should be here by now. He and the *buwe* stayed behind to finish the chores this morning." Dad insisted they take care of the goats instead of Hen. Part of the plan to domesticate her, no doubt. "He's probably painting the house with the other men. Why do you ask?"

"Just wondering."

"I see." Hen drew the words out, letting them hang in the air so her new friend would know she knew. "Just checking on his whereabouts."

"Not just his whereabouts, I suppose." Her head down, Lenora scooped up another seedling and stuck it in a hole. "Does he have a special friend?"

Her voice squeaked on the last word. Hen stifled a giggle. Poor thing. "You don't have to be embarrassed. He's my bruder, and I don't know what you could possibly see in him. There's no accounting for taste—"

"Hen!"

"I don't know for sure, but I don't think so. He goes to lots of singings. He's only nineteen. I'm surprised you don't have one."

"There was someone who was interested, but I never felt. . ."

"Like he was someone you could live with until death do you part?"

"Exactly." She brushed dirt from her hands as if brushing the thought away. "I felt bad even taking one buggy ride with him. I knew from the start there was no spark."

"They make it sound so easy, don't they? Use your *rumspringa* to find the person you'll spend the rest of your life with. As if."

"At sixteen I couldn't even decide whether to wear my lilac dress or my teal one to a singing." Lenora threw up her hands and shrugged. "Let alone who I wanted to spend the rest of my life with."

"I mostly wanted to spend the rest of my life with my goats."

They both laughed.

"So, has Micah been baptized?"

Lenora was definitely taking this opportunity to get all her questions answered. This one was an important one. "He's taking the classes now. He'll be baptized in the fall. What about you?"

"I've been baptized. I'm nineteen too, but I was in a hurry because I wanted to teach school back home."

"Gut for you." The thought of wanting to spend—willingly spend, *volunteering* to spend—all day cooped up indoors in a schoolhouse in charge of a bunch of kids boggled the mind. Hen shivered. It was bad enough as a kid who had no choice. "Do you miss it?"

"I do. I miss the noise and the silly things the kinner do." Lenora's smile faded. "I miss that sense of satisfaction when they get an answer right and I know I helped them get there. But family comes first. Daadi needed us."

So true. There were days when Hen longed to hop on a train and ride it coast to coast. To visit other goat farms, wildlife refuges, and zoos. To soak up everything she could about animals, domestic and exotic. To enroll in classes at a college. To learn everything there was to know about veterinary medicine.

At least Lenora's dreams were allowed by her district.

"Our school will need a new teacher and assistant in the fall. My schweschder Ruby helped out for the past few weeks because the assistant got married." Two long weeks in which Hen scrubbed floors, cooked, washed dishes, and did laundry. Aunt Ginny's company made it tolerable, but a steady diet of housework was enough to make Hen want to run away from home. "The teacher is going back to Bird-in-Hand to get married this summer. Ruby and her special friend are likely getting hitched soon."

"I wish I could take over, but I can't." Lenora sat back on her heels. "I need to be here with Daadi while Nicholas is out on calls with Dr. McDonald."

"True. That makes sense. I wasn't really thinking."

"Don't you want to do it?"

"Me? Nee, nee, never." Hen hooted. Lenora would get to know her, and then she'd know what a crazy idea that was. "I want to be outside with my animals. Not inside with little human animals."

Lenora laughed so hard she snorted. "You should see your face. You'd think I'd asked you to eat live snakes."

"I love boplin. I want a passel of my own. I just don't want to be stuck inside on beautiful spring days, when it's snowball weather, or when the leaves are turning orange and gold and it's time to harvest pumpkins."

"In other words, never."

"Jah. Never. My own boplin I can take outside whenever I want." Her children would live outside—boys and girls. She and her husband, who would have to like animals as much as she did, would have big herds of goats. Pigs, chickens, a few cows for milk, and maybe even some sheep too. "I'll teach them to milk the goats, to clip their hooves and shave their udders, and to make goat milk soap and goat milk fudge and goat milk cheese."

And the girls would sew, bake, do laundry, and clean house too. Of course. She wasn't completely crazy. If she didn't teach them to do those things—even if she didn't like housekeeping—they would never marry, and it would be her fault. Besides, she had to make room for the thought that her daughters might like to sew and cook. If she'd learned anything being Hen the goat whisperer, it was the value of loving people as they were instead of trying to change them into what they weren't.

The bell announcing lunchtime clanged, interrupting Hen's ruminations. "We better go help serve before someone calls us out for being slugs."

Lenora eased to her feet. She flung her hands out. "If they do, we'll simply show them the beautiful garden we're planting. We've done a lot. Besides, Ginny will have the meal organized."

Speaking of women who loved to cook and clean. "I'll find Moses and talk to him as soon as we finish lunch. Then I'll come back out to work on this some more."

"I should help wash dishes, so you'll probably make it out here first."

They made plans as they ran up the back porch steps and into the kitchen, which was busier than the grocery store the day before Thanksgiving. Hen squeezed her way through to the sink to wash up before grabbing a tray of sandwiches and heading to the picnic tables in the front yard.

The tray would serve as her cover while she searched for Moses. With any luck, he was nowhere near her father.

"Dochder."

There was no mistaking that voice or the tone.

Her heart clanging, Hen forced herself to pivot in the direction from which it came.

Her dad sat at a table with Moses. And Nicholas.

One big double whammy coming up.

CHAPTER 10

Nothing to do except face whatever angry hymn Dad was singing now. Hen straightened her shoulders, raised her head, and strode to the table. Nicholas had one hand on a gorgeous white cat stretched out on the table. Moses kept glancing at him as if trying to decide who he was. Hen plastered a smile on her face. "You must be starving." She held out the platter. "You have your choice of ham, roast beef, or chicken salad. It's my aunt Ginny's chicken salad. She slathers the homemade sourdough bread with Dijon mustard—"

"Don't pretend you spent the morning making food in the kitchen." Dad helped himself to a sandwich without checking to see which kind. Not a good sign. He had white paint on his shirt and pants, but then all the men had worn their oldest clothes for the frolic. "I can guess from the dirt on your face and apron that you've been planting in the garden."

"I'm helping—"

"Moses tells me you hired him to draw up plans for an Angora goat shed you're building."

Sweat trickled down Hen's temple onto her cheek. She couldn't explain her reasoning in front of Moses. She did her best to not look at him or Nicholas, but her gaze jumped in their direction. Moses grinned. Nicholas scratched between the cat's ears, his gaze firmly pinned to the feline. "I asked him to do plans, jah, but nothing is firm yet."

"I've seen the plans." Her father's tone was neutral, even. "Do you have any idea how much such a shed would cost?"

"I was going to research those numbers before I talked to you about the plans." And figure out how to do the work herself with the most cost-effective material. She only needed 196 square feet of land near the barn and two acres of pasture. Surely Dad could spare that. "We're still just brainstorming."

"I asked Moses." Dad touched the rolled-up blueprint paper. "More than you could ever save from selling your soap and cheese."

Moses did have the numbers in his head still. If only Hen could ask what that number was. With Dad sitting across from him, she didn't dare. Dad had no idea how much money Hen had saved since starting her herd when she graduated from school at fourteen—even with using part of the proceeds to help with the family's needs.

"That's the point, don't you see? If we expand to a second herd of Angora goats, we can bring in more revenue from the wool products. With the products we make from goat milk and the wool products, we could even open our own store in Smicksburg. Why be a vendor and split profits with existing stores? You have to spend money to make money. It's an investment. Besides, I have—"

"That's enough. Who puts these ideas in your head?" His cool stare chilled Hen to the bone. Yet he didn't raise his voice. "Have you been on the internet again?"

Breathless, Hen shut her mouth. She'd done it again. Embarrassed him in front of other men in the district. Her enthusiasm only served to get her in trouble. If Micah had come up with this idea, Dad would've heard him out. He'd give it careful consideration.

Gott, it's not fair. How God must laugh at that silly whine. Nobody said life would be fair. Far from it. Fair would mean her mother was still here, still gently polishing Hen's jagged edges. Gently calming the rough waters between father and daughter.

"Well?"

He expected an answer. "Nee, I—"

"We'll talk about this when we get home." Dad nudged the plans toward Moses. "I'm sorry my dochder got ahead of herself on this. Don't worry, I'll pay you for your work."

"I can pay him."

"Pay me for what?" Moses' rheumy eyes squinted against the midday sun. His forehead wrinkled. "You'll have to see Jeanette in the office. She handles the money."

"Jeanette works at the post office now. You don't have an office anymore, Daadi." His voice soft, pain flitting across his face, Nicholas patted his grandfather's arm. "Remember? You're retired."

"Then why are they paying me?" Moses grumbled. "A man don't get paid for sitting around doing nothing."

"I'm sorry for the confusion." Hen's heart contracted. What a terrible disease. So far it had spared her grandparents, but it could still dig its claws into them or Dad someday. Or Aunt Ginny. She forced a smile. "I asked you to do something special for me, but my dat's right. We'll get back to you on it."

Dad nodded his agreement. His anger seemed to have dissipated like a pop-up summer shower. Maybe he too saw the error of their dissension in the face of others' suffering. He pointed at the platter. "Are you hungry, Moses? My dochder has a platter of tasty sandwiches."

"I reckon I could eat. Amos, you should eat too. You're too skinny."

Nicholas' hand on the cat stopped moving. "I'm Nicholas. Amos is my dat, your *suh*. He's in Bird-in-Hand."

Did it help to remind Moses when he mixed up things? What did the doctors say? Filing that question away for her next trip to the library in Punxsutawney, Hen held out the platter. With shaking fingers, Moses selected a ham sandwich.

Nicholas smiled. It transformed his face. Like Ruby said, he was a handsome man. Not that it mattered. "What do you suggest?"

Hen held his gaze. It seemed as if he'd thrown her a lifeline. He had no reason to do such a thing. "My aenti makes delicious chicken salad. Who's your friend?"

"This is Snowball. She's an excellent mouser." Snowball raised her head, yawned, and meowed as if to say hello. "I know because she keeps bringing me her kills so I can congratulate her."

"Nice to meet you, Snowball." Hen avoided her dad's gaze. He didn't abide much by including animals in conversations. "Maybe Nicholas will share his sandwich with you."

"Sounds gut to me." Nicholas took a sandwich then helped himself to a second one. "Denki for helping my schweschder with the garden."

"*Gern gschehme.*" Neutral ground. A good meeting place. Hen forced a smile. "We're having fun. Which I always thought of as being the point of frolics. To make work fun."

Dad humphed. Hen peeked in his direction. He had a bemused expression on his face. "You should bring Nicholas and Moses some more tea. We worked up a powerful thirst painting."

What had Dad seen that had him smiling like Willow and Tigger when they caught mice?

Or what did he think he saw?

"I'll do that right away." Hen balanced the platter in one hand. She reached for the plans Dad had shoved aside. "I'll just clear these out of your way."

"You do that." Dad didn't stop her, but neither did his tone approve.

Hen didn't reply. That way she didn't have to lie.

Those plans were going home with her. They would give her a blueprint for how to construct her DIY shed. She'd tuck them away until she came up with a new strategy to convince Dad that her plan was a good one—no, a great one.

But right now she had another mission to complete. A woman such as herself was capable of multitasking. After sliding the plans under a blanket in the buggy, she headed to the kitchen. She would refill the platter and pick up a pitcher of tea. After she found Adele. Her friend was on dishwashing detail. Perfectly kept as usual, Adele's strawberry blond hair remained tucked under her crisp prayer cap. Hen didn't start out the day that neat, let alone stay that way after lunch. She snatched up a dish towel and grabbed a bowl. "Hey, have you seen Micah anywhere?"

"Last time I saw him he was stuffing his face with a snickerdoodle the size of my hand." Adele laid a saucepan in the drying rack. "That boy can eat. I think I served him four sandwiches, potato salad, coleslaw—"

"Listen, we have to figure out how to get him to notice Lenora."

Adele turned back to the sink. She rubbed her wet, sudsy hands together. "Our new friend is interested?"

Her tone was. . .noncommittal. Maybe she didn't think matchmaking was a good idea. Nah, this was Adele. She loved a good romance. Or maybe she was thinking of the stinking beau who'd dumped her and moved to Montana recently.

"I know it must be hard thinking about beaus and all right now—"

"Nee, nee, I'm fine." Adele scrubbed a platter so hard the pretty purple flowers that decorated it were in danger. "Tell me, tell me."

Whew. Hen related their conversation in the garden. "I guess I can see why. He's funny, smart, and hardworking. Lining up a wedding might get Dat's mind off me not having a special friend, since Ruby and Peter can't seem to take the next step."

"I can see what Lenora sees in Micah." Adele dried her hands and laid the towel on the counter. Something in her tone made Hen study her friend. Her cheeks were pink, her smile brittle. Her cornflower-blue eyes dark. "He's a catch."

Adele's beau had added insult to injury by breaking up with her on Christmas Eve. Montana seemed like an awfully long way to go to get away from a person as nice as Adele.

"I wish I could do something to make you feel better—"

"I told you I'm fine."

Prickly fine. "Okay. I guess it's hard to think of a bruder like that. It's kind of icky." Better to move the conversation along. Hen rubbed the saucepan again even though it was more than dry. "Maybe I'll ask him to carry a stack of bags of peat moss around to the back for me."

"He'll think that's odd since you claim to never need his help for anything. You think you're as strong as he is."

"I have a twinge in my back from bending over planting all morning."

Which was true. Normally she'd ignore it, but today she'd let her younger brother help her out.

Hen found Micah preparing to climb a ladder to the catwalk the men had built in order to paint the house's second story. He had paint on his faded blue cotton shirt, his denim pants, and his forehead. He was the picture of a hardworking man.

She explained the problem.

"Can't it wait?" Micah picked up a gallon paint can and poured some into the roller pan. "We're only about halfway through with painting. If we don't get a move on, we won't finish today. It's supposed to rain tomorrow."

"It'll only take you a few minutes, and it would really help us out."

"It's no wonder you hurt your back." He set the roller pan on the ground next to the catwalk. "You're always trying to lift more than your own weight. I'm happy to save you from yourself."

He really was a nice man—for a brother—but that didn't keep him from patting himself on the back for being right. Hen offered a demure smile and murmured, "Denki. You're such a gut bruder."

"Flattery will get you everywhere." Micah guffawed as he wiped his hands on a rag and draped it on a nearby sawhorse.

They made a quick detour so Micah could grab the bags and stack them on his broad shoulders. Then Hen led the way around the house out to the garden, her brother behind her whistling something that vaguely sounded like "Yankee Doodle Dandy."

Lenora had started on the tomato plants. Adele squatted in the next row surrounded by a dozen bell pepper plants.

"Oh, hi." Lenora popped to her feet. Her hands went to her face. She shoved a lock of chestnut hair under her prayer cap. "Micah, what are you doing here?"

Not the most welcoming question.

"*Hallo*, Lenora." His expression puzzled, Micah's gaze circled from Lenora to Adele and back to Hen. "Hen wanted help carrying out the peat moss."

Lenora opened her mouth. She shut it. Her face turned tomato red. Her eyebrows rose. "Oh, well, I see."

It was obvious she didn't.

"Hey, Adele, haven't seen you in a while." Micah had already moved on. "You haven't been over for supper in a long time."

Focused on her work, Adele patted soil around a pepper plant with a firm touch. "You know, busy, busy."

Micah ducked his head. "Still, you should drop by. Aunt Ginny is here now. I reckon we could get her to make her sour cream noodle bake you like so much."

Why was he talking to Adele instead of Lenora? "Lenora, you and Nicholas should come over too." Hen jumped in. "Aunt Ginny likes nothing more than cooking for a big crowd. You can compare recipes. I know how you love to cook."

"Love to cook?" Lenora stumbled over the words. "Mostly I like to bake—"

"Maybe you can bring a peach cobbler. Micah loves peach cobbler, don't you, Micah?"

Micah dumped the bags on the ground next to the rototiller. "Sure."

"Lenora was a schoolteacher back in Bird-in-Hand."

"Gut for you, Lenora." Micah made a show of surveying the sky, now laden with glowering clouds. "That rain might come early."

He started away then turned back. "Like I said, Aenti Ginny loves cooking for a crowd. Hen can let you know when she's making sour cream noodle bake."

Good. Good. An invitation.

The only problem was Micah's gaze was fixed on Adele—not Lenora.

Adele's glance bounced up from the pepper plants and right back down. "That would be nice."

"It would." Lenora's voice trailed off. "Denki."

"Uh, you too, you too." His hand rubbing his neck, Micah cleared his throat. "Nicholas had breakfast with us after he fixed up Jack—"

"He didn't fix up Jack, Dat and me did—mostly." Hen crossed her arms. Women gave, men got the credit. Micah wasn't even there. "And I came over here to help with Moses while Nicholas was off working."

"Jah, jah, I heard."

Waving one hand over his shoulder, Micah pivoted and stomped away.

As soon as Micah was out of earshot, Lenora stuck her hands on her hips. "What was that all about? The peat moss is for the flower beds. We'll use straw around the tomato plants but not until they get bigger."

"I needed a reason for Micah to come back here." Hen scrambled to explain. Surely Lenora would appreciate her efforts, once she understood them. "I wanted him to meet you."

"I already met him after church at the softball game." Lenora's voice rose a notch. "When I was wearing my Sunday dress and bonnet. I wasn't all dirty with my *kapp* crooked and my hair hanging out."

"You look gut. I'm sure he didn't notice—"

"Nee, because he was too busy trying to get Adele to come to supper at your house."

"I'm sorry, Lenora. I'm not sure what was up with that." Adele stood and brushed off her hands. As usual, her dress was clean and neat, her prayer cap perfect, and her hair still neatly hidden behind it. "Me and

Hen have been best friends since first grade. Micah sees me as another schweschder, I reckon. He probably feels sorry for me. Everybody in the world knows my friend dumped me and ran off to Montana."

Not everyone in the world. Just in Pennsylvania. The Plain grapevine was that good.

"Ach. I'm sorry that happened to you." Lenora flopped down among a cluster of zucchini plants next to the plot. "That must've been heartbreaking."

"Okay, so that didn't go so well. I can admit it." Hen scratched her forehead. She tapped her index fingers on her cheek. "I'll do better, I promise."

"Nee, nee, it's not necessary." Lenora tugged off her sneaker and dumped out soil. She tossed it aside. The other sneaker followed in short order. "I know a moonstruck man when I see one."

"What?" Hen and Adele spoke in unison.

"Your bruder likes Adele." Lenora pointed first at Hen, then at Adele. "I can't believe you haven't noticed."

Apparently family was indeed the last to know.

CHAPTER 11

Whether it was exhaustion from the previous day's hard work or the stifling stillness of an impending storm, no one had much to say at the supper table. Nicholas helped himself to food left by the women who'd made far too much for the frolic. The three of them would have to eat until they were stuffed for days, to make sure nothing went to waste. Grandpa muttered to himself while pushing potato salad around his plate. Her expression morose, Lenora picked at her coleslaw. Even Daisy forwent her usual guard duty watching for food that fell to the floor and needed to be captured. Instead she panted in front of the open windows that brought no relief in the form of a breeze.

Mealtime at the Byler house back home was loud and busy, full of laughter and jokes as the family shared their day's ups and downs. Dad pretended to criticize Mom's cooking. Mom promised to never cook again. The younger girls vying for turns to talk about school. The boys arguing good-naturedly about who caught the biggest fish. They all loved to fish. Nicholas missed that. Lenora probably did too. "These baked beans are really gut." People always liked to talk about food, didn't they? "I wonder who made them."

"I think it was Hen's aenti Ginny." Lenora laid her fork down without taking a bite. She picked up her glass of water. "She puts her homemade barbecue sauce in them."

"Well, they're gut."

Grandpa didn't weigh in on the beans. Heaving a sigh, he shredded the bread on his ham sandwich.

So much for food. What about the weather? "It's weird that it's so hot the first week of May."

"I wish it would just rain and get it over with." Lenora tossed her napkin on the table and stood. "Adele Plank brought watermelon. What's left is chilling in the refrigerator. It should be icy cold. You two go sit on the porch and eat some while I clean up. It'll be cooler out there."

"Gut idea. Do you need some help cleaning up?"

Lenora stared at Nicholas like he'd grown a horn in the middle of his forehead. "Of course not. It was leftovers. Hardly any dishes at all." Her attempt at a smile was grim. "I mean, denki, but I'm capable of handling kitchen duties."

Even if it was just her. Kitchen chores at home were shared by half a dozen women and girls. Many hands made quick work. As did the storytelling and giggles. More for Lenora to miss.

"At least let me get the watermelon."

"Go ahead. That's fine."

For once Grandpa didn't have to be asked three times or cajoled into doing something. He left a full plate of food and trudged out to the back porch without comment. Daisy followed. She took her duties guarding him seriously. Nicholas meted out generous portions of fruit in big bowls and carried them outside where he took the Adirondack chair next to Grandpa's. Daisy had picked a spot under the closest maple tree. Smart dog. Shade and more of a breeze.

"Mmm-mmm-mm." Grandpa held up a chunk of juicy watermelon on the end of his fork. "Better than ice cream."

Nicholas tried his. "I don't know if it's better than ice cream, but it's really gut. It's too early for homegrown. I wonder where it came from."

"Who cares?" Grandpa leaned forward. He spit a seed over the railing into the honeysuckle vines growing on trellises. "I reckon you can't beat that."

A shiny memory presented itself. Grandpa and Grandma came to visit when one of the little sisters was born on a warm July evening. Grandpa had made the same challenge. Even Dad had competed in the seed-spitting contest—much to Mom's feigned disgust.

"I reckon I can." Nicholas selected a chunk with a good number of seeds, chewed, swallowed, and prepared to spit. "I have a special technique."

He leaned forward and let it rip. His seed landed somewhere beyond the vines. "Woo-hoo!" He held his fork up high like a trophy for all to see. "I win."

"Hey, no woo-hooing and no winning until I see where it went."

Nicholas rose and went to the railing. Grandpa joined him. His arm shot out. "There it is. I see it. That's mine. I beat you."

A seed nestled in a honeysuckle leaf. Nicholas shook his finger. "How do you know it's yours? That could be mine."

"No cheating, *kinnskinner*."

Grandpa remembered who Nicholas was. In this moment. This sweet moment. "Fine. Let's do it from here so we can keep track of the trajectory."

"Big fancy words won't get you the win." Grandpa scooped up a chunk with his fingers and popped it in his mouth. A few seconds later the seed flew like a bird toward the newly mowed grass. Cackling, Grandpa pointed. "I reckon you can't beat that."

Nicholas did his best, but Grandpa was right. His best fell short—this time. They continued to compete, the hot weather forgotten, until only a few pieces of watermelon remained. Nicholas plopped into his rocking chair. With a lazy meow, Snowball joined him. The cat curled up in his lap, oblivious to the fact that her body was like a hot oven on his legs. "You win. For an old man, you have a gut set of lungs."

"Who are you calling old?" Grandpa turned and leaned against the railing. The vague confusion that so often marred his sun-lined face was missing. "I don't know why your dat thinks I need babysitters. It's a little rough sometimes with your mammi gone, but I can take care of myself."

"Dat doesn't like to think of you here alone." Nicholas trod carefully. Grandpa knew he had dementia. The doctors had told him so. In this lucid moment he chose to ignore or deny the diagnosis. He was allowed. "And I don't mind. The change was gut for me."

Not so good for Lenora. If only they could convince Grandpa to move to Bird-in-Hand. He could live in the *dawdi haus* now that Mom's parents had moved to Pinecraft. Dad had tried. The other aunts and uncles had tried. Grandpa's heels remained dug into the dirt so far they might never budge.

"I should've thanked you and Lenora for coming. I didn't. Forgive an ornery old man who misses his fraa."

"Who are you calling old?" Nicholas swallowed a lump the size of a cantaloupe. "Do you remember the seed-spitting contest we had when our little schweschder was born? You and me and Lenora?"

Grandpa's face clouded. "I do. Like it was yesterday instead of ten years ago. I know my memory isn't as gut as it used to be. It's funny—not funny ha ha but funny sad that I remember things that happened a long time ago better than last week or even last year."

"It's an awful disease, for sure and for certain."

The screen door opened. Lenora slipped out, carrying the plastic container of watermelon. "Anyone want seconds? How about you, Daadi?"

Confusion, then anger, flitted across Grandpa's face. He straightened. His bowl clattered to the porch floor. Daisy hopped up and barked. "Who are you? What are you doing in my house?"

"Hush, Daisy, hush. It's Lenora, Daadi, your kinnskind, my schweschder." Trying to avoid seeing the stricken expression on his sister's face, Nicholas bent and picked up the bowl. It hadn't broken. It should have. Like Lenora's heart. And his. "She was cleaning up after supper, remember?"

"I'm tired. I'm going to bed." Grandpa tugged the bowl from Nicholas' hand. He squeezed past him. At the door, he handed it to Lenora. "*Guder nacht*, Lenora."

He went inside. Daisy hightailed it after him.

Grandpa was still in there, in that steadily shrinking, bent body. Maybe Daisy would give him comfort where human comfort was lacking.

Lenora didn't have a free hand, or she might have covered her mouth. As it was, the sob was small and quiet.

Thunder rumbled in the distance. Big, fat raindrops splattered on the porch steps like someone in heaven needed a good cry.

CHAPTER 12

Such a good day couldn't be allowed to end on that note.

Nicholas took the watermelon and the bowl from Lenora. He stacked them with his on the table Grandpa had fashioned from aspen and placed between the Adirondack chairs. "Have a seat. Take a load off."

"It's been a long day. I'm tired." One hand on the screen door, Lenora shoved straggling hair under her cap with the other. "I should just go to bed too. Tomorrow's another day."

Despite the urge to hug her, Nicholas let his arms hang loose at his sides. He'd never learned to show affection. None of them had. Dad and Mom loved their children, but hugs weren't in their nature. "We were spitting seeds. Competing. He won. He remembered doing it when we were kids. He remembered you."

"I heard you—both of you—laughing. It sounded gut. Sweet." Lenora slipped over to the railing where she leaned out and cupped her hands, trying to catch the rain. "I would've come out sooner, but I didn't want to interrupt and spoil your fun."

Nicholas joined her. He ran his hands over the honeysuckle vines. The water pooled on the leaves dampened his fingers. A fresh breeze caught raindrops and flung them in his face. He closed his eyes and let it cool him and his aching heart. "We have to take the gut moments when they come."

"But we never know when that will be, or how long they'll last."

"Which makes them all the more precious."

"I don't want to complain."

"Don't call it complaining. Call it venting. We all need to do that once in a while." Nicholas wiped the rain from his face with his sleeve, wiping away the once dried sweat of hard work. It couldn't erase the angst at a loved one slipping away. "It's just the two of us, and we have to be able to talk to someone about how hard this is."

"You go off to work each day. I'm here all day long."

"With just Daadi."

"Even if he wasn't. . .the way he is, I'd still feel a loss. I miss my kids at the school. I miss teaching. I miss Mamm and Dat and the kinner and my friends."

She was right. Nicholas did have the better end of the deal. Lenora was alone all day with no friends or family and only a few chores to keep her busy. Nicholas was busy doing something he loved. He came home tired to the bone. She'd given up that thing she loved. "Maybe you could talk to Mamm and Dat. Maybe Lizzie and the cousins could take turns."

Their sister Lizzie was only seventeen, but she had a good head on her shoulders. Dad had decided she was too young for this job.

"The teaching job is already taken. Besides, a revolving door of caregivers would only confuse Daadi more."

"We could try again to convince him to move to Bird-in-Hand."

"Dat talked to him about it until he was blue in the face. Daadi wouldn't budge." Lenora touched an early honeysuckle bloom that hadn't opened yet. So fragile. "Besides, if you think he's confused now, imagine what he would be like if we took him home and stuck him in the dawdi haus. He would be lost. He'd probably try to go home. Then we'd be in a real mess."

"Is that why you were so gloomy at the supper table?"

The rain came down harder then. Lightning crackled. Thunder boomed. Lenora didn't flinch. "Nee. Something happened at the frolic yesterday."

She stopped.

"What? What happened?"

His sister edged toward the porch steps. Rain sluiced down storm gutters. The downpour got steadily louder. She grabbed the porch post and flung herself into the deluge, still hanging on. "This feels so gut." She sputtered and laughed. "Come on, let's play in the rain."

"First tell me what happened." Nicholas tugged her back to the porch's top step. "Then I'll gladly take a dousing."

"It's so weird to talk to a man about it."

"I'm your bruder."

"It's the sort of thing you tell a schweschder or a girlfriend. Not a guy."

Aha. Not something on which Nicholas wanted to be the receiving end, either. "Courting stuff."

"Hen tried to matchmake." A flush crept across Lenora's cheeks. "It made everything awkward."

"I can imagine." He could. Their mother wasn't above taking a turn at matchmaking. "Who was she targeting?"

"Me and Micah."

His sister, of all people. Hen didn't even know Lenora. Why would Hen feel the need to stick her nose in his sister's love life? Nicholas didn't even want his nose anywhere near it. "I can't imagine Micah needs help in that department. He's so—"

"Able to take care of himself. I agree. I think she was trying to help me. She was trying to be nice."

"That's not my idea of nice."

"I made the mistake of asking her a bunch of questions about him." Lenora ducked her head. "It's my fault, really. She had good intentions."

"But that didn't mean you wanted her to orchestrate a get-together over tomato plants."

"Nee, but I think that's just the way Hen is. She goes all out. She doesn't have a slow setting. She's all about speed."

"I can see that." Her enthusiasm for goats was so consuming it was amazing her father could withstand it. Nicholas had been tempted, and he'd never owned a goat. "I did get the impression you liked Micah that first time you met after church."

"Seriously? I liked what I saw, but I don't know him. Just like he doesn't know me. Which doesn't matter, as it turns out."

"Why doesn't it matter?" The entire conversation sent Nicholas hurtling back to being sixteen and attending his first singing. Awkward didn't even begin to cover it. He was the last one who should be giving courting advice. He hadn't managed a second date more than twice. "Maybe Hen's little nudge is enough to get Micah thinking about it."

Lenora hooted. "He likes someone else."

"How do you know?"

By the time Lenora finished relating the incident, Nicholas was ready to throw in the towel. He was in over his head. He racked his brain for something comforting to say. "He likes Adele because he's had all these years to know her. With time he'll realize you're much nicer. You'll see."

"You goose. You sound just like Mom. For your information, Adele's nice. And sweet. And smart. I think she helps Hen keep a more even keel." Lenora grabbed Nicholas' arm and pulled him into the rain. "Time to cool off!"

Hen and "even keel" didn't belong in the same sentence, but Nicholas didn't argue. He followed his sister into the yard. Anything to make her smile.

Lenora didn't just smile. She laughed. She skipped around the yard chanting, "It's raining, it's pouring, the old man is boring. He bumped his head, went to bed, and didn't get up till morning."

She wasn't talking about Grandpa. Life with him was anything but boring.

Don't think about it. Just don't think about it.

Rain soaked Nicholas' clothes. It ran down his forehead and tickled his nose. He laughed. First seed spitting. Now playing in the rain. They were regressing to their childhood. Under the circumstances, it wasn't a bad thing or even surprising. Adulthood was hard. Harder for some than others. Why that was, the deacon couldn't really explain. Nicholas understood that suffering and trials honed a person's faith. An untested faith was a weak faith. But why did some seem to float through life with hardly a scratch or a scar? Why did Grandpa have this disease? Why had Adam lost his wife far too soon, left to raise seven children on his own? Why did Hen have to figure out how to make her way without a mother?

That was just an itty-bitty, thin slice of the pain and suffering that existed in this world.

Why, Gott?

CHAPTER 13

Hen rolled her eyes, even though no one was there to see it. Micah, the weather forecaster. The rain her brother predicted at the frolic had arrived right on time. And it wasn't just rain. It was a deluge accompanied by its three sisters—wind, thunder, and lightning. She scooped up Petunia and tucked the tiny kid under her rain poncho. The goat had decided to squeeze her petite body through a slit in the fence just big enough for her to escape the enclosure—in the middle of a cloudburst just as the sun disappeared in the west. "Come on, you little pipsqueak, stop wiggling."

Animals were so much easier than people. Chasing a goat kid around the yard in a thunderstorm was a million times easier than fixing the mess of Hen's own making at the frolic. In a million years, it never occurred to her that Micah liked Adele.

Why didn't it? Was she that dense? Apparently. Adele was a hard worker, faithful, good at all the things Hen wasn't, from sewing to canning to baking. Which raised the question of why she was even friends with Hen. Probably because she latched on to her in first grade before Hen's propensity for getting into trouble became apparent. Plus, Adele was a kind person, too kind to rebuff Hen's clumsy attempts to be her friend.

The moral of the story, Aunt Ginny would say, if she knew, which she didn't, was for Hen not to stick her nose where it didn't belong, let nature take its course, to be a good friend and stay out of it, et cetera, ad nauseam, as Mom used to say.

Too late.

Rain driven by a strong wind pummeled her, making it hard to see.

Hen ducked her head and trudged to the goat shed. Somehow she had to fix that which she had put asunder. Such a good word from the King James Bible. That which God united let no man put asunder.

Get a grip, Hen, you're losing it.

No, she was tired. Hot tea. Warm nightgown.

Her rubber boots made a squishy, squishy sound with every step. It took all her strength to lift the latch and open the door. She quickly deposited the runaway with her twin sibling, Penny. "No more running away. Got it?"

Petunia didn't appear the least bit contrite. Hen tightened the hood around her face and ventured back into the storm. Getting out of her wet clothes was next. A hot cup of cinnamon spice tea and a dry nightgown would do nicely.

Nor did Aunt Ginny know about the previous day's scene at the picnic table with Dad, Moses, and Nicholas. Unless Dad told her. He'd been even quieter than usual at the supper table. His promise that they would discuss her transgressions later had not materialized. Maybe he was as tired as she was.

Or fed up with her uppity attitude and inappropriate outbursts in front of other menfolk. Like Nicholas. What had he thought of the exchange with her father? Was he embarrassed by it? Did he agree with her father? Fine. Most men did.

The wind ripped the door from Hen's hands. It banged against the wall. Maybe God agreed with her dad too. Hen grappled with it until it finally latched.

She turned to navigate the raging stream that now flowed through their backyard. On the other side, her father, head down, his hand on his hat, strode toward the barn. They'd already fed and watered the livestock. She'd come out to check on everybody one more time. Why was he out in this cloudburst? "Dat. Dat! What are you doing?"

He glanced back for a second then forged ahead. "Micah thinks Lucy is in labor," he yelled. His voice lifted and carried on the wind. "She didn't eat today, and he said she was ornery as all get out when he tried to cajole her into it."

So why didn't he mention it to Hen? Probably because he was still ticked with her over her blatant attempt to matchmake. She'd tried to apologize before supper, but he'd barged past her, washed his hands, and started talking to Dad about the horse they were breaking for an Englisch farmer east of Smicksburg.

Hen followed her father into the barn, where the rain beat a steady rhythm on the roof, but it was warm and dry. Lucy greeted them with a nervous whinny. Her partner Jade whinnied in return. The first-time father was nervous too. Lucy's belly had dropped a few days earlier. She'd been grouchy—but then who wouldn't be carrying a hundred-pound foal after 340 days of pregnancy?

Hen shucked off her rain slicker and hung it on a hook next to her father's. "Did her water break?"

"Micah didn't think it had, but she's been alternating between pacing and lying down in the same place all day."

The equine version of nesting, in other words.

"Is he coming back out?"

"Nee. He has a cough and a headache. Your aenti Ginny demanded that he take some of her medicine and go to bed. No ifs, ands, or buts."

That was Aunt Ginny.

"And Mena and the twins? Luke?"

"Already asleep. Ginny didn't see any reason to wake them up. They've all seen foals born before."

His tone was neutral. He pulled open the stall gate, its squeak punctuating the words.

"Mom would've woken them up." Her hand on the gate, Hen closed her eyes for a second. They'd been on the verge of having a nice moment together, just the two of them. Nothing to do now but forge ahead. "It's a special occasion. A beautiful one, seeing new life come into this world. She always thought we should all share in it."

"I reckon you're right." His voice still had that hollow sound. Like something had sucked all the feeling out of the words and let them dry and brittle. "Give your aenti grace. She's not trying to be your mamm. She's herself, and she's a blessing to us."

"I know—"

"We need to check Lucy's udder."

Conversation over. Hen followed her dad into the stall. Lucy didn't seem happy to see her. Hen approached with one hand out. "Hey, sweet mamm, how're you feeling?"

Tossing her head, her eyes wide and anxious, the sorrel neighed. Hen ran her hands along the mare's back. "I understand. You and me both, girl."

Murmuring sweet nothings, she smoothed and patted until Lucy calmed down. "Okay, here we go." She took a peek at the mare's underside. "The udder is bulging and tight. The teats are waxy, but I don't see any colostrum dripping."

That was a good thing. The foal would need that colostrum for its mom's antibodies after it was born.

A *whish* of fluids splashed Hen's rubber boots. "There we go. No worries, friend, that's what rubber boots are for." Now that Lucy's water had broken, they could expect the foal to follow in about thirty minutes. Quick and easy. The hot tea and warm nightgown wouldn't have to wait long. She kissed Lucy's muzzle. "It'll all be over soon."

Dad cleaned out the roomy stall and added a thick layer of clean straw while Hen brought out the first aid kit. It had been two years since one of their horses foaled. The kit still contained scissors, disinfectant, string, antiseptic, and towels.

She checked the battery-operated clock over her father's workbench. Ten minutes had passed. Lucy still stomped back and forth. Occasionally she ducked her head as if to study her belly. "Soon, Lucy, soon."

Lucy didn't seem convinced. Another five minutes passed. The mare whinnied and tossed her head. She nipped at her flank. Her tail lifted and fell. "She's really agitated." A tendril of worry curled around Hen's throat. Watching an animal in pain was hard. She'd do anything to make it easier, if only she could. "Hang in there, Lucy, hang in there."

"She's done this before." Dad poured steaming coffee from a large thermos into its cup. "Have some kaffi and relax. Foals are like boplin, they come when they're gut and ready."

With all the grace of a bulldozer, Lucy flopped onto the straw. Her legs sprawled. Hen grabbed the opportunity to take a better gander. "I can see the membrane, but only one foot. There should be two feet by now."

Dad set his coffee cup down and strode to her side. He squatted, hand on Lucy's swollen belly. "You're right. That's not gut." He glanced back at the clock. "I'm thinking the foal is in a bad position. That looks like a fetlock and hock."

"Back legs instead of front."

"Appears so." He hauled himself to his feet. "I need to get to the phone shack and call Doc McDonald."

"He's too far away. At least forty minutes by car. The foal will die if we don't get it out of there soon." The clock was ticking. Lucy could die too. "We have to rotate—"

"I'll call Nicholas. He's only fifteen minutes from here on horseback."

Whinnying, Lucy raised her head. Her legs flailed. "I know, I know. We're getting you help. How do we know if Nicholas has any experience with repositioning a foal?"

"I've never done it. Have you?"

"Nee—"

"Then he'll know more about it than either one of us."

"What if he doesn't have the phone in the house?"

"He brought it into our house."

Please, Gott, let him be a rule breaker on purpose. It's his job. Animals can need him day or night. Please make him answer.

Some people might think it wrong to pray for animals, but they were God's creatures too. During her baptism classes, Hen had asked the deacon if animals went to heaven, a question that seemed to pain him a great deal. He finally admitted he didn't know the answer. He insisted they didn't need to know it because God's will was God's will. Hen's argument that animals were God's creation and just as important as humans didn't sway him. "If he doesn't answer, I'll ride over and get him."

No matter how awkward it would be. She would do what was best for Lucy. Nicholas would do his job.

"I'll do it." Dad's trot turned into a lope to the door. He shoved it open and paused with a glance back. "Get her up and walking around. Don't let her strain. We have to get that foal repositioned before she tries to deliver it."

Then he was gone into the storm.

Easier said than done. "Come on, sweet Lucy, up you go."

Lucy wasn't having any of that. She flailed and nipped at Hen's hand. Hen jerked back. "Easy, girl, easy. You have to get up. You want that baby to stay inside while we get help, don't you?"

She tried again. Lucy's teeth showed. She might decide to take a bite of Hen's arm. "I know you're upset, but please don't bite me."

This time Lucy stood. She allowed herself to be led around the stall. "Good girl. Good job." Hen rubbed her flank. She kissed the horse's forehead and smoothed her mane. "It'll be fine. Dat is getting help."

God willing. Could Nicholas help? Now was not the time for smallness. Not the time for self-interest. *Please Gott, let him help.*

She checked Lucy's underside. Two legs now but no head.

Please hurry, please hurry.

The barn door slid open. Dad rushed inside and slammed it shut. "He's on his way."

"Did you ask him if he had any experience with this?"

"I didn't get a chance. As soon as I told him the problem, he said he was coming and hung up."

Nicholas knew what it meant. Time was not on their side. "Did you tell him to hurry?"

"He knows."

He might know, but time didn't. If he didn't hurry, it would be too late.

CHAPTER 14

Rain pelted Nicholas' face. The wind ripped his hood from his head. He ducked lower on the saddle. "Come on, Sable, come on." Sable probably thought he was nuts. Racing down an unlit, unpaved road in the black night of a storm invited disaster. Nicholas eased up on the reins, letting the aging horse slow to a canter. "I'm sorry, buddy, I don't mean to ride you so hard, but it's an emergency. I'll make it up to you later. I promise. A warm, dry blanket and extra hay."

The stallion probably couldn't hear Nicholas, but if he did, he understood. Nicholas' dad laughed at him for talking to animals as if they understood. *"Let me know if they answer back."*

Dad was smart about a lot of things but not this.

Nicholas was caught between rushing ahead to save a foal and taking good care of Sable. Horses were loyal creatures. They would gallop until their hearts gave out. "It's okay. You're doing fine. We're doing fine."

But how was Lucy doing? The question tightened around Nicholas' neck like a noose. The last time he witnessed a difficult equine birth, the perfectly formed, otherwise healthy foal had died from lack of oxygen after being in the birth canal too long. The memory of the chestnut foal's small muzzle, tiny ears, and fragile limbs was burned into his brain, along with the sobs of the six-year-old daughter of the owner, who kept asking why the baby horse didn't get up.

Hen wasn't six, and she would know the answer to the question. But she wouldn't be any less heartbroken. Would she blame Nicholas? It was easy to imagine her despair. Her face showed every emotion, every thought.

The loss of a foal would wound her deeply, and everyone would know it. She'd be sure Dr. McDonald should never have given the job to Nicholas.

Maybe she'd be right. If only he had more book learning. When Grandpa died—Nicholas squashed that thought before it could fully form. God willing, Grandpa would be with them for many years. Nicholas could read books. He didn't have to go to classes. All the material was online.

Another challenge. He had to go to the library in Pittsburgh to get the books and access the computers. Between Grandpa and the job, he had no time for road trips. Could they mail the books to him? He could read them at night after Grandpa and Lenora were in bed.

Round and round, his thoughts circled, faster and faster. Hen had mentioned finding information online. She too broke the rules, but she was a woman. More room existed for Nicholas because of his job. She had no excuse.

No wonder she was frustrated.

How did someone as stoic, staid, and even-keeled as Adam Miller end up with a firecracker-roman-candle-sparkler combo for a daughter? The emotions flitting across Adam's face while Hen dug her hole deeper arguing for the Angora goat enclosure had consumed his features. Adam had squinted, frowned, and rubbed his forehead then his neck. His features had turned icy and frozen, then hot and molten.

Like an unschooled man trying to decipher a mathematical equation that had stumped the world's most learned mathematicians.

The woman went so far as to try to fit her brother and Lenora together as a couple. A woman she'd met only twice. She saw something, and she jumped on it full speed ahead.

She had a good heart and no mother to steer her into womanhood. Adam had no wife to help him mold her into a suitable Plain wife and mother. Neither needed any more pain. Not tonight. The loss of an animal was hard, but it didn't compare to the bigger losses people faced every day. Nicholas couldn't help with those losses. This one he could try. He couldn't be the one to disappoint her—either of them. Any animal owner, of course. But especially Hen.

Why? That was a question for another time.

Lightning crackled across the sky, casting light on a sky filled with angry clouds. Thunder boomed. Nicholas crouched closer to the saddle—as if it would help.

Minutes later the solar lights on the Millers' porch came into view, acting as beacons guiding Nicholas over the long driveway and up to the barn.

Denki, Gott.

He dismounted. The barn doors slid open.

"You're here. Finally." Henrietta shoved the doors completely open. Her brown hair straggled down her back under her saggy prayer cap. The hem of her dress was soaked and muddy. She looked like a half-drowned kitten. "It took you long enough."

"Henrietta!" Adam's voice boomed from the depths of the barn. "Let the poor man in before he drowns."

"Get in here. Hurry."

He did as he was told. Henrietta grabbed Sable's reins before Nicholas could speak. "I'll dry off your horse, put a blanket over him, and get him some water. You go to Lucy. She needs you."

Lucy tossed her head and trotted to the far end of the stall at Nicholas' approach. She whinnied and nipped at her sides. "I know, I know." He slipped closer with caution. She was in pain and instinctively wary. "We need to get her to lie down so I can examine her."

"Have you ever done this before?" Adam grasped Lucy's halter. "Repositioned a foal?"

"I've observed it."

"I told you, Dat. We should've called Doc McDonald and waited," Henrietta called out. "A novice could do more harm than gut."

She wasn't wrong, but they had no choice. "Dr. McDonald is in Pittsburgh for a conference."

Nicholas was it. No pressure.

With Adam's help, Nicholas talked Lucy into lying down. He pulled on gloves and did an exam. "It's facing the wrong way."

"We knew that." Henrietta squeezed into the stall. "What are you going to do about it?"

"A manual correction." *Gott, help me.* "Talk to her, Hen, comfort her. Adam, help me raise her hind legs. That'll move her intestines back and give me more room to work."

His heart clamoring in his chest, Nicholas went to work. Sweat dripped in his eyes, even though he was cold and wet. *Gott, let this work, Please Gott, let this work.* He rotated the foal and gently pulled. The head appeared.

"It's coming, it's coming," Henrietta whispered. "It's working, Dat, it's working."

"Jah, I see. Praise Gott." Adam's gaze remained focused on the horse. "Come on, little gaul, come on."

Please, Gott, please, Gott.

Another gentle pull. Nicholas held his breath.

Please, Gott. Please, Gott.

The rest of the foal appeared. *Denki. Denki. Denki.*

With a whinny, Lucy stood.

"Back away, back away, let her do the rest."

"Is he breathing?" Henrietta's voice sounded strangled. "I can't tell. Can you tell?"

"She. It's a filly, and jah, she's breathing."

The foal shook her head and sat up.

"Hallelujah!" Henrietta clapped her hands. She danced around the stall in a fit of delight. "You did it, Lucy, you did it!"

With some help. But that was okay.

"Easy, Henrietta." Adam's tone didn't contain the admonition it seemed to always carry when he said his daughter's name. He even smiled. "You'll scare them both."

Nicholas took care of tying the placenta in a knot so it wouldn't flap around Lucy's hocks and scare her. Dr. McDonald was a good teacher. His instructions came to mind easily, now that the crisis had passed. The weight would help the afterbirth separate naturally without tearing the uterus. Then Nicholas could examine it to make sure nothing had been left behind that could cause Lucy problems in the future.

"She's beautiful." Henrietta knelt next to Nicholas. "Isn't she beautiful?"

"She's gorgeous. She's a mini Lucy." Nicholas sucked in a long breath and let it out. Now that the adrenaline had faded, his legs and arms felt like soggy cereal. So did his brain.

It was worth it. This was what made being a veterinarian—if he could imagine that for a moment in Dr. McDonald's absence—so satisfying. God's design was perfect, but sometimes His creatures needed a bit of help. Being able to offer that assistance touched a chord in Nicholas' heart like nothing else.

"I love that tiny face. Those tiny hooves." Henrietta's smile stretched wide. It transformed her plain face. Nicholas stared. She was as beautiful as this newborn baby she'd help deliver. Her forehead wrinkled. "What are you staring at? Do I have manure on my face?"

"Nee, nee." Keenly aware of Adam's presence, Nicholas scrambled to his feet. "I need to get washed up. Keep an eye on the placenta. I need to examine it when it disengages."

"Denki." Henrietta followed him to the stall's gate. "I'm sorry I was so surly when you first got here."

"No need to apologize. You were worried."

"You did a gut job. As gut as Doc McDonald would have done, for sure and for certain."

For Hen to admit that was a huge concession. No matter how much she wanted the job, Hen was willing to admit when she was wrong about something. That fact made her all the prettier.

She grinned at him. Nicholas grinned back. She was so happy. Which somehow made him happy.

Whoa. Back up the buggy. A man on his way out of town didn't enthuse over a woman. He reeled in the grin like a kite caught in blustery autumn gale. "Denki. I appreciate that."

The words sounded wooden, even to him.

Hen's smile faltered. She leaned against the railing and studied mother and daughter. "Can you imagine being pregnant with a horse for almost a year and then having it die?"

Until tonight, he couldn't imagine having a conversation with the word *pregnant* in it with a young, single Plain woman. Or anyone not in the medical field, for that matter. Still, she had a point. Being a man, he probably couldn't imagine it. "Nee. It would be a tragedy."

"Henrietta, go in the house and fix us some kaffi and something to eat." The admonition had returned to Adam's voice. "Be quiet about it. No need to wake up the whole house. You can heat up the soup your aenti made for supper, can't you?"

Somehow Adam managed to make that question a criticism. Hen's spectacular smile disappeared. She ducked her head. "Jah, I can."

Her expression woebegone, Hen planted a kiss on Lucy's muzzle, made a wide berth around Nicholas, and trudged from the stall.

"My dochder speaks without thinking. It's one of the many reasons I wish her *mudder* was here to school her in the proper behavior of a young woman." The pain Adam so obviously wanted to hide slipped into his words, overcoming his attempt to be matter of fact. "I'm sorry if she made you uncomfortable."

What exactly did it say about Nicholas that he most certainly was envious of a horse? Not a question he could entertain with her father waiting for a response. "I appreciate that she's plainspoken." It was refreshing, in a way. Figuring out what women were thinking was another one of those incomprehensible mathematical equations Nicholas had seen on a sample GED test. Besides, she was excited and thankful and enthusiastic about the birth of an animal. All good qualities. Not a conversation Nicholas should have with her father. "I've never been gut at talking to. . .a woman."

Which was why he was twenty-three, single, and available to move to Smicksburg to take care of his ailing grandfather. He'd taken a few buggy rides, but they'd been awkward from the minute he arrived at the girl's house down to the second he dropped her off. One girl practically raced in the other direction the next time he saw her at a singing. Another hid behind a taller friend. Nicholas could take a hint.

Henrietta was different. She would understand why Nicholas wanted to go to a veterinary medicine college. She probably daydreamed about going herself—if her life were different. Like Nicholas, her faith and her family likely kept her from pursuing her dream. Something else they had in common.

"The placenta just dropped."

Whew. A change of topic was in order. The afterbirth was complete. "Everything appears gut. We shouldn't have to worry about infection."

The foal chose that moment to scramble to her feet. She wobbled, plopped back down, then tried again. This time she struck a pose, weight distributed on four spindly legs, and whinnied a tiny squeak.

Lucy whinnied in response. Her offspring staggered over to her mom in search of milk. "She knows where to find a drink. That's gut." Adam's smile returned. Hen had inherited her smile from her father. "You've earned your keep tonight. Tell Doc I'll come into town before the end of the week to settle my bill. When I do, I'll let him know you did a fine job standing in for him. He couldn't have done better himself. 'Course I won't tell him that."

Not only did he smile, he winked.

"Denki," Nicholas managed after a few seconds. "No rush on the bill. Dr. McDonald knows you're good for it."

"Come into the house. Eat some hot soup before you head out in this weather."

"Denki, but I should get home." And far from a woman who was starting to grow on him—perhaps a little too much for a man on his way to vet school. "I have to be at work early in the morning."

"Understood." Adam's perplexed expression said the opposite. "Again, I hope Hen didn't make you uncomfortable."

"Nee, not at all."

At least not in the way her father meant.

CHAPTER 15

Sunshine burst through the kitchen's windows as if denying any knowledge of the thunderstorms that had inundated the countryside for two days. It couldn't however, erase Hen's memories of the evening earlier in the week spent helping Nicholas deliver Lucy's beautiful foal. His diligence and his joy had matched her own. Maybe even exceeded it. Seeing the expression on his face had been like seeing her own reflection in a mirror. Everyone found these events beautiful, but this was different. Special. To her at least. What about Nicholas? Who knew? It was downright perplexing. Did it mean something? If so, what? Sighing, Hen took the pan of molds filled with fresh lavender-scented goat milk soap from the counter and set it on the kitchen table next to the plastic wrap and labels.

"That's an awful big sigh for someone who's simply making soap." Aunt Ginny took a bite of Hen's latest concoction of peanut butter goat milk fudge, closed her eyes with a blissful expression, and hummed her approval. "What's going on, kind? You've been in another borough all morning. You've been making soap since you were five, and you almost put in too much sodium peroxide. Does this have something to do with a certain vet's assistant? Your dat said the two of you worked really gut together delivering Lucy's foal."

Maybe it was simply the crazy, emotional turn of events that made Hen's memory seem brighter, shinier, sweeter. Until she knew for sure, Hen couldn't tell her aunt about it. Maybe not even then. She could, however, admit to her other dilemma of her own making in order to nudge Aunt Ginny in another direction. "Nee, Nicholas did his job. Dat helped. I helped. It worked out. Nee, I was just thinking about. . . Fact is, I stepped in some doo-doo the other day at the Byler frolic."

"Ah. That wouldn't be all that unusual, considering the time you spend tending to livestock every day. Which pile of doo-doo are we talking about?" Aunt Ginny snatched another piece of fudge and tucked it in her mouth. She chortled as if she'd told the best joke ever. "I could eat a pound of this fudge. Definitely offer samples at the Smicksburg Spring Open House. People will be hooked. They'll snap it up by the ton."

"Aunt Ginny! It's not funny." Hen picked up Tigger, who'd decided to hop on the table and investigate the treats, and gently settled him on the floor. If her mother were here, the cat wouldn't be allowed in the house. Thank goodness Ruby and the kids had taken Buster with them to go swimming at the pond in celebration of the end of the school year. "Scat, cat. I'm trying to tell you something, Aenti. I need your advice."

"Sorry, sorry." Aunt Ginny wiped her hands on a towel and adopted her most somber expression. Only the faint wiggle of her double chin gave away how hard she was trying to suppress a giggle. "Tell me."

By the time Hen finished explaining her attempt at matchmaking, Aunt Ginny's chins shook with laughter. She had one hand on her chest; the other fanned her face. "I think I'm having a hot flash. Ach, goodness, kind, you are oblivious, aren't you?"

"Oblivious? Nee, nee, I'm not. I know Micah." Hen popped a purple-and-white-swirled soap from its mold, laid it in the plastic, and wrapped it with sharp, efficient movements born of much practice. "I've never seen one iota of spark or interest between Adele and my bruder. Besides, Adele would've told me if she was interested in Micah."

Or maybe not. Maybe she was afraid Hen would laugh at her or be mad. Why would Hen be mad? "I tried to ask her about it, but she laughed it off, like I was being silly. Why wouldn't she own up to a crush on Micah?"

"Maybe because you two have been united in teasing him and treating him as an annoying little brother with cooties since you were six years old." Aunt Ginny slid half a dozen pieces of fudge into a plastic sandwich bag, affixed a handmade label decorated with a Hen's Goat Goodies logo created by Adele, and laid the bag next to a growing pile. "Maybe she's embarrassed to admit that she realized he's grown into a hardworking, faithful, kind, well-spoken man who is handsome enough to make women do a double take on the sidewalks in town. I've seen it with my own two eyes."

"I'm certainly glad it wasn't with someone else's two eyes or three or four eyes." On most days their aunt was more like a sister to Hen and a better sport when it came to teasing than Ruby was. "She was with Nathan for two years. He breaks up with her, and suddenly she's goo-goo eyes for Micah?"

"Did it not occur to you that the reason it didn't work out with that young man is because Adele's heart belonged to someone else? Someone like Micah?"

"Did I hear my name?" Micah strode into the kitchen, smelling of horse and manure. Tigger immediately pounced on his muddy boots. Micah scooped up the kitten, rubbed his belly, and settled him on the pieced-rag rug at the back door. Meowing in protest, Tigger rolled over on his back, legs in the air. "It must really be a boring day, if you're talking about me."

"What are you doing here?" Hen pretended to focus on sniffing a eucalyptus and spearmint soap—her favorite calming scent. She needed it. "You're supposed to be in Punxsutawney training Tom Drucker's colt."

"The colt has a stone bruise on one foot. He's lame, so we postponed." Micah opened the propane-driven refrigerator's door and leaned down as if browsing. After a few seconds he pulled out a platter that held a goat cheese log flavored with rosemary and thyme. "This will hit the spot. Are there crackers?"

"Hey, put that back." Flapping her apron at her brother, Hen flew across the kitchen to save her creation from his clutches. "That's for the open house in town."

Making goat cheese involved a ton of work, but it was worth it. Tourists and Smicksburg residents alike bought it as fast as Hen could make it. The cash register in her brain went *ca-ching* every time she smelled its pungent aroma. Making cheese and soap had the added benefit of counting as "women's work" in her father's mind. Dad would be in a good mood at supper.

"Hey, hey, okay." Micah slid the platter back onto the shelf. He pulled out a plastic container of smoked chicken drumsticks instead. "By the way, Schweschder, I never got a chance to speak to you about the frolic. You owe me an apology. What's more, I hope you apologized to Lenora. You embarrassed her and me."

The days had passed in a frenzy of work for Dad and Micah, training horses on English farms twenty and thirty miles away. Hen's hope that Micah had been too busy to think about what had happened—might even forget about it—were dashed. She backpedaled. "I didn't mean—"

"You stuck your nose where it doesn't belong. You made Lenora, Adele, and me uncomfortable." His tone, his words, his stance with his hands on his hips, chest thrust out, presented a clear picture of how much Micah looked like their father. Moreover, how he acted and sounded like him. His poor children. "There's a reason the Gmay frowns on matchmaking. People get hurt."

"I didn't mean—"

"Did you see Lenora's face? I did."

"Let the poor woman finish a sentence, Micah." Aunt Ginny rose from the table. Her knees popped, and her chair echoed with a creak. She tugged the drumsticks from her nephew's hand. "You're right, absolutely right, but you've made your point. Let her apologize, forgive, and let it go. I'll fix you a PB&J sandwich to tide you over until supper. You can take it and a glass of cold tea out to the porch. It's a beautiful day to eat outside."

Ever the peacemaker. Hen heaved a breath. "Denki, Aenti."

"She interfered where she shouldn't." Micah turned his scowl on Aunt Ginny. "You don't think that's right, do you?"

"Nee, but you've made your point." Aunt Ginny wasn't one to be cowed, especially by a still-wet-behind-the-ears nephew. "Her sin is between her and Gott. Allow her to get a word in edgewise to apologize so we can get on with life."

Thankful for her aunt's wise words, Hen swallowed her portion of thick pride with a glass of humility. "I *am* sorry. I never meant to cause Lenora any pain. I like her. She takes care of Moses and the house, and she selflessly gave up her job teaching to do it."

"You're doing it again." Micah threw up his hands. "Will you never learn? Stop trying to sell me on Lenora."

"I'm not, really, I'm not." Or maybe she was. Because it made so much more sense than Adele. "Sorry, sorry. I just want the people around me to be happy."

"Then worry about making Dat happy by giving up these crazy plans for more and bigger herds of goats. Stop embarrassing him in front of people like Nicholas Byler. Get yourself a beau and get married." Micah accepted the PB&J sandwich and tea from Aunt Ginny. He stalked past Hen, headed for the back door. "Then everyone would be happy, even you."

"Well, well, ach, I just. . ." Hen sputtered. Micah stepped over Tigger and was out the door and gone before she could summon a worthy retort. What did Micah know about anything? "What a judgmental know-it-all!"

"Hmmm. . .maybe." Aunt Ginny busied herself putting away the peanut butter and jam. "Or maybe he's trying to be a gut bruder who really does want his schweschder to be happy. Maybe he's speaking his mind because he feels like it's important. Maybe he loves you."

Ach. Love. Hen lined up almond, black raspberry–vanilla, cucumber-melon, coffee, vanilla, and apple-cinnamon scented soaps in rows. Each had its label affixed. Each its own color and scent. So unlike her messy life. What did she know about love, really? Plain families didn't proclaim their love. They showed it through their actions. And with other words in roundabout, convoluted sentences that a person had to hike ten miles up and down, back and forth, in order to translate to three little words: *I. Love. You.*

This was her little brother Micah. Nah. That wasn't it. "Come on, don't tell me you agree with him?"

"I know for a fact your dat only wants you to be happy."

"He thinks what made him happy will make me happy. Should make me happy. He wants me to not embarrass him. He doesn't want people talking about how the bishop can't keep his dochder in hand, that she'll be an old maid because she's a terrible housekeeper who smells like goat and wanders around with manure and dirt on her face."

"That may all be true, but in his heart, your daed worries about all those things because he loves you and wants you to have a *mann* and kinner and the life that every Plain woman grows up wanting." Aunt Ginny folded her arms and drilled Hen with the most severe gaze she'd ever seen on her aunt's face. "I know because I'm a mudder, and that's what I want for my *dechder*. Someday you'll understand."

Hen did want a husband and children. She wanted a big family and a farm full of animals they would raise together. Goats and pigs and cows and chickens and horses and dogs and cats. Couldn't she be a goat whisperer and a wife and mother too?

"Stop thinking so hard. You'll give yourself a headache." Aunt Ginny patted Hen's shoulder. "Have a piece of fudge. Chocolate makes everything better."

On that they could agree. Hen took her advice. The sweet fudge melted on her tongue, dousing the sour taste left by her conversation with Micah.

"So what about the other doo-doo? The one involving a certain vet's assistant." Aunt Ginny smiled as if she enjoyed opening a jar of canned green beans and finding worms instead. "Nicholas seems like a nice man. He loves animals almost as much as you do. That's something you have in common."

"Ha! Now *you're* doing it." Hen jabbed her index finger at her aunt. "You're matchmaking. Now who has to ask forgiveness for her sin?"

"I'm asking you to think about it. If Nicholas were to ask you to take a buggy ride with him, would you do it?"

Maybe. Yes. No. But maybe. Had they turned a corner that evening in the barn? Or was it her imagination? The image of his face when Lucy's foal finally made an appearance flashed in Hen's mind. His delight at the foal's pretty face and delicate form mirrored her own. He had a heart for animals, and he wore it on his sleeve. He'd left his home in Bird-in-Hand to come to Smicksburg to take care of his grandfather. He had a heart for family. He was a hard worker who hopped on a horse and rode through a storm to help a mare deliver her foal. He flaunted rules because having a phone in the house for animal emergencies was more important than toeing the line.

Could it be that her list now had more pluses than minuses?

It didn't matter. Men had to make the first move in the Plain world. Nicholas never would. Not unless he found an opinionated, rumpled, stinky, ordinary-looking woman attractive.

Just suppose he did. A shiver ran through Hen. Suppose she allowed herself to care for him. And then he died. It would tear her heart from her chest. The way Mom's death had. She'd have that forlorn visage that dad had worn now for three years.

Would the risk be worth it?

"So?" Aunt Ginny's thick eyebrows rose and fell. Her nose wrinkled. "You didn't answer my question."

"So, I need to drain the next batch of cheese. Do you mind starting on the caramel toffees? I'd like to try dipping them in chocolate this time. We'll need to melt the chocolate."

"Uh-huh."

"Didn't you hear what Micah said?" Hen used clothespins to clip a clean flour-sack dishcloth to the edges of her colander. Then she put it inside a four-quart Cambro bucket. "The Gmay frowns on matchmaking. People get hurt."

They also got hurt if they cared about someone. If they loved someone. People died. She fell for that one once. She couldn't fall for it again.

Fool me once, shame on you. Fool me twice, shame on me.

That person would not be Hen.

CHAPTER 16

One person's emergency was another person's *You're kidding me, right?* Trying to hide his smile, Nicholas ducked his head and counted the hens pecking at bugs in Mrs. Lowell's front yard while Dr. McDonald attempted to get a word in edgewise as the woman demanded to know why her best layer hadn't produced an egg in more than a week.

"I'm telling you, Matilda is sick. She's given me eggs every day for almost four years." Mrs. Lowell clutched the Rhode Island Red hen against her overalls-covered bosom. "Now she's just sitting there scowling at me like 'What do you want?' when I go in the coop to gather the eggs. You're a vet. Do something. Give her some medicine. Maybe she's constipated. Should I give her some fresh fruit?"

Dr. McDonald's efforts to answer were hamstrung by the onslaught of words. He put up both hands. "Mrs. Lowell. Mrs. Lowell! You say Matilda has been laying for four years?"

"Yes. She's my best producer. Better than Lydia or Camilla or any of the others." Mrs. Lowell smoothed Matilda's feathers and landed a kiss on her head. "Aren't you, sweet pea, you're the best, aren't you?"

"The fact is, most layers will give you three to five years of production. After that, their bodies are worn out. They can't do it anymore."

"Matilda's better than that. She should have at least another year of laying. No way I'm retiring her and putting her out to pasture this early." Mrs. Lowell shook her finger at Dr. McDonald. "I knew I should've called Dr. Nelson in Pittsburgh. You're a quack."

Nicholas had taken Mrs. Lowell's call. He'd encouraged Mrs. Lowell to bring her "sick" hen into the clinic, but she'd insisted Matilda was too ill to travel. The vet needed to come out immediately, which Dr. McDonald had graciously agreed to do after Nicholas handed him the phone so he could listen to the woman's litany of problems for five minutes.

"What are you feeding her?" Nicholas interceded to give his boss a chance to regain his composure. It was hard to tell if his pinched lips and wrinkled nose resulted from the brilliant midmorning sun, anger, or the effort it took not to laugh. "Have you changed it?"

"Only the best feed for my babies. This feed has higher levels of calcium and protein and contains crushed oyster shells plus grit for their digestion." Mrs. Lowell sounded like a commercial for chicken feed. With her overalls, plaid shirt, work boots, and long gray braids hanging from under an oversized straw hat, she was dressed perfectly for the part. "It has a carefully balanced ratio of amino acids and minerals. I also give them raw cucumber peels, spinach, and tomatoes, plus cracked corn as a special treat."

"Sounds good." Nicholas took Matilda from her owner. The hen's eyes were clear, her feathers shiny, and she had no problem trying to peck his hand. "Easy, Matilda, I come in peace."

She settled into his arms. "How often are you feeding them?"

"Twice a day. On average they get about three pounds of feed a week. That's what the experts recommend."

She might be strident, but Mrs. Lowell knew her stuff. The yard was mowed, the road recently graded, and the farmhouse freshly painted. Mums, daisies, and black-eyed Susans crowded a flower bed to one side. Two sleek Morgans watched from the corral like interested spectators at a tennis match.

Mrs. Lowell was a responsible farmer who took raising livestock seriously. If only all of them did. Nicholas grasped for a response that made sense. "What about the coop? Are you keeping it clean?"

"Absolutely. What kind of animal owner do you think I am?"

Nicholas glanced at Dr. McDonald. He offered a shrug and a faint smile. Nicholas was on his own. "The days are getting longer. That should help. Matilda likely wants about fourteen hours a day for optimate egg producing."

"There's not much I can do about that."

"True, I'm just trying to consider all the possibilities for Matilda's ailment. What about the other layers? You mentioned Lydia and Camilla. Do you have others?"

"Twelve in all. Rhode Island Red and Plymouth Rock, some of the best breeds for layers. But Matilda was my first and best."

"And so she's your oldest?"

"Well, yes. . ."

"I'm afraid age has caught up with poor Matilda. In the wild she might live ten years. She'd produce fewer eggs per year but lay them longer. Raising chickens for the purpose of selling their eggs reduces their lifespan and their productive years. It's a hard fact of life."

"In other words, you have no idea why she's not producing eggs." Mrs. Lowell held out her arms. "Come to Mama, Matilda. Don't listen to this silly man. Don't you worry, sweet pea, I'll get you a second opinion."

"I'm sorry we can't be more helpful." Nicholas tipped his straw hat to her. "You're doing a great job. These chickens are living high on the hog—so to speak. They're lucky to have you as their owner."

"Aww, posh. Now you're just sweet-talking me to make sure you get your fee." Despite her words, Mrs. Lowell's saggy jowls pinked. She might have smiled. "Don't worry, I don't expect nothing for free when it comes to the medical profession."

"Actually, this one's on the house since we weren't able to be more helpful." Dr. McDonald offered her a courtly bow. "I hope you get to feeling better, Matilda."

As they walked away, a rooster blasted them with a *cock-a-doodle-doo* that left Nicholas' ears ringing.

"Another satisfied customer," Dr. McDonald murmured. "Right back atcha, fella."

Nicholas followed his boss to the clinic's van. He waited until they were on the road to test the waters. "I hope I didn't overstep back there. I thought maybe I could help."

"You did help." Dr. McDonald chuckled as he flipped down the visor to block the sun. "I'm pleased with how much you know about chickens. As usual, you've done your homework. I'm constantly amazed at your knowledge, considering you've never been to college, let alone veterinary school."

Reading between the lines didn't require literacy. In other words,

Nicholas' knowledge was amazing, considering his formal education stopped after eighth grade. "Like I said when you interviewed me, I grew up taking care of animals for my dad and various relatives. Plus I do a ton of reading."

"And it shows." Dr. McDonald made the sharp turn from the Lowell farm's dirt road onto the highway and accelerated to stay ahead of an oncoming horse and buggy. "It just seems like. . ."

"Seems like what?"

"I don't mean to offend, I hope you know."

"I know. Go ahead."

"It seems a shame you can't finish your education and become a full-fledged vet." Dr. McDonald glanced at Nicholas and back at the road. "With your brain and your instinct and your love of animals, you're made to be a veterinarian. Have you ever given any thought to furthering your education?"

A thousand and one times. During countless sleepless hours. Since he was ten and helped his dog Snoopy deliver six puppies in the middle of a blizzard. While helping a sow farrow a litter of a dozen piglets. While nursing a gash on a dog's leg and a horse with colic. It was termed a calling for a reason. A vocation, not simply an occupation. It called to him. Nicholas heaved a sigh. "I've thought about it."

"What's holding you back? Is it money? Given what you earn working for me, I have no doubt you'd be eligible for financial aid. You can get your GED—that's the General Education Development—"

"I know what it is." He'd researched it when the calling had been so strong he couldn't avoid it anymore. "Getting a high school diploma equivalent won't help."

"Why not?"

"My community doesn't believe in higher education. We learn everything we need to know at home. After our formal education ends, we begin vocational training at home in occupations helpful to our way of life such as farming, building furniture, making tack and gear for horses, training horses, working as farriers, working on construction crews building houses, to name a few."

"Surely they wouldn't object to you becoming a vet. The Amish need vets. An Amish vet would be a plus, in my way of thinking."

"The education is the rub. Even a vet tech requires more education."

"And there's no getting around it? No special dispensation you can get from the bishop or something?"

"No. Under the Ordnung—the rules—in my district, it's not possible." The words tasted like an overripe lime in Nicholas' mouth. He'd talked to his dad. He'd talked to his bishop. He'd even talked to the deacon. No go. "If I decide to go to college, I have to leave my community. I'll be under the *meidung* or shunning. In other words, I'd be leaving the church, and I couldn't see my family anymore."

One day Grandpa would be gone. What would Nicholas do then? How could he even contemplate that scenario? He would stay with Grandpa for however long he was needed.

"That seems totally out of proportion for someone who's trying to do something good. Who's trying to better himself." Dr. McDonald shook his head hard. "I don't mean to be critical, but I really don't understand. How can education be bad for you? How can following your dream be a bad thing?"

Even though Dr. McDonald had lived among the Amish his entire life, his lack of understanding didn't come as a surprise. "We don't have anything against education, but we protect our way of life by staying disconnected from the world. That means staying off the electrical grid, having our own schools and teachers, and choosing jobs that keep us close to home and family."

Nicholas glanced at his boss. He squinted against the sun, but it was apparent he was listening intently. He really wanted to understand.

"We always put our faith first. It's faith, family, and community, then self. It's not about me or my dreams. It's called dying to self. It means I will always put others first. When I was baptized, I vowed to follow those rules."

"So if you choose veterinary medicine college, you give up your faith, your family, and your community?"

"Yes."

Dr. McDonald tapped the wheel in a soft one, one-two, one-two-three rhythm. "I'm no theologian, but I sit in the pew every Sunday morning with my wife and kids. One thing I'm clear on is no one can take your faith from you. It's yours and yours alone. If you leave the Amish church, you don't stop being a believer. That's between you and God. You might practice your faith differently, but you'd still practice. If you really believe."

"That may be true for your religion, but the only way I know is the Amish way." Nicholas sank deeper into the seat. He leaned his head against the headrest. The last person he expected to talk religion with was Carson McDonald. How had they found their way to this place in the conversation? "Right now it's moot, anyway. As I mentioned in my interview, I came to Smicksburg with my sister to take care of my grandpa. As long as he needs me, I'm not going anywhere."

"Family over self. I get that." Dr. McDonald drove past Old Smicksburg Park on Highway 954. He slowed and turned onto Clarion Street in the tiny borough of Smicksburg, official population fifty-two. "But you also have to think of the long game. You'll want to get married one day and have kids. You need an occupation that will allow you to feed your family. This one won't do it."

One thing at a time. Nicholas didn't even have a special friend. "I appreciate your thoughts on this subject—really, I do."

"In other words, mind my own business." Dr. McDonald had a belly laugh that suited a man with a stomach that hung over his belt buckle. "I'll change the subject. The Indiana County Humane Society is having a booth at the Spring Open House on Saturday. They're bringing dogs and cats available for adoption. They asked if I'd like to have a rep there to encourage people to spay and neuter their pets. I can't do it; my sons both have baseball games. Would you mind? I'll pay you for it, of course."

Spend a day hanging out with dogs and cats in need of permanent homes? A worthy cause Nicholas could support. It wouldn't make Lenora happy. She likely wanted a day off from caring for Grandpa alone. Maybe they could bring him into town too. The doctor said social interaction would help slow the inexorable march of dementia. "I'd be happy to. I haven't been to an open house here. I'm interested to see what the vendors have to offer."

"Everything imaginable. The businesses will have their doors open and displays outside. Vendors who don't have shops will have booths on a portion of the street they'll close for the day. It's a little early for a lot of the produce, but my wife can spend more money on stuff at the craft fair than you can believe. Leather goods, paintings, candles, quilts, wooden toys, jams and jellies, nuts, pottery, goat milk soap, goat milk cheese, goat milk candy. . ."

Dr. McDonald heaved a breath and kept going, but Nicholas' attention stayed with the mention of goat milk soap, cheese, and candy. Did that mean Hen would be there? She couldn't be the only person in Indiana County with a goat herd, but she might be the closest to Smicksburg. Ever since delivering Lucy's foal, he'd found it hard to dismiss the images of Hen collected in his mind's eye. So concerned, her brown eyes big, her fingers tightly clasped in her lap, biting her lip. Then that transformation. Pure joy radiated from her face. A childlike enthusiasm and excitement for something she'd no doubt seen many times before.

"Nicholas? Nicholas!"

Nicholas jumped. "Yes?"

"We're here. Are you getting out? I need you to fill out the paperwork on Miss Matilda. And give me a rundown on what I have on the schedule tomorrow. Also, can you clean up the dog kennels? Bertram, the Martins' terrier, left a mess."

"No problem. I'm on it."

No time for daydreaming now. He might see Hen on Saturday. He might not. For some reason he hoped it was the former. Why? Good question. Not one he intended to answer—for now.

CHAPTER 17

The prance in her sister's step was a dead giveaway. Hen gave up trying to sleep in the midst of Ruby's late-night return from a buggy ride with Peter. At least that was the assumption. Hen sat up, threw off the Star of Bethlehem quilt she held close to her even when the nights warmed because it was the last one Mom had made, and turned on the propane lamp. With a loud meow of protest, Tigger leaped from the pillow where he'd been curled around Hen's head and landed in her lap. Somewhere, Mom was shaking her head at the thought of a cat sleeping on her oldest daughter's pillow.

"Sorry. Did I wake you?" Not sounding at all sorry, Ruby flitted around the room, grabbed her nightgown from the hook, tossed it on her bunk bed, removed her bonnet, and picked the pins from her cap and laid them on the chest of drawers, all the while humming and grinning so wide her cheeks had to hurt. "I'll be quick about it."

"I can't wait that long. I have to get up early in the morning. The driver will be here at dark thirty to load the goats in his truck along with all our wares for the open house." Her brothers and Ruby would take the buggy and arrive later. Hen patted the spot next to her on the bed. "Sit and spill the beans. I know you just came back from a buggy ride with Peter. What has you so fired up that you look like you're about to explode?"

Ruby pirouetted across the room and finally plopped down. Her eyes shining, she clasped her hands in her lap and heaved a breath. "Peter and I went to see the deacon tonight. Our banns will be announced on Sunday."

"Awww, you're getting married." Hen wrapped her arms around her sister in a fierce hug. Not happy at being caught in the middle, Tigger hopped down, trotted across the room, and took up residence on Ruby's pillow. "Congratulations, Schweschder. It's about time. Does Dat know?"

"Being he's the bishop, he was next in line." Tears streaked Ruby's face. Sniffing, she patted her face with a crumpled hankie. "I wish Mamm was here. I'm so happy, and yet my heart hurts."

Hen's heart squeezed in commiseration. Ruby should be sharing this wonderful news with their mother. Unfair. Why did that word always find a way to wiggle its way into her thoughts? She knew better. Life wasn't fair. *In this world you will have trouble. But don't worry, I have overcome the world.* Or something to that effect. If Mom was in heaven, she'd be making her famous lemon meringue pie and washing the stained-glass windows with her special vinegar-water combination, making them sparkle. If only, if only, if only. Ruby didn't need to know of these crazy thoughts strewn across Hen's mind like pick-up sticks. "She knows. She's celebrating with you right now."

"Do you really think so? I'd like to think Mamm, Mammi Jolene, Onkel Paul, and the bopli are huddled together, peeking at us, and cheering us on."

What would Dad say about that? He didn't know everything. No one did. God's ways were mysterious. Scripture also said that. "I pray with all my heart."

Even when her heart was so full of prickly porcupine spines it bled.

"There's so much to do, I don't even know where to begin." The admission brought on a fresh onslaught of happy tears. "When I first started my rumspringa, I used to daydream about Mamm and me making all the preparations for my wedding. She would sew our dresses. We'd clean the house from top to bottom. We'd make lists of groceries. Dat and the buwe would clean the yard and mow—"

"I just heard the gut news." Aunt Ginny burst into the room. Dressed in a baggy nightgown, her silver hair loose to her waist, she trotted straight for Ruby. More hugs ensued. "I'm so full of joy I could burst like a balloon! I couldn't wait until morning to congratulate you. It's so perfect that I'm here to help out with all the preparations."

"That is *wunderbarr.*" Ruby wiped her nose and offered them a tremulous smile. "We have one month to get ready. Peter wants to get married in June because his construction crew has two weeks between projects—unless the weather slows them down."

Despite the tears, Ruby glowed with happiness. She'd waited a long time for marriage. She and Peter had started courting when they were seventeen. Neither of them ever dated anyone else. They likely planned to marry much earlier, but Mom's death had postponed those plans. "That gives us plenty of time to prep. Tomorrow I'll go into town and buy postcards—"

"Nee, no need. I have a stack in my round-robin writing materials. I never go anywhere without them." Aunt Ginny squeezed onto the bed next to Ruby. "You can use them for the *save the date*. You need to start writing them ASAP, so the out-of-town folks can make plans to attend. In the morning you and I will start making lists. Groceries. Chores. Who'll do what. You need to reserve the church benches and the portable wedding kitchen."

She rubbed her hands together. "This is so exciting. I can't wait to get started."

Hen tried to imagine. She couldn't. She'd never daydreamed about making wedding preparations with Mom. Her daydreams were occupied by plans for her goat herds. She wanted to marry. She wanted children, but having them always seemed like something she'd do later.

Nicholas' face with his knowing gray eyes flashed in her mind. She tried to shoo it away, but it refused to go. Someone like Nicholas wouldn't be available for much longer. He had husband material written all over him in big black letters. He was kind to animals. Mena liked him. He worked hard. He was smart. He'd been baptized. And mostly, he loved animals. "How did you know Peter was the one? You never courted anyone else. You never even considered another man ever, as far as I can tell."

Are you sure he's the one?

Her smile growing, Ruby clasped her hands to her chest. "I can't explain it, really. He isn't a big talker. But when he does talk, he makes it count. He's solid as a rock. His parents were right to name him Peter like the apostle. He makes me feel like I'm at the center of his world. That sounds so prideful, but I know he'd do anything for me. That's an amazing feeling. And I feel the same way about him. I can't imagine being with anyone else. He's the one."

Not flashy romance novel love. Solid. No fireworks. Not swept off her feet. And yet a happily-ever-after.

"What if. . . ?" No Hen didn't dare. She couldn't dump her fears on her sister. "Never mind."

"Nee, what is it?" Aunt Ginny reached in front of Ruby and patted Hen's hand. "You look like the sky is falling. That's not like you. Ruby will still be your schweschder. You'll still see each other."

"She's probably thinking about how she'll have to take charge of the house. The cooking, cleaning, the sewing, the laundry." Ruby's tone had turned tart. "It's your turn. The goats will have to share you."

Of course they would. "That's not fair. I help with all the chores." Hen plucked at the patch on her nightgown. She'd repaired the rip herself. She could sew. She simply didn't care for it. "It's just that I worry—don't tell me it's a sin and demand I stop—about the future. What if something happens to Peter down the road—"

"Why would you say such a thing?" Ruby hopped up from the bed, spun around, and planted her hands on her hips. "Nothing will happen to Peter. We'll get married, have kinner, and live our lives together—Gott willing."

"It's that last part that worries me. Gott willing. I can't help but think of what happened to Mamm. Don't you think she and Dat felt the same way? I reckon Dat never thought he'd be raising kinner by himself when he proposed to Mamm."

"That wasn't Gott's will," Aunt Ginny intervened. "He allowed it to happen, but disease and illness happen in a fallen world."

Not news. Dad had given that sermon many times. Why was it so hard to accept?

"Mamm had to die because Eve ate the apple?" Hen stood and paced. "I know I'm being silly. We're supposed to be stoic and accept Gott's plan for us. I know Gott can bring good from anything. I know it in my head. It's my heart I'm having trouble with. It won't get on board."

Aunt Ginny stepped into Hen's path. She held out her arms. Hen had no choice but to accept her offering. "It's okay, my dear maedel. You have a soft, sensitive heart. Gott knows that. He gave it to you. You want to protect your heart from being hurt again. That's understandable. But one day a man will take over protecting it for you, and you'll let him because it would hurt too much to let him go."

"I'm sorry I snapped at you." Ruby added her hug to Aunt Ginny's.

"I should've said that I'll take whatever time Gott gives me with Peter. I pray that it's a very long time, but a little will be far better than none."

"You're brave." Hen hugged her back. "And I'm happy for you and Peter. I promise to help with the preparations instead of running off to tend to my goats."

"I'll hold you to that." Ruby stepped back. "Now we better get to bed."

Almost as soon as Hen turned off the propane lamp, Ruby's even breathing filled the silence. Hen stared into the darkness. *I'm sorry, Gott, for being such a fraidy-cat. I love my goats, but I don't want to spend all my love on them. Make me brave. Please.* Aamen.

P.S. Please help me figure out who "the one" is. Aamen.

P.P.S. And if it's Nicholas, could You give me a sign? Or if I missed the sign, could You bop me upside the head to let me know? Denki. Aamen—and this time I really mean it.

She tugged Mom's quilt into her arms and buried her face in it. The quilt had been washed many times. Yet it still held Mom's light, flowery scent—if only in Hen's imagination. The picture of her bent over the quilt, stretched on the wooden frame, needle in hand, floated from the treasure chest in Hen's mind. She was laughing at a story told by Grandma Martha, God bless her soul. Grandma had a lot of them, and she liked to tell and retell them. Mom's easy laugh soaked into the quilt along with her soft touch and her sweet scent.

Ach, Mom, we love Aunt Ginny, but even she could use your help these days.

CHAPTER 18

Oh, so tempting. The one-year-old Boston terrier mix named Raindrop fit in the crook of Nicholas' arm. The pup couldn't weigh more than twelve pounds. She licked Nicholas' fingers. Her butterscotch fur was soft as velvet. She whimpered. *Take me home. Feed me. Love me.* Nicholas chuckled and kissed her nose. "Sorry, little one, if I take you, I'll have to take your buddies too."

That would include four other dogs and three cats the Indiana County Humane Society had brought to the Smicksburg Spring Open House. Attila the basset hound. Pepper the retriever. Dale the dachshund. And Teddy the mutt. All were under two years old but varied in size from little Raindrop to Teddy at forty-five pounds. Clover, Candy, and Minnie—the kittens—were all shorthairs in black, white, and calico respectively. All spayed or neutered, thanks to the humane society's diligent efforts and vets like Dr. McDonald.

"Raindrop has taken a liking to you." Betty, one of two humane society volunteers working the event, set an oversized travel mug on the table that held adoption questionnaires, information on spay and neuter vouchers, microchipping information, Q&As on animal care, and bowls of free dog and cat treats. She scratched behind the puppy's ears. "Are you sure you don't want to take her off our hands before the crowds descend? Puppies always go first. People forget they grow up."

Raindrop would likely weigh twenty-five pounds when full grown. She would need a place to roam and do her business, and someone with whom she could play—canine or otherwise. Daisy would like to have a buddy, once she got used to the idea. Nicholas could provide the rest. Families living in small houses with small yards, or even apartments, couldn't. They often returned animals—an awful fate to befall animals through no fault of their own. "My sister wouldn't be happy with me if I brought another animal home. We already have a dog and two cats along with all the livestock."

"Maybe you should invite her to come by." Betty took Raindrop from Nicholas. She laid her on a blanket in her roomy cage. Raindrop immediately hopped up and chased her tail in a case of puppy zoomies. "She might change her mind if she saw her. It could even be her idea."

Betty was good at her job, but all five dogs had sweet faces and tails that whapped like crazy if someone even pretended to pay attention to them. They all deserved forever homes. To pick one over the others would be impossible. Lenora would come by later with Grandpa. If she showed interest in adopting another animal, Nicholas would fall over backward. "We'll see."

"Puppies, Mommy, puppies!" Their first visitors of the day had arrived. A young boy with a mass of blond curls and two missing front teeth raced ahead of a woman pushing a stroller. Two other couples weren't far behind. The boy squeezed past the two tables under the society's shade canopy and made a beeline for the cages. "Can we have one, Mommy, can we?"

"Jeremy, get back here." A huffing and puffing woman approached from a few yards behind. She was pushing a stroller that held a chubby-cheeked, sleeping baby wearing a sunbonnet. "You'll get bit. Get out of there."

The dogs naturally started barking all at once, Attila the basset leading the pack with his baying. Eyes wide, Jeremy screeched and jumped back. Betty was helping a couple who were interested in Clover. She telegraphed an SOS to Nicholas. His job was to talk spay and neuter, but the other society volunteer was late. Very late.

Nicholas squatted next to the boy. "When you approach dogs you don't know, it's important to do it slowly, or they'll feel threatened. They don't know you either. Give them a chance to figure out you are friend, not foe." He held out his hand for Pepper to sniff. His tail wagging, Pepper obliged with a sniff and a welcoming bark. "Pepper, this is Jeremy. Jeremy, meet Pepper."

Jeremy imitated Nicholas' actions. He and the dog were immediately best friends.

Nicholas stood. The boy's mom, who was in a family way, frowned. "We can't get a dog. Especially not a big dog."

"What about this one?" Jeremy pointed to the dachshund. "He's small."

"Honey, I have too much on my plate already." She scowled at Nicholas as if he were at fault. "If I'd known you were here, I would've gone the other way. He's been begging for a dog since last year. He asked Santa for one for Christmas and was so disappointed on Christmas Day I thought he would never believe in him or me again."

"I'm sorry, ma'am." Why was he apologizing? Because she looked as if she hadn't had a good night's sleep since Jeremy's birth. "You could try for something smaller and less labor intensive, like a hamster."

"Another mouth to feed. I don't think so."

Hamsters ate a tiny amount of fresh fruit, vegetables, and seeds most days, with an occasional hard-boiled egg for protein. "I understand. It's not the right time."

"No, it's not." The woman patted her belly. "He'll have to be happy with a new baby brother to play with."

"More dirty diapers. Pee-u." Jeremy scoffed. "All babies do is cry, eat, sleep, and poop."

Technically he was right. Ignoring a wave of embarrassment, Nicholas managed to smile at the boy's mother. "They're having a boxcar derby demonstration over by the furniture store. Maybe Jeremy would like that."

"Good idea. Jeremy, let's go see if we can get some information on the boxcar derby. Maybe your dad can find the time to help you build one."

"No, no! I want a dog, please can I have a dog, pretty please?" Tears flowing now, Jeremy jumped up and down. "You said I could have a dog when I got older. I'm older now."

"Jeremy Riley Childress, stop that right now." His mother squeezed past the tables, grabbed her son by the arm, and dragged him kicking and sobbing to the stroller. "If you don't stop, we're going home. No cider. No kettle corn. No snow cone. No nothing."

"Maybe I can help."

Nicholas whirled at the sound of that voice. Just the right amount of concern mixed with enthusiasm. Hen approached. She held out a snack-size plastic bag with two pieces of homemade candy in it. The bag had a business card attached to it with a red ribbon wound through a punched hole. Mrs. Childress took it before Jeremy could. "What's this?"

"It's fudge made with chocolate, peanut butter, and goat's milk."

"You should always ask a parent first before giving a child anything edible. What if he was allergic to peanuts?"

Hen's face filled with consternation. "I'm so sorry. Is he?"

"No, but that's not the point." Mrs. Childress held the bag out of her son's reach. "Anyway, I don't think it will make up for a puppy."

"I also have six goats in a mini petting zoo over by my booth." Her smile reappearing, Hen winked at Jeremy. The little boy's face scrunched up in an attempt to return the favor. She grinned. "Have you ever petted a goat?"

Jeremy shook his head. "Can I take a goat home?"

"No, you can't, but you can pet them. They're members of my family, so they would be sad if I let you take them home. So would I."

"Can we, Mom, can we?"

Mrs. Childress was busy eating a piece of fudge. She closed her eyes. "Mmmm, mmm, mm-mm. Yes, we can. I want to get some more of this fudge and some goat cheese."

"We're halfway down the block on the right. Hen's Goat Goodies."

Jeremy took off. His mother yelled at him to slow down, heaved a sigh, and pushed the stroller at a trot after him.

"Another satisfied customer." Hen appeared pleased with herself. Even so, her smile turned cool when she approached Nicholas. "No need to thank me."

"I wasn't going to." Now why did he say that? She had helped out. She simply took him by surprise. Which was silly. He knew she would be at the open house. "I mean, denki. You have a way with people."

"That's not what my dat says. He says I'm too loud and bossy, that I talk too much." She shrugged and held out a bag of fudge. "I'm drumming up business for our booth. Be sure to stop by if you or Lenora or your daadi have a hankering for goat milk soap, candies, cheeses, fudge, and kefir."

Just drumming up another customer. Nothing more. Nothing less. Fine. Nicholas took the bag. "Denki—"

"Hi, Betty, how's it going?" Hen pivoted and strolled toward the booth volunteer. "What beautiful creatures are you showcasing today?"

"We have some cuties, Hen. You'll love them all. I don't know why I couldn't talk that couple into adopting Miss Clover." Betty stroked the feline. Her purr revved even louder. "It's still early, though."

"Awwww. Who wouldn't want this kitty? Miss Clover is beautiful." Hen took the animal from Betty. "Oh my, you are gorgeous. And sweet as sugar cookies. Unfortunately, Willow and Tigger don't play well with other cats. We've learned that the hard way. Plus we have a new batch of kittens who will need homes soon."

"You should talk to our vet assistant about spaying or neutering them." Betty jabbed a thumb at Nicholas. "You can apply for one of our vouchers and get a discounted rate on spaying and neutering."

Her eyebrows raised, Hen turned to Nicholas. "Your friend here is also a good salesperson, but I don't think Dat will go for spending two hundred dollars per cat to fix half a dozen cats."

It was a steep price, even with the discount, but it was cheaper than feeding and caring for seven cats and their future litters. Nicholas started to say as much, but the two women had moved on. They bonded over the problem of people dumping their animals in the country instead of being responsible pet owners. Hen was doing a good job of ignoring Nicholas. The brief respite the night the foal was born had ended. Hen had to hold, pet, and kiss every one of the society's animals. When she scooped up Raindrop, the wide smile on her face said it all. The puppy had charmed her apron off.

"She's a cutie, isn't she? I reckon Mena would love a puppy." They could always talk about animals, couldn't they? Nicholas scratched Raindrop under her chin. "Does Buster want a friend?"

"Mena would love her. So would Buster. So would I." Her tone a bit friendlier, Hen chewed her lower lip. She held the dog up to her face and kissed her nose. "How could anyone not love this little goober at first sight?"

"So you'll adopt her?" Betty snapped up a questionnaire and held it out with a pen. "Just fill this out, and we'll get the process started."

"Oh, how I wish." Hen rubbed her cheek against Raindrop's fur. "Dat would have a cow. Which I would take care of, for sure and for certain."

Her eyebrows popped up again. She tapped her index finger on her cheek and grinned. "Ah, I have an idea. Maybe I can convince Ruby to take her. She's getting married next month, and she could take Raindrop with her to her new house."

"Is she here?" Hit with the strangest urge to touch Hen's face, pink from the May sun, Nicholas stuck his hands behind his back. She was at her prettiest when she talked about anything animal related. He'd never met a woman who matched his enthusiasm for them. Sure, some women liked cute dogs and cats, but they usually didn't want the added responsibility of caring for them. Nor did they want them in the house. His mom and sisters certainly didn't. "Maybe we could take Raindrop to meet her."

"She's at our booth with Mena and the boys." Hen's voice rose in her excitement. "But you don't need to come with me. I can convince Ruby on my own."

"We can't let a nonvolunteer take an animal from the booth." Betty rolled her eyes. "When it comes to you, it's a stupid rule, but if something happened to Raindrop, it would be my hide. Can you go, Nicholas?"

"I'd be happy to tag along." Even if Hen didn't want him to. "Between the two of us, surely we can convince her. Especially if we take Raindrop to meet her personally."

And then they could walk to the booth together. Nicholas waited for his pleasure at the thought to wane. It didn't. "We'll get the job done. Are you sure you're okay on your own?"

"Just don't let her get away from you. I think she has a bit of jackrabbit in her." Betty laughed at her own observation. "Here comes Johnny-come-lately, my covolunteer. Nice of you to show up, Tanya."

Tanya had a long story about how her car wouldn't start and then. . . Nicholas didn't wait to hear the rest of it. He put a leash on Raindrop, just in case, tucked the puppy under his arm, and joined Hen for the walk to her booth. The crowd had swelled in the hour since shops opened their doors to the public. Nicholas followed Hen as she wove around people who paused to greet friends or slurp their overfull coffee travel mugs. Which meant Hen had to stop to hand out bags of her fudge to them.

"It goes great with hot coffee or tea," she told one English couple—not that they needed much encouragement to accept free homemade candy. "The peanut butter and goat's milk are good for you too."

Maybe so, but fudge is fudge. Nicholas kept that thought to himself.

"Cute puppy." The woman petted Raindrop with one hand and

popped fudge into her mouth with the other. "For a cute couple. You're Amish, right?"

"Yes, yes, I mean yes we're Amish," Hen stuttered. Her pink cheeks turned a deep red. "But we're not, I mean, we're not a couple."

"The puppy isn't ours either." Nicholas spotted a half-full trash can. Maybe he could climb into it and hide until the embarrassment subsided. "Her name is Raindrop. She's available for adoption. The Indiana County Humane Society has a booth back there."

He pointed in the right direction. He was talking way too fast. The woman and her companion laughed. "We can't adopt a puppy. We live in a condo in Pittsburgh. We're just visiting for the weekend."

"Hey, can we get a selfie with you two? Our friends will love your outfits." The guy whipped out his phone. "Come on, Shelby, scoot around so you can get in the shot."

"No, no, we don't do that." Hen stuck out her hand as if to ward him off. "Please don't."

"Joe, you know better," the woman scolded. "We saw it on the website. Something about graven images, whatever that means."

"Thanks for understanding." Nicholas forced himself to smile. At this event and all the others, it was a losing battle. Everywhere he turned someone took his picture. As long as he didn't seek it out, it wasn't his fault—or sin. "And thanks for asking."

"No worries." They started off in the other direction. The woman turned back. "If you're not a couple right now, you will be soon. It's written on both of your faces. You're too cute for words in those quaint getups. I bet you sell a lot of candy that way."

Her laughter lingered in the air even after they were swallowed up in the crowd. Hen's elbow dug into Nicholas' side. He forced himself to glance at her. She grinned. "I don't know about you, but I think my 'getup' is probably more comfortable than the skintight yoga pants and skimpy little top she was wearing."

"Jah, jah, you're right." Nicholas managed a brusque laugh. If Hen could ignore the comment about them being a couple, so could he. "Who is she to judge?"

The sun had decorated Hen's nose with a swathe of new freckles. It was impossible to ignore them. Nicholas cleared his throat. "I was thinking about what you said about your father. He's a bishop and all, but none of us is perfect. There's more than one perspective on your behavior. You're assertive, you speak up, you're outgoing, and you like people." It might not be smart to disagree with his new bishop who was also Hen's father, but so be it. "They're good qualities to have if you're trying to get customers to buy something. Being friendly and liking people are helpful in business."

Hen ducked her head. Her shoulders hunched. He'd managed to embarrass her. That wasn't Nicholas' intent. "I just mean—"

"Nee, denki. You're the same way, I reckon, even though you're not in sales."

Their pace had slowed. People surged around them. A man carrying a big box grunted and grumbled. "You're blocking the road, lovebirds."

Why did everyone make that assumption? "Sorry," Nicholas murmured.

"We better get a move on." Hen charged ahead. "Mena will eat all the candy when Ruby's tending to customers."

Nicholas lengthened his stride to keep up. Raindrop chose that moment to whimper. She wiggled free from Nicholas' grasp, catapulted to the ground, and shot between two toddler wagons pulled by English women carrying the babies who should've been in the wagons.

"Get back here!" Nicholas dashed after her, barely avoiding shoppers loaded down with bags. "Raindrop, stop!"

CHAPTER 19

Raindrop had no sense of impending danger—like being stepped on or tripping someone. Ears flopping, tongue hanging out, leash dragging behind her, she dodged traffic like a pro. As a full-grown adult, Nicholas wasn't as agile. He might need to get more exercise.

Hen apparently had no such problem. She darted ahead of Nicholas. He picked up his pace, trying to match her zigs and zags among strollers, wheelchairs, walkers, toddler wagons, and folks loaded down with big bags, without a single mishap.

Until a boy on a scooter zigged at the same time she did. Hen flailed and hit the deck. The kid missed her by a mouse's whisker. Nicholas danced out of his way at the last half second. "Hen!"

"I'm fine, I'm fine," she yelled. "Don't let Raindrop get away. Someone will snatch her up, for sure."

She was hurt. Nicholas wavered. Leaving a woman holding her ankle on the asphalt didn't suit. But Hen was right. "I'll be back for you."

Nicholas wove in and out of traffic until Raindrop came into sight again. Several strangers tried to scoop her up, but the puppy was too small and too determined. She didn't slow down.

Until she came to Hen's Goat Goodies. The sound of goats bleating filled the air.

The goat pen.

"No you don't, you little beast!" Despite her dress's long skirt, Ruby shot across the asphalt and cut the wayward puppy off at the pass. She scooped her up just before she reached the pen. The goats bleated and scattered to the other side of the portable enclosure. That only encouraged Raindrop. She barked and wiggled, struggling to free herself. "Who do you belong to, stinker?" Ruby's gaze went to Nicholas. Chuckling, she shook her head. "I should've known." She hugged the dog to her chest. "Where is Hen? I assume she's somewhere nearby. Where animals roam, so does she."

"She fell. I have to go help her." Nicholas skidded to a stop. "Can you keep an eye on Raindrop until I get back?"

"Raindrop? Trouble would be a better name. But sure. We've been busy. So don't dawdle."

Nicholas never dawdled. He didn't have time.

Squeezing through the crowd going the opposite direction proved no less difficult. By the time he reached the spot where Hen had fallen, she was on her feet and headed in his direction. A small cluster of people around her quickly melted away. "Are you okay?"

"Did you catch Raindrop?"

"Jah. She's fine. I'm more concerned about you." Nicholas cast around for the boy on the scooter. He was nowhere in sight. "I can't believe that kid didn't stop."

"No biggie. I sprained my dignity, but I think my ankle is just strained." All the same, she limped as she came toward Nicholas. "I ripped my dress, and I'm a little dirty. I won't be able to hand out more samples. I'll scare the customers away."

"Let Ruby or the boys do it." Nicholas took her arm. He didn't bother to survey the area. If someone objected, so be it. He tucked her arm over his shoulder and his around her waist. It was almost like holding her. She was warm, her body sturdy but soft. This was the closest he'd ever been to a woman not related to him. "We'll get you to the booth, and then I'll see if the snow cone vendors or the pop vendors will give me some ice."

"That's not necessary." She tugged free. "Denki, but I'm not some fragile maedel who can't take care of herself."

"I never said you were." He'd overstepped. Nicholas raised both hands in surrender. Heat sizzled through him from his head to his toes. He backed away. "But I do know that you need to ice down that strain, or it will swell."

Hen hopped a few feet then stopped. "Ach, ach, fine."

So she did need help. Just didn't like it. Nicholas repositioned himself so she could put her weight on him. Even the tips of her ears had turned red. She cleared her throat. "You can breathe. I won't break. I promise."

"I know that. I just—"

"I know. Me too."

What did she know? He sure didn't. Nicholas sucked in air. "Ready?"

"Ready."

The trek to the Hen's Goat Goodies seemed to take forever, and yet it was over in a flash. Shoppers made way for the wounded Amish girl leaning on her Amish guy. Englischers snapped photos with their phones. Nicholas didn't bother to duck his head.

"Hen! What have you done now?" One arm wrapped around Raindrop propped on her hip, Ruby pulled a chair away from the booth table. Raindrop struggled to free herself from her grip. Ruby wasn't having any of it. She thrust her at Hen. "Sit and take this crazy hund."

"I'm not a hund, so don't talk to me like one, and Raindrop's not crazy." Hen crossed her arms. "She needs a forever home."

Ruby's eyes narrowed. Her scowl grew. "Oh no you don't. Dat will have a conniption fit if we bring even one more critter home."

"Not the Miller house. Your house. The one you'll live in with Peter. You'll be lonesome without me and Mena and the boys. A puppy will keep you company."

"I'll have Peter to keep me company." Giving up on Hen, Ruby held out Raindrop to Nicholas. "Regardless of what my schweschder says, I'm not interested in another pet. Peter feeds cats that hang around on his property, and he has a hund someone dumped from a pickup truck. A car hit him, broke one of his hind legs. Peter had to pay some steep vet bills."

"That's right. Lucky's his name." Hen stood and hobbled into the enclosure, where a white goat with a black face tried to pluck off her apron. "Lucky's had a rough life. He could use some company."

"Lucky is fine being a lone guard hund."

"Hey, why don't I go get some ice for your ankle, Hen?" Nicholas succeeded in getting a word in edgewise. "It's important to ice it down every few hours for the next forty-eight hours."

"Dillon, Devon, go get ice from Mrs. Simpson at the concessions booth." Ruby made swishing motions with her apron. "Stay together and come right back."

The twins took off. Ruby turned to Nicholas. "I'm sure you know what you're doing, but you are a vet, not a doctor."

"Everyone knows what to do about a strain." Hen held the kid goat in her arms like a baby. "Stop trying to change the subject."

She was right. "Raindrop is such a gut hund." When she wasn't running away or attempting to squeeze into a goat pen. "And the poor thing needs a family. She can't stay at the humane society forever."

"It's a no-kill shelter. They'll keep her until someone comes along. And they will. Puppy-dog eyes get to hund lovers every time."

Ruby's tone left no doubt that she was not among that number.

"Can I hold her?" Mena scooted past Ruby and held out her arms. "Buster would love a friend. He could teach Raindrop everything she needs to know about everything."

"What do dogs need to know?" Ruby scoffed. "They eat, they sleep, and they do their business. They bark at cars. They chase cats and squirrels. That's pretty much it."

"Don't listen to her." Mena put one hand over Raindrop's ears. "She's a mean old lady."

"Am not."

At that moment a flurry of customers arrived at the booth. Ruby turned to attend to them. While Hen and Luke went to help her, Mena stuck with Raindrop. She wound her leash around her wrist and let her sniff at the goats. "Does it cost anything to adopt a puppy?"

"The humane society is having a special today." Nicholas wanted to give her his undivided attention, but for some reason his gaze kept drifting toward Hen. She stood on one foot, one hand on a canopy pole, sweet-talking an English lady in a muumuu and Crocs into buying three different scents of goat milk soap and a goat cheese log. "It's two hundred dollars with their coupon."

The little girl's blue eyes widened behind her smudged glasses. Her lower lip protruded. "That's a lot of money. We've never paid for our dogs. They just show up at the house for free. Like someone knew we would be gut friends."

"The difference is the humane society foots the bill for spaying or neutering, deworming, tick and flea treatment, microchipping, ear mite treatment, heartworm medicine, and any vaccinations they might need."

Which cost far more than what they charged for adoption, but a little girl wouldn't understand that. "I imagine Buster hasn't had all that done to him."

"I don't know. He didn't have tags when he showed up." Mena wiped her glasses on her apron, which sported a smorgasbord of stains chronicling what she'd eaten and drunk so far that day. Blueberry jam, maple syrup, something greasy, and what might have been pop—if Nicholas was a good guesser. "He's nice, though. He never complains. He makes a gut pillow at night too."

"I reckon he does. Like my hund Daisy." Nicholas eyed Hen. She was engaged in conversation with a tiny girl who wasn't convinced she wanted to pet a goat. "She's not as big as Buster, but her hair is longer, so I reckon she's softer."

Really, he had no idea, but any conversation that kept him at Hen's Goat Goodies was fine.

"Baby goats are called kids because they're a lot like people kids," Hen explained to the girl. "They like to sit in your lap and cuddle. They'll fall asleep on you. If they butt you, it's because they want to play."

"They won't bite me?" The girl grasped Hen's hand as if it anchored her in a strong wind. "My brother's dog bit me on the ankle."

"Naughty dog." Hen opened the gate with her free hand. "If you're nice to Tulip, Lollie, and their friends, they'll be nice to you."

The girl put one foot into the pen, then the other. Tulip skipped toward her. The girl cowered behind Hen. "She wants to make friends, Elspeth, don't you want to be friends?"

Elspeth nodded. The goat licked her hand. She squealed—a squeal of delight. "She kissed my hand. She likes me."

"She does, indeed."

Hen knelt in the now dirty hay, one hand on Tulip, the other on Elspeth's shoulder. "Tulip, meet Elspeth, Elspeth, Tulip. I can tell you'll be best friends."

"Can she come to my house?"

"No, but you can come by our farm and visit, if your mom wants."

Elspeth's mom nodded. "I like for them to be exposed to animals. We live in Pittsburgh in a small house, so the best we can do is a cat."

"Oh, we love cats, don't we, Elspeth?" Hen smiled at the little girl. "Cats are special. They think they're in charge of everyone and everything."

"I do. Snooty is funny. If you give her food she doesn't like, she spits it out and walks away with her tail in the air."

"Queen Snooty, yep."

"Yep." Her fear gone, Elspeth's eyes shone. She had her arm around Tulip as if she planned to walk her all the way to Pittsburgh. "I want a dog, but Mom says no."

"The Indiana County Humane Society has several dogs here at the open house that are up for adoption." Nicholas jumped into the conversation. "Including this puppy. Mena, can you introduce Raindrop to Elspeth's mom?"

"No, no, Raindrop wants to stay with me." Mena clutched the puppy to her chest and wailed. "Hen, do something."

"I think there's some confusion here." Hen hobbled from the pen, with Elspeth right behind her. "The puppy's spoken for. But ICHS has several others at their booth. At least they did. If you're really serious about adopting a dog, you better hurry."

"I never said we were adopting a dog." Elspeth's mother grabbed her daughter's hand. "Let's go."

"But Mom—"

"I'll buy you a snow cone—"

"Mom—a"

"And a bag of caramel kettle corn."

Off they went, leaving Raindrop in Mena's arms.

"Yay. Yay. Yay!" The girl rocked the puppy in a celebratory dance. "Denki, Hen!"

"Hen!" Ruby was in the middle of making change for a Plain woman with five stairstep children, but that didn't keep her from expressing her opinion. "We don't need another hund, especially a puppy. Are you going to potty train her?"

"Nee, Mena is."

Ruby groaned.

Mena grinned and Hen joined her, along with Nicholas. A flock of happy folks.

"There you are."

Lenora. Nicholas had forgotten about his sister and Grandpa Moses. Nicholas whirled to see them trudging toward the booth. He rushed to greet them. "*Guder daag*. Sorry, I meant to get back to the ICHS booth sooner."

"Guder daag. It's not the end of the world." Lenora's gaze skipped around the booth. A sly smirk spread across her face. "I reckon you're where you should be. But, just so you know, Betty and Tanya are anxious for you to come back and talk spay and neuter with their visitors."

"I'm sure they are." Nicholas patted Mena's shoulder. "They'll be happy when they find out Raindrop has a new home. Ruby or Hen, one of you will have to come fill out the paperwork and make the payment."

"I'll do it." Still limping, Hen exited the pen. "It's my idea. I'll pay for it."

"That's your Angora goat money. Another reason this is a bad idea." Ruby thrummed her fingers on the table. "Even if I was in favor of the idea, I couldn't help either. All our funds are going into the wedding."

She was definitely warming up to the idea. . .a little.

"I have two dollars," Mena volunteered. "And eight cents."

"What if I pay the fee for you?" The idea burst forth before Nicholas could examine it for flaws. "Mena, you and Hen can pay me back by volunteering at the clinic. Our animal care attendant is out on maternity leave. We could use some help."

Usually the volunteers were adults, but Mena could work under Hen's supervision.

"You mean it?" Mena jumped up from her chair. "Let's go."

"Whoa, whoa." The consternation on Ruby's face didn't bode well. "It's nice of you to offer, but I don't think our daed would be thrilled about it."

"He doesn't want me working at the clinic." Hen slipped over to Mena's side. "But he didn't say anything about us volunteering. And Mena will be there to. . ."

To chaperone.

Their paths would cross more often. Even if Nicholas intended to leave one day in the distant future, he could still have friends now. Couldn't he? A person who saw the world the way he did. He'd never had that before. Might never have it again.

Ruby, on the other hand, didn't appear convinced. Hen took Raindrop from Mena and held her up. "Take a gander at this cute gumdrop. How can you resist this adorable face?" Her cajoling tone was reminiscent of the English boy Jeremy's. "It's not like it would be charity. We're working off our debt. Dat should like *that* idea."

Ruby tut-tutted. "You're kidding yourself if you think Dat will like any of this."

"What do you say, Hen?" Nicholas stared at her, using the most piercing arrow in his arsenal.

She stared back. Finally she gave a sharp, resolute nod. "I say denki for your help."

"Gern gschehme."

Whew. Nicholas heaved a breath. He raised his face to a sudden May breeze that carried the scent of barbecue and hot dogs. It seemed warmer. As if it blew from the south instead of the north now. Softer, kinder, and with a promise of better days to come.

"I'm tired of standing here."

Grandpa. Nicholas grabbed the closest chair. "I'm sorry. Here, sit down. You probably need to rest."

Ignoring the chair, Grandpa stamped his feet. He wore a coat that was too warm, and his straw hat was so crooked it threatened to slide off. "I thought we were going to get hamburgers and French fries."

"We are—"

"You're that Miller maedel." He pointed his gnarled finger at Hen. "You owe me for the plans."

"Daadi—"

"It's okay, It's okay." Hen grinned as if she'd just unloaded a truckful of Angora goats. She took Grandpa's arm. "Let's talk on our way to the ICHS booth."

"Sounds gut." Grandpa's frown disappeared. He stood taller. "We have work to do."

"We do, indeed."

This, on the other hand, was not good.

CHAPTER 20

Digging the hole deeper. That's what her dad would call this. Hen tucked the adoption papers into her crocheted bag. She snapped the leash on Raindrop, thanked Betty, and hobbled over to the chair where Moses sat waiting. She helped him up and tucked her free arm in the crook of his arm. Might as well go for broke. Moses still remembered the plans he'd drawn up for her. She still wanted them for when she could afford to build the shed, even if she didn't have Dad's blessing yet. "Let's go eat hamburgers."

Moses shuffled faster. "And potato salad. And apple pie."

"Sounds yummy." Actually, her hunger ebbed the longer she contemplated what Dad would say when she returned home. The chase scene through the crowded streets of Smicksburg. The collision with a boy on a scooter. Nicholas' arm around her waist. The thought sent a jolt of heat coursing through her. The adoption of the puppy who started the dominoes falling. "I'm glad your appetite is back."

"I eat enough for two men—three men." Moses threw his shoulders back. His head came up. "A hardworking man needs to keep his energy up."

The burst of energy lasted until they reached the district's school fundraising booth in the Amish furniture store's parking lot where several mothers put together the plates they were selling to help pay the teachers and make repairs at the school. The fathers were behind the booth, grilling the burgers and hot dogs. Breathing a sigh of relief, Hen guided Moses to the closest bench. He plopped down. "Mary, get me a root beer, will you?"

Lenora simply nodded. Nicholas opened his mouth. After a second he shrugged. "Can I get you something, Hen?"

"Nee, denki, I ate too much cheese and crackers and fudge." She patted her belly. The truth was she felt nauseous. If Ruby didn't tell Dad about Hen's "behavior," someone else would. "I'll sit with Moses while you get the food."

"If you change your mind, let me know." Nicholas cocked his head toward the line. At least a dozen people were waiting their turns. "There's plenty of time for that."

His smile sent another rush of heat through her. Would this happen every time their paths crossed now? She closed her eyes, and the memory came rushing back. He had a strong grip. Leaning against him was like being supported by a solid tree trunk.

"Where did Amos go?" Moses squinted against the sun. His expression grew grim. "Did that boy run off again?"

"Nicholas and Lenora are getting your hamburger." Favoring her throbbing ankle, Hen eased on to the bench across from him. "And some root beer."

"Who are you?"

"*Mei naame iss* Henrietta. They call me Hen. I'm a friend of your kinskinner."

"*Schee dich zu dreffe.*"

"Nice to meet you too." If sadness and regret pressed this hard against her soul, how much harder it must make Lenora's and Nicholas' souls ache. "You must be thirsty. They'll have your pop in no time."

He didn't respond. Hen let her gaze wander over the people eating at the dozen or so picnic tables spread out in front of the booth. Lots of familiar faces. *Ach.* Esther Drucker made her way toward Hen and Moses. Smiling. Beware of that woman when she smiled. That was what Mom always said.

"Henrietta. Say, was that you I saw running down the street earlier?" Esther smoothed the ribbons hanging from her bonnet. "I wouldn't have believed it if I hadn't seen it with my own eyes. That newcomer Nicholas Byler was chasing you. Whatever happened?"

"He wasn't chasing me." Hen pulled Raindrop onto her lap. Her tongue rough and wet, the puppy licked her hand in appreciation. "We were both chasing this little goober. Meet Raindrop, the newest member of the Miller family."

Esther's face grew more pinched. She likely couldn't fathom the idea of an animal being a member of a family. "Darla Hershberger said she saw Nicholas with his arm around you. In broad daylight."

Gossipmonger. Hen touched her fingers to her chin. No, she hadn't said the word aloud. *Whew. Denki, Gott.* "A boy on a scooter knocked me over. I hurt my ankle."

"Uh-huh."

Did she think Hen was stupid? Did she really think Hen would spurn the Gmay's rules of decorum so blatantly? Fury flickered through Hen's veins. "You don't believe me? Are you calling me a liar?"

"No need to get snippy." Esther's eyes narrowed. She crossed her arms. "I just know what I saw, and Darla wouldn't lie. She has no reason to."

While Hen did? "I was chasing a puppy."

"Well, I'm sure your daed will sort it out." Esther sniffed, whirled, and stalked away.

The inference was clear. *Your daed, the bishop.*

Living in a small, close-knit community had many pluses, this was not one of them. She should go. She'd left Ruby to handle the booth far too long.

When Lenora and Nicholas returned with laden plates, Hen stood and gingerly put weight on her ankle. "I didn't realize it was so late. Your grandpa is tired and hungry. I'll talk with him another time." She winked at Moses. "I know better than to get between a hungry man and his burger."

"Are you sure?" Nicholas set Moses' plate in front of him. Lenora added his cup of root beer. "I thought you wanted to talk to him about the shed?"

"He's too tired."

Nicholas' smile disappeared. "Ach. I see."

Moses winced. "Where's my fraa?"

"Mammi stayed home today," Nicholas said without missing a beat. He nodded at Hen. "I hope all goes well at your house."

Somehow he knew what lay ahead for Hen. She scrapped up a smile. "Me too."

"You'll be at the clinic on Tuesday?"

She had to be. She'd made a deal with him. Even if it meant learning how to harness the sudden wave of awareness that overcame her every time she peeked at him. "I hope so."

"I'll see you then. I hope. You and Mena, I mean."

"Jah, of course, me and Mena. She'll love it."

So would Hen. If Dad let them go.

Back at the booth, business hadn't slowed down. By the time the open house ended, they'd sold all the soaps, cheeses, and fudge, along with Ruby's hand-embroidered table runners, crocheted bags, and baby quilts, as well as jams, jellies, pickles, and hot sauce from the canned goods left over from the previous summer. Ruby didn't say a word about Raindrop's presence. Apparently the day had worn her out, because she slept under the table for the rest of the afternoon.

The day ended too soon, given what lay ahead.

By the time they loaded the goats into their English driver's truck and their booth, chairs, and other items into the van, it was nearly suppertime.

No one had much to say on the ride home. Which was fine with Hen. She needed time to figure out how she felt about Nicholas. She'd started out disliking him as a know-it-all, bossy guy who took the job she wanted. The job she couldn't have even if he hadn't shown up when he did. Now he'd given her the gift of a puppy and a chance to volunteer at the clinic. To learn more about animal care. He'd helped her after she fell and hadn't made her feel like a klutz.

That was all well and good, but that didn't mean he cared a whit about her. He was kind to everyone. Looming over all her warm, squishy thoughts was the knowledge that there were no guarantees—even if they managed to find their way to be together.

When they turned onto the dirt road, Ruby rubbed her eyes and yawned. "Are you telling Dat, or am I? It would probably be better if you did."

For whom? "If you are talking about Raindrop, I will, of course."

At the mention of his name, the puppy raised her head, yawned, and snuggled closer to Mena's chest.

Who could resist such a cute little girl?

Knowing Dad, he would find a way.

He was seated at the supper table when Hen entered the kitchen, Ruby, and Mena close behind. The boys had stopped at the barn first to check with Micah about their chores.

"How did it go?" Aunt Ginny set a basket of rolls on the table. Her tone held a less-than-subtle hint of warning. "Did you sell much?"

"We sold out of everything." Hen limped to the sink to wash her hands. "We had a lot of people from Pittsburgh. The chamber did a gut job of promoting the open house. It smells gut in here. I'm starving."

It did smell like baking bread, scalloped potatoes, and pork chops, but Hen's appetite had not reappeared. Steering the conversation away from the open house seemed her only hope.

"I'm surprised you had time to help in the booth, what with chasing a hund through the streets of Smicksburg, linking arms with a man for the whole world to see, and then adopting the puppy with money you don't have." Dad picked up a fork and jabbed the air with it. "I suppose you were pestering Nicholas' daadi for his thoughts on building the goat shed, while you were at it."

The Plain grapevine in Smicksburg could be counted on to beat the best of the best in all of Pennsylvania's Plain communities. Hen picked up the platter of pork chops and carried them to the table. *Count to ten. No twenty. Or thirty.* "That's some mixed-up gossip."

"If you wanted another hund, you should've waited for the next one dumped down the road from us. You know it wouldn't take long. It costs money to adopt a hund from that humane society. How did you pay for it?"

"We're volunteering at the clinic." Grinning like a mama cat with a new litter, Mena skipped over to Dad. She held out Raindrop. "Isn't she sweet? She'll be Buster's little schweschder."

Raindrop woofed and licked Dad's hand. *Puppy-dog eyes. Please let puppy-dog eyes win.*

Dad accepted her offering. Hope flickered through Hen. Then he fixed her with a fierce stare. "What's Philomena talking about?"

Hen explained the agreement she'd made with Nicholas. "It was his idea, wasn't it Ruby?"

"Leave me out of this." Ruby busied herself at the stove, her back to the table. "You ignored my advice."

"You basically borrowed money from a man you hardly know." Dad's voice dropped into a low, brusque tone it always had when he was upset. Raindrop nosed his hand. Dad obliged by petting her, but his expression didn't change. "Now you're beholden to Nicholas for it. And he's offering to let you work it off in a clinic he doesn't own. How do you know he has that authority?"

"They need help right now. He says Dr. McDonald likes free help as long as a staff member oversees them."

His scowl fading, Dad pursed his lips. He tugged on his beard. Aunt Ginny leaned in front of him and set a bowl of scalloped potatoes on the table. She touched his arm. "It seems like a gut plan to me, Adam. Nicholas is Plain. He'll be a gut person to oversee Hen. . .and Mena, of course."

Dad's forehead wrinkled. He tapped his fingers on the table. "You've signed adoption papers with the humane society. You've made an agreement with Nicholas. That can't be undone."

"We can keep Raindrop!" Mena squealed. "I can work at the clinic."

"Until the debt is paid." Dad's voice was still gruff, but his hand ruffled Raindrop's ears. "But I won't let your unseemly behavior go unpunished, Hen."

Hen picked up a pitcher of water. On second thought, she returned it to the countertop. Being punished like a child. Dad would say for acting like one. She raised her chin and straightened her shoulders. "Jah, Dat."

"No more working in the barn. No more taking care of the goats. No more taking care of the chickens." Anger faded from his face, replaced with determined firmness. "Your work is in the house, cooking, baking, cleaning, and sewing. Ruby will be gone soon. You won't be able to slough it off on her anymore. These are the chores a grown woman should be doing in preparation for marriage. It's time you focused on them."

"But Dat—"

"No buts. You can care for the gardens, but that's it. Mena's old enough to mow the grass. She'll take care of the chickens. The buwe will take over with the goats and the rest of the livestock."

No one moved. No one spoke. Mena had frozen with one hand on Tigger's back. Ruby stared out the kitchen window. Her face creased with sorrow, Aunt Ginny remained behind Dad.

What would Dad do if he saw Hen in the barn? Or mucking Jack's stall? Take a switch to her behind? Shame and embarrassment ran in a torrent through her. *Gott, I can't take this.* She bit her lip, concentrating on the pain to keep the tears from falling. *This is my fault, but I can't bear it. Why make me like this if it's wrong? How can Dat treat me like a kind? I'm not a kind.*

So don't act like one. That was what Dad would say. What would Nicholas say? Would he say it was her fault? Men were the heads of the household. Women were to obey them. The Ordnung said so. Children obeyed their parents. And all was right in the world.

Except in Hen's world.

"Dochder, do you understand?"

"For how long?"

"From now on. Ruby's not coming back." His steely gaze still cut through her, but his voice softened. "The house is your responsibility now. This isn't a punishment. I should've done this a long time ago, but I thought you'd grown out of it. It's for your own good. You're a young woman, not a teenager on your rumspringa."

Forever. Hen cleared her throat. "I understand."

"Gut. I'm glad that's settled." Dad nudged Raindrop until she hopped from his lap. "Philomena, it's your job to keep this little hund fed, watered, and out of trouble. She's to be an outdoor dog. Understood?"

Mena scooped up Raindrop and danced around the room. "I will, I promise." She spun toward the back door. "I'll take her to meet Buster right now."

"Nee, it's time to eat."

To be five again. Hen hurried to the kitchen sink. She turned on the water under the pretense of washing her hands again. Heaving a breath, she splashed her face with water. *Sei so gut, Gott, don't let me cry, sei so gut.*

Aunt Ginny touched her shoulder. Hen forced herself to meet her gaze. Aunt Ginny smiled and patted her cheek. She didn't say a word, but that smile. It said so much. *I'll be there with you. It's okay. You'll survive. I understand.*

Until she had to return to her husband and home.

Hen nodded. Aunt Ginny handed her a towel. "The potatoes are getting cold. Will you bring the beets and the green salad to the table?"

Not trusting her voice, Hen nodded again.

"I made your favorite salted caramel chocolate chip cookie bars for dessert." Aunt Ginny picked up the water pitcher. "I thought we'd have ice cream with them on the porch after we get the kitchen cleaned up."

"You spoil her." Despite his words, Dad sounded almost lighthearted.

"But those caramel chocolate chip bars are my favorite too, so I'll let it go this time."

Was he trying to be nice?

Hen peeked at him as she approached the table. His face was etched with fatigue, his eyes sad, and his shoulders drooped.

He wasn't enjoying this either.

I'll do better, Gott, I promise.

"Tell him, Dochder, not Me."

Why was that so hard to do? Give grace where grace was needed?

God did it all the time.

CHAPTER 21

Which was harder, celebrating Mother's Day without a mother or striving to be happy for all those who still had mothers attending the Sunday service? Hen wiggled on the backless bench in the Planks' barn. Beams of sunlight bursting through wooden slats warmed her neck. The smell of hay mingled with manure and dust. No breeze stirred the stuffy air. She stifled a sigh. Instead of temptation, Dad should be preaching about jealousy and coveting the motherly relations others still enjoyed. She scraped a smidgen of strawberry jam from her apron and tried to concentrate. God must be so disappointed in her. *I'm sorry. I don't know how to change these feelings. Help me, Gott.*

Don't think about it, just don't think about it. Listen to the message.

How could she, when every time she heard Dad's voice she had to stave off anger at the way he'd rearranged her life with no thought for her happiness? So she was different from other Plain girls. Hadn't God made her that way? No milking the does. No playing with the kids. No allowing Sam to follow her around. No feeding Jack sliced apples. Her father had hit the bulls-eye when he chose this so-called not-a-punishment. He might think it was best for her, but he was so very wrong.

He wanted to teach her a lesson. She already knew this lesson. She simply didn't like it.

Round and round the merry-go-round.

Don't think about it, don't think about it.

Hen let her gaze wander through the crowded benches. Moses, as one of the eldest men in the Gmay, sat in the front row. His head down, his eyes closed, his chest rising and falling, he snored softly. Nicholas sat one row back, directly behind his grandfather. Good placement in case he fell off his bench.

Nicholas was spiffy in his black jacket, pants, and hat.

Stop it. The last thing she should think about in church during a sermon on temptation was Nicholas. Despite being exhausted the previous night, she'd had trouble sleeping. Every time she closed her eyes, she saw Nicholas holding Raindrop or talking to Mena or chatting with the English couple who thought they were "dating."

What if they were? What would that be like?

An elbow poked her side. Hen glanced at Aunt Ginny, who gave her the two-high-wooly-eyebrows frown. Hen mouthed *sorry*, straightened, and stared at Dad pacing in front of the ninety-plus members of their Gmay.

If it bothered him to preach on this holiday, it didn't show. It hadn't shown when he rushed them into the buggy and whisked them to the Planks' house either. He hadn't even blinked at the container filled with three dozen cupcakes decorated with red and yellow sugar roses that Aunt Ginny held in her lap. At the moment, he was busy mining the depths of Hebrews 2:18 and Matthew 4:5–7 reminding his fellow believers to be careful of temptation in all its forms.

If Dad knew how tempted Hen was to spring to her feet and limp from the Planks' barn, he wouldn't be happy. But would he be surprised? Or would he be tempted to join her in driving the buggy to the cemetery at a breakneck speed, arriving just as the tears began to stream?

Hen entwined her fingers in her lap, letting her nails dig into the tender skin of her palms. She concentrated on the pain. *"She's gone. She's in Gott's hands. Gott's will be done."* That's what Dad had told her and the other kids the day they lowered the casket into the ground.

A cold, crisp, clear spring day without a cloud in a sky so blue it hurt Hen's eyes.

Aunt Ginny's hand covered Hen's. Hen glanced at her. With a gaze full of a sweetness that brought Hen's tears precariously close to the surface, Aunt Ginny squeezed and nodded.

She knew. Hen swallowed her tears. She tugged Mena into her lap and put her arms around her. Mena didn't protest. She snuggled closer. The little girl didn't remember her mother. She didn't suffer from a sense of loss. She had a slew of older sisters, cousins, and aunts to fill that void.

But she didn't have a mother. *Stop it.*

How easy to say, "Thy will be done." How hard to mean it. Would God strike her dead for daring to question His plan for her? For daring to question His will? Hen fought the urge to push Mena aside and bow her head, in preparation for a lightning strike.

God was also merciful. Otherwise He would've done it a long time ago.

"You're squeezing me too hard." Mena's loud whisper echoed down the row. Ruby glanced their way and frowned.

"Sorry." Loosening her grip, Hen heaved a breath. "Sorry."

Finally the last hymn, which went on for a good ten minutes, ended. They knelt and prayed one last time. The never-ending service was done. Hen grabbed Mena's hand. Together they squeezed past Aunt Ginny, who'd stopped to chat with some other women in the aisle.

Outside, the day had warmed. A breeze wafted through trees loaded with new green leaves. Hen stared up at the same brilliant blue sky that had shared Mom's funeral with her.

"What's the matter, Schweschder?" Mena tugged at her hand. "Do you need an eppy?"

Cookies were the answer to most of Mena's problems. Hen managed a chuckle. "It's ice cream and cupcakes today for Mother's Day—but not until after you eat a sandwich. You can run ahead to the kitchen to help get the sandwiches ready. Don't eat all the pickles! I'm right behind you."

Mena shot ahead. Church lunch was ham, bologna, or peanut butter spread sandwiches, crackers and cheese, chips, pickles, and coffee or tea. Simple and easy. Not much prep. Still, she was expected to help. All the women were.

Favoring her still-sore ankle, Hen meandered left until she reached a massive oak tree at the edge of the yard. She leaned against its solid, unshakable trunk, the bark rough under her shaking fingers. Pain beat in time with her heart, making it hard to raise her feet. It had been three and a half years. It shouldn't hurt so much.

The memory of another's grief loomed in her mind's eye.

She carried a load of dirty clothes toward the laundry room. The chug-a-chug-a *of the wringer wash machine floated from the room, music to Hen's ears. The smell of homemade soap and bleach hung fresh and clean in the air. In those days, chores weren't so bad because she and Ruby shared them with Mom.*

Hen trotted faster. The sooner she delivered the laundry, the sooner she could go outside. It was her turn to hang the laundry. Mom made it fun by challenging Hen to sing hymns at the top of her lungs—even though she couldn't carry a tune in a bucket.

Broken sobs reached her ears.

She slowed, then changed her mind, and ran.

"Mamm? Mamm?"

Piles of dirty clothes strewn around her, Mom knelt on the floor. Her hunched shoulders shook. Her hands covered her face. Hen dropped the clothes. "Mamm, what's the matter?"

Mom lowered her hands. Her eyes were red and swollen, her cheeks wet. "Ach, I'm sorry. I didn't mean for you to see."

Hen sank to the floor next to her mother. "Why are you crying?"

Mom put her hands on her chest, one on top of the other. "There's a hole in my heart."

"Where Stephen should be?"

She nodded. "My heart refuses to heal, even though I know Gott took him home. He's warm and safe and happy forever."

Her voice broke. Hen let her hand creep toward her mother. How did a person fix a hurt so deep? Mom took her offering and held tight. Hen searched for words, any words, anything close to the right words. "He's been gone for six months."

Far longer than he was on this earth.

"There's no timeline for grief. It lasts as long as you need it to last. It's different for everyone. But I think for a mudder it may last forever. A mudder goes on, but she knows a piece of her heart is missing."

"You'll never get it back?"

"Jah, I'll get it back. If it's Gott's will, I'll be in heaven with Stephen one day."

That thought had given Mom solace, for which Hen had been happy. She'd figured it would be many years later when this reunion would occur. Now Mom was in heaven, and Hen was here in Smicksburg at a Mother's Day celebration with a big piece of her heart missing.

"Hey there, Hen." Nicholas strode across the grass toward her. "How's Raindrop doing? Was your dat okay with you adopting her?"

Hen blinked away tears. The memory retreated, leaving behind a sweet sadness. She focused on the here and now—Nicholas approaching even as people filled the picnic tables in the Planks' front yard. Their ears would perk up, and their eyes widen after the grapevine's cache of titillating gossip from the Spring Open House. Dad cared what people thought. He had enough on his heart today. She wouldn't add to his discomfort—no matter how he chose to punish her.

Even if the sight of Nicholas' tall, muscular frame brought back another memory. The feel of his arm around her waist. He had big, warm hands and strong arms. Her breath caught again, just as it had that day, limping, leaning on him while the whole world watched. Heat warmed her that had nothing to do with the sun. Nothing to do with his strength. His nearness set off an unfamiliar yearning.

Too many feelings to handle at once. She couldn't cause Dad further pain on this day. Hen covered her cheeks with both hands. *Gott, I'm sorry. So sorry.*

Tell him, not Me.

"I have to go in."

"What's the matter? Are you sick? Your face is pale under the sunburn." Nicholas' hand reached toward her, wavered in the space between, then dropped. "Your freckles are about to pop off your face."

"I'm fine." For a woman who'd just heard a soft whisper in her ear that sounded so much like a caring God. Hen cleared her throat. "It was warm in the barn."

"Jah. The breeze feels gut out here, even with the sun. It's a beautiful day."

"It is. Beautiful." Hen's throat hurt. Her eyes burned with unshed tears. "Raindrop is well on her way to being a spoiled brat."

"And your dat isn't mad you brought her home?"

"He spoils her the most."

"Is he okay with the payment plan?"

"Nee, but he'll let it stand. We gave our word, and he would never have us break it."

"He's a gut man."

She couldn't bear to share the rest. Not now. It was nothing compared to losing her mother. "He is. I better get inside and help with lunch."

"The men are going to clean up afterward. We're planning to serve the cupcakes and ice cream so the women can sit and visit in honor of Mother's Day."

"I know." Hen forced a smile. Men who mostly could no more express their feelings with words chose this way of honoring the women they loved for being mothers—what Plain folks considered women's greatest contribution in life. Giving them a break from chores. It was simple. But nice. "It's wunderbarr."

Nicholas' smile faded. A softness erased the sun lines from his face. The understanding in his eyes warmed her. "This must be a hard day for you and yours."

"I should get in there. The women still have to prepare and serve the meal." Hen ducked past him. She hobbled across the yard and up the porch steps. Nicholas followed. The man had no sense of decorum. Or it didn't bother him that inquiring eyes watched and tucked away their conclusions for later discussion. Hen pulled the screen door open. "Have a seat. The sandwiches will be out any minute."

"Hen."

Ignoring the impulse—the yearning—to let him comfort her, Hen let the screen door close.

CHAPTER 22

Many enthusiastic people volunteered at the humane society. Dr. McDonald rarely allowed them at his clinic, even though it was small, and he was the only vet in the area. Nicholas could understand that. Volunteers who loved animals wanted to pet and cuddle and hand out free advice. They weren't keen on cleaning kennels, doing laundry, and sterilizing surgical implements. They complained, or worse, whined when they didn't get to "work" with the animals. Dr. McDonald had agreed to Hen and Mena, only because they were so shorthanded, and Nicholas assured him he would supervise their work closely.

Hen and Mena made it easy. They arrived punctually at seven thirty at the employee back door entrance. Mena smiled so wide her face must hurt. "Hmmm, it smells gut in here. Like lavender and. . .nutmeg."

"Gut nose." Nicholas clapped. "Dr. McDonald's wife is a big believer that essential oils leave a gut impression." He led them down the hallway toward the laundry area. Hen was no longer hobbling. That was good. She'd be on her feet for her three-hour shift. "But don't get too used to it. What with parvo diarrhea, pee accidents, anal glands, and abscesses, the odors here are rank. Mostly I smell disinfectants, but even that is better than the alternative."

"I work with manure and stinky livestock all the time." Hen shrugged. "My nose is immune to it."

"Gut." Nicholas stopped in front of a commercial-size washer and dryer. "The blankets used to keep dogs and cats warm during procedures or while sick in kennels need to be washed."

Mena's hand shot up. "Me, me, can I do it?" She jumped up and down. "Ruby only lets me collect the dirty clothes."

"That's because you're not tall enough yet." Hen laughed and squeezed the girl in a one-armed hug. "Your time to use the wringer wash machine will come. Believe me, you'll be less excited about it when it does."

"Okay, Mena does laundry." Nicholas ticked the chore off an imaginary list on his fingers. "You can start the sterilization of the instruments, Hen, and then we'll work on cleaning the kennels."

"Just point me in the right direction."

"I'm glad you don't seem to mind. The new volunteers at the humane society don't come back after they find out they have to deal with animal waste."

Hen snorted and shook her head. "I've been mucking horse stalls, cleaning out chicken coops and goat pens, and cleaning the bathroom at home my whole life."

Plain women were different. Nicholas shouldn't have to remind himself of that. "Gut. You can sterilize instruments first. Dr. McDonald has two spay appointments this afternoon. After that you can both work on the kennels."

"You'll show us how the machines work?"

"I will."

He showed them both the washer and dryer first so he could get Mena started. Then they moved on to the autoclave machine. "I've already washed the instruments with hot, soapy water and rinsed them. The next step is to sterilize them."

As he explained, he placed the instruments from the previous day's surgeries into the autoclave. Hen studied his movements with an unnerving intensity. The way he had when he was first learning. She would be a good student. Did she ever wish she could go to vet school? Did a Plain woman have those dreams too? "So your ankle is better?"

"Jah." She lifted her skirt a bit. "I have it wrapped in an elastic bandage since I'll be on my feet today, but the swelling is down and it doesn't hurt as much."

"How is Raindrop settling in?"

"You should've seen her last night." Hen peered over his shoulder then wrote something down. "Dat was sitting on the front porch talking to Aenti Ginny about the wedding when the pup hops on his lap, rolls over on her back, and presents her belly for rubbing."

"What did your dat do?"

"He obliged. That hund has him wrapped around her little paw." Smiling ruefully, she turned the page in her notebook. "I wish I knew how Raindrop does it."

"He's still not so happy with you. You didn't tell me the whole story Sunday, did you?"

"Nee." Her smile faded, replaced with a grimace. "I'm now confined to the house, doing housework. . .forever."

Nicholas' stomach twisted in a knot. He was partly to blame for this punishment. He pivoted and headed for the treatment room where the kennels were located. "Forever. That can't be."

"Micah is to oversee the boys, who'll take care of the goats. Mena has the chickens." Hen followed close behind. Her voice quivered. Did Adam know how much his choice of punishment hurt his daughter? "Micah has the horses too. Dat says it's for my own gut."

Nicholas handed her rubber gloves and a garbage bag. "I'm sorry."

"Me too." She donned the gloves and shook open the bag. "But it's not your fault."

"I encouraged you to adopt her. Volunteering here was my idea. I'm responsible. I didn't think of the consequences." Nicholas filled one bucket with hot, soapy water, and the other with rinse water. "Do you think maybe he'll relent, eventually?"

"We'll never see eye to eye on it. Aunt Ginny says I'm just making life harder for myself." Hen removed toys, bedding, and debris from the first kennel. She went to work with the brush and a spray bottle of cleanser. "Nee, I don't think he'll relent. He's determined I should act like a Plain woman."

She managed to sound philosophical about it, but if she scrubbed the kennel any harder, the brush's bristles would fall off. "I'm not sorry about Raindrop. Buster loves her, Mena loves her, and the boys do too."

"After the soap and water, we'll use this vinegar solution to disinfect." Nicholas held up the spray bottle. "Then we'll rinse and dry."

"Do you usually do all of this?"

"With the animal care assistant, jah. I'm two rungs below the certified vet technician who works with Dr. McDonald three days a week. I don't have a vet assistant certification. Linda works at a clinic in Pittsburgh the other days. I don't mind, though. Like you, I've been doing this since I was old enough to hold a shovel and push a wheelbarrow in the barn."

A shrill bell rang. Pounding followed.

"Somebody's early." Drying his hands as he walked, Nicholas headed for the front door. "We don't open for another twenty minutes."

"Maybe it's an emergency." Hen's excited voice followed him down the hall. "Let me know if I can help."

The pounding grew increasingly frantic. Nicholas broke into a lope. "Coming, coming."

He unlocked the door to find one of their regular customers, Audrey Roberts, at the door. She struggled to hold up under the weight of her boxer. "Cipher got away from me and ran into the street." She hiccupped a sob. "A car hit him. The guy didn't even stop!"

Nicholas took the dog, who weighed seventy pounds, from his petite owner. His biceps strained under the weight. "I've got him. Come on in."

Cipher was deadweight in his arms. Nicholas lugged him into the treatment room. Just as he laid him on the stainless table, the boxer raised his head and whimpered. "I've got you, Cipher, I've got you."

"Ach, what happened?" Hen rushed into the exam area. "What can I do to help?"

"This is Cipher and his owner Audrey," Nicholas explained. "Can you help her keep Cipher calm while I call Dr. McDonald? Don't let him get up."

"You poor thing, you'll be all right," Hen crooned. She gently smoothed her hands up and down the dog's back and legs. Cipher whimpered again. "I think his back leg is broken."

"I think so too." Audrey stood at the head of the table, petting and kissing her dog's head and face. "You have to help him. He's my best friend. I can't lose him. Please, help him."

A minute later Nicholas had Dr. McDonald on the line. He explained the situation.

"I'm fifteen minutes out. I'll call Linda. She should be on her way in. Make Cipher as comfortable as possible. Try not to move him. He could have spinal injuries as well as internal injuries."

"He's conscious, moving around, and whimpering." Nicholas paced as he spoke. His own leg hurt, as if in response to the animal's cries. "I could go ahead with X-rays so you can review them as soon as you get here."

"No. Just keep him calm. You could make his injuries worse. What you can do is handle Elvis. He's our first scheduled appointment this morning."

Nicholas stopped pacing. He rubbed the back of his neck where a sudden pain pulsed. Elvis' owner had called the previous day to say the cat had been vomiting and was losing weight. Elvis was what vets called an angry cat. He hated strangers. He hated the clinic. He hated the shots and lab work and Dr. McDonald. He hated everyone.

"Nicholas?"

"I'll take care of Elvis."

"Good." Dr. McDonald hung up.

The vet arrived in less than ten minutes. Linda was right behind him. They shooed everyone from the treatment room. A few minutes later, Linda stuck her head through the door. "We'll have to put a pin in and repair some muscle and tendon damage. We're moving him to the surgery suite." She directed the remark to Audrey, but Nicholas knew what she meant. He was on his own with Elvis. Linda gave Audrey a thumbs-up. "Have a seat in the waiting room. We'll let you know as soon as we've finished."

Instead of returning to cleaning kennels, Hen led Audrey to the waiting room. "I can sit with you if you don't want to be alone." She was so empathetic when it came to pets and better at showing it than Nicholas. "Can I get you a cup of coffee?"

"I'm fine." Audrey sniffed. "Really, I'm sure you have work to do."

Hen grabbed a box of tissues from Tilly at the receptionist's desk. She handed them to Audrey. "If you need anything at all, let me know."

Nicholas smiled and sent her a thumbs-up to signal his approval of her handling of the situation. Mrs. Epperson pushed through the door a second later, Elvis' big carrier clutched in her arms. He rushed to take it from her. Growls greeted him—from Elvis, not Mrs. Epperson. "How's he doing today?"

"I'm fine, fine. It's Elvis. The poor baby can't keep his food down. I'm afraid he's wasting away."

The elderly lady had forgotten to put in her hearing aids—again. So be it. "I'll take a look at him right away."

"I hope you can get to him immediately. Poor thing is in dire shape."

Dr. McDonald had tried without success to convince Mrs. Epperson to cut back on Elvis' food. He was considered obese, which wasn't good for the cat. As if he heard Nicholas' thoughts, Elvis hissed and yowled louder. He sounded like a wild animal daring anyone to invade his territory at their peril. They weren't even to the exam room yet.

Nicholas contemplated his next move. He needed help. "Hen, could you assist me in the exam room, please?"

He never spoke in *Deutsch* in front of Englischers. It would be rude.

Her expression eager, Hen popped up from her seat. "If you need anything, Audrey, let Tilly know, and she can get me the message."

Tilly's usual smile dissolved into a puzzled frown. "Who are you?"

Nicholas intervened with quick introductions. Grinning, Hen walked into the exam room on Nicholas' heels. Mrs. Epperson followed. It didn't matter. Even her sweet admonitions wouldn't be enough to calm her pet.

"We need to do blood work on Elvis. To do that we have to restrain him." Nicholas held up a hard plastic face mask. "I need to get this on his face so he can't bite me."

"Why don't we just scruff him?" Hen reached for the carrier's front door. "He'll be just like a kitten scruffed by his mama."

"Nee!" Nicholas pushed her hand away. "Not this cat. He'll struggle hard with his head down. He won't be able to breathe. We don't open the front door because he might dart out and get away. That puts staff and patients at risk for getting bit or scratched, especially those of us who have to catch him."

"He can't be that bad. Poor guy is just misunderstood." Hen bent closer. Elvis hissed, screeched, and batted at the door. Eyes wide, Hen jolted back. "Okay, Mr. Grumpy. You're not making any friends here."

Nicholas pointed to a heavy blanket. "Use that to cover him up as soon as I open the top lid. We'll lift him out. Then we'll work on the face mask."

At first Elvis fought hard, but then, as Nicholas anticipated, he burrowed into the blanket, thinking he could hide. Nicholas was able to find his face. "Hold him tight. Don't let him move."

He slipped the mask on Elvis' face, strapped it behind his ears, and cinched it down. "Now his teeth are covered, but he still has room to breathe. He'll probably get it off at some point, but for now, it's safe to weigh him."

With Hen's help, Nicholas lowered Elvis onto the scale and removed the blanket long enough to weigh the feline. Despite the vomiting, he still weighed twenty pounds. Once he was back on the table, Nicholas performed a quick exam while Hen held his legs. "This will have to do until Dr. McDonald can examine him."

Together they slid him back into the carrier. "Good job." Nicholas heaved a sigh of relief. Hen's hand shot up in a high five. He returned the favor. "By the way, we're not done yet."

"No? I was afraid of that." Hen's face glowed. Her eyes were bright, her cheeks red with exertion and enthusiasm. "Actually, I'd love a chance to get to know him better. Cats like me. I've never seen one like this. How does a cat get like that? Was he a stray?"

"Nope, not feral. Mrs. Epperson adopted him from a friend's litter ten years ago. He just doesn't like people. Right, Mrs. Epperson?"

"He's had an upset tummy for days." Her face lined with worry, Mrs. Epperson patted the carrier table with a hand covered with thick blue veins and brown age spots. "I give him only the best canned cat food. It's all my fault."

"It's okay. It's not your fault. As cats get older, their digestive tracts can become more sensitive." Nicholas studied her woebegone face. Her worry didn't dissipate. "I wish you would remember to wear your hearing aids."

"My purse is right here." She patted a huge black patent leather bag that could serve as an overnight bag. "Why would I forget it?"

Nicholas exchanged sympathetic glances with Hen. She wrinkled her freckled nose. "So how *do* we do blood work on this wild cat?"

"Very carefully." Nicholas opened the lid on top. "Keep him wrapped in the blanket while I find a spot where I can draw the blood."

As Nicholas suspected, Elvis had worked his way out of the face mask. Hen did a great job of immobilizing him long enough for Nicholas to draw the blood. They moved him into a kennel with the heavy blanket to make it easier to get him out later. "I saw some dental decay when I examined his mouth." Nicholas closed the kennel and latched it. With the fading adrenaline came a wave of fatigue. And this was the first appointment of the day. "Dr. McDonald will want to do some more tests. We'll probably have to sedate him."

"How did you learn so much about how to treat cats like Elvis?" Hen gestured with both hands toward Elvis' kennel. She seemed to still have plenty of adrenaline for both of them. "I'd love working here."

Her voice trailed off. She'd have loved working at the clinic if Nicholas hadn't taken the job from her. In a way, he owed her an apology. "I bought used textbooks relating to veterinary medicine and studied them. But it's true I've gained hands-on knowledge here. I'm sorry I took that chance from you."

"You didn't really. My dat would never have let me take the job."

Her shoulders slumped. She stared at her empty hands. Nicholas fought the urge to slide his arms around her to comfort her. "I know what it's like to not be able to do the things you most want to do in life."

Hen followed him into the laundry room where Mena was busy folding blankets. "What do you mean? What would you do?"

Nicholas picked up a stack of blankets. They were soft and warm and smelled of fresh, clean soap. "I'd go to veterinary medicine college and become a vet." He added Mena and Hen to the short list of people outside his family who knew of this aspiration. "My dat feels about that the way your dat feels about you working here. Only more so—"

"Because you'd have to leave the faith."

"Jah. I don't understand why. Why can't we do both?"

"I only know what my dat says." Rolling her eyes, Hen pointed at the ceiling. "The big, bad world is out there."

"Jah, the big, bad world." Nicholas turned away. "I'll show you where to put these, Mena."

"Do you really think you'll do it?" Hen stopped at the autoclave. "The instruments are ready."

"I'll show you how to store them as soon as we finish with the laundry."

Leave everyone he loved? Leave his faith. In this moment, he'd never felt closer to a woman not family. What if he wanted to explore *that* feeling, taste it on the tip of his tongue, inhale its scent, find out where these feelings led? "Right now, family comes first. Daadi needs me. I don't want to think about when he doesn't."

When he passed away.

"But you still think about the future. I don't think any of us can not think about it."

Nicholas met her gaze.

"Me too, me too." She whispered the words as if God Himself might hear them. "Gott forgive me."

CHAPTER 23

Cracking eight dozen eggs before seven o'clock on the first morning in June wasn't a physically draining job. More sticky and occasionally frustrating. Like when a bit of shell fell in the whites. Hen touched the shell with the tip of her finger. It stuck, and the whites let it go. No problem. A puny breeze lifted the curtains in the open windows, carrying away the lingering scent of the bacon, fried eggs, and toast they'd eaten for breakfast. Raindrop slept on her back, feet in the air on the back door rug. Tigger stretched out, long and lean, snoozing on the narrow windowsill. All was right in their world. So why did the minutes tick by so slowly for Hen? Why did that sneaky suspicion she was missing out on all the good stuff outdoors niggle at her?

Make the best of it. That's what Aunt Ginny kept saying. Dad would relent. Eventually.

Eventually was far too long. Tulip would be a doe before Hen knew it.

"Isn't this fun?" Hen forced a silly face so Ruby would know she was being funny—trying to be funny. No sense in spoiling the wedding prep frolic for her sister. "I love sticky in the morning."

Ruby didn't answer. For a morning person—and a woman getting married in seventeen days—she'd been quiet since they went to work after breakfast to prepare for the horde of women who would arrive in an hour to help make twenty pounds of noodles for the wedding.

"Hey, earth to Ruby. Are you still asleep?"

"Nee." That single syllable overflowed a bucket of something not quite right.

"What's the matter, Schweschder? Did you get up on the wrong side of the bed?"

"Nee."

"Not sleeping."

"Nee."

"Talk to me." Hen plunged her hands in a tub of soapy water in the sink, rinsed them off, and dried them on a dish towel. "What's the matter? Maybe I can help."

Ruby pivoted and leaned against the counter. Shoulders hunched, she crossed her arms. "This will sound stupid and selfish."

"I know all about stupid and selfish."

A glimmer of a smile appeared on Ruby's face. "True."

"Hey."

"I'm getting married. I try not to let it bother me, but it does. Mamm isn't here to see it. I know what you and Aunt Ginny said, but I can't help it." The smile gone, Ruby's voice broke. She swiped at her eyes with the back of her hand. "I know I should be happy she's with bopli Stephen in heaven. She's been gone so long I can hardly remember her face anymore. I'm forgetting her."

Not having photos was especially hard when a loved one died. Hen leaned against the counter next to her sister so that their shoulders touched. "I'm not getting married, and I feel exactly the same way. I don't think it's selfish. It seems like it's human. Or am I just making excuses for a weak faith?"

"My faith isn't weak." Ruby straightened. She turned back to the counter and the eggs. "I just can't help imagining what it would be like to have her here. She always liked Peter. She used to try to get me to spill the beans about us courting, but I never told her. She'd be so happy. She would help me with my dress. And help me decide my colors and the flavor of the cake. It's stupid, I know. Why fret over what can't be changed?"

"Like I said. Human." Hen picked up an egg then laid it back down. "I hated Mother's Day this year just as much as I did in the previous two years. I didn't want to celebrate with all those people who still had their mamms. I know that's selfish. Did you feel that way?"

"I tried not to."

"Me too. It must be even harder for Dat."

"That's why I keep telling you to stop making life so hard for him." Ruby cracked an egg against the ceramic bowl a little harder than necessary. "He has enough to worry about—"

"I don't do it on purpose."

"Maybe not, but sauntering down the street with a man's arm around you in broad daylight isn't a good way to make life easier for him."

Hen hadn't planned it. The same heat that scorched her body every time she thought about those few moments leaning against Nicholas returned. The same yearning to feel it again. Did Ruby feel that way when Peter touched her? Not a question Hen could ask, not even of her sister. "I hurt my ankle. Nicholas was only trying to help me. It was innocent."

It didn't feel innocent. It felt wonderful and scary at the same time.

"But it didn't appear innocent. Can't you see that?" The egg in Ruby's hand broke. The yolk oozed through her fingers. "Ach, see what you made me do?"

"What I made you do? I was just trying to make you feel better—"

Head down, Ruby leaned her forearms on the counter, her dirty hands dripping in the sink. "I know, I know. I don't know why I'm so riled up all the time."

"Your life is changing. You're getting married. You're moving away from home. I can't even imagine." As much as Hen wanted both events to occur for herself. "No wonder you have the jitters."

"The jitters are normal." Aunt Ginny's voice was sweet and warm like hot, mulled cider on the coldest day of winter. "So are your feelings about your mamm."

Two twenty-pound bags of flour in her arms, she trudged across the kitchen with Mena on her heels carrying a small bag of sugar. "What you have to remember is your mamm would've wanted you to be happy. She wouldn't have wanted you to mope around because she's not here. She's sitting at the foot of the throne, hanging out with Mary and Elizabeth. She's holding Stephen in her lap and teaching him songs. She's not pining to come back to earth with all its turmoil and pain and misery. Much as we like to make it about us, it's really not. She's exactly where she belongs. Where all of us belong."

Aunt Ginny puffed as if such a long string of words had emptied out her lungs. Or maybe it was carrying big sacks of flour up a flight of wooden stairs from the basement. Hen should've done it for her. "I know, but—"

"She's right, Hen. We both just said we were being selfish." Ruby moved another basket of eggs closer. "We know we're selfish. So we just need to get over it."

"You're right." Her aunt Ginny was always right. Ruby, not as much, but she was the one getting married with no mom to help her get ready—physically or in her heart. "You're both right."

"Gut, I'm glad we're all agreed. Now help me with this flour."

"Do you think bopli Stephen is older? Or do you stay the same age when you go to heaven?" Mena stood on tiptoes to shove the bag of sugar onto the counter. "Is Cooper the cat there and Peanuts the hund?"

"Ach, kind, do you think I'm an expert on these things? You should ask your dat." Aunt Ginny handed one of her bags to Hen and unloaded the other onto the shelf next to a plethora of ingredients used in baking. "I imagine heaven as being a place of never-ending joy and peace. I don't worry about the particulars. I doubt anyone who makes it to the promised land does."

"But—"

"Finish the eggs, maed, lickety-split. We have time for a wedding committee meeting before the others get here."

Aunt Ginny did love her committee meetings.

Adele, Ruby's friends, and a few other women from the meal prep committee were coming over for a noodle frolic. Which would sound like an odd frolic to English people, but they needed at least twenty pounds of homemade noodles for the menu. Making them from scratch took many hands.

While Mena helped Ruby finish up the eggs, Hen pulled the pasta maker from the bottom shelf next to a stack of cookie sheets and cake pans. Mom had received the stainless-steel appliance as a gift from her sisters on her last birthday.

Hen set it on the table. She ran her fingers over the base then turned the handle. Her job consisted of running dough balls through the pasta maker to make thin sheets after some of the other women mixed the dough. They knew better than to allow her to handle the mixing. Her past attempts at baking led to salt being substituted for sugar in an apple pie and triple the necessary baking powder in a cookie recipe—to name a few. Ruby insisted Hen did it on purpose to get out of baking chores. Not true. Her bored mind simply wandered.

Her mom never said a word to the aunties, but she didn't really want the pasta maker. "Noodles are best made by hand with love," she'd confided in Hen after her birthday supper ended and everyone had gone home. She'd contemplated the cabinets and shelves for a few seconds, then slid the new appliance onto the bottom shelf in the far corner. "Just because it's more convenient doesn't mean it's better."

Mom felt that way about many modern conveniences. Which made sense. She was Plain, after all. It was almost comical to watch her face when their English friends talked about popping frozen dishes into a microwave oven. She'd nod, but the wrinkle between her eyebrows and the downturn of her lips gave her away. Even if she could, she would never use a microwave.

Hen's hands went to her throat. It hurt. To have her mom here now to roll out the dough on a flour-covered counter, all the while singing her favorite English hymn, "How Great Thou Art," would be such a gift.

Tears teetered. *No, no, no, no.* Just pollen floating through the open windows irritating her eyes and nose. She rushed to the sink, filled a glass with water, and gulped down half of it.

"Stop mooning around and get over here," Aunt Ginny called from the table. "Now's not the time for dawdling."

"I don't dawdle." Hen swiped at her face with her sleeve and turned around. "I was thinking maybe we should cut the noodles by hand. Mom always said they were better that way."

"Your mom wasn't talking about making twenty pounds of noodles." Still peering at her paperwork, Aunt Ginny smiled. "I promise she'll forgive you for using the pasta maker for any meal serving more than a dozen people."

"Sorry, Mamm," Hen murmured under her breath as she hurried back to the table. "But Aenti Ginny is right."

"What did you say?"

"Nothing."

Nothing and everything. Mom was busy mopping around the throne of the Lord and making Jesus and the disciples her favorite lemon meringue pie. She had other things to think about besides making noodles using a pasta maker. Someday Hen would like to help her. And get all the answers to Mena's questions while she did.

One thing for sure—Cooper the cat and Peanuts the dog would be there. And every other animal Hen had loved.

Mena could count on that. They were God's creatures, for sure and for certain.

CHAPTER 24

"I'm working on my grocery list. We'll need two hundred pounds of chicken."

Aunt Ginny had already moved on from the pasta maker discussion. Which was fine with Hen. She would slip that memory of her mother pooh-poohing the appliance into her treasure box to cherish when she was alone.

Her aunt had papers strewn across the table, along with three colors of highlighters, two pencils, an eraser, a pen, and a thick stack of purple, pink, orange, and pale blue sticky notes. She was nothing, if not prepared, for the wedding committee meeting. "We'll also need two hundred pounds of potatoes. We'll ask your aunt Millie to check the Pittsburgh newspaper for prices. They might be on sale. You'd be amazed at how much a dollar off can add up when you're talking about two hundred pounds of anything."

She tossed out the numbers like they were nothing. Which they were, if a person compared. They expected about 115 people—many traveling from across Pennsylvania as well as other states—for Ruby's wedding. That was rather small for a Plain wedding, but it still required an experienced, keen mind to do the planning. That's why Aunt Ginny was in charge. Hen tapped her index finger on her cheek and pretended to contemplate. "Are you sure that's enough?"

"That's just for the noon meal."

Aunt Ginny didn't look up, so she didn't catch Hen's weak attempt at humor. She applied the pencil's eraser to something scribbled on the notebook paper in front of her. "We'll need another fifty pounds of chicken for supper. I hope your dat has the men lined up to handle the grilling.

It'd be nice to have six or seven. That way they could get it done before the service starts at nine. It'll be hot."

"Knowing Dat, he has them all lined up. He probably has them practicing with gas grills and his favorite marinade."

"I hope so. We have seventeen days left until the wedding. It's starting to get tight." Aunt Ginny shoved her glasses up her nose for the fiftieth time. She really should get them adjusted. "What about you, Hen? How's the cleaning coming?"

"Fine." As fine as could be, considering she'd been given the worst jobs on the prep list. She lobbied for yardwork, but the boys won those slots—of course. "Me, Adele, Lenora, and the cousins finished the windows. We'll do the floors and floorboards when we get closer. We'll wash the rugs and curtains next week. After that, we'll wash all the bedding and clean the guest bedrooms."

Aunt Ginny's family would stay with them for three or four days, taking up the two empty bedrooms and sharing the boys' bedrooms. Every room would be cleaned and dusted down to the floorboards.

It would be worth it. Hen hadn't seen Aunt Ginny's kids in at least a year. With all the other relatives coming, it would be a family reunion as well as a wedding.

With Adele, Mena, and her local cousins belting out songs and whispering silly boy stuff and Mena stopping every five minutes to cuddle Raindrop, the window washing had been fun. Not that Hen would ever admit that to her aunt.

"Gut work. Stay on it." Aunt Ginny held up a paper filled with more scribbles. "Ruby, you've got your witnesses, your table servers, and your special helpers. Have you picked out your colors?"

"We have seven table servers. They'll wear burgundy. The special helpers are wearing yellow." Ruby turned from the counter where she'd been lining up the ingredients for the noodles. Arms crossed, she leaned against it. "My dress is pale teal, so Cora and Leah are wearing a dark teal. Peter will wear an evergreen shirt with his black pants. His witnesses are wearing a dark navy-blue shirt."

"Have you started sewing yet?"

"Nee, we've been busy cleaning out our house and moving the furniture that Peter bought from his onkel."

"Can't that wait?" Hen scooped up Raindrop and settled the puppy in her lap before she could untie her sneakers for the third time in an hour. She was determined to see the laces as worthy adversaries. "You won't need it until after the wedding."

"His onkel wanted the furniture out of their house right away because they have the farm on the market. Prospective buyers are coming. They'll think the furniture comes with the house." Ruby wrung her hands. The closer the wedding came, the more she did that. Peter had bought a small house on a twenty-acre farm only ten miles from his parents' place, but it needed a lot of work. "They're moving to Pinecraft in three weeks."

"That's fine, that's fine," Aunt Ginny intervened. "I can sew your dress. I know Hen is no help in that department."

"Also, Peter and I want to decorate the cake." Her hands just as quickly at rest in her lap, Ruby smiled that dreamy smile that made her appear far too young to be getting hitched. "We have a theme we're working on."

"Did you decide on a flavor?"

"German chocolate with chocolate frosting. Peter's favorite."

That's what love did to a person. Hen hid her own smile. Ruby didn't even like chocolate that much. Her favorite was carrot cake with cream cheese frosting.

"Gut, gut. Moving on, the wedding cook kitchen is booked." Aunt Ginny marked off items on her list. "I know you don't like to cook, Hen, but it's all women in the kitchen in the three days before the wedding. We need at least twenty-five cooks for the mashed potatoes, stuffing, coleslaw, barbecue beans, corn, and lettuce salad. The bread, cakes, pies, and puddings will be made ahead, of course.

"We have enough home-canned chicken broth in the basement for the stuffing, canned rhubarb for the pies and custard, and canned apples we can use for apple butter. I counted enough jars of jam down there to cover what we need as well."

Nobody ate like Plain folks at a wedding.

"We're here, we're here." With Adele leading the way, a passel of women and children burst through the doorway, bringing chatter, laughter, and general hilarity. "Let the fun begin."

With a ferocious—albeit tiny—woof, Raindrop hopped from Hen's lap, bringing the wedding planning committee meeting to an abrupt end.

"We can have fun without you," Hen teased as she took a casserole dish from Adele, who'd been one of the women designated to bring lunch. Hen lifted the foil and sniffed. Spicy hamburger meat, pungent onion, salsa. Taco casserole, her favorite. "Such *hochmut*."

"Adele doesn't seem prideful to me at all." Lenora followed close behind. She carried a bag of tortilla chips, another of avocados, and a Mason jar of homemade hot sauce. "In fact, she's the picture of humility."

"Denki, Lenora, but I don't need defending. I know just how to deal with turncoat friends like this one." Adele pretended to take back the dish. "No taco casserole for you, my friend. So sad too, because I added extra cheddar cheese, black olives, and green onion, just for you."

"And I made your favorite strawberry lemonade to drink, so don't be so touchy." Hen settled the dish on a cast-iron trivet on the table before it landed upside down on the floor. "Aunt Ginny also made your favorite salted caramel chocolate chip cookie bars, by the way. Ruby has all the ingredients assembled for the noodles. Let's get started while the kitchen is still cool."

"Easy for you to say." Ruby waved her hand toward the pasta maker. "You don't have to do anything until the dough is ready. I cracked most of the eggs, boiled the water, and lined up the ingredients."

"I cracked some of those eggs, missy." Hen mock-bowed to her sister. "You lined up salt, boiling water, and flour. Such a strain—not. No standing around congratulating yourself. Get busy."

Ruby responded as all mature women did. She stuck out her tongue.

To which Hen responded in kind. Ruby, Lenora, and Adele went to work beating the egg yolks with salt and boiling water while Aunt Ginny and her friends dumped flour in four storage container bowls big enough to hold four pounds each.

In no time at all, the wet and dry ingredients were combined so the women could begin forming the dough balls.

"So I see Raindrop is settling in nicely." Adele already had flour on her cheek. A trickle of sweat glistened on her forehead. "How do you like volunteering at the clinic? Have you seen much of Nicholas?"

Hen's first day at the clinic stood as one of the best days of her life. She didn't want to leave—ever. She intended to tell Adele about it later when they were alone. Feeding the grapevine was not on Hen's to-do list.

She shot her friend a meaningful glance. "I'm learning so much about caring for animals."

"From Nicholas?"

Adele hadn't caught her drift. She wasn't usually so dense. Hen tried out a more forceful stare. "From the clinic staff."

"Nicholas let me hold a hamster," Mena volunteered. "And he showed Hen how to hook up an IV to an angry cat who was de–de–hy. . .thirsty."

"Dehydrated." Hen stifled a sigh. Mena was too young to understand about grapevines and gossip. "It was no big deal. He did it. I just watched."

"Nee. He said you did a gut job keeping Elvis from scratching him."

"Ah, he was trying to flatter you." Adele high-fived Aunt Ginny like a teenager. "Has he asked you to take a buggy ride yet?"

"He's not going to ask me to do anything. We're just working together."

"But you wish it were more. I know you do." Adele brought a tray of dough balls to Hen. They'd set for the prescribed ten minutes and were ready for the pasta maker. She patted Hen's prayer cap. "Admit it. You think he's cute."

"Come on, that's my bruder you're talking about." Lenora covered her ears with both hands and sang, "La-la-la-la."

"Sorry, Lenora, but it's true." Adele and the other women laughed. "Has Nicholas said anything to you? Is he interested in Hen?"

"Seriously, you wouldn't like it if we poked at you like this." The heat that rolled through Hen had nothing to do with the boiling water. "Nothing is going on between Nicholas and me."

He'd been busy taking care of a dog hit by a car, an angry cat, and a puppy that swallowed the squeaker from one of its toys.

"He said he liked Hen's freckles." Mena again. The child had a big mouth to match her big ears. "He said she could easy be a vet's assistant if he ever left."

"Left?" Lenora's forehead wrinkled. So did her nose. "Where would he go? Did he say he was going somewhere?"

"Nee, he didn't. It was hypothetical." Hen jumped in before Mena could make it worse. "We were just talking."

"Talking about going to vet school. That's where you go to learn how to take care of animals." Mena pushed a chair from the table to the cabinets. She then climbed onto the chair. She opened the door, grabbed a glass from the cabinet, set it on the counter, and climbed down. "Adele, will you put some lemonade in my glass for me?"

"Of course I will. You could've asked me to get the glass down for you." Adele dropped a kiss on the little girl's cap. "You don't want to fall off a chair and break your neck, maedel."

"Nicholas likes Hen."

A chorus of "aha" filled the air on the heels of the child's statement. Next they'd be singing "Sitting in a tree, k-i-s-s-i-n-g," like grade schoolers.

Adele poured the girl's lemonade and handed it to her. "How do you know?"

"He watches her with this funny look on his face, like his tummy hurts."

"Jah, that's it." Aunt Ginny clapped. The other women laughed and joined in a rousing round of applause.

"Isn't it time for you to collect the eggs?" Hen took the glass from Mena's hand and pointed at the back door. "While you're out, make sure the boys milked the does and moved the kids back in with them. And say hi to Sam and Sassy for me."

Did they miss her as much as she missed them?

"Can I feed Jack?"

"That's up to Micah."

"What's up to me?" Micah clomped into the room. His straw hat had a dark sweat ring, and his faded blue shirt was soaked as well. He and the rest of the male Millers had been plowing and preparing fields for alfalfa and corn. "I have very little say about what goes on around here."

"Ha ha." He had way more say than Hen did or would ever have. He'd joined Dad in blocking her plan for expanding to two goat herds. "Mena wants to feed Jack."

"He's already been fed." Micah helped himself to a tall glass of strawberry lemonade. "So have your precious goats and the chickens. But Mena can still collect the eggs."

"Do the mamms' udders need shaving? Have you clipped their hooves?"

His chin jutting, Micah slid his hat back on his head. "You're not the only one who knows how to take care of goats."

Maybe so, but Hen was family to them. "But I'm the only one who wants to."

"No bickering at Ruby's noodle frolic." Adele spoke up. "Hen, didn't you say your dat made the rules? Not Micah."

Adele was siding with her brother. Now who was the turncoat?

"Adele's right." Micah shot a grin at Hen's best friend. "Denki for pointing that out. But then, you're almost always right."

What was going on here? The two were eying each other like chocolate fudge sundaes. "That's true. So Micah, why *are* you in the kitchen bothering us when you should be outside surveying your domain?"

No it wasn't fair, and sarcasm was likely a sin, but Hen couldn't help herself. *Sorry, Gott.*

"I reckon he smelled your aenti Ginny's caramel chocolate chip bars." All smiles, Adele picked up the platter and took it to Micah. "I had one. They're so gut I asked your aenti for the recipe."

Seriously, what was wrong with Adele? She'd known Micah since he was in diapers. She should be on Hen's side. She was the one banished from the goat shed. Tulip missed her. Sam wandered the yard crowing for her. Buster howled.

"I do like a gut eppy." A goofy grin on his face, Micah took his time browsing the selection. He pointed at one. "Do you think that's the biggest one?"

Adele, who was standing far closer to him than Hen liked, shook her head and pointed at another one. "Nee, take this one. Or take two. I know us maed won't eat them all."

"Don't give away all our dessert—"

"I'll get you some more lemonade," Lenora interrupted. "You must be parched after working in the fields."

Now she was getting into the act. What about Hen's little brother could possibly be so entrancing?

Lenora rushed to fill Micah's glass and delivered it just as Adele took a step back. The two nearly collided. Lemonade sloshed on the floor. Lenora stepped in it.

Now they had a sticky mess to clean up. Served them right.

"He was out there all of two hours." Hen stomped across the room. She grabbed Micah's arm. "Off you go, and take the eppies with you. In fact, take the whole platter. Share them with Luke and the boys. These maed don't deserve them."

"Whoa, what's got your dander up?" Micah allowed himself to be led into the hallway. As soon as they were out of earshot, he halted. "I came to tell you Nicholas is here. He says he came by to check on Jack."

Nicholas was here. At the farm. Now. When Hen had no chance of leaving a frolic without everyone knowing. Besides, she wasn't allowed in the barn. "And?"

"And he hasn't checked on the gaul all this time. Plus he said he needs to ask you a question about Jack's feeding schedule—even after I told him Luke has been feeding him."

"He wants to ask me a question?"

"Jah." Micah waggled his eyebrows and winked at the same time in a form of facial gymnastics. It probably hurt. "You."

"I can't go out there."

"Jah, you can. Dat is at the Connors' training their new stallion. Luke is with him. You're not doing any work, you're just answering a question at the assistant vet's request. I have the boys with me planting the corn."

He made a good argument. Dad shouldn't be mad under these circumstances. "And the frolic?"

"Aunt Ginny will figure it out."

Aunt Ginny, whose original reason for coming to stay was to help marry off Hen. Aunt Ginny, who knew it would make Dad happy to see a certain vet assistant with his oldest daughter. Now who was matchmaking?

"Did he really ask for me?"

"Would I make that up?"

"What's going on with you and Adele?"

"You figure it out." Micah helped himself to a cookie bar. He held out the platter. "Give one to Nicholas."

He took off. At the front door he turned back. "Close your mouth. You'll eat a fly."

Her brother, the matchmaker.

CHAPTER 25

Jack was doing great, which was more than Nicholas could say for himself. The Morgan trotted over to the corral railing, neighed a welcome, and tossed his regal head as if to say, "Where've you been?"

"I've been thinking, that's where I've been." Thinking about how he shouldn't have come to the Miller farm. His head knew that, but his heart had decided to take charge. Nicholas held out an apple slice on the palm of his hand. Jack took it with a delicate nibble that showed his well-worn teeth. "I shouldn't even be here now. I happen to know you're doing fine for an old geezer."

Jack arched his long neck. His head dipped. "No offense, buddy. I can't think straight. That's the problem. I need to think straight. What do you know about it? You've got it good, what with the likes of Hen and Mena taking care of your every need."

He had no business showing up at the Miller farm in hopes of talking to Hen. He'd just seen her at the clinic at the end of last week. Working with her was a treat. She knew her stuff, despite no formal training. She was a natural. Plus she had a contagious laugh and cute freckles.

Cute freckles?

Lord, have mercy on me, sei so gut.

Did God help a man who was considering leaving his faith? Did God give him this desire to do something outside the bounds imposed by the Ordnung, the rules of faith for his community? Or did Beelzebub tempt him? Did Nicholas want what he wanted because he was a selfish man who hadn't learned to die to self and put his wants aside?

A Plain man who couldn't answer these questions shouldn't be anywhere near a woman of faith. It was tantamount to leading her on. Or leading her away. Both were wrong.

All this presupposed that she was interested in him. A Grand Canyon leap. Was this another way in which Nicholas was weak?

"Do you think banging my head against that tree over there would rid me of these thoughts?" Nicholas jerked his thumb toward a black cherry tree. Jack's head dipped again. Nicholas chuckled and patted the horse's muzzle. "You'd agree to anything to get another slice of apple, wouldn't you?"

"He's also a big fan of raw carrots."

Nicholas jumped. The apple slices fell to the ground inside the corral fence. Jack helped himself. Laughing, Nicholas swiveled. "I thought I was alone."

Hen approached. She carried a platter that held at least two dozen dessert bars. Raindrop, a tiger kitten, and a rooster followed. Hen truly was the pied piper of animals. "I figured. I try to limit my personal conversations with Jack to private moments. Otherwise my dat thinks I'm nuts."

She held out the platter. Nicholas helped himself. His mouth watered, but he waited for the first bite. "Do you think I'm nuts?"

Stomping his feet, Jack whinnied. He had an opinion on the subject, but it was hard to say what it was.

"I think animals are much better listeners than humans." Hen smoothed Jack's forelock. He nuzzled her hand in a velvety kiss. "They're also better friends."

"Agreed." Nicholas took a bite of the bar. Gooey caramel, chocolate chips, with just a touch of saltiness melted in his mouth. "Ummm, umm, um. Did Micah send you out here?"

"He said you had a question about Jack's feedings."

Nicholas silently thanked Micah for being willing to deliver a message. "I did say that."

"So what's the question?"

"Is he eating the beet pulp?"

"Micah could've answered that question." Her expression baleful, Hen hunched her shoulders. "I'm not allowed to feed him anymore, remember?"

"Jah, I remember, but knowing you as I think I do, I assumed you are keeping on top of his feeding habits by having the boys report back to you."

A weak argument for a weak excuse to bring her out here.

Hen set the platter on an upside-down plastic bucket next to the corral gate. She leaned on the railing. "At first I was worried Dat would be upset if he found me out here. Then I realized he, Micah, and Aenti Ginny are all angling to put me right here, right now."

What an odd conclusion. A bishop didn't generally approve of single Plain men and women spending time together alone—except for when courting. "I don't know what you mean."

"They're matchmaking." Hen, always so straightforward, stared at a stand of red maples beyond the corral, at the sky, at the barn—everywhere but at Nicholas. "Ruby is younger, and she's getting married first. They're afraid I might never find a match. That's why my aenti came to Smicksburg. To help Dat marry me off."

Leave it to Hen to lay it out for Nicholas. She was plainspoken—even when it might be embarrassing. She spared not even herself. The urge to head her off at the pass pressed on Nicholas. He should set the record straight. Wasn't that why he'd come? "Why would they think that?"

"It probably has something to do with my inability to be presentable." Hen did a slow spin. Her apron sported something yellow and dried, what might be chocolate, and another stain that might be coffee. At nine in the morning, her prayer cap was wilted. A blotch of flour adorned her forehead. "I'm messy by nature. According to Dat, no man wants a messy fraa."

"Your dat is a gut man." Nicholas studied his dirty boots. No answers wrote themselves in the dust that had hitched a ride there. "But he's not the last word on what men want in a fraa. He can only speak for himself."

Hen lowered her head, as if studying her equally dirty sneakers. "You think?"

"I know."

"How?"

Because his heart spoke truth to him. Adam Miller should know outward appearances meant nothing. He was a bishop. "I know next to nothing about women and fraas. I'm the last man who should talk about the Bible and scripture, but I remember there being something about Gott telling Samuel not to consider outward appearance, because God doesn't care about it. He looks at our hearts."

Hen raised her head and peered at the sky. "I wonder what He would say about my heart."

"You love animals. I don't know what Gott thinks about that, but it tells me all I need to know." She would take this admission all wrong, and it would be Nicholas' fault. "Before you say anything—"

"Hen, there you are!" Ruby had a set of lungs. Her shout likely rattled the barn rafters. "You're not supposed to be out here. Get back to the house."

"She's bossy, isn't she?" Nicholas swiveled to stare at Hen's sister. She had her hands cupped around her mouth like a megaphone. As if her sharp tone wasn't enough. "You better go before she breaks an eardrum shouting so loud."

"She's not wrong." Hen offered him a rueful half smile. "I'm supposed to be making noodles for her wedding luncheon."

"You still have a couple of weeks to do that."

"Hen!"

"Coming!" Hen turned to leave.

"We need to finish this conversation."

"I can't. I have to make noodles from dough balls on a pasta maker my mamm didn't want."

No going down that rabbit hole. "What if I came by and picked you up tonight. . .late."

Hen stopped. Her body rigid, she didn't turn around. "A buggy ride?"

"So we can talk." Nicholas' tongue refused to connect with his brain. "About. . .things."

About the *us* he wished they could have, about the reasons there couldn't be an *us*. He would never ask a woman to leave her Plain community, not even a woman for whom he had feelings. Feelings he'd never had for any other woman. Feelings he couldn't explain. Not even to himself. "Sei so gut."

"Okay."

She took off as if propelled by those two syllables.

Or maybe it was the smirk on Ruby's face that made her race across the yard like a skunk had crossed her path.

A buggy ride.

Hen clasped her hands to her mouth to hide a smile that refused to fade. She scooped up Tigger and hugged the kitten to her chest as she trotted up the porch steps. Sam crowed behind her. She pivoted. "I know, I know. I miss you too. I promise to visit soon."

A quick visit.

Petunia and her siblings bleated in the distance. *I know.* What would Dad say if she argued that he was punishing the goats as much as he was punishing her? He'd tell her it was silly to think animals had feelings like human beings.

But they did. They loved people. They missed them when they were gone. They could see Hen in the distance. Their feelings were hurt by her failure to visit. *I'll visit. Soon. I promise.*

Hen kissed Tigger's head, ruffled his fur, and laid him on the Adirondack chair's cushion. "Hang out here. There are too many women in the kitchen. You'll get stepped on. I'll snuggle you later."

Tigger yawned and curled into a ball. No argument there.

A wave of laughter tumbled over Hen as she entered the kitchen. Who knew about what. Still laughing, Adele held out another tray of dough balls. "There you are. I thought maybe Micah decided to hand all the livestock chores back to you."

"Nee, he likes being in charge." Plus he would never go against Dad's wishes.

At least he didn't rub her nose in it.

Hen took the tray and went to work. Suddenly thankful for the machine, she flattened the dough balls enough to feed them through the pasta maker, which further flattened them to the perfect thickness. She liked her noodles on the chewy side. She laid the noodles over the wooden racks and glanced at the clock on the far wall. Two hours to air-dry. Because of the eggs, they had to be careful not to leave them out too long. No one wanted to give guests salmonella poisoning.

Her technique might be lacking, but not even the pickiest grandma at the frolic could argue with her efficiency. The women's chatter buzzed her ears, but the threads of conversation danced in the lukewarm breeze, impossible to capture and hold.

Buggy ride. Buggy ride with the know-it-all vet assistant who took her job.

Why did it sound so inviting?

"Hen? Hen!"

She glanced up. Adele approached with the taco casserole gripped between pot holders. "Casserole's hot. Time to eat."

"I'm not hungry."

"You? Not hungry?" Adele snorted. Pursing her lips, she stared at Hen with piercing eyes. "What's going on? Your face is red. Do you have a fever? You're not coming down with a stomach bug, are you?"

Her feelings for Nicholas did feel like the flu. "Nee."

"What did Micah say to you?"

Hen wiped her hands on her apron. She poured herself a glass of water and concentrated on taking a few small sips.

"Hen!"

"Not here. Not now."

"We need another jar of salsa. Come to the basement with me."

Like it took two of them to carry up a pint jar of salsa. Not to mention that the jar Lenora brought would be more than enough. "You can never have enough salsa."

In the cool semidarkness of the basement, Hen plopped into a canvas camping chair. "I don't know what I'm thinking."

"What, why, what happened?" Adele sat on the wooden steps. "Is something going on with Micah? Is it bad? Spill it, maedel."

"It's not Micah."

"Oh. Whew!"

"It's Nicholas."

"Ah." Adele's pique disappeared. She leaned forward, elbows on her knees. "Tell me, tell me."

Saving the buggy ride for last, Hen zipped through the recent events at the clinic.

"That's wunderbarr. But what's that have to do with Micah pulling you away from making noodles?"

"Nicholas. Nicholas is out there. He said he needed to ask me a question."

Adele squealed. "A question. What question?"

"About Jack."

"Oh."

"Nee, I think it was an excuse. He started talking about veterinarian stuff and how gut I was at it. Then he was saying something about veterinary college."

"And?"

"And then Ruby called me back."

Adele groaned.

"Wait. He said we needed to finish the conversation. He asked me if we could take a buggy ride. Tonight."

"You waited until now to tell me this?" Adele hopped up. She flung her arms in the air. "Seriously, maedel. You did that on purpose."

"Nee, I wanted to set the stage, so you'd understand why he asked me."

"He asked you because he likes you."

"Maybe." Hen leaned back. She studied the naked light bulb. It shone brightly despite the thin layer of dust that covered it. "I think there's something he wants to tell me."

Adele stuck her hands on her hips. Her expression perplexed, she cocked her head. "Jah, that he likes you."

"Nee. Jah. But I think. . . I think he's thinking about. . .one day leaving."

"That can't be right."

"Hey, you two, what are you doing down there?" Lenora's high-pitched voice filtered down the stairs. "Food's getting cold. We're starving."

"Coming." Adele shook her head. Her smile had become a frown. "Leave to go where?"

Hen explained.

The frown turned into a scowl. "If that's the case, my friend, guard your heart."

If anyone knew how it felt to have her heart returned to sender, it was Adele. Hen crossed her arms. If only it were that simple. A heart ignored reason. "He wants to be a vet. But he won't leave Moses."

"I would hope not. But that would have him here long enough to break a heart."

"Or to ask a woman to leave with him."

"Surely he's not the sort of man who would do such a thing."

"Surely."

"You wouldn't consider it, would you?"

Would she? Hen's stomach roiled. Dad. Mena. The twins. Luke and Micah. Aunt Ginny. Her aunts, uncles, cousins, nieces, nephews. Tulip,

Willow, Tigger, Buster, Sam, Sassy, Jack, Lucy, Raindrop. Her extended, ever-growing family. It had never occurred to her, ever. "Nee."

"Gut." Adele held out her hand.

Hen allowed her friend to pull her to her feet. "Denki for listening."

"It's hard. I know."

"I know you do." Hen pulled her into a quick hug. "I'm sorry. I understand now better than I did before."

"I don't wish it on anyone, especially my gut friend."

Staring up at the doorway at the top of the stairs, Hen paused. "Do I still take the buggy ride?"

"Absolutely." Adele nudged her forward. "What if we got it all wrong?"

Good point. When it came to men, the possibility was very real.

CHAPTER 26

A shiver of anticipation shook Hen. Or maybe it was the cool after-dark breeze. Even in June, evenings in Pennsylvania could have a touch of chill. She tucked her light shawl tighter around her shoulders and trotted down the porch steps. Nicholas pulled the buggy up next to her. Woofing in protest, Buster followed. "Stay here. I'll be back." Hen patted his shaggy head. "Guard the house for me while I'm gone."

Buster woofed again. Nicholas' horse neighed as if in response. No doubt he told the dog he could be trusted to take care of his precious cargo.

Nicholas tipped his hat. "Hallo."

"Hallo." Legs like pudding, Hen pulled herself into the buggy on the second try. *Just breathe.* She sucked in air. She hiccupped. Loudly. *Nee, nee, nee.* "I'm sorry. I don't know why that happened."

And hiccupped again. *Gott, have mercy, sei so gut.*

"It happens." Nicholas had the audacity to chuckle. "Maybe it's the brisk air. Or is it possible you're nervous?"

"Me, nervous? Nee." Hen brushed damp palms against her best evergreen dress. "Not in the least."

Hiccup.

"I just wondered because I was wishing I had a paper sack."

"Why?"

"To breathe into. Isn't that what you're supposed to do when you're hyperventilating?"

"You're nervous?" *Hiccup.* Hen swallowed against a nervous desire to howl with laughter. "You don't seem like it."

"It's dark. You can't see me." Nicholas shoved his Sunday go-to-meeting hat back on his forehead. "I also think the cheesy chicken casserole I ate for supper might decide to reappear. Along with the green salad and the apple crisp."

"Ach. Isn't going for a buggy ride supposed to be fun?"

"I've never found it to be."

"Me neither." Hen loosened her fingers and splayed them across her lap. "Not that I have much experience. One ride and I never got asked a second time."

"Maed ran in the other direction after a ride with me."

Another experience they had in common. Hen's shoulders relaxed. "We're a pair."

Hiccup.

Nicholas chuckled. "Try holding your breath."

It didn't work.

To Nicholas' credit, he ignored the next one. "I'm new at doing this around here. You'll have to tell me which way is best for a ride at night."

Hen waited for the next hiccup to pass. She directed him to an old dirt road that led to what had once been an English family's home until it was condemned because of mold infestations. When her grandparents bought the property, they tore down the old house and built in a spot closer to a nice pond.

Nicholas didn't have much more to say. Hen racked her brain. "How's Moses?"

"He has gut days and bad days."

"Don't we all?"

"He asked me yesterday where that freckle-faced girl was who likes goats. He thinks you're a family member."

Somehow, that would be nice. Hen wiggled in her seat. She had a family. But then a person could never have enough family. Imagining herself as part of Nicholas' family on the basis of one buggy ride? Adele's words echoed in Hen's brain. *"Don't even think about getting attached until you know what his plans are."* How to broach the subject? Straightforward worked best. "Why did you want to take me for a buggy ride?"

Katydids sang. Bullfrogs croaked. Leaves rustled in the maple and oak trees. The fishy odor of dogwood scented the breeze. The pause lasted so long, it seemed Nicholas wouldn't answer. He clucked and shook the reins. The horse picked up his pace.

The buggy's wooden wheels creaked. The *clip-clop* of hooves, a familiar, always soothing sound, did nothing to quiet Hen's misgivings.

She'd stepped in doo-doo again. "I'm sorry. I'm always jumping in without thinking." *Hiccup.* Embarrassment singed her skin from head to toe. "Really, I didn't mean to put you on the spot."

"It's not you." Nicholas craned his head from side to side. He glanced her way, then back at the road. "I didn't want to give you the wrong impression."

Hiccup. Hiccup.

"What impression should a woman have when a man asks her to take a buggy ride?"

"That's the problem. I couldn't figure out how to have a conversation with you. . .privately. Without making you think something was going on that wasn't going on." Nicholas' voice turned gruff. "I mean it would be going on, I would like it to be going on, but it can't because I'm not sure how long I'll be around. If you see what I mean."

"Nee. I don't think I do. I'm sorry. I'm *schtumm* sometimes."

"Nee, you're not. You're smart." Nicholas pulled off the road and halted the buggy in an open space between thick stands of pines. His eyes shone in the light of a three-quarter moon. "I'm just bad at explaining. I really could use that paper bag."

"Me too. It might help with the hiccups."

Hen held her breath while they sat in silence for a few minutes. It didn't help. "Why don't you try starting at the beginning?"

"A while back I had decided to leave my family, get my GED, go to college for a bachelor's degree, and then apply to a college of veterinary medicine. When I told my dat and mamm about it, they were horrified." His head bent, Nicholas fixed his gaze on the reins in his hands. "They wanted me to talk to our bishop. I said I would, but it wouldn't make a difference. Two days later Dat announced he needed me to come to Smicksburg with Lenora to take care of Daadi."

"He didn't say it was to keep you from going to college?"

"Nee, but he could've sent my bruder John. He's only a year younger." Nicholas' tone turned rueful. "He's working for a big Englisch farm managing their dairy herd. Dat said it was too gut a job to give up."

It made sense because it was exactly what Hen's father would've done. As a father and as a bishop. "Where were you working?"

"As a vet assistant."

Which explained why Dr. McDonald hired him. Shame welled up in Hen. She'd been so sure it was because Nicholas was a man. "A gut job too. But one that would only encourage you to pursue your plan to leave."

"Jah. Dat was so angry when I took the job with Dr. McDonald."

"I can imagine." Hen studied the stars. Suddenly it hit her. The hiccups had fled as quickly as they'd come. So had her nerves. This conversation was bigger than her. "I know how I'd feel if Micah announced he planned to leave us, our community, and his faith. I'd be heartbroken. So would Dat. Your daed isn't angry. He's crushed that you would even consider leaving."

"I know that. And yet, the dream still won't leave me alone. That's how much I want it." The want was so deeply ingrained in his words they trembled with it. "I knew it's a long shot, what with only having formal education to the eighth grade. I had signed up to take my GED the day Dat told me I was leaving."

"Did you argue with him?"

"Nee. Family comes first. Daadi comes ahead of my *narrisch* dreams."

"They're not narrisch, which is why I respect that you put your daadi first."

"Die to self."

Gelassenheit, one of the pillars of their faith. Humility. Put faith ahead of personal wants. "Die to self."

Hen leaned against the buggy seat. She inhaled air thick with the lovely scent of summer-sweet flowers. A dog barked in the distance. He sounded lonely. "I've often dreamed of going to veterinary school too."

"That doesn't surprise me. That's why I knew you'd understand."

"I understand, but I banished the dream, because I couldn't leave my family. Dat has had enough loss. I couldn't hurt him like that." As much as Dad infuriated her, he also served as her safe place in a storm. She measured every other man against him and every action she took against his standards—even when she failed to live up to them. Which was most of the time. "I love all my family, including my animals, too much."

"You didn't mention your faith as a reason for staying."

He hadn't mentioned it either. Trusting him with her doubts was like teetering on a ledge so narrow, her toes hung over a dark, bottomless pit below. "Why are we talking about this? What does it have to do with buggy rides?"

Heaving a sigh, he rubbed his temples. "Let's get down and walk a bit."

Not an answer, but Hen hopped down. She stopped to pat the beautiful Morgan's muzzle and smooth his tangled mane. He whinnied his thanks. Sweat tickled her temples despite the cool breeze. *Just a ride. Just a walk.*

"Stay on the road." Nicholas clasped her hand and tugged her away from the grassy ditch that divided the meadow from the road's shoulder. "We don't want to fall in the dark."

"There's plenty of moonlight. We're fine." His touch was more likely to send her tumbling than the uneven terrain. Her heart hammered in her chest. She cleared her throat. "Tell me what you're trying so hard not to tell me."

"I like you. Despite everything, I like you."

"You don't have to sound so surprised." Hen freed her hand. Was Nicholas simply another man who couldn't abide Hen being Hen? "I know I'm different. I try harder than you may think to follow the rules, but most of the time I end up being who I am."

She didn't do it on purpose. She didn't set out to be different. No matter what Dad might think.

"I don't mean it that way." Nicholas slowed. The shadows cast by the trees hid the three-quarter moon and his expression. "You know as well as I do that we didn't get off to a gut start."

"Because you acted so high and mighty, like you knew it all." Snarky words delivered in a snarky tone. She wasn't making it any better. "I mean—"

"Because you acted so high and mighty, like I couldn't possibly take care of Jack better than you."

Some facts couldn't be disputed, even if a woman more skilled in womanly arts would let him think he was better at what he likely considered a man's job. Hen wasn't and she couldn't. "You can't."

"I know that now, but I also know I can help. I also know how much you care about your animals, love them. I didn't know that then." Nicholas ran the words together as if trying to keep her from interrupting. "You're gut with people too. You may be messy, and you're opinionated, but you have a gut heart."

"Funny, that doesn't sound like a compliment. Anything else you want to criticize?"

"I'm not criticizing, I'm explaining."

"Huh. Sure."

"You don't like to cook, bake, sew, or clean, like most Plain women. You're not like any Plain woman I've ever known. But those facts don't bother me."

A Plain man who didn't mind a Plain woman who didn't want to do what women were supposed to do—and love doing it. "It's hard for me to believe—"

"I know. Me too. But you love animals as much as I do. They're your friends. Your family. You made me realize that's more important to me."

They were alike in that. "I've never known a Plain man like you either."

Silence reigned for a few seconds. If what Nicholas was confessing was true, then he found her passion for animals to be a strong point, instead of a fault. She would never have to apologize for it. Or pretend otherwise. The thought was almost too much to bear. Hen picked up her pace, matching the *katy-katy-did* rhythm of the katydids' song.

"So is it a gut thing?" Hen asked. Her uneven stride wasn't even a problem for him. She'd never walked with a man who could match her steps so well. She groaned at the thought. Another thing they shouldn't be doing. "Me being different?"

"Your being different doesn't bother me. It's a gut thing."

"Then what does bother you?"

"I like you. I think about you. I'm worried I might get too attached, so much that I can't leave when. . ." His voice grew hoarse. "When Daadi passes, I want to go away to college. Knowing that, I don't want to lead you on."

"You don't want to hurt my feelings?"

"Jah. I mean, nee I don't." He sounded as confused as Hen felt. "Of course I don't, but it's hard to resist feelings so strong, but I know I must. It's the right thing to do."

"I see." Sort of. In stories of knights and ladies-in-waiting, this would be called a noble gesture. In the real world, it left the woman lonely. And peeved. "It doesn't feel gut, knowing you like me, but you still want to leave. Why tell me? Why not leave me in the dark? Why were you so insistent on having this conversation, you came to the farm and made up an excuse to talk to me in the middle of the day?"

The blissful unknowing instead of a squashed dream.

"I thought you might have noticed by the way I act. I wanted you to know why I can't—"

"Why? It only makes it worse."

"What worse?"

"That I feel the same way." There. She'd said it. Flat out. "It stinks."

"You like me?"

"I do."

The two syllables clanged like English church bells on Sunday morning.

"I mean—"

"I know what you mean." Nicholas took Hen's arm, forcing her to stop and face him. "I'd ask you to come with me, but I would never want to cause another person to leave the church."

Which brought them back to the subject Hen had wanted to avoid. She tugged free of his grasp, whirled, and started back to the buggy. "I should get home."

Nicholas kept pace. "Why don't you want to talk about your faith?"

She halted again. How to explain? Especially under a night sky filled with moon and stars and a countryside replete with God's creations from opossums to raccoons to beetles to mosquitoes to wolves to coneflowers and poplars and elms. "Because my faith is weak, and I don't want to influence you."

His huff held disbelief. "Explain. Sei so gut."

The words poured out then. The loss of her baby brother. Her mother's death. The empty words that didn't warm her frozen heart. "I keep thinking I'll get past it. That's what everyone says. Time will heal. Gott knows. Gott understands. His will be done."

They'd arrived at the buggy. Nicholas took Hen's hand before she could climb in. "I know we're supposed to accept God's will and His plan, but if somebody said it was easy, they're wrong. I've never had a loss like you have, so I don't know how I'd react. I just know the thought of my mamm dying makes me feel sick to my stomach."

Knowing hurt. Would not knowing hurt more? It took guts for

Nicholas to bare his soul to her. His confession held a few delicate stalks of sweet-smelling flowers. Her eccentricities didn't keep Nicholas from liking her. Enough to want to court her under other circumstances.

"I'm glad you told me about your plans." Hen squeezed his hand and let go. "It's nice to know a man could like me despite my faults and flaws."

"I don't see faults and flaws." Nicholas rearranged Hen's shawl so it covered her shoulders again. "I see a person who loves hard and long. A woman filled with kindness and joy and a sense of humor. The important things."

A shiver ran through Hen. The urge to touch Nicholas overwhelmed. Better not to. Better not to know that feeling when the opportunity would not present itself again. Better to only imagine it than to know how wonderful it was. "We should go."

"Jah. We should." Still, he didn't move. Regret lined his moonlit face. "I wish there was another way."

"Aenti Ginny would say pray and let Gott lead the way."

"Which means we have to accept Gott's leading."

"We do."

"The world is full of what-ifs and roads not taken." He touched Hen's cheek for a fleeting second. His fingers were warm, his expression uncertain. "I know I'm going to regret this one."

Her throat tight with checked sobs, Hen backed away. She slipped around him and climbed into the buggy. She couldn't give her heart to a man who had dreams that didn't include her. "Take me home now, sei so gut."

CHAPTER 27

"If I see one more potato, I may never eat another one again—not even Aunt Ginny's Dijon mustard potato salad." Hen held up the offending item, examined it for any remaining peel, found none, and tossed it in a huge extra-strength foil pan already full of raw, peeled potatoes. "My fingers are numb, and my shoulders on fire."

"I'd rather peel potatoes than chop up and season two hundred pounds of raw chicken." Adele flung a fat potato into her pan, only slightly less full than Hen's. "Wouldn't you?"

Hen stretched and craned her neck. It popped. It had been a long day already. Her eyes wanted to close, and her muscles ached with fatigue. Even Buster and Raindrop had given up on racing from stranger to stranger to smell their shoes and greet them, tails wagging a thousand miles a minute. They now shared a corner of the tent, backs touching as they curled up in one big ball and one small one. "Absolutely. How long do you think we've been doing this?"

"I have no idea. I want to curl up and take a nap like Tigger." Lenora nudged with one sneaker the cat stretched out next to her chair, oblivious to the conversation overhead. "I don't mind peeling potatoes, but the heat is making me sleepy."

This was just the latest in a long list of tasks to be accomplished on the last day before Ruby's wedding. Hen and the other women helped set up the wedding cook kitchen, coolers, dishes, and tables in the morning while the men erected a thirty-by-sixty tent along with the tables and chairs that went in it.

Then Aunt Ginny had appointed Hen to lead the potato peeling detail. She'd rather work with the men setting up tables and chairs, but that would surely mean running into Nicholas. She couldn't have that. She'd managed to avoid speaking to him for nearly two weeks. It meant giving up clinic visits with the excuse that there was too much work to be done preparing for the wedding. It meant squashing all the feelings that welled up inside her every time she pictured his face close to hers on that moonlit buggy ride.

If she thought about it, if she examined her feelings too closely, she'd know for sure one thing. She'd handled it wrong. She should've urged him not to abandon his faith or his family—if for no other reason than the most important one—because she had a responsibility as a sister in Christ to hold him accountable for the vows he'd taken when he was baptized. She'd been so caught up in her own faith battle, she hadn't considered fully the implications of him abandoning his faith.

She was the most selfish person on earth.

"Earth to Hen. Stop mooning over the potatoes." Adele pointed her peeler at the last remaining twenty-pound bag. It was less than half full. "We're almost done. Can I get a hallelujah?"

"I'll give you a hallelujah and add an amen." Lenora wiped droplets of sweat from her forehead with her sleeve. The sun was low on the horizon now, so the tent erected for the potato peeling contingent—as well as the dishwashers—didn't protect them from its glare. "We're blessed to be sitting while doing our assigned task, I suppose. Nicholas helped put up the big tent first. Then he had to set up tables and chairs all evening."

The simple mention of his name sent a tsunami of hurt, concern, uncertainty, regret, and guilt through Hen. She grabbed another potato from the burlap bag. Head bent, she attacked it with pretend enthusiasm.

"Speaking of Nicholas, it's been almost two weeks, and you still refuse to talk about the buggy ride you took with him. What gives? Every time I ask you about it, you look like you're coming down with the flu and change the subject." Adele's technique of peeling the skin in a lovely spiral was envied by all the potato peelers—except Hen, who preferred quick, hard strokes. "I know courting is supposed to be private, but this is your best friend asking."

"You and my bruder are courting?" Her eyes wide, Lenora dropped her potato. It fell into the grass and had to be rescued. "He hasn't said a word. In fact, he's been holed up in his room at night, every night. When I ask him what he's doing, he says he's reading."

Studying his veterinarian books. "We're not courting." Hen fought to keep her tone neutral. "That's how rumors get started."

"So what happened? Was it what we thought it was?" With a furtive glance at Lenora, Adele flung a long strip of peel into the pile that would later be thrown into the compost. "Don't keep us in suspense, maedel."

We were right. He'd rather do something else with his life, that's what.

Grateful she hadn't said those words aloud, Hen dunked her peeler in a bowl of water to rinse the starch off. The sound of laughter made her swivel. Ruby and Peter strolled by. Peter carried an enormous plastic cake container. Likely the wedding cake the two of them had decorated together.

They seemed so happy.

How would it feel for Ruby to know her entire life would change in the next twenty-four hours? From single woman to one in body and spirit with the man she loved? The only man who might be willing to consider such a risk with Hen had other plans. The smile on Nicholas' face when he talked about vet school—she couldn't compete with that. If he chose not to pursue his dream because of her, he would come to resent her one day.

On the other hand, a good sister in Christ would pray for him to cling to his faith, that he not leave his church, family, and community. Some might even suggest she had a responsibility to tell the bishop—her own father—of Nicholas' plan.

A plan he'd shared with Hen in strictest confidence. There was no doubt about that.

It was all so confusing. Was this God's plan? To show her that she did have faith? A strong faith? She would never leave her church, her community, or her family. Even if she still had to come to terms with the scars left by her mother and little Stephen's deaths. Even if it meant spending her life as an aunt, sister, and daughter but never a wife and mother.

Maybe her love of animals was meant to be enough.

The thought sent sharp, painful arrows of regret and sorrow winging their way to Hen's heart. Only a few months ago she'd been sure caring for her goats and opening a shop in town would be a perfect life for her. Husband and children would come along at some point. She could have it all—eventually.

If Dad knew, he would diagnose her with a severe case of hubris.

And he'd be right.

"Hen? Hen!" Adele flicked potato water at Hen. Drops splattered her face. "Stop mooning over him and tell us what happened."

"I'm not mooning. There's nothing to moon over. Nothing happened." She attacked her potato with fierce but even strokes. "We're not courting."

"Why not?" Her forehead wrinkled. Adele frowned. "What happened on that buggy ride? Was it what you thought it was?"

"It's about veterinary college, isn't it?" Lenora's face crumpled. She jabbed the air with her peeler. "He's thinking of leaving us, isn't he? If he leaves the church, my parents will be so devastated—"

"He's not going anywhere anytime soon." Hen managed a reassuring smile. "He would never abandon you and Moses. You know that."

He wouldn't leave until Moses passed and Lenora went home to her family. That could be in a few months or a few years. However long, Hen would have to deal with it—with him—with grace and move on.

"You're right. I do. He's a gut bruder and kinskinner. It's just that he's been so moody lately. He doesn't seem content." Chagrin colored Lenora's words. "When I ask him if something's wrong, he says everything is gut. He has a gut job. He likes Dr. McDonald. He likes living here. That's what he says. So why is it so obvious he's unhappy?"

"A Plain man his age is usually thinking about taking a fraa and having kinner." Adele stood. She put her hand on her hip like an old lady and straightened slowly.

Her expression reflected the sentiment she didn't add. So were Plain women. Like Hen and her. Hen stood as well. She stretched her arms over her head, left, then right. "What if. . .what if it's not meant to be? Do you ever think that maybe God's plan is for us to be an aenti, not a mamm?"

"I didn't used to. Not until Nathan." Adele shrugged. She flopped into her chair. "I wasted so much time thinking he was the one Gott had for me. Now I'm not sure I'd trust my instincts. I don't want to get my heart broken again."

"I'm so sorry." Lenora patted the other woman's shoulder. "I know how you feel. But for different reasons. I thought there might be a beau for me in Bird-in-Hand. It was just a feeling. Nothing had happened.

But then I moved here where I don't know anyone, and the chances of meeting someone seem so small."

Hen studied Adele's face. Something was going on there. "You don't know if you can trust your feelings because there's someone you think might actually be *the* one?"

Adele smiled primly. "Courting is private."

"Aha. Aha. I knew it!" Hen clapped and hooted. "It's Micah, isn't it? Come on, admit it, it's Micah."

Adele frowned and tilted her head toward Lenora.

Right, right. Hen went back to peeling potatoes.

"It's okay." Her smile fierce, Lenora jabbed her peeler into a potato and dug out an eye. "I couldn't expect the first nice man I run into here in Smicksburg to be the one. I was just lonely, I think. The right man will come along in Gott's time."

If only Hen could be as sure. "And then there's me. A Plain woman who doesn't like to cook, sew, clean, or bake." She tried to laugh. The sound fell flat and brittle. "The one man I like. . ."

"Is what?" Lenora dropped her peeler on the table. She shook her head. "I don't get it. If my bruder took you on a buggy ride, he must like you, and you must like him. What are you not telling me?"

If he wanted Lenora to know about his plan, he'd tell her. At some point he wouldn't be able to avoid it. Hen couldn't be the one. "You'll have to ask—"

Bleating filled the air. Led by Tulip, goats skipped, hopped, jumped, and butted their way into the tent. Squawking and flapping his wings, Sam followed. Buster and Raindrop immediately rolled to their feet and barked. Tigger yowled and shot from the tent, fleeing to parts unknown.

Lenny, the oldest and biggest goat, butted the bag of potatoes. It fell over. The potatoes rolled all over the ground. Mama goat Nora butted a potato pan. Raw potatoes flew.

Little Lulu pranced on a chair. It fell over and sent her tumbling to the ground. Her brother Bubba careened into a table. It toppled and landed on its side.

The goats had invaded the tent.

CHAPTER 28

"Hen, do something!" Adele flapped her arms. "Get them out of here!"

"The goats got out, the goats got out!" Mena raced into the tent. Her face red, prayer cap askew, the little girl skidded to a stop on dirty, bare feet and gasped for breath. "They want you, Hen!"

"So I noticed." Hen couldn't help herself. She laughed. They were simply doing what goats did, after all. "Come here, you naughty little kids." She scooped up Tulip with one arm and her sister Lily with the other. "That's enough. All of you, stop it right now."

They didn't stop, of course. They were having too much fun. Hen couldn't be too terribly mad at them. They saved her from either lying to her friends or betraying a confidence. "How did they get out?"

"I visit them." Huffing, the little girl fell to her knees in a futile effort to grab Rosie. The half-grown doe eluded her. "They miss you. They're sad. I make them feel better."

Hen tightened her hold on the two squirmy kids. "And?"

"The gate didn't get shut."

"I see." Sweet Mena, the goat whisperer in training, had good intentions. If Hen could get them back into their pen before Dad saw them and before any damage was done, then no harm would've been done. Mena didn't need to be in the doghouse—so to speak—too. "Help Lenora and straighten up while I get these silly critters back where they belong."

"I'm sorry, Schweschder, I'm sorry." Her dirty face pinched with worry, Mena hopped to her feet and ran after Lenny. He sprang up on a table and bleated so loudly they could probably hear him in the wedding kitchen. "I'll be more careful."

"You're forgiven. Stop chasing them and let me get them rounded up."

"Jah, jah, I will."

"Gut luck!" Adele chortled. Lenora was busy shooing goats from atop two of the tables and under another one. Both of Hen's friends were laughing. At least they weren't bored and sleepy anymore. Or thinking about Hen's love life—or lack thereof. "You'll need it."

"Come on, all of you. Now, let's go." Arms tight around her wiggling prisoners, Hen marched from the tent. "Mama Goat, your kids are leaving. You better catch up."

Amazingly, Mama Goat bleated and followed. Where she went, Lenny went.

Hen took a quick right turn to avoid the big tent where the men had set up the tables and chairs. Making a mess in there would not only bring out Dad but also Aunt Ginny—and no one in her right mind would irritate Aunt Ginny on this day of all days.

With a loud *cock-a-doodle-doo* and a flap of his wings, Sam sped ahead of her, like a parade marshal who took his job seriously. Still laughing, Hen followed. "Let's get you all back home before Dat sees you and decides it's time to turn you from dairy goats to meat goats."

Where Lenny went, the other goats were sure to follow. Goats were like that. They played follow the leader. Which could be good or bad, depending on what trouble the leader decided to pursue. Which made goats fun. Why couldn't everyone see that?

Hen cuddled her squirmy captives close to her chest. "You're the best, even at your worst, do you know that?" Tulip bleated, a plaintive sound as if she was sad she'd lost her freedom so quickly. "I know. I'm sorry. You missed me, didn't you? I miss you too." She hugged them tighter. "I miss all of you, my sweet boplin."

Babies. Hen swallowed hard against a sudden ache in her throat. They weren't babies. Not really. And they couldn't take the place of a real baby of her own flesh and blood, the product of a sworn union of death-do-us-part love. "That's okay," she whispered. "I still love you."

"The goat whisperer at work."

Nicholas' voice held suppressed laughter. Hen forced her gaze to meet his. He stood a few yards away, the corral and the goat pen behind him.

A dark sweat ring decorated his straw hat. His faded blue shirt stretched tight across his chest muscles. The folded sleeves revealed big biceps. A day outdoors had given him a fresh tan, making his gray eyes lighter and his teeth whiter in contrast.

Of course, Hen was a mess, as usual, sweaty, covered with goat hair, dirt, and potato juice. Nothing to be done about that. She halted. "They broke out of their pen."

"So I see." Grinning, Nicholas didn't budge from her path—even when Sam squawked and flapped his wings at him. "Lucky for everyone, they'll follow you anywhere."

"I better get them back to their pen before Dat decides to send them packing."

Hen attempted to circle around him. Nicholas moved with her. "Even Buster and Raindrop are following along."

"They're herding the goats for me." A smile snuck up on Hen. Buster rounded up stragglers and urged them forward. What Buster did, Raindrop did. Animals sometimes worked together better than humans. "It's nice to know I can count on them."

Nicholas' smile faded. He ducked his head and kicked a clod of dirt with a dusty boot.

"That wasn't directed at you." Or maybe it was. "Not everything's about you."

A little white lie.

Nicholas raised his head and stared at the startling blue sky decorated with a few lacy clouds that drifted slowly east to west. "How did they get out?"

So Hen wasn't the only one who changed the subject these days.

"Mena didn't get the gate locked." He was so close Hen could smell his earthy scent mixed with soap. "I think they missed me."

Nicholas' response was somewhere between a mumble and a whisper. It sounded suspiciously like *"I know the feeling."*

Hen halted a second time. Confused, Sam strutted around in a circle. The goats bleated. Buster woofed. Of course Raindrop did the same—twice and louder. "What did you say?"

"Nothing. I didn't say anything."

So why did red suffuse his face along with what undoubtedly was guilt?

Hen resumed walking. This time she picked up her pace. "That's not fair."

"I know." He petted Petunia, who baaed her pleasure. "I didn't think our conversation would mean you would stop coming to the clinic."

"Mena came. Luke brought her."

"I'm aware. But the agreement was that both of you would come. You're not living up to the agreement."

"It's unfair for you to insist. You're the one responsible. You know why I can't."

"Just because I don't want to. . .act on. . .my feelings. . ." Nicholas' voice had gone jerky. The red hue on his face deepened. Instead of petting Tulip, he touched Hen's arm. "That doesn't mean we have to avoid seeing each other."

Hen pulled away from his touch. "I can't."

"Why?"

"You figure it out." She wouldn't pour her heart out to a man who'd made his decision. His future didn't include her. It didn't include his Plain faith or family. "Instead of sticking your nose in my business, you should be searching your own heart to make sure you understand fully what it will mean if you leave your faith. You were baptized. You took vows before your church and God."

"I know. I was there."

"Then how can you simply walk away? Is veterinary school worth incurring Gott's displeasure, His wrath?"

"Nobody said it was simple or easy. You of all people should understand that." He sounded hurt. How dare he sound hurt? "I've prayed. I've talked to Gott until my mouth is parched and my throat hurts. I'm not smart enough to understand His plan for me."

"Dying to self isn't that hard to understand. Putting others first. Obedience. Humility. Think of your mamm and dat. Of your schweschdre and brieder. Think of the gut life you had back in Bird-in-Hand. Wouldn't dying to self be worth it if it means living the rest of your life in the company of people you love and who love you?"

He barked a mirthless laugh. "The skillet calling the kettle black?"

"I know." To her everlasting shame, Hen's voice broke. "I know I also want what I want. But I would never leave my faith or my family. I try to work within the allowable space, no matter how small and tight it feels.

"I'm worried for you. Your soul is more important than what I want or need. Gott wants you. Your church and your community want and need you. Your family wants and needs you. Think about that. Stand that up against your want and need to be a vet. See how they stack up."

"You've given this a lot of thought."

She had, but the words weren't hers. She would never have found them hiding in the disarray in her mind and soul. *Denki, Gott.* "I have to get these critters home."

"Home." He let the single syllable float on the air as if hearing the word for the first time and not quite grasping its meaning. "Let me help."

"Nee." She picked up her pace. "Let's go, Sam. Come on Buster, Raindrop, let's get these goats back where they belong."

This time Nicholas didn't try to stop her. Nor did he follow.

Hen breathed a sigh of relief. She hugged her sweet kids close and let the tears seep into their soft fur until they reached the pen. Once they were safely inside, she wiped her face on her sleeve, straightened her shoulders, and headed back. She'd said her piece.

Whatever happened now was up to Nicholas.

CHAPTER 29

It didn't matter how dirty Hen's apron was or how crooked and wrinkled her prayer cap. Nor how cranky, opinionated, and fierce she acted. Nor that she'd skewered Nicholas with her words. Frozen to the spot, he watched her go, her beloved goats, dogs, and rooster joining her in a parade that would be comical if it didn't hurt his heart so much to watch her leave him behind.

Nope. Their conversation and the looks she gave him only served to reignite the argument's smoldering embers. The argument he'd been having with himself morning, noon, and night, since he folded and, against his better judgment, asked her to take an ill-advised buggy ride with him.

He'd stirred up her hopes. Not just wrong but cruel.

He could do nothing about it now, except stay out of her way so he didn't make it worse—like he'd done just now.

What had he been doing before he ran into her? It took a minute for his brain to catch up with his adrenaline-deflated body. To tell Lenora that Grandpa wanted to go home. That was it. He spun around and headed for the smaller tent. It was empty, except for a few peels that had fallen in the grass. Where was she?

"Lenora's in the wedding wagon helping to make the stuffing," Ginny called out as she bustled past the tent en route to who knew where. Despite having greeted Nicholas, Moses, and Lenora at six a.m. earlier in the day, she looked as fresh as the first rose of spring. "Or were you searching for Hen?"

That last part was tinged with what sounded distinctly like hope.

Nicholas scurried to catch up with her. "Why would I be looking for Hen?"

"Suh, you're not fooling a single soul." She cackled as she took a sharp left toward the house. "Neither of you. You've been courting since the night Lucy's filly was born."

"We have not."

"Maybe you didn't know it—you're both denser than a loaf of rye bread—but you were. You are." She clucked and shook her head so hard her prayer cap threatened to slide to one side. "What is it about young people these days? They have to make things so much harder than they have to be."

"I'm not trying to make things harder—"

"Then stop pussyfooting around and put the poor maedel out of her misery." Ginny stomped up the back porch steps. She pivoted and stared down at him through smudged glasses. "I'm too tired to be prim and proper the way a Plain woman not your mamm or your aenti should be, but here it is. Stop being selfish. Stop putting on airs. Stop being a malcontent. Be happy where you are. No one is promised another day, let alone another second. Your blessings are here. Now. All around you. Thank Gott and get on with it."

Her scowl fierce, she brushed her hands together as if ridding them of something particularly disgusting. "I've said my piece. Do with it what you will."

"I never meant to be selfish or conceited or whatever—"

"I know that. The thing is I have to go home after this wedding." Her expression turned pensive. "My mann needs me. My kinner need me. I have a life too."

What did that have to do with his predicament? "What's keeping you here?"

"Hen. Hen's keeping me here. She's lost. Her dat asked me to help her find her way. As soon as I saw the two of you together I knew I wasn't needed. Adam just needs to be patient. Or so I thought. Don't disappoint me now, you hear?"

With that she pivoted once again, opened the screen door, and stepped inside.

"One more thing. Before you do what you're thinking about doing, talk to Adam. He's your bishop while you're in Smicksburg. He can help you."

"He may be the bishop, but he's also her daed."

The door shut, leaving Nicholas with his mouth open and his hand up. Did he have the guts to talk to Adam? Could the bishop separate himself from role as father—a role that was riddled with tension and a certain air of disappointment when it came to his oldest daughter?

The door flew open. "He's on the other side of the wedding kitchen getting the grills ready for tomorrow."

"Denki. I—"

The door closed again.

After a quick stop to ask Lenora to take Moses home, Nicholas went to find Adam. It only took a couple of minutes, no matter how fervently Nicholas wished it weren't so. Hen's father was in the middle of pushing a commercial-sized gas grill across a field that had been mowed earlier in the day. Several other men were at work setting up temporary spotlights powered by a portable gas generator. The smell of fresh cut grass eased the tension in Nicholas' shoulders. God's green earth. He strode toward the spot where Adam had stopped at the end of a row of a dozen grills of equal size.

Adam glanced up before Nicholas could speak. "Nicholas. Gut to see you. Are you volunteering for grill duty?" He lifted his straw hat and wiped his forehead on his sleeve. "We can use all the help we can get. Does Moses have a grill, by any chance?"

"Jah, I mean nee. Jah, I'm happy to help with the grilling, but nee, Moses doesn't have a gas grill. He has a smoker and a griddle, though."

"That's okay. At least three more are on the way." Adam grabbed a wire brush and opened the grill's lid. He applied elbow grease to the racks. "We can use you as a runner. We're starting at four a.m. We hope to be done by nine, when the service begins."

Adam had to be done. He was officiating the service.

"I'll be here."

"It'll be a long day."

"Jah."

"I reckon you didn't come out here to talk about grilling. What's up?"

"You're busy, we can talk another time." Ginny's words echoed in Adam's head. Right now, she'd be shaking her finger at him and chanting *chicken, bawk, bawk, chicken*. "After the wedding. Down the road."

"I'm done for now." Adam laid the brush aside. He gestured toward the house. "It's a gut time for a break. I need a tall glass of cold water. Walk with me."

"Finish what you start." That's what Nicholas' dad always said. Nicholas matched Adam's stride. "It's hard to know where to start."

"The beginning's always a good place."

"I'm overwhelmed with the desire to go to veterinary medicine college."

There. It was out there, hanging in the summer air, thick and foreboding.

"Ah, it's that kind of talk." Adam bypassed the wedding kitchen and the house. Instead, he veered toward the road that would take them away from the clusters of people working, laughing, and talking. "We need a longer walk for that."

"I'm sorry. My timing is terrible, but Ginny—"

"Ginny, jah. My schweschder can be almost as bossy as I am." Chuckling, he pulled down his hat's brim against the setting sun. "So this also has to do with my eldest dochder."

Nicholas spilled it all then. The words, pent up for so long, gushed out. The faster he talked, the slower they walked. Adam was a good listener, occasionally throwing in an "I see" or an "ach" but nothing more.

"That's it, in a nutshell. I know you have a hard line to walk in this, with Hen being your dochder, but I needed to talk to you as a bishop while I'm here."

Adam ambled over to the split-log fence that separated the dirt road from a field of half-grown corn. His expression revealed little as he leaned his upper arms against it, hands clasped.

"My dochder can't be the center of this discussion." All humor had faded from his voice, replaced with a serious yet gentle tone. "When were you baptized?"

"Two years ago."

"Not so long ago that you've forgotten your vows, then."

"Nee, I haven't forgotten."

"It sounds like it. You promised before God and His church that you would support the Ordnung with the Lord's help, faithfully attend the services of the church, help to counsel and work in it, and not to forsake it, whether it leads you to life or to death, did you not?"

The memories welled up. The stillness of family, friends, neighbors, spread out on benches that filled the barn. The bits of dust and hay that floated in the air, lit by shafts of light penetrating the slats of wood. Drops of sweat tickling his temples. "I did."

"Did you not vow that you recognized this to be a Christian order, church, and fellowship under which you now submit yourself?"

"I did," The two syllables were barely a croak. Nicholas cleared his throat and tried again. "I did."

"Did you renounce the world, the devil with all his subtle ways, as well as your own flesh and blood, and desire to serve Jesus Christ alone, who died on the cross for you?"

A shudder went through Nicholas. "Jah. I did. That hasn't changed."

"If you're considering going out into the world, knowing the consequences, then jah, something has changed. You've been changed." Adam swiveled and shot Nicholas a penetrating stare. "Maybe it's spending so much time working for an Englisch veterinarian. Maybe it's reading so many Englisch books. I can't know that. Only you can examine your heart and know where you've gone astray."

"Is it so wrong to want to be a veterinarian?" He sounded like a whiny child who didn't get what he wanted for his birthday. "I care for animals. They're creatures of Gott too."

"You know the answer to that question. Not in itself. It's what the job represents for you. It's more important to you than your faith in Jesus Christ and your commitment to your church. That's what troubles me. You had a chance to explore life outside your community during your rumspringa. You chose to go ahead with baptism. Why?"

"I was trying to do the right thing. I believed everything I studied in the confessions of faith, and I knew that's what my parents, my whole family, my friends, everyone wanted. I thought if I went through it these longings would disappear. But they didn't."

"Did you ever think maybe these seeds of doubt were planted by Satan himself?"

"Wanting to be a vet?" The idea blew through Nicholas like a hot July wind whipped up by a threatening storm. "Wouldn't he choose something far more sinister than wanting to take care of sick animals?"

"He knows you better than yourself. He knows your weak spots. He knows exactly which buttons to push. He seizes intentions that seem good and innocent and twists them into an idol that you begin to worship. You're focused on what you want instead of what God wants for you."

Cold fingers of guilt and remorse trailed down Nicholas' spine. "How do I get rid of this longing, the feeling that it's what I'm meant to be?"

"Stop seeing at it as the be-all, end-all. You're not Gott. He cares for His creatures, which includes animals. You're only His vessel. Nothing more and nothing less. You're like a kid who wants what he can't have. It consumes you." Adam straightened. His hands flew up as his voice gained strength. As if his words rang out for the trees, the birds, and the wildflowers. This was the Adam who delivered messages on Sunday mornings. "The grass is always greener on the other side of the fence. If you don't take the time to truly see the blessing of the green grass in your own backyard.

"Start thinking about it from the perspective of what you *can* do, what *is* allowed, the blessing you *can* be to the people you love and who love you. Contentment is learned. It's not always easy, but it's always possible. Believe me. I know."

The words stung, yet they rang with a truth that couldn't be denied. Adam had lost his wife and a baby son. Yet he'd learned to accept as God's will his role as a widower raising seven children without his beloved soulmate. And as a bishop chosen by God to serve his Gmay.

"I want to make clear that I would tell you exactly the same thing if this discussion didn't have an impact on my dochder." His voice softened to a near whisper. "I admit I've committed the sin of worrying about her future. I've tried so hard to do right by her. Not having my fraa to guide me is no excuse for sometimes being too harsh. I pray Gott forgives me if I've done wrong by her and for doubting Him when it comes to Henrietta. He made her who she is. He has a plan for her, as much as it pains me sometimes."

"Understood." Nicholas shifted from one foot to the other. He craned his neck. This was an admission best reserved for a father-daughter talk—one likely to never happen. "You've given me a lot to think about."

"Think hard. Ask yourself what series of events had to occur for you to end up in Smicksburg, working for a vet, taking care of animals on my farm, and meeting likely the only Plain woman in the state as smitten by animals as you are? A woman who is determined to make her poor father mad with her constant begging to expand our goat herd, open a store in town, and who brings home a puppy—with your encouragement—that is yet another mouth to feed in her menagerie?"

"You think all of this is Gott's plan?"

"I'm not smart enough to know Gott's plan. None of us are. I'm just asking you to study scripture, starting with Romans 12:2. To think, to contemplate, to pray, before you make a decision that will change not only your life but the lives of everyone who loves you and your very soul."

As hard as it was to accept, it was good advice. "Denki."

"No need to thank me. Whatever happens is between Gott and you." Adam straightened. "It's almost dark. Someone is surely wondering where I am. You too, I reckon. I have a really powerful thirst now."

"I'm sorry. This wasn't the best time to buttonhole you."

"Nee, it was a conversation that couldn't wait. It needed to be had."

"I know what the right thing to do is." Nicholas forced himself to meet the bishop's gaze. "It's as if I needed someone else to say it. To convince me. That's crazy."

"That's our sin nature, my friend." Adam clapped Nicholas on the back. "I'll pray for you. You'll need it."

"I'll take your words to heart. I promise."

He laughed. "I was referring to Henrietta."

"I haven't made any—"

"Don't tell me. I'm her daed. I don't want to know what you decide. After all, courting is private."

His hopeful tone suggested he and his sister Ginny were certain the need for matchmaking was at an end.

If only Nicholas could be as certain.

CHAPTER 30

Something wet and rough grazed Hen's cheek. Smelly dog breath filled her nose. She opened her eyes. Raindrop woofed and licked Hen's chin. "Okay, okay, I'm awake."

Awake, but not awake. The dream refused to fade. She closed her eyes again, seeing herself propped up in her bed, her long hair loose around her shoulders. She held a beautiful baby girl in her arms. Joy filled her. *"You're so sweet, so perfect. Ten fingers. Ten toes. Denki, Gott, denki."* The words lingered in the air like a lullaby sang hundreds of thousands of times through the ages. *"You look like your dat."*

The baby stared up at her, gray eyes full of wonder. Her heart ready to burst, Hen smoothed a tuft of chestnut hair. It sprang back up.

"What will you name her?" Hen glanced up. Her mother stood at the foot of the bed. "I like Joy, don't you?"

She hadn't aged. Hen shook her head, as if she could clear her vision. "Mamm? Mamm, you're here. How?"

Bleating overpowered her mother's response. Startled, Hen glanced down. In her arms she held a baby goat. "Nee, nee, nee."

She ripped her gaze from the squirmy goat. Mom was gone.

Barking replaced the bleating. Hen opened her eyes and sat up. Raindrop. Only Raindrop shared her narrow bunk bed. She woofed more softly and licked Hen's cheek.

Hen wrapped her in a quick hug and let go. "Denki for waking me up."

Even if it meant letting go of her mother. It was only a dream. Nothing more than a dream until they came face-to-face in heaven—God willing.

Still, a sense of wonder buoyed Hen's spirits. For a few seconds she'd held a baby—Nicholas' baby—in her arms. Why had the baby turned into a goat?

It didn't take much smarts to figure that out. She put her dreams ahead of having a family of her own. Just as Nicholas was putting his dreams ahead of faith and family.

The day hadn't even started, and Hen's head already hurt.

"Woof, woof." Her tail wagging, Raindrop hopped from the bed, zipped across the room, slid to a stop at the door, whirled, and barked.

"I know, I know. It's Ruby's time, not mine. I'm coming. I'm right behind you. I promise."

The dog took her at her word, apparently, and disappeared down the hall. Hen heaved a breath and glanced around the room. Ruby's bed was empty. Her big day had arrived. Hen rubbed sleep from her eyes. They burned. She stretched and regretted it. Her shoulders and arms still ached from the previous day's preparations that had kept her and everyone else up too late. Hen grasped the windup alarm clock on the end table next to her bed. Five a.m. She'd overslept.

Why hadn't Ruby awakened her? Hen threw back the sheet and sprang from the bed.

She took the dark teal dress she'd made—under Aunt Ginny's supervision—from the hook. Her uneven hem and dropped stitches didn't show much. It didn't matter. Everyone would be watching Ruby and Peter. It took two minutes for Hen to dress, but bundling her hair on top of her head in a neat bun was a different story. Another task other women seemed to do naturally well was a daily battle for her.

If Nicholas left, where would that leave Hen? Would she meet someone else? Or was this God's plan to show her that she did have faith? A strong faith? She would never leave her church, her community, or her family. Even if it meant spending her life as an aunt, sister, and daughter, but never a wife and mother.

Maybe her love of animals was meant to be enough.

This day wasn't about her or Nicholas. It belonged to Ruby, who had her priorities straight. Ruby, who followed the rules. Ruby, who carried the load when their mother died and Hen abdicated, putting her wishes and needs ahead of her family's.

Hot, mournful shame cloaked Hen. No wonder God didn't think she was ready for a true relationship and marriage. Starting tomorrow, Hen would be in charge of the Miller household. It was time to accept that responsibility and figure out how to live with it.

Hen dressed in a rush and went in search of her sister. The kitchen was empty, which wasn't surprising. Breakfast dishes had been washed and left on the counter to dry. The smell of coffee and bacon still hung in the air. Food didn't appeal to Hen, but she grabbed an oversized mug and filled it with coffee, a liberal dose of milk, and a tablespoon of sugar. A person needed to be fortified to survive a wedding celebration.

The beehive of activity would be in the wedding cook kitchen. Carrying her mug, Hen padded outside where the predawn dusk still hung over the farm. Tigger hopped from one of the chairs and met her at the top of the porch steps illuminated by solar panel–driven lights. Kerosene lanterns lit the path to the kitchen trailer. Beyond it, smoke curled from a dozen or more gas grills surrounded by men sipping from coffee travel mugs. Their conversation and laughter carried on a light breeze. The sound of community and family.

Unexpected tears gathered in Hen's eyes. A person should never take for granted moments like this. Not one person was promised another day, not even another moment, of these family times. Mom knew that. She had only three weeks to snuggle baby Stephen. Only three weeks to sing off-key lullabies to him when he had a tummy ache deep in the night. Only three weeks to smell the sweet scent of his hair, touch the soft skin on his tiny belly, and count his miniature toes. Then God had taken him home again.

Hen inhaled fresh air not yet warmed by the sun. She straightened her prayer cap and wiped her face. *Thy will be done. Come what may.*

An enormous plastic container filled with seasoned, raw chicken pieces in her arms, Aunt Ginny descended the trailer steps. "There you are. Can you take this to your dat? I need to get back to the mashed potatoes."

"Why didn't you wake me?" Hen exchanged her mug for the container. Aunt Ginny sipped and murmured appreciatively. Hen laughed. "You're welcome. My alarm didn't go off."

"Ruby said you tossed and turned and mumbled in your sleep all night. She turned the alarm off." Aunt Ginny headed back up the steps to the trailer. "She thought you needed to sleep a few more minutes. I was about to come get you."

"She must not have slept either, then. Where is she?"

"She was too excited. She's running on adrenaline and caffeine, I expect. She's inside putting the finishing touches on the cake she and Peter decorated."

Given Aunt Ginny's red cheeks, bright eyes, and breathless words, it seemed likely she'd already consumed her share of coffee. Hen needed her ability to juggle a dozen details at any given moment. "I reckon Dat's just as excited. His first dochder to marry. And him, getting to perform the ceremony."

"You'll see when you deliver that chicken." Aunt Ginny made shooing motions. "Go on, git. Then you can help with the table centerpieces and decorating the *eck*."

Good idea. Decorating Peter and Ruby's corner table would give Hen the opportunity to make sure Ruby wasn't trying to fix her up by seating her across from one of Peter's bachelor friends. The tradition of matching up couples next to the newlyweds' table should end when the person in question passed the twenty-two-year mark. There would be a new addition to the single men at the table—Nicholas. Would he avoid it? Avoid her? Would his choice be a message to her? Hen shook her head. *Stop. Just stop.* Obsessing didn't help one whit.

The closer Hen came to the area cordoned off for the gas grills, the more the mouthwatering aroma of grilling chicken filled her nose. Talking and laughing, fathers and sons worked side by side turning out pound after pound of grilled chicken. Her stomach rumbled. Hen ignored it. She let her gaze roam over the men, most of whom she'd known her whole life. This ritual happened over and over again each year at Plain weddings. The good times began long before the wedding itself. Nicholas stood next to the Planks' grill, tongs in one hand, a travel mug in the other. Hen froze. What was he doing here?

Helping, of course. He had every right to join in. He was smiling and nodding his head at something one of the other men was saying. How could he be so happy, knowing he planned to walk away from all this? English folks catered their wedding receptions, didn't they?

She'd said her piece. How he chose to live his life was in God's hands. Hen resumed her mission; only this time, she scurried toward her dad's grill. He manhandled perfectly golden-brown chicken quarters dripping with juice from his grill to a foil-lined pan. The scents of chili powder, cumin, onion powder, and garlic powder mingled in the air, teasing her nose and her taste buds. She waited until he finished to speak. "Aenti Ginny sent me with more—she didn't want you to run out."

His glasses splattered with grease, Dad glanced up then went back to his work. "Tell her to keep them coming." Nothing in his tone to suggest this day was any different from any other. "I want to be done by nine o'clock."

"You'll be done in plenty of time to prepare for the service." Hen handed him the bucket. "Aenti Ginny says everything is going like clockwork, but I better get back."

Before Nicholas noticed her. Not that he would make a scene in front of her dad. Surely he wouldn't do that.

"Only because she planned everything down to the last detail from the time the banns were announced." Dad plucked a plump chicken breast from the bucket and laid it on the grill. It sizzled, a lovely sound. "That's the advantage of doing things the right way and not going off half cocked."

There it was. That finely veiled criticism. Hen bit back a retort. She picked up the empty container. "Do you need anything else? More kaffi? Foil? Clean washrags?"

"Nee."

She turned to go.

"Henrietta."

Not now, Dat, please not now. She paused, turned back. "Jah."

"Tomorrow you'll be in charge of the cleanup."

"I know."

"Your aenti is headed back home the day after. Your onkel needs her there."

Hen's heart squeezed. Her next breath took a concerted effort. She exhaled. "I'll miss her, but the kossins probably miss her more. They need her too."

"Jah, they do." Dad laid down his tongs. He rolled up his left sleeve with methodical care. "I had a long conversation with Nicholas yesterday."

Hen glanced toward the man in question. He'd turned with his back to her. He was too far away to hear their conversation. Even so, she had no desire to discuss this topic with her father now or ever.

"What we talked about was just between him and me. But I suspect you know most of it." Dad picked up his insulated coffee mug, but he didn't drink from it. "It's not my place to meddle in courting, but I hought it only right that you should know that the topic came up."

He was talking to her adult to adult. Maybe she wasn't the only one attempting to turn over a new leaf. "I appreciate that."

Hen started to back away then stopped. "I know we can't take on another herd of goats right now. I've stared at the numbers until I'm seeing double. To buy them, build the new shed, and the extra feed, it's not feasible—for now."

"I'm glad you were able to study your plan objectively and come to your own decision. I know it's not the one you wanted. That's a sign that you're maturing." His tone somber, he laid one big hand over his heart. "I know I've been hard on you, but it's because I want what's best for you. I don't deny you have a gut head for business. I admit I haven't allowed for that. I want you to be like your mamm. She loved being a fraa and a mudder. That's what all Plain women are expected to be. That doesn't mean you can't also have a business, at least until you have your own kinner. Or even with their help one day. When the right man presents himself."

"That's my hope too." Tears blurred Hen's vision. She took a surreptitious swipe at her eyes. *Not now. Not now.* "But it has to be the right man, doesn't it?"

"It does." Dad laid his mug aside and moved closer. "It has to be a man who is sure of his faith, who will put faith, community, and family before his own desires."

Nicholas had told her dad about his plans. Hen gripped her hands together. Had Dad tried to convince Nicholas not to break his baptismal vows? Had he been successful? It wasn't her place to ask. "Anyone who's been through baptism classes knows this to be the case."

His expression solemn, Dad stared down at her. No doubt it was the district's bishop who spoke to her in this moment, not her father. "Is that why you've chosen to let go of your plans for the Angora goats?"

"Jah. And because you are my daed, and you know better than I do what's best."

"Are you trying to butter me up?" He smiled—a small smile—but still a smile. "Don't answer that. God has a plan for you, Dochder."

Hen couldn't barf on her dad's boots the way she'd promised to barf on Aunt Ginny's sneakers if she said those words. "Sometimes I wonder if that's true," she blurted. Her hand went to her mouth. How could she have said this aloud to a man doing double duty in her life? She let it drop. "How could He let Mamm die of something so minor? How could He tear Stephen from her arms? I can't help but still feel angry about it. He could've stopped it. Why didn't He?"

"Ach, kind, do you think you're the only one who's ever felt that way?" Dad loomed over her, his eyes red from lack of sleep and smoke from the grill. And maybe something else. "Do you think it was easy for me to believe after your bopli bruder died? After your mamm died? Do you think I didn't want to shake my fist and scream at the heavens?"

"Did you shake your fist and scream?"

"Nee, I had you and the rest of my kinner to think of. There are things we can't understand, will never understand. Gott has given me many blessings. Who am I to curse Him when He allows tragedy to strike in this fallen world? That doesn't mean I like it. But I know I'm stronger than I ever was, having lived this life. These trials make me a better bishop. They make you a better person. You have an enormous heart for people who are hurting. You love with a fierceness that can only come from having lost. You have a compassion I envy—Gott help me."

His voice caught. He turned back to the grill. "The chicken is burning."

In those few moments her father had revealed more of himself to her than he'd done in the full sum of her life. He had trusted her with his grief. She could trust him to guide her. She might never understand Gott. She wasn't meant to. But if Dad could rely on Him, so could she. "No matter how hard I find it to believe, I've never given up on my faith. I will never leave it. Or my community or my family. I will persevere."

"I'm glad to hear that." The lines around Dad's eyes and mouth softened. His Adam's apple bobbed. "As your bishop but also as your daed. My heart is strong, but I'd rather not test it again. Not so soon."

"Me neither," Hen whispered. "I'm sorry I've been a trial to you."

"It's all right. It helps me to hone my skills for dealing with other members of the district who have these same sorts of issues." He deftly turned over chicken quarters, breasts, legs, thighs, and wings. They sizzled. Smoke rose. The aroma made Hen's mouth water. Dad smiled. A true, sunny smile. "Besides, I think your life is about to change in ways you can't imagine. You'll see. I have faith."

Dad swiveled and winked at her. Hen's mouth flopped open. Flustered, she managed to nod in return. "Gut to know. What—"

"You'll see. Gott's plan unfolds in His time. Not ours."

He handed her the empty bucket. "Put the handle over your arm so you can carry in a pan of the grilled pieces. Then bring me some more ready to grill."

She did as he said. "Denki, Dat."

"Don't thank me. Thank Gott."

CHAPTER 31

Neither a numb behind, a rumbling stomach, or an aching back dimmed the anticipation. Hen squeezed Ruby's hand. Heaving a breath, her sister squeezed back. She'd slid onto the bench occupied by their cousin Charlotte; Aunt Ginny, who had Mena on her lap; and Hen after joining Peter for half an hour outside in a meeting with the deacon and minister to receive their admonitions and blessings. The three-hour service was almost over. Only the five minutes they'd all been waiting for remained.

Dad, also known as the bishop, motioned for them to come forward. Ruby stood first. Hen and Ruby's best friend Nina, serving as her attendants, followed. Peter stood to Dad's left with his two younger brothers as his attendants. His face was scarlet. It matched his bride-to-be's. Hen sneaked a glance at the crowd. Friends and family from at least ten districts, some from as far away as Missouri and Colorado, filled the benches. The doors were open to allow for the overflow seating. Her gaze stopped midway back. Nicholas shared a bench with Moses, Micah, Uncle Joel, and Xavier, his and Aunt Ginny's youngest. Moses' bearded chin rested on his chest. His snoring carried in the respectful silence.

To Nicholas' credit, he didn't smile at the snores. In fact, he didn't seem to notice them at all. What was he thinking about? Would it prick his conscience at all as the ceremony was performed uniting Ruby and Peter in holy matrimony? That he would never take those vows with a Plain woman if he carried out his plan? Did he think of what he would miss, or was he focused on how wonderful his life would be when he was unfettered by his district's Ordnung?

Whatever his thoughts, they didn't show on his face. Henrietta forced her own gaze back to Dat. She gritted her teeth. For Ruby's sake, she had to keep it together. Willing a neutral expression, she focused on her father as he motioned for Ruby and Peter to face him.

Everyone knew the words that would come next. They'd heard them at dozens and dozens of weddings over the years. Still, every time Hen had to tame tears that threatened.

"Do you, Ruby Miller, promise that should he be afflicted with bodily weakness, sickness, or some similar circumstance, that you will care for him as is fitting a Christian fraa?"

Ruby's firm "jah" likely could be heard in the last row beyond the barn doors. Peter's was equally assured.

"Do you solemnly promise, with one another that you will love and be patient with each other, and shall not separate from each other until the dear God shall part you from one another through death?"

Again their responses rang out. A few more seconds and it was over. Now married, Peter returned to his seat, and Hen followed Ruby to hers. So simple. No fuss, no muss, as Aunt Ginny liked to say.

Dad prayed for the newly married couple. Then he, the deacon, and the minister offered their blessings. Ruby grasped Hen's hand so hard, her fingers hurt, but she didn't mind. "Congratulations, Schweschder," Hen whispered. "You did it."

"Denki." Ruby's eyes shimmered with unshed tears. She ducked her head, but not before Hen saw her tremulous smile. "I thought I would faint."

Finally, they knelt for the concluding prayer. Would Dad be embarrassed if Hen yelled "hallelujah"? In all likelihood. She had to be satisfied with Mena's loud "I'm so glad that's over. Can we have cake now?"

Aunt Ginny, who looked as if she agreed with her niece, nudged Mena toward the flow of people leaving the barn. "Go, run off some of that energy, wiggle worm. Then go to the dishwashers' tent. You can help dry dishes."

"And eat cake?"

"Eventually." Aunt Ginny chuckled. "But not before your schweschder Ruby and her mann, Peter, get theirs."

Apparently satisfied, Mena wove her way through the crowd and disappeared from sight. Hen and Nina escorted Ruby from the barn at a more sedate pace. Peter joined up with them, his brothers trailing behind him.

"Are you ready to go to the eck, or do you need to make a stop first?" A polite way of asking if she needed to visit the bathroom. Once Ruby was seated, the attendants were done with their duties. Hen would check with Aunt Ginny to see where she was needed next. She'd draw the duty of floating helper—going where she was needed. "Congratulations to you both, by the way."

Ruby responded with a tight hug. "You're next," she murmured. "I know it in my heart."

Maybe. "Gott's will be done."

A standard response, surely, but a person had to learn to do more than parrot it.

"I'll take care of her." With a teary-eyed smile, Nina linked arms with Ruby. "I think there's someone waiting to talk to you."

Puzzled, Hen surveyed the steady flow of wedding guests spreading across the yard, headed for tables and chairs under the big tent or into the house to help with chores. Nicholas stood next to the table where Moses sat, his chin propped up on the palms of his hands like a man in a deep funk.

Nicholas had spoken to her father after she'd chewed him out. Maybe something Dad had said had softened his heart or changed his mind. Or maybe God had worked a change in him.

If it could happen to her, it could happen to him.

"I better see if they have enough servers. I see Aenti Ginny in the tent." Her aunt was already moving toward the house. She was light on her feet when she wanted to be.

"You're not going to sit at the eck?" Ruby called after her. "Should we save you a seat?"

"Nee, Aenti Ginny has work for me to do."

After she tested the waters with Nicholas. Hen spied the table filled with water pitchers to be used for refills by the servers currently picking up their first load of serving dishes from the helpers who passed them out from the kitchen. She grabbed a pitcher and marched over to Nicholas' table.

"*Guder mariye.*" She picked up a glass and filled it. "I guess I should say *guder nammidaag.*"

"Or guder daag." His expression inscrutable, Nicholas accepted the glass she offered. What was he thinking? At least he didn't run away. "*Wie bischt?*"

So now they would make polite talk like people who barely knew each other. "*Ich bin gut.* Wie bischt?"

"Gut, gut."

"You're gut. She's gut. Everybody's gut. Now can you two stop yammering so you can bring me some food?" Moses tugged the glass from Nicholas' hand. Water slopped on his pants. He gulped down what remained and burped. "My throat was parched, and I'm starving. That service went on forever."

Sometimes older folks lost the filter that kept them from saying what everyone else was thinking. Hen chuckled. Nicholas' expression lightened. He laughed. Moses scowled. "You think that's funny. You try having a bad back, sore knees, and a bladder the size of a peanut."

"It's hard, I'm sure." Avoiding Nicholas' gaze, which was sure to make her laugh again, Hen pressed her lips together to keep another giggle from burbling up. She poured more water for both of them. "The food is on its way, I promise."

"They may be serving inside first." Nicholas cocked his head toward the house. "Maybe we can intercept someone who can bring food to a starving elder."

Servers had been assigned to bring serving bowls to the outside tables at the same time that others served inside. Hen opened her mouth to say so. Nicholas shook his head. Ah. "Let's see what we can do."

"We'll be right back." Nicholas squeezed his grandfather's shoulder. "Stay right here. Don't go anywhere."

"I'm not one of the kinner, always running off." His tone sour, Moses grunted. "Next you'll be telling me I can't drive a buggy on my own. Who do you think you are? My dat?"

"Nee, nee. I just don't want your food to get cold while I search for you." Nicholas' soothing, patient tone belied the fact that Moses was in fact guilty of wandering off and being unable to find his way home, according to Lenora, who was in charge of finding him when Nicholas was working. He wasn't supposed to drive the buggy anymore either, for the same reason. "I'll be right back."

Hen settled the pitcher on the table in case Moses wanted more and headed toward the house.

"Let's take the long way around." Nicholas' touched her arm so briefly she couldn't be sure he'd actually done it. "Less traffic."

So to speak. She did as he suggested. Not that there weren't people everywhere at the moment. "Your daadi is in rare form today."

"Today and every day, but that's not what I want to talk about." Nicholas' voice dropped to just above a whisper. "I wanted to say I'm sorry."

"Sorry for what?" Hen marched past the house. The vegetable garden would be a good place for whatever Nicholas had to say. If anyone saw them, she was simply picking a few tomatoes for the green salad. "You are who you are. You can't change that."

Hen reached the end of the house. She turned the corner. Micah and Adele faced each other next to tomato plants that sprawled against stakes designed to keep them upright over a bed of hay. Her brother had his hand on her best friend's shoulder. If their faces were any closer together, their noses would touch. They glanced up at the same time. And immediately pulled apart.

"Ach, sorry. I'm so sorry." Hen tried to backtrack. She stepped on Nicholas' boot and stumbled. "Turn around."

"Nee, nee." Adele pushed away from Micah. She whirled and trotted toward the house. "I was just picking some more tomatoes for the green salad."

"Jah, she was." Micah followed her. "I was. . . I came out to. . .help."

Neither one of them had a single tomato in their hands. It didn't seem right to mention that. Why hadn't Adele told Hen? Hen told her everything. "I was after tomatoes myself."

"Oh, gut, gut, I saw several ripe ones." Adele grabbed the screen door. "I'll tell Lenora. She's in charge of making more green salads. Ginny's afraid we underestimated. . ."

Her voice trailed away as the screen door closed behind her. Leaving Micah on the other side.

He grabbed it and let himself in.

Nicholas trailed after Hen. "That was awkward."

"I can't wait to chew Adele out. She hasn't breathed a word to me." The loving gaze between the two attested to one central fact. This had been going on for a while. They were in love. It was written in big, cursive letters across their foreheads. "In fact, she said she was afraid to trust her instincts, leading me to believe she's been avoiding courting my bruder or anyone else."

"Maybe this was the first time it got. . .serious." Nicholas followed Hen to the garden's edge. "Or it would've been if you hadn't so rudely interrupted."

"I wasn't expecting anyone to be in the garden. Plus you didn't see the way they stared at each other."

"You think you're the only one with courting on your mind at a wedding?"

"I don't have courting on my mind."

"If you say so. We were talking about people changing. Surely you don't believe a person can't change." He squatted next to the patch where Hen bent over and picked a plump tomato from a massive plant weighed down with fruit in various stages of ripening. It was so big the stakes could barely support it. "People are constantly growing and learning and becoming more mature. It's called growing up."

He was right, of course. Hen was changing. Growing, growing up, putting aside childish pursuits. Her heart twinged. Her goat business was an adult proposition. A way to earn money to support her family. If a man led it, her dad's perspective would be different. She would do as her father instructed her, because that's what good daughters did, but not because she was wrong. Obedience. One of the pillars of their faith, along with humility. "Jah, a person can change. I'm working on changing. But you haven't told me you wish to change. Just the opposite."

"I had a talk with your daed last night. He gave me much food for thought."

"He mentioned that—not what was said. He wouldn't violate a confidence." Hen rushed to clarify as she laid another tomato in the grass. "He said to be open to compromises. To seek new ways to think about what I want from life."

"That's what I've been doing." Nicholas took a tomato from her pile. He bit into it. Juice and seeds dribbled down his chin. "Hmmm. So gut fresh off the plant. Sweeter than an apple. A fruit masquerading as a vegetable. Things aren't always what they seem if we take the time to really examine them."

"That is true." Hen grasped the ends of her apron and turned it into a makeshift bowl she could hold with one hand. She placed the tomatoes into it and rose to her feet. "I know you aren't who I first thought you were."

Nicholas held out the tomato. Hen took a bite. Her taste buds applauded the tangy juice and pulp. He grinned. "I thought you were a bossy, know-it-all Plain woman who didn't know her place."

"And I thought you were a bossy, know-it-all Plain man too big for your britches." Hen managed to suppress a smile. He couldn't sweet-talk her after playing with her heart on their one and only buggy ride. "A wolf in the chicken coop."

"I guess we were both right about the bossy, know-it-all part, but I've learned you have a heart bigger than any woman I've ever known." Nicholas touched her cheek. "You're kind. You love people and animals. You are passionate about what you believe. You're someone I'd like to know better."

"What are you saying?" Hen's breath caught in her throat. Her heart pumped so loudly Nicholas must have heard it. "Are you saying you're not leaving to go to veterinary college?"

"I'm saying don't give up on me." His hand dropped, but she could still feel his touch. It ran down her cheek to her neck and across her collarbone. "I'm saying I'm trying to figure it out. Gott willing, Daadi will be with us for a long time yet. Even if Gott takes him home soon, I find I've come to care for Smicksburg and the patients we have at the clinic. I care about their owners too. I know Gott has a plan for me. I think I was too quick to make my own plan without waiting to see what He has for me."

"But you're not sure?"

"Don't you see? I'm making progress."

Hen stepped back. "I see. But I can't hang my heart on someone who isn't a sure thing."

"You won't go with me on another buggy ride tonight after the festivities are over?"

"Come see me when you're sure."

She brushed past him and trudged toward the house.

"Hen."

Every muscle in her body wanted to turn back. Hen kept walking forward. It was the only direction that made sense.

CHAPTER 32

Weddings were usually more fun. Nicholas pushed mashed potatoes around his plate, mixing them with noodles and the last of his stuffing. His appetite had nose-dived after his not-an-argument talk with Hen. Couldn't she see he'd taken her father's words to heart? He intended to reevaluate his faith, work on it, and shift his priorities. Letting go of dreams was hard work. Hen of all people should understand that. He dropped his fork on his plate and picked up his water glass.

"Why the sourpuss face?" Moses wiped up the last of the gravy on his plate with a roll. He stuffed it in his mouth and chewed loudly. "Your schweschder is a gut cook, but she can't do better than this."

"The food is gut." Nicholas forced a smile. Moses remembered for the moment who Lenora was and that she was doing the cooking. They could count that as a blessing. They were also fortunate their grandfather's appetite hadn't been affected by the medication the neurologist prescribed to slow the inevitable march of his disease. "It's been a long day, that's all. Let me know when you're ready to head home."

"Not before dessert. I saw banana cream pie. I'm not missing that." Moses finished off the last bite of his corn. "Why didn't you sit at the eck? Young single man like you should be sitting across from a girl right now. A wedding is the perfect place to find a girl to court. They're all moony eyed after the ceremony."

Because Moses might wander off if left unsupervised. Because Nicholas wasn't in any position to court. Because if he were, Hen would be the only woman he wanted to court, and she'd shut him down quicker than he could say buggy ride. "There will be more weddings later."

"Hey, Bruder, there you are." Lenora threaded her way around the tables in the crowded tent. When she reached theirs, she slipped into the empty chair closest to Nicholas. She leaned in. "Do you mind taking Daadi home without me?"

"I was planning on it. I figured you'd still have a ton of dishes to wash. Who'll give you a ride home?"

"I finished my shift dishwashing." She sounded breathless. His sister's eyes sparkled. Her cheeks were pink. The smile that had been missing for the past few months was on display. "Don't worry about the ride. I think Nina and Ruby put their heads together. They seated me across from—"

"Nee, never mind." Nicholas had formed the question before the obvious answer smacked him between the eyes. Nina and Ruby had been matchmaking. Lenora had a buggy ride on her itinerary for later in the day. "I'm such a dolt. Say no more. Be careful."

"Are you sure?"

"Positive. Have fun."

"Denki." She stood. "I think I will."

Who would it be? None of his business. As her big brother, he'd like to think he should make sure the man was suitable, but it didn't work that way.

"You've got a sourpuss face if I've ever seen one." Moses stacked his dishes and peered around the tent as if expecting someone to appear and cart them away. "I told you that you should've been sitting at the eck like your sister. She's a smart maedel. You're a goose."

A goose. "I'm not ready for courting right now."

"You're twenty-three. You don't get ready soon, you'll be an old bachelor, cooking and cleaning for yourself." Grandpa snorted. "Shove those medicine textbooks under your bed and get yourself a girlfriend before it's too late."

How did Grandpa know about the textbooks? "It's not that simple."

"More than simple. You've been baptized. You're of age. You've had a gut job. The only thing missing is a fraa." Grandpa hailed a server carrying a tray loaded with saucers of chocolate cake with vanilla frosting. "One for me and two for my kinnskind, the sourpuss. We need to sweeten him up so he can get himself a fraa."

Fortunately the woman carrying the tray appeared to be well into midlife. She wouldn't be embarrassed by an old man's blather. Nicholas finished his cake first and waited while Grandpa scraped his plate with his fork. It appeared he might lick it clean, but at the last minute he swerved and stacked it on Nicholas'.

"Come on, sourpuss, let's go home. I'm stuffed to the brim and ready for a nap."

Nicholas had no problem with this plan. He could barely keep his eyes open on the ride home. Daisy met him at the front porch—or rather met Grandpa. The dog followed him into the house and disappeared into Grandpa's bedroom.

Good ideas shouldn't be ignored. In his bedroom, Nicholas shucked off his boots, hung up his hat, and sprawled on the bed. Then he tossed and turned for ten minutes. Every time he closed his eyes he pictured Hen's face rosy with summer heat and the excitement of her sister's wedding.

Walking Jack. Cheering on Lucy and her foal. Risking scratches from the cats. Pied piper. Goat whisperer. Adam's words spun in Nicholas' head. Vows. He took the baptism vows. He meant them.

Ruby and Peter had taken another set of vows earlier in the day. Nicholas wanted to take those vows too. In sickness and health for the rest of his days. And hers.

He sat up and reached for the stack of books on the side table. One by one he slid them under his bed. He still had plenty to learn from the textbooks but not so he could attend college. Instead he would educate himself so he could be the best vet assistant in the state.

Under all those books was the one he needed most. Moses' Bible. Nicholas adjusted his pillow so he could lean against the headboard. Adam's words ringing in his head, he opened the Bible to Romans chapter 12. *"And be not conformed to this world: but be ye transformed by the renewing of your mind, that ye may prove what is that good, and acceptable, and perfect, will of God."*

Be not conformed to the world. Be transformed by the renewing of his mind. What did that mean? Time to find out.

For his sake. And for Hen's.

CHAPTER 33

Anything to "accidentally" run into Hen. Even if that meant a thirty-minute van drive to Mack Park on the Indiana County Fairgrounds for the Fourth of July Star Spangled Celebration. Nicholas yawned and stretched—as much as he dared in a van stuffed to the legal limit with Lenora, himself, and nine members of the Troyer family.

Hen had been faithful about her volunteer duties at the clinic in the weeks since their conversation at Ruby's wedding. However, she'd studiously avoided any personal conversation. Anytime Nicholas tried to broach the subject of a buggy ride, she'd scurried away in search of another task to accomplish.

As well she should. But how could he tell her he spent time before bed each night, reading from his grandfather's family Bible, studying scripture, and praying instead of scouring the mountain of veterinary medicine books that called his name. He asked God to forgive him for his hubris and show him His plan, not only for Nicholas but for Hen and for the two of them together—if such a plan existed.

"We're here. They said there'd be arts and crafts, bouncy houses, and sack races for the kinner; vendors; and a cornhole tournament." Her eyes wide, Lenora leaned past Nicholas. "I hope they have funnel cakes, cotton candy, and caramel apples. And those fried pickles you like."

"You're thinking of a county fair. This is a Fourth of July celebration." Nicholas laughed. His sister was more excited than a child on her first trip to an amusement park. "The flyer said food trucks will sell hamburgers, hot dogs, and fries. All-American food. There was also mention of an apple pie eating contest."

"That would be perfect for you. I don't know anyone who can eat more pie than you can." Lenora waggled her finger at him. "But maybe you should find Hen first and enter the sack races with her."

A Plain man and woman, hip to hip, arms around each other's waists, hopping around with their legs in burlap sacks in front of a crowd—that would go over big with the elders. Nicholas snorted. "You're narrisch."

"It's all in fun."

"I'll let you explain that to the bishop."

"On second thought, maybe we should stick to the cornhole tournament." Lenora shoved the van door open and scrambled out. "Come on, come on. Time's a-wastin'."

Nicholas clambered after her. She'd been in a good mood since Ruby's wedding, but she hadn't let out even a peep about the buggy ride. He'd peeked out the window at the sound of people talking a few times since then, but he couldn't tell who was in the buggy. Not his business, but curiosity threatened to get the better of him.

A day of respite from caring for Grandpa likely added to Lenora's carefree attitude. Grandpa's coworker from the days when he owned his own construction company had jumped at the chance to spend the day with his best friend—even though Grandpa wasn't convinced at first he knew who Abel Glick was.

Nicholas needed this day too. He needed to find Hen and convince her he'd turned the corner and found his way back home—this home. He wasn't going anywhere. "I'm coming. They won't run out of hot dogs and fries, I promise."

A steady stream of chattering English and Plain folks trying to corral excited children traipsed from their cars to the fairgrounds. The mingled scents of barbecue, burgers, kettle corn, and other treats greeted Nicholas before he neared the food trucks. Red, white, and blue bunting and U.S. flags in all sizes decorated every building, booth, pavilion, and tent. Music blared. The song sounded like one he'd heard on the radio station at work. Dr. McDonald liked what he called "oldy-moldy rock n' roll."

"Come on, slowpoke, I want to hit the food trucks first. I'm starving." Despite having shorter legs, Lenora charged ahead by several strides. "Adele and the others are supposed to meet me there at twelve thirty."

"Then go. If all else fails, we'll find each other outside the arena gates for the fireworks." Unless Lenora was meeting her special friend. "Unless you have other plans."

"Nee, no plans. Are you off to find Hen?" Grinning, his sister walked backward for a few steps. "Did I tell you she's a vendor? She's selling her Goat Goodies."

Nicholas didn't rise to the bait. "Gut for her."

"Even Mena got into the act. The sponsors said kid entrepreneurs were welcome, so Mena's selling pot holders she made herself."

Lenora offered him an exuberant wave and pivoted. "Have fun."

And she was off. Now to find the vendor area. Nicholas passed canopied booths filled with jewelry, pottery, quilts, candles, framed, original artwork, macrame wall hangings and plant holders, and enough other stuff to make his head spin. He wove his way between baby strollers and clusters of people who'd stop to chat. Many wore red, white, and blue clothing and hats with sayings like HAPPY BIRTHDAY, AMERICA emblazoned on them. Everybody smiled. He smiled back.

"Would you like to try a free chocolate peanut butter goat milk fudge sample?"

Nicholas spun around. Hen stood behind him with one arm wrapped around her basket of samples and the other holding out a snack-sized baggie of fudge. "There you are."

Hen's eyebrows rose. A smile tugged at the corners of her mouth—or maybe that was Nicholas' imagination. "Jah, here I am."

At least she didn't embarrass him by asking why he would be searching for her. There seemed nothing else to do, so he accepted the baggie. "Denki."

"If you like it, come by Goat Goodies and buy some." She smiled then, the sincere smile of a vendor intent on making a sale. She reeled off her spiel like the practiced saleswoman she was. As if Nicholas was just another customer to be lured into a sale.

"I'll do that. In fact, why don't you show me where your booth is?"

"It's about six booths down and two over. I'm sure you can find it."

"Hen, sei so gut."

The crowd flowed around them. A lady dressed in stars and stripes from head to toe stopped and took their photo without so much as a by-your-leave. If Hen noticed, she didn't say. The tug-of-war playing out on her face couldn't have been more obvious.

Finally, she shifted the basket to her other arm. "I'm happy to show you. Maybe you can buy some of Mena's pot holders. I'm sure Lenora could use a few more—what Plain woman who cooks morning, noon, and night couldn't?"

"Lenora was just saying she needed more pot holders."

Hen led the way, zigzagging around people like an experienced festivalgoer. Nicholas did his best to keep up. "So how's it going? Lots of sales?"

"Nee, not really." She glanced back for a split second and nearly collided with a man eating a cheesesteak sandwich dripping with cheese and caramelized onions. "Oops, sorry. It's hard to compete when people have their choice of Tastykakes, shoofly pie, sticky buns, apple dumplings, and whoopie pies—and that's after they stuff themselves with stromboli, tomato pie, scrapple, bacon cheeseburgers, and the cheesesteak sandwiches."

"Your treats are portable, though. They can buy your candy and cheese to take home for later. They'll need the soap to clean up."

"I like the way you think." Hen squeezed past a couple sharing a banana split in the middle of the walkway. "Excuse me, excuse me."

"How's it going being in charge of the house now that Ruby's married and your aunt Ginny returned home?"

"The hard part is missing Aenti Ginny and Ruby. I miss having them to talk to." Her smile dissolved. She stared at the ground. "As far as the rest goes, it's not that big of an adjustment, considering that Dat forbade me to take care of the livestock after. . ." Her cheeks, already pink from the sun, reddened. "My cooking is actually getting better—at least the buwe are eating it without complaining."

"That's a gut sign."

She slipped around the corner. "Here we are."

Luke, Dillon, and Devon lounged on canvas camping chairs behind tables laden with Goat Goodies. They stood, chorused a rousing hello, and immediately clamored to leave.

"Fine, but stay together and come back after you've seen the booths and bring back some lunch for your little schweschder." Hen made shooing motions. "Don't make yourself sick on cotton candy and caramel corn."

Mena had her own table and her own small canopy next to the bigger one. She popped up and ran to meet them. "Nicholas, you came, you came. Hen said you—"

"I was just saying that you did a great job with your pot holders." Hen held up a partially completed pot holder made of multicolored cloth loops stretched and woven together on a small loom. "How many have you sold?"

"Twenty-three." She grinned, revealing she'd lost another tooth since her last visit to the clinic. "I wanna buy goats."

"Gut for you." Nicholas offered a high five. Mena accepted with an exuberant, sticky hand slap. "I'd like a set of four. I'll save them to give to Lenora for Christmas."

"Yay!" Mena squealed. "Do you want to pick them out?"

"Nee, I trust your judgment."

Nicholas followed Hen toward the back of the bigger canopy. She'd busied herself adding more bars of soaps to the display. The scents of lavender, eucalyptus, and peppermint floated in a soft breeze like a cleansing breath. "Seems like the buwe made a few sales while you were out drumming up business."

He sounded so lame.

"How's your daadi doing?"

So she too wanted to make small talk. He would oblige. "As well as can be expected."

She nodded without pausing in the task at hand.

Time was a-wastin', as Lenora had so aptly put it. "Could we talk?"

"Here?" Hen waved her hand toward the tables. "I have work to do."

"I'll talk. You work."

"Fine, talk."

"I thought long and hard about what you said. I took what your dat said to heart. I took what you said to heart. I read scripture and prayed. I'm sure I'm not going anywhere. I can't. Not and leave you." Heat, having nothing to do with the hot July sun, burned through Nicholas. *Sei so gut, Gott, soften her heart, open it to my pleadings.* "I won't leave. I'm as sure about that as I am that the sun will set in the west tonight and rise in the east in the morning."

The orange-lime soap in Hen's hand fell to the ground. Her fingers fluttered. Head bent, she stared at the bar of soap without moving to pick it up. "That's gut to know."

"I'd like to say more, but as you said, this isn't the place."

"How do you feel about selling goat milk soap?" Hen raised her head and met his gaze head-on. Nicholas stared back. Sighing, she scooped up the soap, settled into a chair, and pointed at another one. "And hawking goat cheese?"

"Jah, Nicholas, how do you feel about hawking pot holders?" Mena skipped in a figure-eight loop around the chairs. "How do you feel about Hen? Is it lieb?"

"Mena!" Hen grabbed the girl and tugged her onto her lap. "Just you never mind, maedel. That's not a question a person asks."

Her face the picture of innocence, Mena wrapped her arms around Hen's neck and leaned her head on her sister's shoulder. "But I want to know. I like weddings. I like when everybody comes and eats a bunch of food. Especially cake. Lots of cake."

"Nobody's talking about weddings. We haven't even courted yet, not—"

"It's okay." Nicholas stopped laughing long enough to reassure Hen. "She's a mini Hen. She says what she thinks when she thinks it. It's nice to know what a maedel is thinking. The fact is I've actually given some thought to selling goat products."

"You have?" Hen's eyebrows arched. Her first genuine smile appeared. "Did it make your head hurt?"

"Ha, very funny." Nicholas' head did hurt, mostly from trying to order his thoughts and find the words to convince her to trust him. "Being a vet assistant pairs well with raising livestock. You can take care of the animals better than most people, knowing so much about animals."

"Interesting."

"Interesting." Mena parroted her sister's tart tone. "I like animals. I can take care of animals."

"Jah, you can, sweet pea, but I think Nicholas is trying to say something more than that." Hen hugged the girl close. "At least I hope he is."

Mena entertained them with more outlandish questions and stories until the boys returned with bags of food and tall plastic cups of birch beer made with fresh birch sap. With its earthy, mint taste it was even better than root beer. Nicholas ate a stromboli, a warm pretzel with mustard, apple dumplings, and two sticky buns. Something about the exchange with Hen had reignited an appetite that had been missing for weeks.

"Do you always eat like this?" Hen licked cinnamon and sugar from her fingers.

"Nee. I need my energy. I'm planning to enter the sack races. I might even try the cornhole tournament. Maybe you could come with me."

"I can't do sack races in a long skirt." Hen stared at him head-on, her eyes dark and questioning. "Besides, I don't think Dat would be happy about it."

"Of course not. I wasn't thinking." Not clearly, not in this moment. "What about cornhole?"

She cocked her head to one side. After a long few seconds, she laid the soap on the table. "I'm a whiz at cornhole."

Nicholas stifled the urge to heave a huge breath. "I suspected as much." Keep it simple. Keep it casual. He turned to Luke and the twins. "Can you boys hold down the fort now that you're full of food and have plenty of birch beer to keep the thirst away?"

"We're gut." Luke was all business now that his hunger was satisfied. "Hen has us trained in what to say, when to say it, and how to say it. Now that Ruby's married, I'm the lead salesman and spokesman for Goat Goodies, don'tcha know."

"Nee, I am, I am." Mena grabbed a dozen sample bags and held them to her chest. Only a few fell into the grass. "I'll get people to come."

"Nee, you won't. You stay with your brieder." Hen took the bags from her. "I can multitask, as the Englischers like to say. You have pot holders to sell."

After instructions that had the boys rolling their eyes in exasperation—apparently they were oft repeated—Hen rearranged her display once again. She moved the baskets around three times until they ended up exactly as they had been in the beginning. Nicholas bit his tongue and bided his time.

"Okay, let's go."

It took all Nicholas' willpower to keep from taking her arm and propelling her from the booth. Instead, he waited until she was several feet from the booth to silently thank God and follow.

No turning back now.

CHAPTER 34

They located the tournament by the noise of a raucous crowd that had gathered, adult libations in hand. A huge banner read CORNAMENT: CORNSTARS, TIME TO SHOW YOUR STUFF. PRIZES FOR TOP-SCORING TEAMS, HOLY MOLY TRIPLE CORNHOLY, AND THE GREAT CORNHOLIO.

"This will be fun." Hen rubbed her hands together. "I like a challenge."

"Are you sure about this?" Nicholas perused the dozens of cornhole boards. Many Plain couples stood in the pitching squares, but Englischers outnumbered them. A few had red faces, loud talk, and loosey-goosey movements that suggested they might have spent some time in the "beer garden" before entering.

"Jah, this is perfect." Hen pointed at an open spot. "Let's show them how it's done."

Their opponents in the first match were the picture of Englischers who frequented fitness gyms. The woman used the man's broad back to balance while she stretched her hamstrings. He stretched his muscled shoulders and arms with the air of a man who was concentrating on the most important pregame ritual known to athletes.

At the referee's bidding, they introduced themselves before the coin toss. Dale and Krystal. Hen won the toss. She trotted to the pitching box next to Krystal's, while Nicholas took up his position at the other box across from Dale.

Hen stepped up to the foul line, red bag in hand. Just as she drew back her arm, Krystal burst into song. "Oops, I did it again." Her friends, lined up behind the couple, joined in at the top of their lungs.

"What's that all about?" Nicholas glanced at his opponent. "I don't think we need music."

Dale grinned and shrugged. "All's fair in love and war and heckling."

Hen took aim again. Her first toss arched nicely. It sailed through the hole without touching the board. The singing stopped. Grinning, Hen raised her arms and did a one-two-one-two victory dance. "Nothing but airmail. Nothin' but corn. Three points."

Krystal grabbed her blue bag and stepped up. "Lucky toss."

Her bag smacked the board above the hole but slid in. Whooping, Krystal cartwheeled twice, did a backflip, and landed with both hands in the air, flashing the victory sign.

Not quite. As soon as Hen picked up her bag, Krystal's cheering crowd started yelling. "You throw like a girl."

Hen frowned but said nothing. Her toss landed within an inch of the hole, good enough for another point. She grinned at her opponent. "Throwing like a girl is a good thing, isn't it?"

And so it went. Each time Krystal's cheering section had a new heckle. "Pilgrim, what are you covering up with that long dress? Did you come over on the *Mayflower*? What's under that bonnet—a bird's nest?"

If it bothered Hen, she didn't let it show. Her unerring tosses landed her last two bags in the hole for a total score of ten. Krystal didn't fare as well, coming in with eight points. That didn't keep her from doing a one-handed cartwheel and a dance called the floss.

Arms crossed, Hen stepped back and shot Nicholas an encouraging smile. "You've got this."

Truth be told, Nicholas hadn't tossed a cornhole bag in at least two years—maybe longer. His failure to mention this might account for Hen's boisterous shout when he stepped up to the box. What would the bishop say to a Plain main silently whispering to God that he not embarrass himself in front of the woman whose heart he was trying to win?

He eyeballed the box, craned his head side to side, breathed deeply, closed one eye, then the other, and finally pulled back and let it fly.

Fly it did, right into Krystal's face.

"Hey, hey, you cornholed me!" Doubling over with laughter, the woman covered her cheek with one hand and jabbed her other index finger at Nicholas. "Good shot. No points for that, Suspenders Man."

Suspenders Man? Nicholas had been called worse. Still, embarrassment made it hard to focus. Hen waved. *You've got this*, she mouthed.

Apparently not, but Nicholas smiled back anyway. She was having fun. That was the point. His shoulders relaxed. He eased up on his grip. *"Throw it like a Frisbee,"* his dad had told him when he was eleven and frustrated that he never hit the hole. *"It's not a baseball. Make sure the bag is evenly placed with the weight equally distributed. Aim for the center of the board. Arch, not flat. Don't release too late. Or too soon. No spin."*

"Anytime now, Farmer Nick."

"I'm not a farmer." Nicholas tossed the bag. It sailed, its trajectory straight and true, landed just above the hole, and slid in. He dusted off his hands and smiled at Dale. "I'm a vet's assistant. Three points."

"Cool."

Dale was as good as his girlfriend. Maybe better. The match seesawed until it came down to the final toss between Hen and Krystal. Some of the Plain spectators had gathered around, creating a less boisterous but just as loyal cheering section. Good-natured heckling became a two-way street. "Do you want to borrow my glasses?" was a favorite, along with "My grandma could throw better than that."

Hen hadn't been kidding when she said she was good. The score was tied 18–18 when she made her final toss. It hit the spot. "Three points. That's twenty-one." She bowed to the crowd. "Better luck next time."

"Whoa, whoa, hold your horses and your buggy, Bonnet Lady." Krystal stomped up to the pitching box. "Foul, foul, you saw that, Referee, you saw it, right? She stepped over the line. Foul. It doesn't count."

"No, I didn't." Hen's tone remained friendly but firm. "I don't believe so. I was very careful."

"Come on, Referee, tell me you're not blind too." Arms flapping, Dale got into the act. "Were you watching, or were you too busy flapping your mouth with your buddies and drinking beer?"

The "official" was an event volunteer. He held up a plastic cup that clearly held pop. "I'm not sure what I saw—"

"Ah, come on," Dale and Krystal spoke in unison. "No fair. We're lodging an official protest."

Nicholas strolled across the grass to where Hen stood, arms crossed, a bemused expression on her face, her cheeks red, and her nose dusted with new freckles from the July sun. She was beautiful. "What do you think?" he murmured in Pennsylvania Deutsch.

"I think it's just a game." Hen leaned closer and whispered in the same language. "I'm thirsty, and I want a root beer float."

"I agree, and that sounds gut."

Hen's hand shot up like a kid who knew the answer in school. "Excuse me, Mr. Referee."

"Yes, ma'am."

"We're just playing for fun. We'll withdraw. Krystal and Dale are great. They can have the win."

"Seriously? You're forfeiting?" Shock gave way to outrage on Krystal's face. "So you're too chicken to let us win fair and square?"

Fair and square would've been to forgo the false claim of a foul, but Nicholas let it go. "Congratulations. Good luck with your next match."

He followed Hen through the crowd that parted with a smattering of applause that grew as they walked away.

"That was different." Hen straightened her bonnet, leaving dirty fingerprints on the sides. "I think I'd rather play at home after church. I'm competitive, but I like to have fun."

Nicholas squeezed her elbow. "I agree, Pilgrim."

"Stop." She tugged loose and used the elbow to nudge him. "Suspenders Man."

"Bonnet Girl."

"Farm Boy."

Heckling was more fun when it involved just the two of them. Nicholas bought Hen a stromboli. She counted out goat soap money for two root beer floats. They strolled until they reached the stage where a country singer named Andrew Mack crooned a ballad about a homesick rodeo rider who wanted to return to his girl in Wyoming. They ate, drank, and listened until Hen wadded up the wrapper and tossed it in a rusted barrel that served as a trash can. "I better get back."

Nicholas slurped the last of his icy float. The mix of root beer and melted vanilla ice cream was the best part. "I'll walk you back."

"That's okay. It'll be time for the concert in the arena in a few minutes. You probably need to meet Lenora and the others. She'll wonder what happened to you."

"Aren't you coming to the concert?"

"We have to pack everything up and load it in the van." She used a napkin to wipe at a blob of marinara sauce on her apron but only succeeded in smearing it. "I'm in charge of taking the kinner to the fireworks after the concert. Dat is coming over for it. He's bringing Aenti Ginny and Onkel Joel. They came up for the holiday weekend. We're meeting at the gate at nine thirty."

He couldn't wait. "What if we meet. . .later. I'd like to talk some more."

A lot more.

Hen crossed her arms, but her gaze didn't waver. "We won't be home until eleven or so."

"You'll have had a very long day." He shouldn't push too hard. It wouldn't be a good conversation if she was worn out. "Is that too late for a buggy ride?"

She smiled. "Maybe we could talk on the porch."

Whew. "I'd like that."

"Me too."

Relief blew through Nicholas. If only he could kiss her.

Tonight. Tonight.

CHAPTER 35

A few more miles. Just a few more miles. Hen fought to keep her eyes open. Her day, which began at five a.m., had included loading the van, unloading it at the fairgrounds, selling her goodies, unexpectedly spending time with Nicholas, loading up the van again, a concert, and fireworks. Her head might explode, her feet hurt, and her back ached, but contentment soothed what ailed her. The goodies sold well. The money would help her family and add a small sum to her savings.

Even Mena's pot holders had sold out. The five-year-old had a head for business and a nice sales pitch. Mena lay across Hen's lap sleeping, while Devon leaned against one of her shoulders, and Dillon against the other. All three had tiny snores like a concert given by a children's trio. Hen leaned her head back and stared out at the darkness that raced by, the miles marked by rushing air and streaks of light on the other side of the window.

And then there was Nicholas. What a wonderful time.

Now he wanted to finish their conversation. He was likely in his buggy now headed toward the farm. Her fatigue fled. She straightened. He said he was ready. He said he was sure. Was she? She sucked in a long breath and closed her eyes for a few seconds. The image of his suntanned face staring at her, his eyes lit with an undeniable emotion stared back at her. She didn't have any experience with this kind of love, but she saw a yearning, a want, a longing, in Nicholas' face. It gave a name to the void in her own heart. He could fill that hole. She wanted to do the same for him.

She opened her eyes and breathed again.

To give up her dream of building a business with her goats hurt. She couldn't deny it. Love was sacrificial, to be sure. Nicholas' sacrifice was greater. He would give up his dream of being a veterinarian. The dream of a different life. Would that make him bitter? Would he hold it against her?

"Are you still awake?" Aunt Ginny whispered. She sat between Micah and Luke. Micah's head kept lolling to one side. Then he'd jerk awake, straighten, and drift off again. It was fun to watch. "Or just pretending?"

"Jah. Barely."

The van hit a bump. The impact jostled Mena. She sat up. "Are we home?"

"Nee, go back to sleep." Hen nudged her back down. "Sleep, lieb, sleep."

The girl sighed and closed her eyes.

One hand cupped around her mouth, Aunt Ginny leaned forward. "Mena said you played cornhole with Nicholas."

Dad's expression had said he was none too happy about it, but he hadn't commented. Hen plucked straw from Mena's loosened hair. "I did. Just one match. We forfeited when the Englisch couple got argumentative."

"That's gut. Did he have anything interesting to say?"

"Aenti, are you fishing for information?" Hen let her stew for a minute. After all, Dad had invited Aunt Ginny to Smicksburg earlier in the year for the express purpose of matchmaking. "Courting is private."

"Then you are courting," Aunt Ginny crowed. "That's wunderbarr."

Fortunately, Dad sat up front with the driver. He hadn't said a word since he slid into his seat. With any luck he couldn't hear this conversation. Uncle Joel sat in the last row, head back, eyes closed. No worries there.

"Hey, hey." Luke opened his eyes, squirmed, and closed them. "Can't a guy get some quiet?"

"Sorry, sorry." Aunt Ginny clapped so softly her hands made no sound. "He's not still thinking of leaving, then?"

"He says not." A glimmer of light in the distance caught Hen's peripheral vision. She slid one arm around Devon and leaned across him to peer out the window. "What. . .what is that?"

"What's what?" Aunt Ginny yawned so loudly her jaw made a cracking sound. "I don't see anything."

"It's bright yellow and orange. . . Is that a fire?" Brilliant flames leapt against a black night illuminated by only a sliver of moon. Hen's heart pumped like an out-of-control racehorse. She twisted in her seat so she could pat her father's shoulder. "Dat, Dat! I think there's a fire. It might be on our property."

"What? I don't. . ." Dad scooted around toward his window. "Jah, I see it. I'm not sure, but I don't think it's the house. I can't tell. I think it's in the field by the barn." Alarm ran his words together faster and faster. "We need to get there right now, Lou."

"You betcha!" The driver hit the gas. "Hold on to your hats—and bonnets."

Hen clutched Mena closer. The boys slid against her. The barn. Jack. The horses Dad was training for their owners. The sheds. Petunia. Penny. Lily. Lenny. The chicken coop. Sam. Sassy. Where would Raindrop and Buster be right now? And Tigger and Willow and her kittens? Hen tried to breathe. Her lungs refused to work. "Drive faster, Lou. Faster, sei so gut. Hurry!"

"You got it, ma'am."

The van jerked forward again. This time everyone woke at once. Mena whined. Devon and Dillon complained. Luke sputtered. Uncle Joel grunted and sat up. "What's going on?"

Hen pointed. Luke pressed up against the window. "Fire!"

"I can't tell what's burning, can you?"

"Jack. Willow. The kitties." Mena rubbed her eyes. Tears trickled down her cheeks. "Don't let it be the barn."

Hen tightened her hold on the child. "Pray, lieb, pray."

Minutes stretched, lasting hours and days. No matter how fast Lou drove, jolting against deep ruts head-on, the van seemed stuck, wheels turning in place. Hen grappled with the desire to scream. To jump from the moving van and sprint ahead of it with sneakers powered by fear and dread. *Gott, sei so gut, sei so gut, sei so gut.*

Was this another example of a trial she'd have to endure to show her faith? *I have faith, Gott, I do. I survived Mamm's death and little Stephen's. I love the animals. They're only animals, but they're family too. Jesus is the gut shepherd. Let Him herd the animals to safety. Have mercy on them. Shower Your grace on them. Sei so gut.*

She could live with the house burning down. Clothes and furniture and bedding could be replaced. They could rebuild. Living with lives lost would be so much harder. They could buy more livestock, but they wouldn't be Petunia or Jack or Buster or Tigger or Sam. It didn't work that way.

They were God's creatures too.

With barely a tap on the brakes, Lou turned into the road that led to the house. The back end of the van lurched and slid. Holding on to the kids, Hen gritted her teeth. Fire and smoke filled her vision. Flames shot up from the stretch of land that lay beyond the fence to their left. It ate up bushes, trees, wildflowers, weeds, tall grasses—anything in its path.

The more it ate, the more it grew, and the faster it spread.

In the scant minutes it took them to arrive at the yard, the fire had consumed a wood fence, destroyed the pony cart and a buggy, and scorched a metal horses' trough.

None of it satisfied the fire's hunger. It lunged forward, ever closer to the barn, the goat sheds, and the chicken coop.

"Hurry, Lou, hurry!" Mena broke free from Hen's grasp. She struggled to free herself from her seat belt. "Raindrop! I have to find her and Buster."

"Dogs know what to do." Hen grabbed her sister's flailing hands. "Calm down, lieb. Stay buckled. Buster will take care of Raindrop, I promise. He's a gut big bruder. You know that."

Mena hiccupped another sob, but she stopped struggling. "And Willow will take care of the kitties?"

"She's a mamm. She'll do her best." *Or die trying.*

"Adam, you call the fire department!" Aunt Ginny undid her seat belt even though they were still moving. "I'll get the kinner started on a water bucket line."

The Dayton District Volunteer Fire Department was less than four miles from Smicksburg, but the volunteer firefighters had to get to the station from their homes. Many would be asleep in their beds when the call came in. It took time for them to get to a fire. Tears welled in Hen's eyes. She blinked them away. "Tell them to hurry."

"Look, there's Nicholas." Devon pointed. "He's got Jack."

Squinting as if that would help her see through the darkness, beyond the flames and thick smoke, Hen peered through the window. Nicholas led Jack up the drive toward the house. The elderly horse reared up, again and again. Fear might kill the poor thing. "Stop, stop, let me out." Hen threw off her seat belt. She scrambled to the door. "This is close enough."

"Wait, Hen, wait." Dad twisted in his seat. "Getting hurt won't help."

"Nicholas needs help. The animals know me. They trust me."

Lou slammed on the brakes. The van jerked to a halt. Hen tumbled forward against Luke. He helped her up. "Go, go."

Hen hurled herself from the van and took off at a dead run. Pounding footsteps behind her said the others followed.

Sei so gut, sei so gut, sei so gut, Gott.

Buster bounded toward her then veered toward the barn. *Denki, Gott.* "Gut, hund, gut!"

Barking, he charged through the open doors. "Buster, nee, get out, get out." Hen panted. "I've got this. Stay safe."

Of course, Buster ignored her, brave to the marrow in his bones.

Flames had penetrated the elderly barn's wooden slats. They shot up the walls and spread across bales and swathes of loose hay on the cement floor. Sweat poured into Hen's eyes. Heat burned her face.

Bits of hay crackled and floated in the hot wind.

A pile of rags caught fire in a whoosh that sent sparks flying onto a bag of feed. The smell of burning alfalfa turned her stomach.

She opened Zane's stall and grabbed a lead rope. His eyes wide and frantic, he neighed and tossed his head. "It's okay, buddy, it's okay." With shaking fingers, she hoisted the lead rope over his head. He shook it and whinnied, the sound like a high scream. "I know, I know. I'm scared too, but together we'll make it. I promise. You can trust me."

Keeping up a steady stream of comforting words, she trotted him from the barn, Buster scampering ahead of them.

Luke raced past her. "Lucy and the foal are in the pasture already," Luke yelled. "I'll get the Sextons' horse and the Richters' too."

"Gut. Hurry!"

Nicholas slowed as he passed her. "I called the Dayton Fire Department. They're already at a fire at the Planks' house." His breathless words carried as the wind picked up and tossed them into the sky. "Something about kids driving around shooting Roman candles from the back of a pickup truck."

"Who's coming, then?"

"Perry. Plumfield. Rural Valley is headed to the Hershbergers'."

Teenagers blowing off steam by starting fires at Plain farms? Intentionally or simply because they didn't bother to think of consequences? It didn't matter. The consequences were the same.

Hen left Zane in the pasture behind the house. He raced off the second she loosened the lead rope. Lucy neighed. Zane responded. They had each other's backs. She whirled and retraced her steps. Luke led two horses toward her. Dad had two more.

Bringing up the rear, Micah had Willow under one arm and two kittens in the crook of the other. Devon corralled a squirmy mess of three kitchens in his arms. Dillon carried Raindrop. "We've got the animals. Make sure Mena stays out of the barn. Hog-tie her if you have to."

"What about Tigger?"

"I didn't see him." Micah kept going. "Willow is scratching me."

"She's scared. I'll look for Tigger."

"Keep Mena out of there. She's going crazy."

Hen picked up speed. Flames enveloped the west side of the barn. They shot from the loft window.

"Mena, Mena, where are you?"

No answer. Hen covered her mouth and nose with her sleeve. She plunged into the burning building. Sparks floated and burst around her. Embers scorched her eyebrows. "Mena, Mena, get out here! Now!"

The stalls that held horses only a few seconds earlier now held flames that couldn't be corralled. Her throat and eyes burning, Hen coughed. "Mena!"

The little girl stumbled into view. She had her arms wrapped around Tigger. The tiger-striped cat yowled. "I got him, I got him."

Hen scooped up the girl and her precious cargo and ran. A wooden pillar crashed behind them. Tigger screeched. Mena screamed.

"It's okay, it's okay." Hen hurtled through the doors. She kept going until they were clear of the smoke billowing from the barn. She glanced back. The old barn, as much the center of their lives as their house, collapsed.

It had been the key to their family's way of life since before Hen was born. At night when she couldn't sleep, she would sit at her window and see it in the light of the moon, and cradle memories of her mom leading her through its doors so they could see a new foal born during the night or a litter of kittens, eyes still closed, meowing as they snuggled close to their mother.

Where Dad taught her to hitch a buggy and saddle a horse. Where he taught her to muck stalls and tend to tack.

Where she spent hours grooming Jack and crying into his mane after Mom died.

The barn would burn to the ground, leaving only a foundation where they would rebuild. Because that's what they did. Fire couldn't take her memories.

"The goats, Schweschder." Mena struggled to free herself. "The chickens!"

"Luke's got the chickens. Put Tigger in the house." Hen settled her sister on her feet, whirled, and shot toward the goat pen. "Aenti needs you to help with the water buckets," she yelled over her shoulder. "Soak down the ground between the barn and the buggy shed. We don't want to have to replace them too."

Aunt Ginny knew what to do. But Mena had much to learn. This would be her first lesson in overcoming life's trials. One she would never forget.

Sirens screamed in the darkness beyond the inferno. "Denki, Gott."

Nicholas knelt in the goat pen, a kid in his arms, surrounded by bleating goats milling about in a frightened frenzy. "How do you want to do this?"

They needed to get them as far from the fire as possible. "We'll move them to the pasture where we have the horses." Hen opened the gate. "When they're scared they stick together."

They could round them up by light of day when the danger had passed.

With Buster's help, they herded the goats from the pen. Still bleating, they surged closer to Hen, following her across the yard, past the house, and toward the gate to the pasture.

"Once again, you're the goat whisperer." Sweat and soot covered Nicholas' face. "They'd follow you anywhere."

"Nee, this time I'm a goat herder." Hen scooped up Petunia and hugged her close. The kid snuggled against her chest. "I'm so glad they're okay. I don't know how I'd bear it if something happened to them."

Together they shooed the goats inside the gate. Hen hugged Lenny, patted Tulip, and scratched between Lily's ears. "Gut goats, you're all such gut goats. Now, behave yourselves, all of you. Stick together. I don't want to have to track you down like the shepherd chasing the one lost sheep."

Petunia nuzzled Hen's neck and bleated. She'd make sure the rest received the message.

Sirens screamed, getting steadily louder. The whirling lights approached the front yard, mingling with a horn honking. A pumper truck and a ladder truck. Dad beat Hen and Nicholas to the first firefighter to hop off the truck. "The barn is gone." His features stoic as always, he cocked his head toward the other buildings. "We're trying to keep it from taking the buggy shed, the other outbuildings, and the house."

"We're on it." The firefighter darted away, yelling orders to the other men.

Dad turned to Hen. "Tell your aenti to soak the yard around the house. Just in case."

Hen ran to deliver the message, Nicholas right behind her.

Aunt Ginny pumped water from the well and handed off buckets to Hen's siblings in an old-fashioned bucket brigade. She paused long enough to point over Hen's shoulder. "Look. More help is coming."

Hen pivoted. A line of headlights shone on the road leading into the front yard. Dozens of sets. One buggy after another. "Your dat called the deacon. He was to go door-to-door to wake up folks."

The adrenaline pumping through Hen's body quieted. Help was on the way. The horses had each other's backs. As did the goats and the chickens and the cats and dogs. So did Hen's community.

The buggies pulled one by one into the yard. Their neighbors piled out.

Stumbling in her haste, Ruby ran toward them. "Are you all right? Is everyone all right?" She threw her arms around Hen and hugged her so hard her ribs protested. "I prayed all the way here, but I couldn't stop my worry and my fear."

"We're okay. We weren't here when the fire started." Hen held on to Ruby for a few more seconds. Her sister smelled of lavender soap and minty toothpaste. Normal, everyday smells. Life would go on, eventually. "I was scared too, for the animals. The rest can be replaced."

Adele and her sisters joined along with a cadre of other women joined the bucket line. The men went to help the firefighters. Everyone moved in sync as if they hadn't been rousted from bed in the dead of night to race across the countryside to help save the house of good friends. Friends who were more. They were family.

Faith. Family. Community. Then self. Those vows in action. *Gott, I understand now. I'll keep it straight from now on, I promise.*

"I better call and check on Lenora and Daadi." Nicholas had goat manure on his shirt and soot smudges on his cheeks. With an apologetic glance at Hen, he pulled a phone from his pants pocket and tapped out a number. After a few seconds, he left a message, disconnected, and returned the phone to his pocket as quickly as he'd grabbed it. "She probably won't go by the phone shack until in the morning."

"Let me ask Simon if she came to the door."

Hen didn't have to look far for the deacon. He strode toward them. "Nicholas, I have a message for you." He spoke fast, his words full of concern. "Your schweschder said to tell you she can't find your daadi. She's searched the house, the barn, and his shop. No sign of him."

"Denki." His tone tight, gruff, Nicholas turned to Hen. "I'm sorry. I have to go."

"If you haven't found him by the time we're finished here, we'll join you in searching for him." Simon nodded toward the buggies. "As soon as I'm done here, I'll come to your house. Then I can spread the word, if needed."

Nicholas thanked him again. He pivoted and headed toward the backyard.

Hen followed. "I'm going with you."

"Nee, you're needed here."

"The whole district is here. There's only you and Lenora until they get done." Hen scurried to keep up. "Besides, Moses likes me. If he's hiding, he'll come out for me. I just have to talk to him about building goat sheds. I'm the Moses whisperer."

A ghost of a smile flitted across Nicholas' face. "That you are, but your family needs you here."

"You're family too. Or you will be." Hen murmured the words more to herself than to Nicholas. She might be stepping out on a narrow cliff with a world of hurt in the canyon below. Would he understand her meaning? "I hope."

Nicholas grabbed her hand. He pulled her forward, so their strides matched. "I hope so too. More than you can know."

In the midst of something so destructive, they'd found the start to something new.

CHAPTER 36

"Take care of Grandpa." A shudder ran through Nicholas. Dad had sent him to Smicksburg with one job. He'd failed.

Gott, sei so gut, show me where he is. Take care of him, sei so gut.

Thy will be done. The sentiment came as an afterthought, but it still counted. At least a person could hope so.

Hen at his side during the seemingly endless ride to the farm served as the one silver lining in this debacle. She hopped from the buggy ahead of him and hurried across the yard to Lenora. Daisy raced to meet them. Barking, the dog ran circles around Hen then backtracked to Nicholas.

Her shoulders hunched, head bent, his sister stood outside Grandpa's shop. "I can't find him. I'm so sorry, Nicholas. I don't know where he is."

"It's not your fault. It's his sickness. We'll find him." Hen hugged Lenora. With one arm still around her waist, Hen turned to Nicholas. "Won't we?"

Her eyes and nose red, Hen was covered with soot. Wet sweat stains marred her dress's bodice. Mud mixed with hay caused the hem to drag. An angry burn stood out against the fair skin on her cheek. She seemed oblivious to it all. She'd never been more beautiful.

Filing the thought away for later, Nicholas leaned over to corral Daisy. "Shush, hund, shush. We'll find Daadi, I promise. When was the last time you saw him?"

"When Abel brought him home right after you left." Her voice tearful, Lenora wiped sweat from her face with the back of her hand. "He said he was tired. He went straight to bed. At least I thought he did."

"Did he say anything about his day?" Hen rubbed Lenora's back. "Was he in a gut mood? Happy? Mad?"

"He thanked Abel for bringing him home. He seemed to know who Abel was." Lenora's voice trembled. "It was obvious he wasn't sure who I was but didn't want to admit it. He didn't say a word about his day."

"Lenora, go through the house and barn again. His shop too. Keep an eye out for places he might be hiding or could've fallen." Nicholas forced himself to slow his words, to exude calm. "Don't just call his name. Search every nook and cranny. He may be sleeping. He may have fallen. He could be unconscious."

Lenora gasped. "Do you think—"

"I don't think anything. I have faith, but I'm doing my best to figure out what might be going on in his muddled brain."

She wiped her nose and nodded. "What will you do?"

"Hen and I'll retrace his ride to and from the Glicks'—if you're okay with that."

"Jah, I feel better, knowing you're searching for him too."

"Don't search around the pond until it gets light." Nicholas had to keep Lenora safe too. He couldn't let both her and Grandpa down. "I don't want you to break an ankle or conk your head."

Or fall into the water.

"I'll get you flashlights to take with you."

Lenora broke away from Hen's grasp. She disappeared into Grandpa's shop. A minute later she returned with two jumbo flashlights. "Don't fall and break an ankle or conk *your* heads." She handed them to Nicholas. "If you find Daadi, leave a message at the phone shack. I'll check it every so often."

"Gut plan. And call me if you find him."

It could happen. Grandpa could amble back to the house as if nothing had been amiss.

Or he could be sprawled in overgrown grass under towering pine trees, unconscious, oblivious to time passing.

Nicholas sprinted toward the buggy, Hen only a few steps behind. Daisy beat them to it. She sprang onto the back bench.

"Down, Daisy. Get down."

Daisy barked twice and lay down.

"I think she wants to lead the search party." Hen climbed in and settled onto the front bench. "It's not a bad idea. She has a much better sense of smell, and she knows Moses' smell."

"She's not a bloodhound, but you're right." Nicholas snapped the reins. Sable went to work. "Dogs have better hearing too, depending on the frequency and distance. We can use all the help we can get."

Once on the road, he forced himself to slow down. His ears pricked up, Sable wanted to pick up the pace. Nicholas would've preferred to do the same, but they needed to examine every foot of land between Grandpa's farm and the Troyers' and beyond. "Easy, gaul, easy. Daadi may be on foot."

"Do you think we should be walking?" Hen turned on a flashlight and directed it at the thickets of trees and bushes that lined the dirt road. She guided it back and forth, casting light on the thin strip of weeds and wildflowers that grew under the trees. "We could easily miss him."

"He may not remember much, but he still has the instincts of a man who's lived his whole life in this place." Nicholas slowed Sable to a walk. "Early memories remain, according to his doctor. It's the recent memories that are slipping away first."

"How awful."

"If it frustrates us, I can only imagine how it makes him feel."

"Moses! Moses, it's me, Hen. Henrietta Miller," Hen yelled. "I'm the one you designed the goat shed for. I need to talk to you. If you can hear me, call out."

Daisy joined in the chorus with her deep bark. Hen swiveled and patted the dog. "Let's see if we can hear him answer."

The dog quieted. Hen probed the thick stands of trees with her flashlight. Birds twittered. Katydids sang. Sable's hooves thudded on the packed dirt road. The buggy's wooden wheels creaked. A soft summer breeze lifted the leaves in a noisy dance. Pine needles rustled.

No voice rose above nature's conversation.

Nicholas swallowed a lump of fear that hurt his throat. "Daadi, Daadi, answer me. It's Nicholas, your kinnskind. If you're listening, call out."

Nothing.

"We'll find him." Hen's soft voice held reassurance and an underlying thread of steel. "Like you said, he could've laid down somewhere to sleep."

"Or he's wandering lost in the acres of woods on our farm or the

Troyers' farm next door." Nicholas worked hard to shutter the fear that echoed in his words. "He has no sense of how far it is to the Glicks'. They're two more farms over."

"Why would he go back to the Glicks'?"

"Maybe he thought he left his tools there. Or maybe he thinks Mammi is there." Nicholas' fingers gripped the reins so hard they hurt. He forced himself to loosen his grip. "Or the answer has no rhyme or reason."

Hen nudged him with her elbow. "Hey, I can see you blaming yourself. This isn't your fault."

"It's my job to take care of him. It *is* my fault."

"You can't be with him every hour of every day."

"Neither can Lenora." Guilt wrapped its gnarly roots around Nicholas' chest, constricting his lungs. "I should've stayed home with him today instead of dropping him off at the Glicks'."

"He needs to get out too. Rolling him up in bubble wrap and keeping him locked in his shop is no way for him to live. A man like your daadi needs his dignity—no matter how far gone his mind is."

"You're right." Her rational argument didn't help much, but her effort was sweet. "I just need to find him."

"We will."

Nicholas took turns with Hen calling Grandpa's name. Darkness gave away to a dusky predawn promise of light. For a time Hen took the reins while Nicholas and Daisy walked along the grassy divide between road and woods. He shone the flashlight into narrow gaps in vegetation. Daisy did her part by startling a fox, an opossum with babies clinging to her back, and a raccoon. She earned pats for not chasing them.

Nicholas turned the flashlight toward the ground in front of him, searching for signs other than paw prints. Signs a human had come this way. No broken branches, no downtrodden weeds. It had been weeks since their last rain. Where there was dirt, it was dry and hard packed.

"Nothing." Longing for a drink of cold water, he climbed back into the buggy. "Not even a single footprint."

"Should we move on to the Troyers'?"

"Jah. Just go slow. We'll keep looking as we go."

Nicholas' eyes burned. The lack of sleep was catching up with him. It didn't matter. He wouldn't sleep again until he found Grandpa, but Hen should be with her family, cleaning up after the mess left by the fire. "I'm sorry. I shouldn't've brought you along."

"What are you talking about?" Scowling, she crossed her arms. "You didn't bring me along. I came on my own two feet."

Like she did everything else. Nicholas managed a soft laugh. "What was I thinking?"

"I don't know. You know me better by now."

"I do." He turned off the flashlight and stowed it in his lap. They might still need it in the Troyers' barn and outbuildings. "At least I think I do. As a matter of fact, I had this entire speech prepared to give to you tonight—last night."

Hen's gaze swiveled to the field that ran alongside the road. "I had a few things I wanted to say to you as well."

"Will they keep until this is over?"

She nodded. "Will your speech?"

"It's engraved on my brain. It's not going anywhere."

He smiled at her. She smiled in return, that wide smile that sent his mind chasing after thoughts of tender kisses.

The sun peeked over the horizon. Squinting, Nicholas surveyed the Troyers' property as they pulled in front of the house. No sign of life. He hopped down and ran up the porch steps two at a time to knock on the door. No answer. "They're probably still at your place," he called out.

"I'm sure Simon passed the word about your daadi." Hen was already securing the buggy. She picked up the flashlights. "They'll be along shortly. In the meantime let's check around the barn and sheds."

With Daisy at his side, Nicholas took the lead. They tromped into the barn.

Daisy shot toward a stack of feed bags. She grabbed a sweat-stained straw hat and raced back to Nicholas. She dropped it at his feet and barked.

"It's his. He was here." Nicholas accepted her find. "Gut hund, gut hund."

"It could be one of the Troyers'."

"Daisy would know the difference. Besides, see these holes?" They were more like tiny rips. "Daadi dropped it in the chicken run. The ornery old rooster pecked those holes in it before he could grab it."

"Then that's a start."

Together, they investigated every nook and cranny in the barn. Nothing.

"Why didn't he pick up his hat? Where'd he go from here?" His chest tight, Nicholas rubbed his forehead. A headache pounded between his eyes. Images of Grandpa unconscious or worse, his body lying in the woods that surrounded the Troyer farm, assailed him. What if he fell into one of the ponds that dotted the land in this area? "If we don't find him soon, we'll have to call Simon and the others to expand the search."

"It'll be all right. He's disoriented and tired, that's all." Hen took his hand and squeezed. "He's in Gott's hands."

"The longer it takes, the more worrisome it is." Nicholas tugged her closer. He rubbed his thumb over the back of her hand. She had the hands of a hard worker. Her fingers were long, thin, and her nails clipped painfully short. "It's selfish, but I'm glad you're here with me now."

"Me too," she whispered. "I'm glad I could be with you."

Nicholas studied her face. Her gaze seemed riveted on their hands. "You have such a loving heart. Ever since the first time we met, I knew you were a kind soul. Even though you didn't like me, you were willing to help get Daadi out of his shop. I liked that."

"Even though you didn't like me much either." Her gaze came up to meet his. Her eyes were dark and warm. "I have that effect on people. The Plain woman who doesn't know her place."

"Your place is with me."

"Right now, you mean?"

"Right now and. . .we'll talk about it later." Right now and forever. As soon as they found his grandfather. It could wait that long—but no longer. "Simon has a shop where he builds furniture. Daadi would feel at home there." Nicholas still couldn't let go of her hand. In that moment she served as a lifeline. "The smell of sawdust, stain, and oils would comfort him."

"Wouldn't it be locked?"

"Let's find out."

They raced across the yard to a smaller building with several windows that would flood the shop with the light necessary for the work done there. The closer they came, the louder Daisy barked. At the shop, she jumped up, front legs on the door.

"She's smelling him." Holding his breath, Nicholas turned the knob and leaned into the door. It opened. He breathed and stepped inside.

"Daadi, Daadi, are you here?"

"Moses, it's me, Hen." Her tone was calm, light, and friendly. "Where are you? I'd love to have a cup of kaffi and a chat about the goat shed."

Daisy added her two cents' worth in woofs.

Nothing.

Where was he? Nothing was more important than finding him and keeping him safe for the rest of his life. Him and their entire family. Nothing beyond the narrow confines of his Plain world could compete for Nicholas' love and attention. That fact buried any thought of ever leaving so deep it would never bother him again. He belonged with the people who loved him, and he loved tenfold in return.

Nicholas trained the flashlight across a finished hickory rocker, a table that still needed staining, and various other pieces awaiting Simon's touch.

A noisy snore broke the silence. Nicholas froze. Hen's eyebrows popped up. A sudden smile stretched across her face. "Does that sound familiar?"

Daisy barked in agreement.

Nicholas whirled. He landed the flashlight's beam on an Adirondack chair occupied by his sleeping grandpa. Clad in a nightshirt and pants, he leaned back, head lolling to one side, slumbering peacefully.

Except for the explosive snores.

Daisy darted ahead of them. She nosed Grandpa's arm. He didn't budge. "Woof, woof."

"Daadi, Daadi." Nicholas touched his arm. No response. He shook him harder. "Daadi, wake up."

Grandpa rolled his head to the other side, but his eyes remained shut. The snoring reached a crescendo.

"Let me."

Hen knelt next to the chair. She patted Grandpa's face. "Moses," she whispered. "Moses, it's me, Hen. Time to wake up. Lenora is fixing breakfast. She wants you home."

Moses' eyes opened. He frowned at first. Then his eyes widened. He smiled and sat up. "Henrietta Miller. Gut to see you. How are the goats?"

"Gut, they're gut. Are you ready to go home?"

He glanced around the workshop. His smile dimmed. He glanced down at his clothes. "I don't. . ." He shook his head. "I dreamed I was in my shop. I was drawing up plans for a barn. Mary rang the dinner bell."

Moses sat up. He adjusted his hat and rubbed his whiskered face. "I have to get home. My fraa is waiting supper. She made my favorite sausage lasagna."

Nicholas opened his mouth. Hen shook her head. Nicholas forced a nod. "I'll get you home in two shakes, Daadi."

"You should eat with us, Henrietta." Moses stood and trotted past his grandson. "My fraa makes the most delicious lasagna. She makes nice garlic bread too. You won't want to miss it."

"Sounds scrumptious." Hen cocked her head toward the door. "I'll walk Moses to the buggy, if you want to call and leave a message for Lenora, Nicholas. She'll be so relieved."

Nicholas pulled his phone from his pocket. Lenora would be delighted—so delighted she wouldn't mind whipping up a pan of sausage lasagna on the fly.

CHAPTER 37

For the first time, Hen's filthy clothes, the stench of sweat and smoke that clung to her skin, and the pain of a burn on her cheek registered. Along with a powerful need for sleep. She leaned against the buggy seat's back and let the rhythmic pounding of Sable's hooves on the dirt road lull her. The sun shone. Cardinals preened while mourning doves cooed in the treetops. A beautiful day after a horrific night. Images of flames devouring the barn, the horses' crazed whinnies, their eyes wild with fear, and Mena's devastated face assailed her. The smell of burning hay and alfalfa made her want to gag. The terrific heat that singed her eyebrows. The taste of sweat and soot in her mouth.

In the light of day, it seemed a terrible nightmare. Only it wasn't. Now they would rebuild. Their community would help. It had been years since Hen had attended a barn raising, but she still remembered the amazing sight of dozens of men heaving the wooden frames upright, muscles bulging, faces red and damp with sweat. Another example of their community coming together as family.

Joy comes in the morning.

There was much work to be done, but for now Hen was content to sit in the buggy next to Nicholas. In fact, she wouldn't mind if the buggy ride never ended. Just the two of them on a journey together. Her stomach and her heart were full.

Moses hadn't objected when Lenora had promised to make lasagna for supper and instead laid out a breakfast spread of waffles, butter, blueberry syrup, scrambled eggs, link sausages, and toast. Copious amounts of coffee with milk and sugar topped off the feast. Nicholas and Lenora's grandfather made no mention of his late-night hike to a neighboring farm. Nor did he seem to notice that he wore a nightshirt. He'd eaten with gusto then excused himself and disappeared upstairs.

Lenora wouldn't allow Hen to help with the cleanup. She insisted Nicholas take her home instead. Nicholas had left a message at the Millers' phone shack as well as Simon's letting them know Moses had been found.

"You're awfully quiet." Nicholas held the reins loosely. His voice was hoarse from smoke and lack of sleep. "Did you doze off?"

"Nee. Just wondering what the next few days, weeks, and years will bring."

Nicholas slowed the buggy. They moved to the side of the road and stopped next to a fenced pasture filled with tall grass, purple ironweed, yellow evening primrose, bee blossom bushes, and lavender milkweed that reached heights of five feet or more—like a bouquet nature had delivered just for Hen.

"What are we doing?"

Instead of answering, Nicholas hopped from the buggy. He came around to her side and held out his hand. "Come on."

She took it and allowed him to help her down—something she hadn't done since she was old enough to catapult from the seat like one of her frisky goats.

Nicholas led her through brilliant orange butterfly weed that had grown into bushes to a spot at the fence. "Instead of bringing flowers to you, I brought you to the flowers." He leaned against the fence. "I don't believe in picking them, but gazing at them fills me with a strange sense of hope. Does it do that to you?"

Hen had never known a man to admit to enjoying flowers for flowers' sake. But then she'd never known a man like Nicholas. "Jah. They make me feel peaceful. Content." She inhaled the sweet fragrance carried by a warm July wind. "As if Gott can create something so beautiful for no other reason than to feed the bees and be pretty. He's way wiser than you or I."

"I hope it's not too prideful of me to say I suspect He brought us together."

"I hope not too, because I want to feel the same way. Except you want to leave this place, this life. You want to leave me behind so you can have your dream." Fighting to keep her voice even, Hen drank in the beauty that filled her gaze as far as she could see. Calm. Content. Peace. God walked through this season with her. Scripture said so. He held her right hand. "I don't want being with me to be something you settle for."

Nicholas edged closer. His hand slid over hers on the fence post. "I'm not settling. I'm reaching beyond pitiful dreams that don't come close to the possibilities I see in front of me when I look at you." He took her arm and tugged her around to face him. "Believe me when I say I will have no regrets if you say jah."

Hen couldn't move. She stared at his hand on her wrist. Her heart slammed against her rib cage. She clung to one thought that kept racing through her mind. *Don't let go, sei so gut, don't ever let go.* "Jah to what?"

"Will you marry me?" Nicholas touched her chin with his free hand. She raised her gaze to meet his. He smiled. "Say jah, sei so gut."

What else could she say? Whatever she'd thought she'd wanted or needed, whatever fears had once hounded her, she knew one thing for certain now. All she would ever need was standing in front of her. Regardless of the risks, she couldn't say no. "Jah."

"Jah? Are you sure, jah?"

"If you can ask me to marry you when I'm standing in front of you covered in soot and stinking of sweat, manure, and smoke, I know you've seen the real me and you aren't put off by it." Hen's voice quivered. This was happening. Really happening. In her heart of hearts, she'd been convinced it might never. "I thank Gott for you. I can't wait to marry you."

"You're more beautiful than ever."

Nicholas drew her into his arms then kissed her cheek. She leaned in until their lips met. Her first kiss. So perfect she never wanted it to end. Her arms went around his neck. His embrace tightened. A warm, lovely light had cast itself on the world around her, a light that could never be extinguished.

Finally, Nicholas leaned away. His smile told her all she needed to know. He felt the same. She could count on him. Yes, life could end unexpectedly at any moment. But in the meantime, they had each other, and they would make the most of every moment.

"They'll say we haven't known each other long enough." Nicholas put his arm around Hen's shoulders. "They'll say we should wait until we know each other better."

"Maybe not." Hen chuckled. She leaned her head against Nicholas' chest. "My dat is desperate to marry me off. He may want to perform the ceremony before you have a chance to change your mind."

"I won't change my mind. That's a promise."

"What about veterinary medicine college?"

"I don't need that kind of schooling to do what I love. That will be the beauty of you and me." Enthusiasm bloomed in Nicholas' voice. "Your dat said something that got me thinking."

"Ach, no, my dat? I can only imagine—"

"Nee, nee, wait. You love animals. I love animals. You want to keep raising dairy goats and start a herd of Angora goats—"

"I know that's a pipe dream. Dat is convinced it's a bad idea to expand at a time when the cost of groceries and everything else has skyrocketed. Average people don't have money for extras. Even the tourists spend less than they used to on what he calls luxury items."

"We can start small. I've got a gut job with Dr. McDonald. He's willing to help me get my certification as a vet assistant through on-the-job training and online courses that I would do in his office—with your dat's and the other elders' blessings, of course." Nicholas' boisterous excitement grew with each word. "Your dat had made it clear he's not interested in having goats. He'll let you take the herd you've raised, and you can start a second small herd. We'll grow it, while we wait for the economy to improve. It always does. Eventually we might even have that shop in town you've been dreaming of."

His enthusiasm was contagious. "You've thought this out, haven't you?"

"I've been able to think of nothing else." Nicholas grabbed her hands. "I can see us now with a few cattle, some pigs, horses, and chickens. Enough for our own needs, but lots of goats for your business."

"My business?" Hen's imagination caught fire. Goat pens, a big kitchen with plenty of room for making soap, cheeses, and candies. A big living room where she'd learn to make wool and wool products. Maybe Dad would loan her Mena to help. An assistant-in-training when she wasn't in school. "You'd be agreeable to such an arrangement?"

"Agreeable? I'm itching to get started. That's why I couldn't wait to ask you. I know I'm getting ahead of myself, but the possibilities are so amazing, I wanted to share them with you."

"Where would we do this?"

"At Daadi's house. With him and Lenora, for as long as she wants to stay. We could outfit Daadi's shop as your workspace."

"You really have thought this out."

"It would do Daadi gut to help with the animals. I've read about programs where people with dementia spend time with animals. They have a calming, comforting effect."

"Just like for the rest of us."

"Exactly. Now you see why I think God's hand was on this. We both wanted something it seemed we were destined to not have. But together we can have it. The best of both worlds. Right here." Nicholas grinned. "In fact, I think that this realization is worthy of another kiss, don't you?"

"Just one?" Hen grinned in return. "A bouquet of kisses?"

"I can do that."

Nicholas' hands went to Hen's waist. He held her there in his firm grip and proceeded to deliver on his promise.

No more words were needed. They might face a future full of challenges, but together they would see it through. They would grow goats, a garden, and a family—not necessarily in that order. Hen couldn't wait to get started.

Award-winning author Kelly Irvin has published more than 30 novels and a dozen novellas. The bestselling novelist worked as a newspaper reporter before spending 22 years in public relations. She now writes fiction full time. She and her husband live in Texas. They are the parents of two kids, four grandkids, and an ornery senior cat.

THE HEART OF THE AMISH

Full of faith, hope, and romance, this series takes you into the Heart of Amish Country.

AVAILABLE NOW

The Flower Quilter by Mindy Steele

Barbara Schwartz struggles to find what brings her joy amidst traditional expectations. But while staying with her grandmother in Indiana, a chance to help landscaper Melvin Bontrager may lead to a unique expression of her artistry—and romance.

Paperback / 978-1-63609-642-1

Ruth's Ginger Snap Surprise by Anne Blackburne

Ruth Helmuth learns that being independent doesn't necessarily mean you can't accept help—especially if it means saving what's most important to you and maybe realizing your dreams in the bargain!

Paperback / 978-1-63609-689-6

The Quilt Room Secret by Lisa Jones Baker

Trini seems to have her life all lined up, owning her own quilt store before the age of thirty—but secret dreams pull her, despite her falling for a handsome farmer. And soon she will be faced with an agonizing choice for her future.

Paperback / 978-1-63609-775-6

Courting an Amish Bishop by Mindy Steele

Simon, a dedicated bishop, and Stella, an herbalist, each have been so busy serving others that they have neglected romance—until now. Brought together to help the sick of the community, is it possible for them to have a second chance at love?

Paperback / 978-1-63609-815-9

Mary's Calico Hope by Anne Blackburne

Mary Yoder is happy with her life despite her disability from a childhood accident, but then a Mennonite doctor comes into her life, challenging everything. Can Mary risk hoping for a future free of pain and a love outside the faith she has already been baptized into?

Paperback / 978-1-63609-855-5

Serenity's Secret by Lisa Jones Baker

Serenity Miller, the flower shop owner of Arthur, Illinois, is content with her path in life. But a brush with danger and a taste of romance make her question the secrets she has always held close.

Paperback / 978-1-63609-958-3

A Stolen Kiss by Mindy Steele

LeEtta Miller's daring impulse to kiss a stranger will lead to events neither she nor Benuel Ropp ever imagined.

Paperback / 978-1-63609-993-4

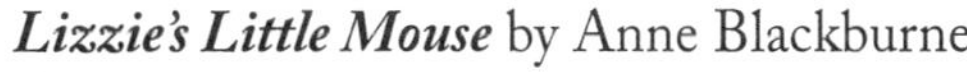

Lizzie's Little Mouse by Anne Blackburne

Lizzie Miller is determined to open a French-inspired bakery. But even on opening day, threats of putting her out of business arrive, and it'll take all her strength and friends to help her overcome the opposition.

Paperback / 979-8-89151-068-5

Hunting for a Husband by Mindy Steele

Leah Wickey moves to Kentucky with a strong desire to find a husband, but when she sets her sights on Joe, could his disabilities get in the way of romance?

Paperback / 979-8-89151-145-3

COMING SOON

Plain Jane's Secret Admirer

by Anne Blackburne

Sweet, shy, and devoted Amish woman Jane Bontrager secretly hates her childhood nickname—"Plain Jane." She doesn't know who started the ugly name back in her school days, but she can never forget how it has made her feel ever since. Jane has a huge crush on Amish buggy maker Samuel Mast, but they are both so shy that they are more likely to turn old and gray alone than to ever get together—especially since Samuel holds a secret or two of his own. What can bridge the gap between two young people who both deserve love and happiness?

Paperback / 979-8-89151-257-3

Christian Fiction for Women

Christian Fiction for Women is your online home for the latest in Christian fiction.

Check us out online for:

- Giveaways
- Recipes
- Info About Upcoming Releases
- Book Trailers
- News and More!

Find Christian Fiction for Women at Your Favorite Social Media Site:

 Search "Christian Fiction for Women"

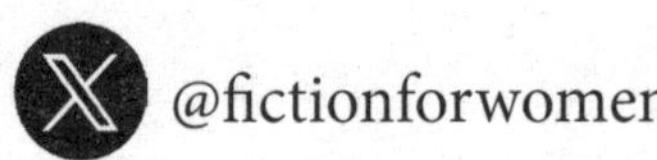 @fictionforwomen